Hervé Le Corre is one of the foremost voices of contemporary French noir. He's the author of several award-winning crime fiction novels, including *Talking to Ghosts* (2014), *After the War* (MacLehose Press, 2015), and *In the Shadow of the Fire* (Europa Editions, 2021).

Award-winning translator **Howard Curtis** has worked on more than sixty books from French, Italian, and Spanish. Among his recent translations for Europa are works by Jean-Claude Izzo and Santiago Gamboa.

T0282063

DOGS AND WOLVES

Hervé Le Corre

DOGS AND WOLVES

*Translated from the French
by Howard Curtis*

Europa
editions

Europa Editions
27 Union Square West, Suite 302
New York NY 10003
www.europaeditions.com
info@europaeditions.com

Translation by Howard Curtis
Original title: *Prendre les loups pour des chiens*
Translation copyright © 2024 by Europa Editions

Library of Congress Cataloging in Publication Data is available
ISBN 978-1-60945-976-5

Le Corre, Hervé
Dogs and Wolves

Cover photo: clearstockconcepts/iStock

Cover design by Ginevra Rapisardi

Prepress by Grafica Punto Print – Rome

Printed in the USA.

CONTENTS

C'était un temps déraisonnable
On avait mis les morts à table
On faisait des châteaux de sable
On prenait des loups pour des chiens
Tout changeait de pôle and d'épaule
La pièce était-elle or non drôle
Moi si j'y tenais mal mon rôle
C'était de n'y comprendre rien[1]

—LOUIS ARAGON, *The War and What Followed*
("Is This How Men Live?")
from *The Unfinished Novel*

[1] It was a time of unreason/We had invited the dead to dinner/We built castles out of sand/We took wolves for dogs/Things kept changing sides/Was the play funny or not/I played my part badly/The whole thing was incomprehensible.

DOGS AND WOLVES

DOGS

They'd released him an hour earlier than planned and since it was raining, he'd had to wait under a kind of bus shelter erected at the intersection, with the entrance of the prison behind him and the only landscape a cornfield on the other side of the road and the parking lot with its gates and its metal detectors and the comings and goings of the visitors, women, children, old people, mixed with the muffled slamming of car doors. He'd leaned out and seen the high walls that ran for nearly four hundred yards, and it had sent a nasty shiver down his spine and he'd sat down on the wooden bench set deep inside the shelter, so that he should see as little as possible, even though all these years he'd dreamed of surveying the whole of the horizon without the slightest obstacle. He had put his big overnight bag down at his feet. It was lumpy and bulging and weighed as much as a dead donkey because of the books he'd sent for during his imprisonment and which he'd been determined to take with him just as he would have taken loyal, loving pets.

He had time to smoke three cigarettes, listening to the rain abate and move away southward with a dull rumble as if a storm was coming. Suddenly, the clouds parted and the light appeared, throwing a glow like fake jewelry over the whole scene, alive with the sucking of tires on wet asphalt. He blinked in the blinding light and gazed at those glittering expanses with the awe of a child looking at a Christmas tree.

When he saw the car slow down and drive into the parking lot and slow down even more, he looked at his watch. He'd already been waiting more than an hour and he hadn't felt the minutes pass. Time was like water that slipped through your hands and disappeared, unlike in prison, where every quarter of an hour stuck to your skin, sweaty and stifling and unhealthy. He watched the little red Renault come back out of the parking lot and stop. It was driven by a woman whose features he could barely make out behind the reflections on the windshield. He didn't need her to flash her headlights to know that she'd come for him. He waved at her and stood up as the car crossed the street and pulled up in front of him.

He leaned down at the same time as the window was lowered and said "Hello" to a pair of very light blue or gray eyes. Very light. All he could see in the shade of the car's interior was that washed-out phosphorescence. She smiled and leaned toward him. She wasn't yet thirty.

"How are you?"

"Better now."

With a broad gesture, he indicated the sky, the trees massed in the distance, lining the road, the dried-up fields. The light, and the heat beating down again. He opened the back door of the car and dropped his bag on the seat. He sat down next to the woman and held out his hand but she moved closer and pecked him on both cheeks. He loved the coolness of her lips on his skin. Something went through him, something rapid but deep, awakening tiny, buried pathways, hidden branches. It was almost painful. An oppressive sense of fulfillment.

"Isn't Fabien here?"

The woman put her sunglasses back on and started the car.

"I'm Jessica."

"Oh, I'm sorry. Franck."

"I know."

"Fabien told me a lot about you in his letters, I . . ."

He fell silent. Better that way. He'd have to get used to it again. Having normal conversations with people. Taking care what you said. Not like with the cops, or the other convicts, no. Just so as not to hurt people, not to rub them up the wrong way.

"Fabien's been in Spain for three weeks. He couldn't put it off, it was urgent. I'll tell you about it. He may be away for two or three more weeks, you never know with him."

"What's he doing in Spain?"

"Business. I'll tell you later. Otherwise he'd have come himself, you can be sure of that. You're his little brother, that's what he always says: 'My little brother.'"

She switched on the car radio, a station that played French singers, and she hummed along to their sentimental songs as if she was the only one in the car. As soon as they were on the highway, going in the direction of Bordeaux, she switched off the air conditioning and the radio and lowered her window and warm air came into the car with a violent, deafening rush. She didn't say anything for a while. Franck was expecting questions about the slammer, what a shithole it was, he was ready to tell her the bare minimum because you never tell the whole truth about what happens in prison. About what you had to see and go through in there. He would have liked her to talk to him, because that would have given him a good reason to turn and look at her without having to ogle her out of the corner of his eye as he was doing now.

She was wearing a man's shirt with the sleeves rolled up over her forearms. It was too big for her and reached down to the tops of her thighs, over a pair of shorts cut out of old jeans. Her legs were tanned, the skin glistened, and he told himself she must have put on a moisturizing cream and that if she hadn't been Fabien's wife he would have put his hand on that softness, even if it meant getting a slap. He constructed a whole porn script in his mind, a script so realistic, with the woman sitting just an inch or two from him, that it made his jeans feel too tight and he had to change position several times to relieve the pressure on his groin.

"You want to stop? There's a service station over there."

He gave a start because part of him took this for an invitation to prolong the fantasy that held him captive. A bumpy path, the shade of a tree, the girl shifting to the back seat, panties coming down, a hand moving up.

"Yeah, I'd like that."

His voice hoarse, filled with embarrassment. He cleared his throat, mouth dry.

She put the turn signal on, a half-smile on her pretty mouth. Ironic or mocking. Or simply calm, relaxed. He didn't know. He hadn't thought about women's smiles for a long time. The meanings they imply, the misinterpretations they give rise to.

"I need a coffee and a smoke," she said.

She pushed her dark glasses back over her hair to look for a parking spot, squinting, bent forward slightly. She parked the car near a picnic table where a couple and three children were sitting in front of cardboard plates that the mother was filling with tomato salad while the father fiddled with his cell phone. The table was cluttered with sachets and bags, cans of soda, packages wrapped in aluminum foil, and the children were throwing their hands into this chaos to grab pieces of bread or paper cups that they held out to their mother for her to give them a drink.

Franck watched the man, who was indifferent to all this bustle, starting to talk on the phone then moving away to continue his conversation, and all you could see was his back, his bent neck, shrugging his shoulders from time to time, his free hand beating the air in front of him.

"Shall we go? Is this bringing back memories?"

Yes, vaguely, the road leading to vacations in Spain when he was nine or ten, when everything was still going well, before the shipwreck, the sandwiches he feasted on, bought in stores along the highway and quickly devoured standing by the car because his father didn't like to stop, the games he and Fabien played on their consoles in the back seat. His big brother Fabien. Four years older. Who taught him all the tricks, always patient. And who later would take the blame whenever they did anything stupid. The blame and the blows. And the tears, too, which he wiped away with the back of his hand, panting, without a word, his father above him, yelling, fist raised. Fabien muttering insults at night in their room, buried beneath the sheets, cursing their father in a low voice, vowing to exact a terrible revenge one day.

The two brothers had never fought. Had hardly ever quarreled. They needed to support each other, the way you cling to someone or something in the current of a river gone crazy or in a wind that uproots trees. There weren't many brothers like them in the world. That was what they'd told each other once on one of those endless nights. Screams, groans, obscene insults. Mom.

And there had been that day, the day it had happened, about four in the afternoon. Fabien running across the supermarket parking lot without turning, the bag full of money, Franck bouncing off the hood of a passing car, leg broken, the security guards lying on top of him.

He hadn't talked despite all the pressure from the cops, all their blackmail, the advice he'd gotten from the court-appointed lawyer.

He had a clean record. The gun was a fake gun, a copy of a Sig-Sauer, a starting pistol. But the bookkeeper, a father of three, had been left a tetraplegic after his fall down the stairs. The case had gone to court in the Gironde. Six years with no remission.

He hadn't talked.

He got out of the car without saying anything in reply, and immediately the slamming of car doors, the calls, the coming and going of people, all that casualness of bare legs and short sleeves and dark glasses dazzled him and he lowered his head beneath the bright, harsh light the sun cast over it all.

Jessica was walking ahead without bothering about him, the strap of her bag pulling on the collar of her shirt and baring a shoulder with no bra strap over it. Franck caught up with her so as not to have the curves of her ass in front of his eyes, curves emphasized by her shorts, the line of her neck emerging from the askew collar, that nakedness that the clothes revealed or implied. They entered the vast hall, drowned in the noise of the customers and the muzak, freezing cold because of the air conditioning, and they staggered in the direction of the toilets through the groups massed in front of the coffee machines and the people standing around, waiting for someone, gazing at the road map of the region on the wall, or else busy on their phones.

Franck shut himself in a cubicle with a damp floor where the toilet bowl was still full of urine and toilet paper, and his excitement receded, faced with this filth saturated by the smell of rim blocks. He peed, quickly buttoned himself again, relieved, calm almost, then watched the toilet bowl clean itself in the din of the flush, his mind empty, no longer knowing where he was or why he was there. At the washstands, there were guys washing their hands, sprinkling water on their faces, looking at themselves in the mirror without seeing themselves or maybe without recognizing themselves. Some seemed in a daze after hours on the road, others rolled their shoulders like toughs. The noise of the hand driers was deafening and the swing door squeaked every time someone came in or went out. Franck rinsed his lowered eyes in the lukewarm water, refusing to see anything around him, scared by all this noise, then he left the place without turning back because that smell of men, that lack of privacy reminded him of prison, but without the raised voices and the shuffle of feet, the guys who made out like they didn't give a fuck about anything.

He went to the freezer aisles and started looking at the sandwiches in their triangular packaging, and he salivated at the sight of the sliced white bread and the garnish and his stomach felt hollow and there was a painful lump in his throat because what he saw was worth more than any cooked meal, any pastry filled with cream or fruit. He made his choice, took a bottle of

water, then went to pay for everything, trying to spot Jessica
in the crowd. He looked in his wallet for the right change but
couldn't find the coins he needed and the cashier waited, looking away, stiff on her seat, sighing with impatience, and he felt
stupid and clumsy, the way he had as a child, when he took
out a ten-euro bill and the girl stuffed it in her cash drawer
and without a word gave him his change with the same almost
abrupt gesture. He saw Jessica through the glass doors in front
of the entrance, smoking in the sun, a paper coffee cup in her
hand.

"Where did you get to?"

"I was buying something."

He showed her his sandwiches and unwrapped one and ate
it in three mouthfuls. He pushed it all down with a gulp of
cold water, and one of his back teeth rang with pain. Jessica
looked at her watch and said it was time they left, they still had
a way to go, and she walked away in the direction of the car,
not bothering about him, as if she were alone. He followed her
at a distance, finishing his snack, hardly chewing it, happy to
stuff his mouth with it then swallow it down with the help of
a little water. It was a greedy pleasure, the pleasure of a little
boy fond of his food, a kind of animal satisfaction that quietly
brought him back to this side of the world, to the blinding light
flooding everything, the noise of the voices and the bustle of
crowds of human beings rushing about in all directions, like
flies on a windowpane, unable to understand that they can't
get through it. He couldn't find words for the invisible walls of
that prison. He only felt his own freedom lift his shoulders and
soften his back, relieving it at last of the weight of those looks
like bags filled with knives, and it seemed to him that he was
walking with a lightness, a grace, maybe, that he had never felt,
like a dancer pacing this overheated blacktop after a star with
a stunning ass. He finished eating by the car while she smoked
another cigarette. She didn't say anything to him as she leaned
on the car door, apparently engrossed by the sight of a group of

fairly elderly tourists getting off a huge red bus, wearing caps and Bermuda shorts and brand-new sneakers, attempting a few stretching exercises as they walked stiffly toward the toilets and the shops.

In a corner of his field of vision he saw Jessica's legs moving as she maneuvered the car back onto the highway, moving her legs up and down on the pedals like scissors, and the desire to slip his hand into the gap between those legs, or even to place his fingers on that brown skin, took hold of him again and forced him to keep his arms folded, and he tried to concentrate on the landscape or the traffic, eyeing the big sedans, the powerful 4×4s overtaking them at ninety miles an hour, or turning to look at the caravans and trailer homes dragging along at sixty and cursing them under his breath. As for her, she said nothing. Her face was suddenly impassive, inscrutable, with bitter lines at the corners of her lips, and behind the dark glasses her eyes were fixed straight ahead, unblinking, as if she were a disturbing figure in a wax museum. She might have been asleep, hypnotized by the ribbon of asphalt unreeling before them, the intermittent whiteness of the barricade tapes.

He wondered for a moment what he could have said or done for her to withdraw into that hostile silence, then he started daydreaming as he looked out at the landscape, imagining himself living in that brick farmhouse he glimpsed below the highway, or in that other one on a hillside, picturing himself walking at dawn amid the vines or in the grass wet with dew beside a deserted road. He began to dream of winter in that drab, dry, yellow landscape, without relief or depth because the shade had fled, never to be seen again. He sat down in a deep armchair, in front of a wood fire, a book on his knees while the icy blue light of a dying day faded beyond the window panes. He walked on frost-hardened earth early in the morning. This was the kind of image he had projected for himself in prison, lying on his cot and seeing the first light of dawn through the skylight. To watch the sun rise. To witness that miracle every day without any barrier—any wall, any window—between yourself and the silent clamor of everything emerging from the darkness.

Then she turned to him and threw a glance behind her. "Can you pass me my smokes? They're in my bag."

It was as if she'd suddenly come back to life. Her fingers were moving on the wheel, her lips half open as if she was starting to breathe again. He gave her a cigarette.

"Help yourself, if you want one."

She lowered the window a little on her side, and he did the same, and they smoked in the whoosh of the hot air rushing in on them. Franck took the opportunity to speak, thinking that whatever he said would be drowned out in that vast tremor anyway.

"What kind of business is Fabien doing in Spain? He didn't say anything about it in his last letter."

"It was decided on quickly, last week. You know how he is, you're his brother. He can be quite secretive, not always easy to deal with. One evening, he told me he was leaving the next morning to meet some guys in Valencia. And since he wanted to make the most of it, he told me he'd stay for at least three weeks because he has friends down there. That was all he'd tell me; no point in even arguing. He wanted to do something with that dough of yours that's been lying around all this time. It was a suggestion from Serge, a Gypsy who's a good friend of my father's. That's all he told me. I think right now, he's probably sweet-talking girls on the beach, I'm not worried about him."

"He just thought about using that money after five years? It's about time. What's he been doing all this time?"

"Odd jobs here and there. He used to help out this scrap metal merchant, the Gypsy I mentioned, then he found a job in Langon, night watchman in a logistics depot, they call it. Three nights a week, for crap pay. Anyway, right now, you can't find anything. He's a cook by trade, but he can't stand the bosses anymore, and he's not interested in lousy pay at the end of the month for long hours."

They hadn't had time to count it. There had been at least fifty or sixty thousand euros in cash in the attaché case. Monday's takings. Monday was a quiet day, and the courier came alone in an unmarked car. Franck had learned that over time, during the ten months he'd spent moving pallets around on his cart and making friends with a security guard named Amine, a huge black guy who swore he'd pull the job one Saturday night with pals of his. Franck had let him talk while they smoked a joint one evening after the depot closed. Other times, too, Amine had given him all the details and even suggested they should pull the job together. He'd shake his head after every drag as if the dope was blurring his neurons or his sight, then he would breathe out everything his lungs had been unable to absorb and close his eyes and laugh silently. Franck would merely smile and nod in agreement while Amine put together his plans, shaking and stomping like a sportsman just before the start of a race or coming onto the pitch. Franck didn't trust him, that genial, talkative guy and his pre-rolled joints filled to the brim with hash he claimed came straight from Sierra Leone.

After leaving the highway at Langon, they drove along a country road that cut through a gloomy forest of pines whose dirty green tops glistened in the sun. At times, there were bare stretches of sand, blackish as if charred and overrun here and there by gray-green gorse. The heat was more intense here, dry and dusty, and an acrid smell of burned earth and resin infiltrated the car. Franck wondered how it was possible to live here, far from everything, and he took fright at this desert bristling with black trunks from which there occasionally emerged a round, dense thicket of tightly packed oaks, survivors on a battlefield planted with halberds.

He yearned for a town, its noise, its crowds, its girls especially, in summer skirts and tops loose over their breasts, he would have looked at all of them, peered at them, an unashamed voyeur, caressing and feeling that warm skin, that round softness with his eyes, not knowing how he would resist the desire to touch them in reality, to lift their skirts and slip his fingers between their thighs and stick in his tongue and the rest. The times he had jerked off on his stinking mattress, tormented by these images and the fantasies he fabricated, the cell suddenly invaded by holograms in flowery skirts pushing back the mass of their hair as they all know how to do with that quick, supple gesture. The times, shaken by the spasms of his wretched orgasm, he had sighed into the hollow of a warm, tanned shoulder only to find himself blowing with his mouth open into the questionable material of his pillow.

Jessica turned abruptly onto a dusty path, its ruts filled with pebbles and broken tiles, which led first past a thicket of oaks then past a parched meadow strewn with the wrecks of cars and rusty trailers and agricultural equipment—an ancient tractor, its faded hood baking in the heat with sad red patches, a harrow, its long tines overrun with bindweed—in the middle of which wild grass and yellow acacias thrived. There were tires, some burst, some piled up in the middle of the brambles. The sky was as white and blinding as molten metal, crushing these heaps of scrap iron.

When the car drew up in front of the house, something emerged from around a corner of the wall. It took Franck a second to realize that it was a dog. A dog such as he'd never seen, not even in movies or videos. Black, its coat smooth, its body bulging with muscles, its square head crowned by ears cut into points like two spearheads. Simply standing on its four legs, it pressed its muzzle against the half-lowered car window and Franck could hear its breathing and the deep growling that rolled in its mouth through bared chops and see up close its eyes fixed on him, protuberant, set in whitish circles where madness gleamed. It didn't move, content to stare at him. It was waiting, quivering with an anger that ran beneath its skin like a fierce charge of electricity.

"Don't open," Jessica said. "Roll the window up. I'll deal with him."

She went around the car and grabbed the dog by the collar and pulled it toward her with some effort, yelling, "Quiet now, Goliath!" and hitting it on the head with the flat of her hand. When she let go of it after a while, the animal sat down, its big head at the level of Jessica's stomach, looking up at her, ears lowered, blinking as if it was afraid of her.

"You can come out, he won't hurt you. He's always like that with people he doesn't know."

Franck tore himself from the car as if from an oven and sweat ran down his back and he mopped it with the material of his shirt. Jessica ordered the dog to lie down under an old bench next to the front door of the house and the animal obeyed but kept its head up and its eyes on Franck.

"When he's gotten used to you, you'll see, he's quite docile. And besides, he's a good guard dog. We're safe with him here."

She went inside and Franck followed her, making sure the dog wasn't moving. His heavy bag was pulling on his arm and beating against his leg, giving him the lopsided, uncertain walk of someone who's disabled.

"I'm here!" Jessica called out.

She had stopped at the foot of a staircase and was listening out. The chatter of a TV could be heard from somewhere in the house but nobody replied, nobody seemed to be there.

"What are those jerks doing?"

She waited a few more seconds then shrugged.

"Never mind. You'll see them later. Come with me. We'll go this way."

She opened the door to the kitchen. The room was dark, the shutters half closed. The table hadn't been cleared after lunch, the sink was full of dirty plates and greasy dishes, and the counter was cluttered with cans, empty sachets, and wine and beer bottles.

"Don't mind the mess. My mom isn't having a good day. I'll see to it later."

She took two beers from the refrigerator, piled up some

plates that had been left on the table, and placed the cans on a corner of the oilcloth. With a sigh, she sat all the way back on a chair, stretched her legs, slipped her sandals from her feet, and wriggled her toes as she opened her can.

"Shit, it's hot," she said. "Don't just stand there like that, sit down. Cheers."

Franck sat down on the other side of the table. He could see nothing now but her tanned shoulders, the neckline of her shirt, the damp shadow between her breasts, glistening with sweat. She drank a long gulp then rolled the aluminum can over the insides of her thighs, slowly, closing her eyes. He drank, too, taking great swigs of the ice-cold beer, and felt the chill of it descend into his stomach and spread throughout his body, and gradually the oppression of the heat gave way to a bitter lucidity he couldn't quite figure out. He no longer knew what he was doing here, in the chaos of this grimy kitchen, within reach of the perfect body of this girl lying back, abandoned, on her chair and cooling her thighs with a beer can. Amid the sickly-sweet odors of the filth surrounding them, he thought he could perceive also Jessica's intimate scent, the perfume of her skin, the aromas of her secret folds.

In almost five years, how many times, driven almost crazy by that desperate desire, had he dreamed of a woman's body so close, so available? He watched her as she lit a cigarette and blew the smoke out in front of her, staring vaguely at the window above the sink overflowing with dishes. She might have been alone, holding her beer between her outstretched legs, her eyes closed now, smoking slowly and flicking the ash onto the floor. He didn't dare move, suddenly dreading to attract her attention, like a little boy who keeps quiet after a harsh reprimand. Then something moved to the right of his field of vision and he gave a start. There in the doorway stood a little girl, watching him gravely, questioning him with her dark eyes, a plastic racket in her hand.

Franck said hello in a low voice, trying to smile at her, but the girl didn't react. Her face remained impassive, eyes still wide open with curiosity or perhaps anxiety, and it occurred to Franck that he didn't know how to behave with children, how to talk to them or how to smile at them—but was he any better at dealing with adults, or people in general?

Jessica's voice drew him back from these questions that had no answers. "Rachel, sweetie, aren't you with Grandma?"

The little girl shook her head, then started twisting her black hair around her finger, one foot behind her, rocking on the tips of her toes as if she didn't dare come into the room. Jessica threw her cigarette butt into her beer can then held out her arms to the little girl, who ran toward her and threw herself between her legs and huddled against her belly. From there, she continued to stare at Franck. Jessica stroked her forehead and kissed her hair, whispering to her that she was hot and that she should have washed herself, but the little girl seemed not to hear her, just kept examining the man who was looking at her from the other side of the table, embarrassed by his own forced smile.

"Do you want a drink?"

Rachel moved away from her mother's knees and opened the refrigerator and took out a big bottle of soda, then stood with this burden in the middle of the room, looking around for a usable glass. Reluctantly, Jessica stood up with a sigh and opened a cupboard that was too high for the little girl and took down a glass and looked at it in the light from the window.

"Here you are, Missy. This one's clean."

Rachel put her glass down on a corner of the table and filled it and drank slowly, turned toward the window. When she had finished, she put the bottle back in the fridge, then went and rinsed her glass at the sink, standing on tiptoe to reach the faucet, and put the glass on the drain board in the middle of what was already there. Then she picked up her racket and left the room without saying a word. The door creaked slightly as it closed.

Jessica had sat down again and lit another cigarette. She sighed some more, blowing the smoke out through her nose.

"She always has to have clean things. She never eats from someone else's plate, not even mine, not even to have a taste, or with a fork that's been used to serve. She always looks through glasses to make sure they're clean. And then she has to put everything away, all the time. You should see her room! I don't know where she gets all these habits from. I didn't bring her up like that, like a princess, I mean. And her dad wasn't the delicate kind. As far as I'm concerned, it's good to be clean, I mean I don't like living in a pigsty. But you're not going to catch a fucking disease because you drink out of someone else's glass, especially if they're family, are you?"

She turned to Franck. She was puffing nervously on her cigarette, waving her hands in front of her.

"How old is she?"

"Eight. She'll be nine in September."

"She seems quiet. She's like you."

Jessica giggled. "She's like me because she's quiet? I don't even know who she gets that from. We're the nervous kind in this family . . . Well, maybe from her grandfather. He hasn't always been like that, but he's quieted down a lot now." She stubbed out her cigarette in a plate. "Well, it's been best for everyone."

She got to her feet. She seemed impatient all of a sudden.

"Come on, let me show you where you'll be staying."

Franck followed her outside. Once again, she walked a few yards in front, without waiting for him. Inside a roughly-built old shed, he saw a trailer raised up on cinder blocks, with a satellite dish on top. Jessica went inside and he hurried to join her there. She was leaning against the little stainless-steel sink and in the light coming in through the open Plexiglass windows at a low angle, all he could see were her legs and the gleam of her eyes, which made him think of those lagoons you see in photographs, more luminous than the sky. He put his bag down on a bench seat and watched her open the closets, run the water, show him where the clean sheets were, explaining that there was a little bathroom on the first floor of the house that he could use. Beneath that low ceiling, her muted voice came to him as if she had spoken in his ear and it seemed to him that this confined space was pushing them into an intimacy that almost embarrassed him. At any moment, he expected to see her undress, like someone making themselves comfortable at home, maybe keeping on only her panties, and come and go barefoot across the linoleum floor, putting away his things, then press herself against him and stick her tongue in his mouth and eagerly unbutton his jeans.

When she left the trailer, telling him to take his time and join them later behind the house because that was where her parents were—those two idiots must be having a nap, even though they were supposed to be keeping an eye on Rachel from the side of the pool—he felt relieved and hurried to stick his head under the faucet in the sink and splash water on his face. The water was warm at first then grew colder as it ran, so he drank it in great gulps until he couldn't breathe.

He put away his few clothes in the chests, taking care to keep them well folded, then put his toiletries in the little cabinet. He stood for a moment looking at his toothbrush and his disposable razor, which he'd placed on the plastic shelf, and the bar of soap on the edge of the tiny washstand and the towel hanging from a chrome bar, like so many tangible signs of peace and freedom. Already, the silence, disturbed only by a purring in the distance, probably a tractor, was welcoming him into a kind of bubble that gradually adjusted itself to him like a new garment that becomes comfortable as soon as you put it on. He no longer had to watch his back in the mirror, dreading to see some randy bigshot or some crazy guy who might be hiding a knife in his towel loom up behind him. He no longer had to wait or to hurry through the enforced closeness, the touches, the nudges, the constant challenge of those bodies that were either threatening or tense with fear.

He left the toilet and felt a kind of well-being in his chest. The trailer was small, with a low ceiling. It looked like a doll's house with that miniature washstand, that two-ring portable stove that would just about do for making tea on a campsite, but he felt the same tranquility as he had in his boyhood room, so long ago, once he had shut the door and left behind him, depending on the evening, his father's cries of rage or else the yelling and slamming of doors or else his mother's sobs as she sat on the steps in front of the door. He and his brother would wait for everything to quiet down, listening out for murmurs and groans in a tomblike silence, to come into the other's room and slip into his bed and plot escapes, acts of revenge, scenarios of another life, far from here, far from everything.

He lay down on the bed, surrounded by the smell of clean sheets, and closed his eyes, thinking of Fabien and how they would party when he got back, before getting out of here and really starting to live. And then because this dump, with that monstrous dog, that girl who looked really hot, and that almost-mute little girl, struck him as weird and dicey. Something in the air, like a lingering odor, the trace of an old stench that sometimes stopped you from breathing deeply. Nothing to do with prison. He couldn't have said truly what he was feeling.

But here, in this hovel, he felt a little at home, alone, really alone, and very calm.

2

When Franck introduced himself to them, the old man and the old woman made no attempt to pretend interest. This was the first time they'd met him, but they didn't make any effort to smile or utter words of welcome. He might simply have come to say hello in passing, like someone you won't see again. They knew perfectly well, though, that he'd just left prison, that he was Fabien's brother. He was going to live with them for a while, they would share their meals with him. They would pass him at the door of the toilets. They didn't move from the deckchairs they were sitting in, and the dog, which had been lying between them, its head in its paws, got up with a growl and Jessica's father made it lie down again, kicking it on the muzzle with his espadrille.

They greeted Franck with a simple "Hello—Roland, Maryse," holding out their soft, moist hands and blinking because he was standing against the blinding sky. Then the man made a show of resuming his interrupted nap, placing his bony arms on his swollen belly, and the woman picked up her pack of cigarettes from the grass beside her, got laboriously to her feet, lit one, and then stood there motionless, smoking and watching Rachel in the above-ground swimming pool a short distance from them.

Now that the woman was standing, Franck could see that she was tall and broad-shouldered, with a round face and reddish hair gathered into a shapeless bun. They might have been seventy. Maybe younger. But to Franck they seemed tired and worn, eaten up from inside, withered like a couple of fruits left in a basket. Old. He would think of them simply as the old man and the old woman. Because of the age difference between them and him, and above all because of that impression they gave of being on their last legs.

Franck searched in the woman's tired features and grainy skin for some resemblance to Jessica but couldn't find any, apart from the faded blue of the eyes, which took away all expression from them, the pupils planted in that transparency like a nail in cold water. Two large breasts drooped beneath a kind of fuchsia top. She stubbed out her cigarette in a resin pot that served as an ashtray, glanced at Rachel, who was floating in the pool, sitting in the hollow of a big rubber ring, then walked away, dragging her feet, on her thick, tanned legs, her cellulite-swollen thighs packed into a pair of white shorts.

Beyond the swimming pool, the dry yellow meadow of dead grass descended in a gentle slope toward the forest, some fifty yards away, which rose like a wall in a dark, tangled mass. The light seemed to cancel itself out as soon as it fell on the tree-tops, so that within the silent forest permanent darkness prevailed. In the pool, Rachel's face glittered with water, and when she jumped up, beating her arms, her hair launched gems that rolled down over her shoulders. In this setting, heavy with sadness and vaguely threatening, she was the one expression of a little life and grace, and Franck couldn't take his eyes off her, though he didn't understand the reassuring sense of contentment he felt in watching her.

He heard the hiss of a can being opened behind him and when he turned he saw the old man in his deckchair with a beer in his hand, frowning in his direction, his eyes buried amid the lines and wrinkles of his tired face. He seemed older than his wife, wearier, with just the remains of a smile, a very old smile, engraved around his eyes.

"What was your name again?"

"Franck."

"Mine's Roland. You're Fabien's brother, right?"

"That's right."

Franck approached him. The man took a big swig of beer, closing his eyes, then sighed noisily, gasping for breath, and ran his hand over the dog's back, his fingers combing its smooth coat.

"I feel embarrassed, coming here like this. It's kind of you to put me up. It won't be for long. As soon as Fabien gets back, I'll work things out with him. I don't want to outstay my welcome."

The old man looked at him, blinking his eyes as if trying to find a hidden meaning in his words, then belched softly and rubbed his stomach.

"No sweat. It makes Jessica happy, and since you're Fabien's brother . . ."

"Of course, but . . ."

"What time do you make it?"

"Nearly six."

The old man stood up with difficulty, his thin arms trembling beneath him as he raised himself from the deckchair. Once he was standing, he motioned with his chin at Rachel, who was still in the pool. "Keep an eye on her," he said. "We don't want her to drown. Her mother would never get over it."

He walked slowly toward the house, stooped a little at first, massaging his back, then gradually rose to his full height. With his feet trapped in espadrilles worn like slippers, he tottered on his crooked legs and seemed about to give way at any moment and throw him to the ground.

Franck approached the pool where Rachel, still sitting on her big rubber ring, was turning around and around in the pool, using her hands like tiny oars. The dog followed him and lay down next to a garden chair covered with a beach towel and observed the edge of the forest, its ears up.

"Aren't you cold after all this time?"

She shook her head without looking at him. She was no longer rowing and the water had grown still around her, making a smooth mirror for the heat-whitened sky. Franck searched for something to say to her but couldn't find anything. He didn't know if the little girl, still now, eyes lowered, was pretending to ignore his presence or was simply lost in thought.

"So you're Rachel? It's a pretty name."

She looked at him at last. Her dark eyes were all-consuming. Vast and deep.

"Were you in prison?"

"Yes, but that's all over now."

He wasn't very pleased with his answer. Or very sure of it. He had been out for six hours now, and he sometimes had the feeling that he was an escapee and they would catch up with him at any moment and throw him back inside for his 1,408th night of incarceration. A night of enforced intimacy and alarms, his sleep interspersed with periods of wakefulness listening to the guy in the upper bunk move about, a guy who had been there for ten days and never slept, silent, bad-tempered, as tense as a cocked gun. Sitting on his mattress, his hands together between his thighs, staring straight ahead. For hours. Or lying there motionless, like a statue on a tomb or a bomb about to explode.

Franck was aware of all this free, vacant space around him, and the emptiness of it distressed him. He felt as if he were floating, like those lost astronauts you see in movies who glide away into the coldness of infinite space, kneading the void with slow gestures, like powerless swimmers. He didn't know what to say or do when faced with this strange, silent little girl— strange because from deep within her mute indifference, she seemed to see and hear and understand everything with the wisdom of a young sorceress.

She went close to the edge then hoisted herself onto the rungs of the chrome ladder. Franck walked around the outside of the pool because he was afraid she would fall. He reached out his arms toward her but she spurned his gesture and jumped to the ground without looking. She grabbed her towel from the chair and the dog lifted its big head toward her with a snap of its jaws then stood up and planted itself in front of her, panting, its half-open mouth giving it a kind of smile. Rachel took the dog's tongue between her thumb and index finger and gently pulled on it and the animal let out a plaintive moan then shook itself.

"Is he good with you?"

Without taking her eyes off the dog, she shrugged and wiped her hair and put the towel around her shoulders like a cape.

Then she gave him her hand and they walked to the house.

Once inside, Rachel rushed upstairs without a word, leaving Franck standing at the foot of the stairs. He could hear the women chatting in the kitchen. Jessica's high-pitched voice and her mother's rough tone. He opened the door and stopped in the doorway. Jessica was doing the dishes. Her mother was smoking, sitting on a chair, her elbows on the table. They were talking vehemently about some asshole, some real son of a bitch they would have to go and see one of these days to set the record straight. They broke off when Franck entered the room. Jessica had her back to him, working away at a plate that kept knocking against the bottom of the sink, displacing a lot of water. The old woman looked him up and down for a long time, the cigarette in her mouth, eyes screwed up because of the smoke.

"Are you looking for a dishcloth?"

He saw Jessica's shoulders shaking in silent mirth while her mother choked with laughter, which then turned into a cavernous cough.

He felt as embarrassed as if he were naked in front of them, and there was a rush of heat to his face. He looked at the old woman, sitting right back in her chair, unable to catch her breath, and told himself that if she started to suffocate, to choke for real right there, in the middle of the room, he wouldn't do a thing to help her in any way, he would watch her die slowly, her face purple like that guy in the slammer who'd hanged himself in his cell and whom he'd seen on the stretcher before he was covered with a sheet. That surge of hatred gave him the courage to say:

"No, not particularly. I wouldn't like to take your work away from you."

Jessica turned and stared at him gravely, as if trying to understand something, then nodded.

Her mother laughed, then stubbed out her cigarette in an already-full ashtray and looked at Franck with an expression of defiance. She glanced at her daughter, still busy at the sink, as if her stooped back could answer her silent question. After a while, she stood up and left the kitchen, dragging her feet. The stairs creaked beneath her and they could hear her breathing and coughing and adding a string of curses to her coughing fit before slamming a door.

"She should see a doctor," Jessica said. "She'll end up dropping dead one day, coughing like that."

"It's the cigarettes."

Franck was standing close to Jessica because he felt that he could sense what was emanating from her body—her heat, her smell—but also because he could see the grain of her skin on her cheeks and on the back of her neck, below the hair gathered on the top of her head and secured with a thick barrette, and on her breasts, which he could easily sense under the black top that barely covered her. Beneath his gluttonous gaze, she pretended to wash and rinse, her eyes fixed on the dishes she was scouring and the swirls of the murky water, and he sensed that she was fully aware of what he wanted, what he was ogling, just three feet from her, this guy who'd just come out of prison and who must have been driven crazy by the thought of girls like her until he'd soiled already-disgusting sheets. And he watched that feigned indifference, convinced that she must know what effect she was having on him, he was sure of it, and that reciprocal certainty created a magnetic link between them that would eventually bring their bodies together.

That evening, after nightfall, they had dinner outside the house, surrounded by clouds of mosquitoes and the disturbing flight of a few hornets excited by the light. The old man grilled cutlets on a barbecue made from a gas can sawed across the middle and placed on metal trestles. At a certain point, he asked Franck to bring him a glass of wine and he seized the opportunity to question him about prison and they chatted calmly while the women, who were waiting at the table, smoked and drank wine. Then Franck asked about the possibilities of work in the area and the old man told him he'd have to see, it was the country here, but there might be something in Bazas or Langon. Fabien had been a night watchman in a haulage company in Langon for six months. Maybe there.

The old man was poking the charcoal and speaking in a hoarse, subdued voice, his face reddened by the barbecue, his thin arms stretched across it like dry branches about to burst into flame.

"I also did time when I was young. Ten months. All because me and two pals had pissed off this girl after a dance in the Médoc, where I was living. Some kind of whore who'd been coming on to us all evening and then went and complained to the cops. A youthful error, they call it. And since I'd already been in trouble a few times, the fucking judge threw the book at me. All because I stuck my finger in a girl's pussy . . ."

He shook his head, still poking the charcoal, causing sparks to fly up and flames to dance.

"Still, I don't regret a thing. I was young, dammit, and if I was young again I'd do the same."

Franck said nothing, watching the charcoal crackle and blaze in contact with the fat melting off the meat. Feeling a little dizzy after his second glass of wine, he remembered the times he'd gotten really smashed, the first time with Fabien and his pals, when he was fifteen, one summer evening by the sea, lit only by torches and the big fire they had made with driftwood and branches and pine cones, then the terror that had seized him on the way back, when he had plunged into the woods, thinking he had found a shortcut, and suddenly lost his way beneath the jagged covering of the pines and the scattered stars, panting, drunkenness hammering at his skull, so dizzy suddenly that he was thrown to the ground. He'd thought he was going to die there, on all fours, vomiting, dripping with phlegm and tears, and it was like that, whining like a puppy, that he had gotten back to the paved road and had seen lights in the distance, hovering in the darkness like fireflies.

He felt something against his thigh and shuddered because he thought it was the dog putting its muzzle there, then felt Rachel's hand, closed into a cold little fist, looking for his and snuggling inside it. She watched the poker raising whirls of sparks and her bright gaze didn't flinch and she held herself motionless and silent between the two men, who had also fallen silent.

"Do you like fire?" Franck asked.

She didn't answer. He simply felt her closed hand move against his palm.

"She doesn't talk much," the old man said. "She's always been a bit like that. You don't like talking, do you?"

He gave her a little pat on the back of her head, and she shrugged and her fist tightened in Franck's hand.

"There are times when we wonder if she isn't a little bit deaf. Maybe we should take her to see a doctor, but her mother doesn't want to. She says she can hear a deer walking in the woods a hundred yards away. And she seems to be doing okay at school."

Franck looked down at Rachel.

"She's like a cat," the old man went on. "Cats hear what they want to hear. When you tell them to come they don't give a damn, but if there's a fucking bird hopping about in the grass, you see their ears prick up."

Rachel fluttered her eyelashes and wiped her nose with the back of her hand, then walked away. The dog followed her. It looked bigger at night, and its shadow looked like another dog dragging after it. They vanished beyond the circle of light given off by a kind of lantern hanging on the front of the house. Franck watched them anxiously as they moved away. He could still feel in his hand a trace of that little life that had been inside it.

They finished late, after midnight, tormented by the mosquitoes. Rachel had fallen asleep in a deckchair and Jessica had sent her to bed. They talked about money, how hard it was to make any. The old man spruced up cars in a barn that he'd converted into a workshop, right next to the shed where the trailer was kept. From time to time he would give a hand to a scrap merchant near Bordeaux, maybe to do a job on a big stolen saloon car that would be sent east two weeks later, but that wasn't enough to make ends meet. Apart from that, Jessica and her mother harvested grapes in the Sauternes area, did the odd cleaning job, and filled in for carers in a retirement home in Bazas, or in a supermarket as cashiers. Sometimes they felt like tipping the senile, bad-tempered old people marinating in their own piss out of their armchairs or beds, or stifling with a pillow those who'd been abandoned there like dogs and who wept in silence or refused to leave their place at the windows of their rooms, or throwing a pack of beer in the face of an arrogant, complaining customer, or slamming shut the cash drawer on the hands of that bitch of a supervisor who kept saying they weren't going fast enough, or tearing down the vines of all those fucking vineyard owners who came to look over the work in their farmer get-up, rubber boots, blue jeans, big velvet jacket, all just casual enough not to get too dirty in the mud as they walked among those who were slaving away, stooped between the rows of vines.

The two women got carried away, talked loudly, refilled their glasses, searched on the table for their cigarettes or a lighter. Nobody was spared: the bosses, the supervisors, their work colleagues, the slackers, the pen-pushers, the kiss-asses, the pushovers, the hypocrites, all those who profited from other people's poverty. To hear them, you would think they were the only ones who had ever paid with their bodies, who had ever really worked and understood the way things functioned, the greed and the laziness, the cowardly compromises, all the filthy rotten mess of the world. With the help of the booze and the cigarettes, they spoke almost with the same voice, thick and rasping, cutting into each other's words. The old man looked at them, sunk in his camping armchair, his eyes shielded behind his screwed-up eyelids, his mouth twisted into a disgusted or vaguely contemptuous pout.

Franck looked at the old woman. Maryse. He'd been trying to remember her first name for a while. She'd cheered up a little with all the drinking. She laughed heartily as she brought up one anecdote after another, sometimes choking and ending up coughing fit to burst. She included him in what she was saying, with a familiarity that made him feel uncomfortable, letting her transparent gaze linger on him as if hoping to catch him off guard. After a while, she went to look for some beers because she was thirsty and there was no more chilled white wine. The four of them toasted, knocking their aluminum cans together. A dull, derisory sound.

"To your freedom," Jessica said.

Franck would have liked to say something in reply but that word—freedom—struck him as so abstract and intimidating that anything he said might seem ridiculous. Then he thought of his brother. Nobody had mentioned him. It was as if he had never existed.

"To Fabien."

He made an effort to smile as he said this, but his cheeks felt as stiff as cardboard, anesthetized by the alcohol.

The old man merely smiled and nodded with a kind of grunt, and the old woman said nothing and took another swig of beer, sitting back in her chair.

"I hope things are going well down there," Jessica said.

Franck felt an icy shiver run through his entire body, and his stomach suddenly seemed disgustingly heavy. He took a swig of beer and stood up as if to propose a toast, but his legs gave way and he had to sit down again and breathe in great mouthfuls of air in an attempt to hold back his rising nausea.

He said he wasn't feeling well and he stood up again slowly, as if carrying a container full to the brim with some kind of toxic liquid. He stood there for a few seconds, looking at the other three, who were already bidding him good night and continuing to empty their cans without taking any more notice of him. He walked away, making an effort to walk straight, his head throbbing with pain, feeling as if a living thing was moving sluggishly in his abdomen. Behind him, the others were silent. They were probably watching him, in surprise perhaps, or contempt. As he got closer to the trailer, he heard the noises of the night. Crickets, owls calling to each other. A breath of cool air came from the forest, and he shivered again, soaked in sweat.

3

He had dreamed of another morning. A dawn he would
have seen grow lighter, casually extinguishing the
stars, gently pushing the night back into the recesses
and holes where it always hides. He would have liked to hear
a rooster crow, a first car pass quickly on the road. For weeks
before he left prison, he had replayed the sweetness of that moment every day. The first morning. Its light, its birdsong.

Imagination is a powerful thing. In the cell, despite the com-
motion of the other two waking or getting up, their yawns, their
sighs, their groans, the piss cascading to the bottom of the pan,
the loud farts you didn't try to suppress, immediately followed
by the foul smell that would linger for a long time, despite this
awakening of caged primates, sometimes he lay there on his
bed with his eyes closed and ran the movie of a summer dawn,
in color and 3D, the clear sky above the trees, the unexpected
gift of a little coolness.

It was the heat that woke him. And the migraine. And the
throbbing of his heart in his throat. With the feeling that he was
stinking and dirty. He remembered that he'd had to get up in
the night to throw up and that he'd thought he would die with
every spasm, soaked in sweat, disgusted with himself. He sat
down on the edge of the bed and waited for his stomach to rise
or fall, for the pain in his skull to throw him to the floor. He
measured his breathing, dreading the possibility that breathing
too deeply would lash his guts and bring them all up in one go.

But he felt his muscles getting stronger. His flesh resuming
its consistency, his center of gravity descending within him.
Once he was on his feet, he thought that his temples were going

to burst with the beating of his arteries and he had to close his eyes.

He opened them again and saw the light streaming in through the door of the barn. "It's all right," he said in a low voice. He dressed and grabbed something to wash himself with from the little bathroom. When he emerged into the sunlight, he stopped for two or three seconds and took advantage of this blinding happiness.

Rachel was sitting in the doorway of the house, looking at him, a big white bowl in her hands. He said hello to her and she replied weakly, turning her eyes away then drinking a mouthful of hot chocolate. When he went closer and made to stroke her hair with his fingertips, she moved her head away. She stood up and walked off slowly, almost on tiptoe. She looked like a little dancer. She turned and looked at Franck over the rim of her bowl. It was just then that the dog appeared. Its muscular back rippled in the sun, giving off midnight-blue glints. It advanced toward Rachel and stopped two meters from her, its nose on the ground, its ears down, without taking its eyes off her. It had a shifty look, sly and menacing, and Franck thought the animal was going to jump on Rachel at any moment. He was already wondering how you could kill a dog like that, already looking around for some object capable of beating it to death or cutting its throat, but he couldn't see anything, and the dog continued looking at Rachel, who had stopped moving and was holding her bowl in front of her with both hands. The animal took a step forward, then another, and Franck's heart skipped a beat, but he stopped himself from moving or even speaking, for fear of triggering the attack.

Rachel still didn't move. Her face expressed nothing. Neither fear nor surprise. In the house, Jessica could be heard calling her. One of the dog's ears turned in that direction. Then Rachel bent down and held out her arms, still holding the bowl, then placed it on the ground and moved back and walked toward Franck. The dog threw itself on the bowl, plunging its big mouth into it with a noise of wet chops, emptying it, licking it clean, then knocking it over with a blow from its muzzle.

"Weren't you afraid?"

She shook her head. The dog lifted its muzzle and sniffed the air, then set off at a trot along the path that led to the road and disappeared behind the wreck of a Renault van.

Jessica came around the corner of the house, carrying a big basket of washing, and hurried when she saw her daughter. She was smoking a joint and wearing big basketball shorts, red and shapeless, and the kind of long openwork top that exposed her breasts. Her features were drawn and she blinked in the sun. Bitter lines at the corners of her mouth. Franck tried to remember the pretty girl who had driven him here the previous day. She walked past him without saying a word. She smelled of dope and coffee.

"Oh, there you are! Can't you even answer when you're called?"

"It was the dog," Franck said.

"What about the dog?"

"He was standing in front of her, and when he went closer I really thought he was going to attack her."

"Is this true?"

Rachel didn't reply. She went and picked up her bowl, then walked back into the house without a word. Franck stroked her head as she passed and she did nothing to avoid him.

"She gave him her bowl of hot chocolate to finish."

"I guess that's what he wanted. He's weird sometimes, that dog, but he isn't aggressive. She's weird, too, never speaking, never answering. They make a fine pair!"

"You can't compare them, it's—"

"Weren't you going to take a shower? I've just had mine, so you'd better hurry before my mother gets into the bathroom, she always takes two hours."

She abruptly turned her back on him and shuffled away in her espadrilles, her basket wedged against one hip. Franck watched, again trying to find in that sluggish demeanor the body that had made him fantasize and given him a hard-on the previous day. Two women in one. Light and shade.

The bathroom smelled of soap, mixed with a stronger fragrance, a sweet, heady scent of violets. An open skylight let in a dazzling diamond-shaped block of sun that fell on the wall, and Franck shook his towel to air the room. He studied his face in the mirror above the washstand. He thought he looked sickly, the skin pale, and around the mouth and the eyes were a few lines he had never noticed before but which here, in this harsh white light that did nobody any favors, implicitly showed him all the time spent and wasted.

He realized that he hadn't really had the opportunity or the desire, in prison, to look at himself in a mirror, when he could find one, concerned more to keep an eye on what might loom up behind him than to detect signs of fatigue or age. He again had the sharp, almost heartrending feeling of newness, as if he were doing certain things for the first time, experiencing sensations previously unknown to him: the heat of the sun, the dazzle of the summer light, the songs of birds that were nowhere to be seen earlier when he had come out of the barn, the peace and quiet of a bathroom, the clean smell of his towel . . .

He started to undress, his muscles rippling in the harsh light and admired himself in the mirror, as most people did in the slammer whenever they passed a mirror that hadn't been broken, probably because that armor of muscles, forged with barbells on the sports field, gave them the illusion of being harder, less vulnerable. Yet they didn't linger in certain corners when certain underworld bigshots came shuffling along in their track pants, escorted by their entourages. A screwdriver, a coffee spoon, even, sharpened patiently on concrete, can tear any flesh, whether or not it's been inflated by bodybuilding.

Entering the shower cubicle, he saw it immediately, hanging

on the mixing faucet by its black cotton strap. He wondered what that white triangle was doing there, but he couldn't stop himself from taking a closer look, examining it and seeking in it traces of the intimacy that had obsessed him for the whole of a day, nestled as it had been in the secret folds of that girl's body. He started sniffing the piece of cloth like a dog being put on a scent, but he wasn't a dog and he couldn't smell anything, so he flung it away because he was hard and already on the verge of orgasm, the blood pounding in his temples, gasping for breath, and the images and ideas that assailed him would end up with his coming, and he'd have to wash it away with copious amounts of scorching hot water.

Too late: it was so violent that he almost fell, stifling a moan. He wondered if he would come as strongly as that inside her, and he recalled Jessica walking away in that outfit that had been thrown over her like dirty linen left on the back of a chair, to the point that he no longer knew if the body he had been sitting next to for more than three hours the day before was only an illusion due to his painful desire for women and sex. He shuddered with disappointment and shame, a boxer fighting his exhausted shadow beneath a flickering light bulb.

When Franck entered the kitchen, his wet towel over his shoulder, his bottle of shower gel in his hand, the old man was there, sitting at the table in front of an empty bowl, in an undershirt, Bermuda shorts and espadrilles. He smiled on seeing him and asked him if he had slept well, then without waiting for the answer told him that there was still some hot coffee and that everything else was on the table. There were bowls in the cupboard. He was in the middle of lighting a cigarette, and the lighter flame wavered in his trembling hand.

Franck poured himself some coffee and sugared and stirred it standing up, leaning on the counter. The old man was smoking, staring into space, sometimes removing pieces of tobacco from his lips with his fingertips.

"Hell, it's going to be hot again," he said, gesturing with

his chin at the light pushing against the half-closed shutters. "Fucking weather."

He shook his head, his sparse, messy hair sticking up like pieces of tow. He looked as if he had only just gotten up and was still stupefied by sleep, waiting for the connections in his brain to form, like those of an old computer that's too slow. Franck told himself the old man might go on rambling like that for a while, shaking in the semi-darkness of the room. Then he added his bowl to the dirty dishes still heaped in the sink and went out. The heat outside the house, the sun bright in the still air, was so dense that it slowed down movements and weighed on your chest, and Franck lowered his shoulders as he walked to the trailer.

He opened the windows to get rid of the sleeping animal smell he had left behind him. He counted his money, 650 euros in savings, sorted the few papers he'd crammed into his bag, lined up on a shelf the books he'd sent for in prison, then sat down on his bed and looked around him at the plastic partition walls with their coating peeling off, the cigarette burns in the covers of the bench seats, the big blisters on the linoleum. It was tiny and shabby, but he knew that no place would ever again seem to him narrower than the cell, even during the few occasions when he had been alone in it, because there, it was within himself that he was truly imprisoned. Here, the hot air moving around him smelled of hay and resin and wood, he could hear the chatter of birds in the trees behind the barn, and all this surrounded him like a friendly presence, a mute solicitude with invisible, discreet, but palpable gestures.

He lay down and closed his eyes and tried to empty his mind of the memories of prison. The image of Fabien inserted itself between the faces of the guys he would pass in the gangways or the exercise yard, swaggering sons of bitches or pathetic losers who dragged their despair around with them, sometimes both at the same time, and that included himself, putting on a wild look or a detached air, some muttering to themselves, others talking loudly, some with their hands in the pockets of their baggy pants, others exchanging obscure signals with mysterious correspondents while the warders looked on wearily.

He fell asleep, unable to remember anything else, his only memories ones of confinement, of being in a cage.

He dreamed someone was knocking at the door of his cell and his heart missed a beat and he found himself sitting on the edge of the bed, gasping for breath. The old man's bony face appeared at the door.

"I need a hand. I could ask a pal, but not before this afternoon."

Franck stood up immediately.

"Of course," he said, and shook what remained of sleep out of his head.

The old man seemed to have perked up, he was alert, determined. He led Franck along the path that went around the outside of the house as far as another barn, this one of brick and with a metallic frame. It might once have housed tractors and agricultural machinery, but it now served as a workshop where a BMW and a big Peugeot saloon were waiting, gleaming and glittering amid a filthy mess of tools and spare parts, wheel rims and tires and pieces of bodywork that seemed to have been scattered haphazardly during a frenzied search.

"We have a delivery to make. The BMW."

Franck went up to the car and glanced inside through the tinted windows. Leather. Wood.

"Here's the key. It's in Bordeaux—well, on the outskirts. Just follow me. On the highway, don't do anything stupid. Keep to eighty, no more than that. The papers are watertight, but I don't want anyone putting them to the test. Besides, you're just out of the can and it wouldn't be advisable to get yourself nabbed the next day for speeding, would it?"

Franck was hardly listening to him. He opened the door of the BMW and sat down and closed his hand on the wheel and stroked it and the warm roundness of the gear shift.

"It was Serge Weiss, a gypsy, who passed it on to me. His mechanic is in Gradignan[2] right now, and he had a customer who couldn't wait. And since we've known each other for ages, he trusted me."

The old man went into a shed and came back out at the wheel of an open-top midnight blue Mercedes 190 coupé, which looked as if it was straight from the factory. Franck bent forward to get a better view of the old man at the wheel. Sunglasses and baseball cap. Surrounded by all that chrome and those reflections of the sun on the bodywork, he looked like any old fool thinking he could still impress people, driving his museum piece.

They retraced as far as the highway the route that Franck had taken the previous evening on the way to the house. In the gentler light of morning, the landscape seemed less gloomy, less gray, as if the night had refreshed all the colors and a little green had been added to the brown and the gray. Occasionally, an isolated house stood out from this monotony, its garden overflowing with dahlias and gladioli or the bright colors of its shutters. They drove through deserted villages where occasionally an old guy in a leather vest, with a beret on his head, watched them passing, hands on his hips. Occasionally, someone came out of a bakery, occasionally a car passed them, or a truck pulling a trailer loaded with lumber.

All around them, the forest rose against the pale sky, striping it with its thousands of green needles. No horizon, still obscured by those countless bars rising from the meager soil. A closed landscape.

Franck had the impression that the car was gliding a fraction of an inch above the roadway in a gentle purr, heedless of the jolts, absorbing them scornfully, taking the bends with indifference. As if it smoothed the blacktop and straightened the bends, turning the winding ribbon of asphalt into a moving

---

[2] Name of the commune on the outskirts of Bordeaux where the prison is located.

walkway. At times, coming out of a bend, with a simple pressure on the accelerator he would leave the old man and his antique two hundred yards behind, and could already hear him cursing, yelling that he was going too fast and would crash this German jewel into a pine.

On the highway, he had to keep an eye on the speedometer to stay at eighty. He had the feeling he was dragging along in a padded box. When he slowed down on arriving at the tollbooth, his heart missed a beat at the sight of cops on the sidewalks of each lane, looking scornfully at vehicles and drivers. Franck concentrated on the payment process, using a credit card the old man had given him. He felt the eyes of the cop resting on him, inscrutable behind his dark glasses. Some distance farther on stood a high-speed blue car with a flashing light on its roof, its driver leaning on the door. As he drove away, Franck looked in the rear-view mirror and saw the cop watching him leave. For a while, he kept his eyes on the traffic behind him but no blue flash was visible, hurrying to intercept him. Instead of that, the old man flashed his lights at him then overtook him and pointed him in the right direction. They left the beltway and took the road to Lacanau, surrounded by the cars of foreign tourists, trailers and RVs rushing toward the coast.

Franck remembered certain trips to the beach, the excitement of the last few miles, the crossing of the hot dunes and the same intact emotion when the ocean appeared before their eyes and he and Fabien ran down into the water, sometimes a long way out at low tide, in spite of their mother yelling at them not to get wet, to wait for them, their father and her, but they continued to run and stopped on the hard wet sand at the exact place where the waves came to die, struck by the coolness of the water and intoxicated by the wind fluttering their T-shirts.

The old man turned onto a narrow road lined with deep ditches, then almost immediately onto a tarred path along which two big vans were parked. They came out onto a vast, graveled open space, in the middle of which rose a huge white house with pale green shutters. All around, along the fence, were a dozen huge trailers, some of them resting on cinder blocks. In front of one of them, three young girls under a parasol were laughing as they did each other's hair, long hennaed hair that rippled down their backs like thin snakes. Two little boys bent over bicycles were having fun making their back wheels skid and raising clouds of dust that hung for a long time in the still air. Other younger kids were advancing with difficulty across the pebbles on tricycles. All half naked, their skin burned by the sun, dark and golden, blue gleams shimmering in their hair.

They got out of their cars and a dog came trotting toward them, barking without conviction, a skinny mongrel with torn ears, its tongue hanging out. It sniffed the wheel of the old man's car and just as it was about to pee on it, the old man launched a kick, which the animal dodged with a leap before running off in the direction of the children. A woman who was standing under the canopy of the house, leaning on a post, rushed inside then came back out again almost immediately, followed by a tall guy with gray hair cut very short, who walked toward the old man. They shook hands and gave each other a kind of hug and exchanged first names. The man's name was Serge. Tall and thin, with powerful shoulders, in leather vest and Bermuda shorts. Tattooed arms: a mermaid and a snake intertwined on one, Maori patterns on the other. He indicated Franck with a movement of his chin.

"Who's he?"

"It's all right. He's Fabien's brother."

"Fabien's brother."

He looked Franck up and down, then turned his gaze back to the old man. His eyes were green with gold flecks, and he had long, thick lashes that fluttered heavily like those of a tired woman.

"What's your name, Fabien's brother?"

"He just got out of the can. Yesterday. He's—"

With a gesture, Serge silenced the old man. He looked straight at Franck, waiting for him to answer.

"My name's Franck. I got out yesterday."

"These things happen," Serge said.

"You have to get out some day," the old man said.

Serge shrugged and went up to Franck and held out his hand. His gold-flecked eyes watched for his reactions.

"Welcome to the land of the free."

He slapped him on the shoulder then turned to the BMW.

"So, what about this crate?"

He walked all the way around it, bending down from time to time, skimming the bodywork, kicking the tires with the tip of his shoe, then sat down at the wheel, started the ignition, examined the dashboard, released the hood. The old man rushed forward to open it and bent over the engine and inspected it anxiously, biting his lower lip. Going to it in his turn, Serge bent and emitted a whistle.

"You could eat off of it. I wish my daughter could do the dishes like that."

He snapped his fingers at Franck.

"Start it."

Franck sat down and turned the key. The engine started to purr. There was a heady scent inside the car—mint, perhaps. From where he was, he could only see Serge's big hand, carrying a big ring adorned with a blood-red stone. The hand went up abruptly.

"It's good!" He straightened up and closed the hood. "How much did we say? Five thousand?"

"No, seven," the old man said. "Seven thousand."

"You're a real vulture. Wait here."

Serge had said this in a low voice, without taking his eyes off the car. He sighed, shrugged his shoulders, and walked back to the house. He went in through a French door, squeezing through the narrow opening like a thief, as if taking care not to be heard.

The old man didn't move, standing directly in the sun, eyes fixed on the house, blinking beneath the peak of his cap. Franck could feel the sweat running down his temples and his back. Not a breath of air. The girls under the parasol had fallen silent and were looking in their direction. When Franck turned his head toward them, they burst into noisy laughter, so he looked away and walked up to the old man.

"What's he doing, printing the banknotes?"

The old man spat on the ground. "I wouldn't put it past him, the son of a bitch."

Serge came back out and stopped in the doorway and looked at them as if he might have heard what they'd just said. He was holding a plastic bag. He walked up to the old man and handed it to him.

"Five thousand. You can count it if you like."

The old man opened the bag and looked inside and fingered the bills heaped in the bottom then closed it again and wrapped it around the money.

"Wasn't it seven thousand?" Franck asked. "Wasn't that what you said?"

The old man shook his head and walked to his car. "Come on," he said. "Let it go."

Franck felt Serge's hand come to rest on his shoulder. It was as heavy as a beam. "Hey, Roland! Is this your accountant you brought with you? Want to leave him with me so I can teach him to count?"

Franck pulled away with an abrupt movement and turned to face the Gypsy. He saw the girls stand up and leave the shade of their parasol to get a better view. The Gypsy looked him up and down and his gold-flecked eyes seemed to gleam with an inner flame. He brought his face up close to Franck's.

"Get out of here, sweetheart, before I bend you over the car and show you how you can earn your two thousand euros. It'll make you a lot more than you got in the slammer. Got that, bitch? Now get out of here and watch your ass."

He had whispered all this in an even, almost gentle voice. Franck had felt the heat of his breath, the disgusting smell of his heavy perfume. He got in the car and the Gypsy leaned down to the old man.

"And don't ever bring this fag here again, Roland. I can't believe he came out of the same cunt as his brother!"

The old man put the car into gear as soon as Franck closed the door behind him. The wheels skidded on the gravel and Serge disappeared in a cloud of dust. Franck saw him put his hands in his pockets then turn his back on them and walk back to the house.

The Gypsy had scared him. He had been scared often enough in prison. He had felt heavy breathing on his neck, heard obscene whispers behind his back, seen gleams of madness in the eyes of guys who were put into his cell, and on the nights after their arrival he wouldn't sleep, keeping under him the fork he had managed to filch and sharpen over time. He'd always told himself that in prison, everything was harsher, more violent, more pitiless because of the confinement, the enforced intimacy, and he had more or less learned to protect himself in that enclosed jungle. But never before in normal life, outside, as a free man, had he had that sensation that a predator could attack him at any moment, in broad daylight, in a dark corner, or in the dead of night, simply because he felt like it, without any other constraint or necessity than that of dominating, humiliating, and knowing he wouldn't be punished. He would have been incapable of saying why he had butted in over those two thousand euros, except to test the animal the way you annoy an aggressive dog or a snake. Except to get himself in a mess, as he had already done too often, as he was so good at doing, only this time without the help or protection of Fabien, and that probably changed everything.

The old man drove nervously, his eye on the rear-view mirror, as if he was afraid of being followed. Eyes alert behind his sunglasses, face set, jaws clenched. As soon as they were on the highway, he started to curse between his teeth and shake his head as if a whole heap of conflicting ideas was knocking about in there.

"Why did you have to open your big mouth? What business was it of yours? You only got here yesterday and you're already interfering?"

"He was cheating you out of two thousand euros. And anyway I didn't like the guy."

"Oh, right, and after what he said to you, did you like him any better?"

"What he said to me is my business."

The old man shook his head some more and gave a crooked smile. "Everyone knows what Serge says and does to people. Outside his clan, he doesn't think much of anyone. Not even me, although he trusts me and he's helped me in the past. But the day I get into trouble with him, I might as well leave the country and hope he never finds me. You humiliated him, and he won't forgive you for that. He's a friend of your brother's, for fuck's sake. They're in business together, and Serge doesn't trust many people. Now you've annoyed him, he's going to stop trusting us. You have no idea how nasty he can get, how crazy. He's the kind of guy who likes to hear you blubber and beg for mercy and only stops when you've stopped moving. And that's the guy you had to go and piss off, you fucking idiot."

"Don't talk to me like that. I thought I was doing the right thing."

"I'll talk to you how I like. When you don't know something, you keep quiet, and that's that. You stay in your place and keep your mouth shut until someone asks you to open it."

They didn't say any more. Franck saw again the Gypsy's gold-flecked eyes, like a wild animal's. Above all, he heard again those words uttered up close to him, icy words despite the hot breath blown on his skin. At the tollbooth, the old man asked him for the credit card he'd lent him on the way out.

As soon as they were in open country, the convertible became a hot bath that even the speed couldn't cool down. The vertical sun pinned them to their seats, and sweat glued them to the leather. Noon had drained the land of its shadows. When they spotted the thicket of hazel trees lining the road, Franck felt relieved. He wanted to be alone again in his trailer, just like when he was a child and he'd hidden after doing something stupid and cursed himself for doing it or for letting himself get caught. But a big black 4×4 loomed up and forced the old man to brake sharply in order to let it pass. They couldn't see anything of its occupants through the tinted windows, and it sped past, swerving and almost mounting the grassy shoulder.

The engine of the Mercedes had stalled, and the old man turned the ignition key to no avail. He looked anxious, and not because of the mechanics. He glanced in the rear-view mirror and Franck turned, but the road was empty and shimmering in the heat. When they set off again, the old man drove at a snail's pace. The dust raised by the 4×4 still hung in the air. Like a fit of anger that refuses to subside.

"Who was that?"

"Nobody. If anyone asks you, say you don't know a thing."

The house was dark and almost cool. They found the old woman sitting with Rachel at the kitchen table in front of what looked like a salade niçoise.

"We got delayed. We're only just starting."

"So I see," the old man grunted. "Did they stay long?"

"No. Half an hour."

The old woman tried to meet his eyes, but he turned his back on her and opened the fridge and took out a bottle of beer, then rummaged in a drawer for an opener.

"Where's Jessica?"

The old woman pointed to the ceiling then shrugged fatalistically. "She's just gone up. She isn't feeling very well. She took a couple of pills."

The two old people exchanged knowing, scornful glances.

The old woman shook her head, then served Rachel, who had been looking at them in turn for a while.

"This is our business," the old man said to Franck. "No need to get involved. We'll sort it."

The old woman threw Franck a furtive glance, hostile and full of contempt.

The old man put a hand on his shoulder. "It's okay. Grab a beer, and come and eat."

"There are plates in the cupboard. Rachel and I made the food. Isn't that right?"

Rachel nodded without looking up from her plate. She lifted four or five grains of rice with the tip of her fork. Her grandmother watched her with an irritable expression, then turned to the old man.

"So how did it go?"

"He coughed up. What do you think?"

"Fucking Gypsy. We shouldn't do business with him anymore."

"Easy to say. Do you have another solution? You know perfectly well he's the one who makes the decisions."

The old woman glanced over at Franck. "We'll talk about it later. Now's not the time. All the same, you did your job, right?"

"Serge can be temperamental sometimes, but he's a guy you can count on."

The old woman nodded and fell silent. Franck had found some plates and flatware and put it all down on the table, making as little noise as possible. Rachel watched him, picking at her salad. The old man sat down, saying that he was hungry, and pulled the big salad bowl toward him.

"Can I get up?" Rachel asked.

Her grandmother pointed at the plate. "No. Finish your food first. She doesn't eat a thing, this girl. Like her mother when she was little. She'll be just the same."

Rachel still had her nose down, her fork in her hand. She heaved a big, unhappy sigh and started eating again, sparingly, moving the tomatoes and leeks to one side of the plate, the rice and the flakes of tuna to the other.

"This is a good salad," Franck said. "You made it, you really should eat some of it."

Rachel shrugged.

"Did you hear what he said? Eat now."

"I want to go see Mom."

"You'll go when you've eaten. You saw for yourself, she doesn't want to see anybody, so now's not the time."

They finished the meal in a mournful silence. The old man kept pouring himself more wine, which he drank in great gulps, clicking his tongue and sighing noisily. He devoured half a camembert then stood up abruptly and announced that he was going to take a nap. His wife also stood up and started clearing the table, roughly. She took Franck's plate away while he was still wiping it with his bread and Rachel's when she'd just speared a slice of tomato with her fork. Rachel stood up, went to the refrigerator and got out a crème caramel and ate it standing up, walking slowly around the table.

Franck would have liked a coffee but he didn't feel up to asking the old woman if there was any or if it had to be made. She had her back to him, tinkering at the sink, a cigarette stuck between her lips—he could see the wreaths of smoke rising above her. He sat there looking at this woman in her white shorts stretched tight over her broad ass and her thighs padded with cellulite and her stooped back and her red hair, and he imagined her mouth, twisted around her cigarette because of the smoke stinging her eyes, no doubt frozen in a grimace that summed up her entire nature: tense, grotesque, repulsive. He already hated the woman, even though this was only his second day here, even though she hadn't said more than twenty words to him and showed him nothing but indifference or contempt. He was surprised by the strength and depth of this feeling, and he told himself that the hate he felt was the product of a kind of intuition. There was something

bad in this woman, something toxic or poisonous that ema-
nated from her.

Rachel left the room and could be heard climbing the stairs.
The old woman broke off what she was doing and listened to
the little girl's footsteps. She shook the ash of her cigarette into
the dishwater, sighed, and muttered: "What the fuck is she doing? I did tell her." She seemed to hesitate for a few seconds,
one hand propped on the sink, the other holding the cigarette,
from which a thread of smoke stretched up, blue and slow and
straight in the still air.

"Go see what she's doing and bring her back down," she
said to Franck. "Jessica doesn't want to see anyone. There's going to be trouble again."

Franck went to the foot of the stairs and heard a few little
knocks at a door followed by Rachel's voice calling her mother
softly. He slowly climbed the stairs and no sooner did he reach
the landing than he saw Rachel slump against the door, whispering "Mom, mom," her ear stuck to the wood, banging it
softly with the flat of her hand then stroking it. He went to
her and crouched down and saw the tears running down her
cheeks. He searched for words, short of breath, not knowing
what to say or how. Rachel was moaning now and Jessica's voice
echoed inside the room, thick and muffled.

"That's enough now. Leave me alone. Go play and stop
crying."

Rachel burst into tears, hitting the door and dropping her
hand with the fingers curved, hooked as if to scratch the wood
and cling to it, still slumped, her bare legs folded beneath her.

Just as Franck was making up his mind to take her in his
arms and move her away, he heard Jessica cry, "Stop bugging me now!" Then the door shook with a loud thump that
made Rachel jump and stop crying abruptly, leaving her open-
mouthed, panting, her eyes wide open. Franck assumed that
Jessica had thrown a shoe in her daughter's direction, or something else she'd had within reach.

"Come on, Rachel."

He lifted her, she didn't weigh anything. She had stopped moving and her body was floppy, and if it weren't for the feverish heat that made her shake, he would have thought he was holding a dead girl in his arms. As he passed the kitchen door, the old woman glanced at him, her hands in the sink. He stopped, hesitated in the doorway, but she turned her back on him and bent over the dishwasher and noisily shifted plates and dishes, unconcerned about anything else.

As soon as they were outside, Rachel began struggling feebly in Franck's arms, so he put her down on the terrace and she stood beside him for a moment, still silent, pensive perhaps, or just numb.

"You mustn't be sad. Your mother's sick, but it'll pass, you'll see. We just have to let her rest. Okay?"

She didn't move. She stood there, frozen, just as he had put her down, like a life-size figurine.

"Don't you want to go over there, under the trees? It won't be so hot."

She didn't react. Franck took a deckchair and carried it over to two big oaks just outside the barns, then turned to Rachel. She seemed to be watching something, over toward the forest, with such intensity that Franck also looked, but he couldn't see anything on the dark edge of the woods, dominated as it was by the motionless mass of the foliage.

"What did you see?"

Rachel gave a start and turned her head toward him. She seemed surprised to see him there and stared at him gravely. Suddenly, she went back inside the house, almost running, came back out a few seconds later, holding a big rag doll in her hand, and came toward Franck.

"This is Lola," she said, holding the doll out to him.

He took it. It was soft and warm. He looked at its big blue eyes and the freckles on its cheeks and the enigmatic smile, benevolent or mocking, that had been drawn on it. Hair made of strands of orange wool were gathered into two stiff braids.

"Is she your favorite?"

She nodded then reached out her hands to get Lola back. She hugged the doll to her then went and lay down in the deckchair.

"What were you looking at in the woods over there?"

She stared at him, her doll lying on her chest. He held her gaze, plumbing the depths of those dark eyes that might be capable of absorbing him entirely.

"Why are you looking at me like that?"

Rachel sighed, then turned her head toward the barns, and from this point on made a show of ignoring him. He would have liked to approach her, break though her silence, drag a smile out of her, but he didn't dare because he didn't have enough gentleness in him to avoid hurting her. He felt as if his skin was covered in scales and might well scratch her. Rough and soiled. Unworthy.

He went back into the house and was struck by the silence there, only interrupted by the intermittent buzzing of unseen flies. The kitchen smelled of dirty water and vinegar. The dishwasher was humming. He turned on the faucet in the sink, filled a glass that was drying on the drain rack, drank the water in long gulps, and filled the glass again. He felt as if he could go on drinking endlessly. Out of breath, he went back into the corridor and listened, wondering where they had all gone, the old nanny goat and her stupid old billy goat, their probably slightly crazy daughter, just the kind of woman who attracted Fabien as surely as carnivorous flowers swallow insects. As open as a trap. He liked that anyway, Fabien—getting his wings singed by girls everyone knew you shouldn't touch, shouldn't even go near, but he liked it, forbidden fruit, he called it, even when there was a knife or gun telling him to back off.

Advancing along the corridor, Franck saw the huge TV screen. It was on, but the sound was turned right down. Men and women in suits were moving about, having a serious discussion in a glass-walled office. Cops in an American series, looking like cool, determined models. And in front of the TV, slumped in his armchair, mouth open, his undershirt riding up his beer belly, the old man, wheezing in his sleep as if he were dying. A hand dangled over the worn leather arm, resting on a bottle of beer he seemed about to grab.

In this silence, the air was heavy, unbreathable. He walked back out into the motionless light and hurried to his trailer, where the dim light could pass for coolness. It was soothing to be alone there, surrounded by the few things he had put away, knowing they were around him like the imagined boundaries of a private territory. He took his clothes off and collapsed flat on his stomach on the bed. He fell asleep immediately and dreamed that the black 4×4 stopped in front of the house, driven by Fabien, although he couldn't see his face through the smoked glass of the windows.

He woke with a start and got up and glanced through the window to check if the 4×4 was there or not. It was already nearly five in the evening. Franck went back to the house, where the TV was still chattering away in the silence. He wondered what Jessica could possibly be doing, shut up in her room. A vision of a naked body lying abandoned on the bed came into his mind but then he recalled Rachel slumped against the door. He climbed the first steps of the stairs, slowly at first, but they creaked and squeaked as if being trodden by a thief, so he climbed the rest two by two until he reached the landing. In the dim light, the heat gathered and made the silence even heavier.

He gave a start when he saw the dog's huge head loom up. It was lying in the middle of the landing, motionless, its long feet stretched out straight in front of it, its ears up, its dull eyes unfathomably dark. Franck stood motionless for about a minute, unsure what to do. The dog was about ten feet from him, as still as a malevolent idol. Sensing the nervous quivering of the tense muscles beneath that smooth coat, he thought about going back downstairs, but instead took a step forward. He wouldn't let it be said he had retreated at the sight of a stationary dog, even a monstrous one, even one that was capable of tearing him to pieces.

At last, the animal let out a big sigh and collapsed onto its side. Franck looked at the pale-blue door behind which Jessica might be asleep, and he went and pressed his ear against it but heard nothing except his own blood throbbing in his temples, and he straightened up, his breath coming in short gasps, knowing that not many feet away she lay collapsed on the bed, dazed and available, in the stifling darkness of the room. He felt the sweat slide over his skin in a shiver, thinking suddenly of the panties abandoned this morning on the mixing faucet of the shower like a confused signal, an involuntary invitation or an obscene provocation to which his body responded instinctively when his soul was telling him to flee.

Just as he was retreating, the door was flung open and he caught a glimpse of her in the dim light, scantily clad, one of her breasts uncovered by her top, which had fallen off her shoulder. Her hair was tangled, the skin of her thighs were pale in the gray light of the landing, and her eyes were shining, as if washed by tears, the dilated pupils almost phosphorescent. Franck saw her back reflected in the cracked mirror of the wardrobe occupying the opposite wall, cut in half diagonally like a queen in a pack of cards. She shrugged her shoulders and turned and walked back to the bed, saying, "Come."

4

He had slept badly, and although he was alone, he had been awakened by Jessica's body. Or rather, by the memory of what she had done with him, what she had let him do. Available, open, abandoned. Silent. Or else moaning through clenched teeth in what sounded like pleasure. Dog and bitch glued together. Claws and teeth. Saliva, fluids, sweat. She had occasionally pushed him away with her elbow, then pulled him back and held him with her mouth. He had plunged into her, feeling at times that he was losing himself. It was like throwing yourself into a blazing fire with no hope of getting out again.

He had never done this. Not this way. He had seen things in movies, he had fucked a few girls in a rush, girls who were resigned or drunk and said they wanted more but could barely stand and fell asleep between two thrusts or walked away to throw up booze and cum, blubbering. There had sometimes been hidden, clandestine, stolen embraces. Above all, he had hoped and dreamed, always disappointed by the over-zealousness of his right hand.

The previous day, leaving the room, he had descended the stairs at the end of the afternoon, his legs shaky, his body damp and sticky, then had flung himself under the cold shower, rubbing himself to awaken the other parts of his body or rid himself of incrusted filth.

It was a storm that brought daylight. It was as if the lighting flashes had lit up the sky, and the rain and the wind awakened nature. For half an hour, in the torn darkness, Franck had listened to that fury explode and the roof of the barn shake over his head. Then it receded the way a gang of screaming kids runs away after banging on doors or letting off firecrackers in letter boxes. A hissing silence returned, full of wet whispers, lapping on sheet metal, like hundreds of little throats swallowing all that water.

As the storm moved northward, he let the obsessive visions of the night fade while a little coolness entered through the windows of the trailer and the light spread everywhere. He heard the shutters of the house open, the chatter of the TV start up. He was hungry. He knew that if he went into the kitchen, he would find the old woman sitting at the table over her bowl of coffee, already wrapped in cigarette smoke, but he didn't care. He got up. The coolness brought by the storm was nothing but a memory now, replaced by warm air bringing him the smells of wet earth.

Once outside, he saw Jessica on the path leading to the forest, with her back to him, facing the mass of trees. She was dressed only in a long T-shirt, and was smoking a cigarette. When he hailed her to say good morning, she jumped, then turned and threw him a hostile look without saying anything. He asked her if she was all right but she pretended not to hear him, almost imperceptibly pulling her head down into her shoulders. He stood for a moment looking at her, hoping she would decide to come to him. The forest was still, filled with shade, only the tops of the trees tinged with the sun's glow.

After drinking three cups of coffee and eating a little cereal, he hung around the meadow, on the edge of the trees, beneath a milky, already scorching sky. The two women and Rachel had gone shopping in Bazas and he felt alone and tired. The old man was tinkering away in his shed. Every now and again Franck heard metallic crashes, the clink of tools being thrown to the floor. He went closer. All he could see of the old man were his legs sticking out from underneath a car propped up on jack stands. The old man was blowing and grunting unintelligibly and his feet, encased in dirty, old, unlaced sneakers, moved in time with his efforts.

"Can I help?"

"No, it's okay. I've nearly finished. I had to take this fucking oil pan off."

Franck crouched down. He saw the old man's gnarled arms raised above him, holding the steel part. A screw fell and rolled along the floor and with a final effort, his back arched, the man loosened the oil pan and put it down next to him.

"Pass me that cloth."

Franck grabbed an oil-stained piece of cloth lying next to a wheel, maybe an old sheet, and handed it to the old man, who wiped his hands and forearms then got out from under the car. He sat up and took two or three deep breaths.

"I'm too fucking old to do this kind of thing. Help me up."

He held out his hand to Franck who grabbed it and helped him to his feet. He stretched his neck, threw out his chest, then massaged his lower back, making faces. He took a pack of small black cigars from a pocket in his overalls and lit one. From the same pocket, he took an envelope and handed it to Franck.

"There's a hundred there. You can check."

Franck opened the envelope, held together with an elastic band. The fifty-euro bills were brand new. He smelled them as he leafed through the wad. They smelled of ink and paper. That was how money smelled before it was soiled by sweaty hands.

"Plus another hundred next week. I didn't want to withdraw it all in one go. It was your brother who told us to give you that to help you before he gets back."

"Where's this money come from?"

"I'm not too sure. Before he left, he just said: 'Give this to my brother, it'll help him start over. Tell him to wait for me.'"

"And the rest?"

The old man blew out his cigar smoke with a sigh. "The rest of what?"

"The rest of the money. There was sixty thousand when we pulled that job. He didn't spend it all in five years."

"I have no idea. Maybe he had a lot of expenses. Or maybe he got involved in schemes that didn't work out. That's why he left for Spain. He had enough money to put into a deal, he said. A deal that Serge pointed him in the direction of—you know, the guy you insulted. He had his plans and we had ours, you have to eat. You know, he didn't talk much, your brother."

"Did he say when he'd be back?"

"Sometimes he's been away for days without saying anything, and then come back without letting us know. This time, he told us he'd be away for nearly a month. For him, it was like a vacation."

"It's weird all the same. I hope he hasn't gotten into any trouble. He was quite good at that. Didn't he say anything to Jessica?"

The old man smiled, his cigar stuck between his lips. "You're the one Jessica confides in now. Why don't you ask her?"

Franck felt himself blush and didn't know how to reply. He simply gave a crooked smile and turned, expecting to see her standing there on the path, watching him slyly, but there was nothing but the trembling of the branches, the movement of an unseen bird.

The old man blew smoke out of the side of his mouth, then threw his cigar away and turned and bent over the engine, an open-end wrench in his hand. Franck found himself watching the man's thin, twisted carcass, each movement of which seemed to be accompanied by a noise of metal as if it were in the process of becoming an outgrowth of the machine. He held the envelope full of money, wondering what he was going to do with it and having no idea. Right now, he felt embarrassed and useless and stupid next to this old man bustling over this car, partly because he hadn't wondered anything like that in a long time, if he ever had.

He moved away and hung about the house for a moment, tormented by the desire to go up to Jessica's room the way you return to the scene of a crime you're not sure you committed to convince yourself that it really happened. He might well find Fabien there, getting dressed or still sprawled on the sheets, and Fabien would say, "Here you are, you motherfucker, I've been waiting for you. So, how was Jessica, was she good? Did you give her a good fucking while I had my back turned?" then he would come to him and grab him and pin him against the wall, crushing his throat with his forearm, and Franck would feel ashamed of himself for taking advantage of his brother's absence but he would fight back, what about his five years inside, he would retort, what about the fact that in spite of all the questioning by the cops and all the threats, he hadn't talked, he had held out even though his lawyer advised him to say what he knew, and not make matters worse by taking all the blame, acting tough and trying to be clever would just annoy the judges, think about that, you could get up to ten years, don't you realize?

He turned his back on the house and the bitter stream of thoughts engulfing him. His heart was racing and there was an acrid taste coating his throat as he walked toward the forest and the dark, tangled mass of the trees came to meet him like an enormous wave. He slipped the envelope into his pants pocket and hurried in beneath the shady vault. The coolness and the darkness took him by surprise. He looked through the gaps in the foliage at the fragments of the sky. It seemed further away than usual, almost unreal. The forest pressed in on him with all its weight of branches and leaves and thick trunks, blotting out any horizon, and the sand on the path slowed his progress, occasionally giving way beneath his feet. From time to time, the cry of a bird could be heard, the distant tapping of a woodpecker, insects buzzing in his ears as they flew past, and he would brush them away with his hand and shake his head. Soon coming to a fork, Franck took the path on the right, which was wider and more concave. The shade became less dense as pines gradually replaced oaks until the forest was nothing more than a forbidding plantation of straight black trunks from the tops of which a hot, milky light fell.

He stopped at the entrance to a circle of galleries supported by wooden posts, camouflaged by bracken and panels of heather and pierced with small, narrow windows. In the middle, an empty space with stakes driven into it and wires run across it that worked wooden levers and pulleys. It looked like some kind of sacred site used for pagan sacrifices or witches' sabbaths. Franck advanced into the middle of the circle, and in the silence, which suddenly seemed deeper than ever, he had the impression that he was being watched by eyes hidden in the shadows of the arrow slits, maybe the hollow eyes of ghosts.

He had seen this kind of construction before. It was a pigeon trap, where hunters lay in wait in the fall, manipulating decoys to attract birds, but to him it seemed that this village of children's huts, this rickety circle made up of odds and ends, imperfect as it was, was surrounding him with some kind of black magic. He turned to get out of there and gave a start. There it was, some sixty feet away, sitting in the middle of the path, panting, its tongue hanging out, its sides lifting in time with its rapid breathing.

"What are you doing there?"

The dog stood up, sniffing the ground. It looked even bigger than before. It stood in the middle of the path, seeming to occupy the whole width of it. Franck whistled softly and the dog raised its head and sniffed the air, no doubt making sure it recognized his smell.

Franck took a step forward, and immediately the animal was on its guard, its legs stiff, all its muscles tense and bulging beneath a black coat that gave off no reflection, seeming to absorb the gray light spread by the jagged vault of the pines. It gave a low growl, its head down, not taking its eyes off Franck. There was nothing around that he could use as a weapon, not even a branch. He thought to go back to the pigeon trap to find something there, and started walking backwards, slowly, but the dog advanced toward him and the distance separating them diminished.

Franck had never been attacked by a dog, or even bitten. Of course he had seen movies where guys held the foaming mouth of a guard dog at arm's length and finally got the better of the monster by strangling it or putting an eye out, but he couldn't remember how they managed to do that when all their strength was already taken up by stopping the animal from tearing their throats out. He froze, and the dog did the same, still on its guard, its legs slightly bent, like springs stretched so taut they have to jerk back. Its eyes gave off no luster, the sockets could just as well have been empty and burned out.

Franck knew that the animal smelled his fear, could even perhaps hear the crazy beating of his heart. He had to try something. A kind of anger rose in him, shaking him out of his terrified inertia. Fucking dog. He wasn't going to let himself get eaten by this mutt, here in the middle of the forest, and die alone with the blood draining from him, or even let himself be intimidated like a child by its ugly mug. "Move and I'll tear your guts out, you motherfucker." He turned to his right and started walking, slowly at first, through bracken that came up to his chest and hid the dog from sight. He described a large circle, stepped over a fallen tree trunk, and crossed a kind of dried-up ditch. He felt his courage return, his breathing keeping pace with his rapid walk. He knew the path was to his left and he started veering in that direction. The oak wood began to encroach on the vertical trunks of the pines.

Then he heard a loping sound behind him. The dog was on his heels, its ears down. As it overtook Franck, it knocked against his leg with its big head then disappeared into the high dry grasses, which closed over it, absorbing it in their silence.

The light burst above the meadow and Franck's heart beat faster when the gray house appeared, its shutters closed. He stopped to watch, pleased to see without being seen. The old woman was hanging the washing. Rachel was passing T-shirts and underwear and clothes pegs to her. The dog was lying next to them, its head turned toward Franck, its nose in the air, sniffing. Franck made up his mind to emerge from the woods. The low green grass rustled as he trod it.

"How's it going? Hot, isn't it?"

Rachel took a shirt from the basket then stopped and watched him as he approached.

"Are you going to pass me that shirt or not? What are you looking at? Come on, get a move on. Always daydreaming."

The old woman tore the shirt from Rachel's hand, and the girl hastened to hand her another clothes peg.

Franck was now about fifteen feet from the clothes line. The old woman's eyes passed over him without stopping, as if he were a dead tree or a scarecrow that had been there for years. Rachel, though, was looking at him on the sly, lowering her eyes to the basket as soon as the old woman turned toward her for another item of washing. Just as he was setting off again toward the house, he heard the old woman's voice.

"What were you doing in the woods?"

She hadn't moved, her two hands resting on the clothes line, and was looking straight at him.

"Nothing. I went for a walk."

She glanced in the direction of the trees.

"Why did you ask me that?"

"No reason. You don't look like the kind of person who hangs around in woods."

"What kind of person do you think I am?"

He said this more sharply than he had intended, with a certain swagger, chin thrust forward. There was a desire in his hands and arms to hit her, to wipe away that ugly mug, but first he wanted to know why she felt such hatred and contempt for him. To know what Fabien had to do with it all.

The old woman stiffened, her lips pursed. She was about to say something, her mouth already open, but changed her mind and made an impatient gesture at Rachel, demanding the next item to hang up. Before he walked away, Frank turned toward the forest, where not a leaf was moving beneath the leaden sun.

The old woman had resumed her work and was no longer bothering with him. The dog had stretched out to its full length, as if dead, its sides convulsed by its heavy breathing. Above it hung a sheet that no breath of air stirred, as still and flat and white as a dividing wall.

As he walked toward the house, he felt the old woman's gaze, heavy between his shoulder blades, and he lowered his head and rounded his back to get rid of that steel tip ready to plant itself in him. As soon as he had closed the door behind him, he reveled in the half-light, the closed shutters, the impression of coolness. Jessica was washing tomatoes in the sink. She turned and looked at him indifferently. She was wearing a man's shirt open wide at the top, which slid from her shoulders and fell over her buttocks. He liked the thought that she might not be wearing anything underneath.

"Where were you?"

"I went for a walk in the woods."

"How was it?"

"Not bad. Until the dog showed up."

"Oh yes? And?"

"I got the feeling it was going to jump me. There it was, in front of me, giving me a sidelong look. I swear, it was growling and everything . . ."

Jessica shrugged and started cutting the tomatoes into the hot oil of a frying pan. She smiled ironically. "A big boy like you afraid of dogs . . ."

"No, not of dogs. This dog. I'm sure it's dangerous. Remember yesterday morning, with the kid."

"He'll never do anything to her. We've had him for a year, and he's never growled at her, or at anyone, so drop it."

They fell silent. Jessica stirred the tomatoes and they sputtered. Rachel came in and huddled against her mother, putting her arms around her thighs. Jessica told her to leave her alone and lay the table instead. Rachel went to a wall cupboard and moved a chair closer to reach it. She climbed on the chair, took some plates and stood there, back arched from the burden she was carrying. Franck was scared she would fall and rushed to her.

"Give me those. Come down."

Rachel came down cautiously, refusing to hold his hand. She put the chair back where she had taken it from, she went to look in a drawer for the flatware and put it on the table. She moved calmly, with a solemn air, concentrating on her task as if afraid of forgetting something. Jessica turned. She watched her daughter bustling about, carefully arranging the glasses, putting rolled-up napkins next to the knives.

"You have to let her manage by herself. Otherwise she'll never be independent."

"She was going to fall off that chair. She's small, don't forget."

"No, she wasn't going to fall. Isn't that right, sweetheart? You weren't going to fall, were you?"

Rachel looked up at her mother and replied with a flutter of the eyelashes.

"I love you, sweetie. You're a real little woman."

Jessica bent down and held out her arms to Rachel, who came and snuggled up to her, head down, letting herself be stroked and kissed, arms dangling. From where he was standing, Franck glimpsed a breast beneath Jessica's oversize shirt. And Jessica knew it. She looked at him for a long time and he didn't turn his eyes away from that plunging neckline. She told Rachel to go wash her hands and as the girl started toward the sink, she said:

"No, not here. In the bathroom."

Rachel obeyed. She left the kitchen, holding her arms away from her body, her hands open with the fingers spread as if she had suddenly dirtied herself. As soon as she was in the corridor, Jessica went to Franck, one hand between her thighs.

"I want it like crazy. Touch."

He touched. She guided his hand, and he started to rub the hot, damp softness he could feel beneath his fingers. She looked him straight in the eyes with an almost threatening intensity, standing firmly on her parted legs, and he could feel her against him, as stiff and still as a store window dummy. Although he was worried about Rachel coming back, he slid his fingers inside the triangle of cloth. Jessica, lips tight, breathed into his neck with a moan that came from deep inside her throat.

They leapt apart on hearing the old woman coming, muttering and complaining about the heat. Franck went to the table and pretended to arrange the place settings and Jessica started cracking eggs over the tomatoes she had fried. The old woman stopped in the doorway and let her weary eyes linger first on one, then on the other. They both made a show of ignoring her. She finished laying the table.

Now the old man came in. Bermuda shorts, undershirt, espadrilles. Oil stains on his belly, yellow patches under his armpits. Black streaks on his face like those special forces guys you sometimes see on TV.

Jessica asked him if he had seen Rachel.

"She's brushing her hair."

"What do you mean, she's brushing her hair?"

"I don't know. She has a brush in her hand, and she's running it through her hair. That's called brushing your hair, isn't it?"

"For fuck's sake, Rachel, come to the table, now. What are you up to?"

They heard a door being closed. Rachel appeared at the door to the kitchen, her long hair hanging loose over her shoulders. In her hand was a blonde doll dressed in a swimsuit.

"What have you been doing? You were gone ages."

She sat down and then sat the doll down facing her, next to her plate. She folded her napkin in a long rectangle so that it made a kind of mattress and laid the doll on it. She passed the tips of her fingers over the doll's eyes, as if to close them, but they stayed open, huge and blue and empty. Then she arranged the doll's hair around her head and on her chest. Then she sat there motionless and silent, her hands flat on the oilskin. The old man sat down with a sigh and ran his big hand with the black nails through Rachel's nicely-brushed hair. The little girl broke away and tidied it.

There they all were, around this table, drinking pastis and cutting themselves slices of sausage, serving themselves eggs and tomatoes, breaking thick pieces of bread with their damp hands, exchanging only the odd word as they passed each other salt or water or slices of melon that Rachel went to fetch from the fridge.

Franck watched them surreptitiously, miming their gestures as if studying a tribe of monkeys from the inside. The old woman sipped her drink with a stubborn or anxious air, staring straight ahead, no doubt lost in bitter thoughts. The old man sighed with pleasure between mouthfuls, refilling his plate, and greedily grabbing the food as it passed in front of him. Jessica ate almost nothing, chewing on a piece of bread and trailing her fork through a spreading egg yolk. She never took her eyes off Rachel, who was giving crumbs to her doll then placing them carefully beside the mattress she had made for it.

Flies buzzed around them and they swatted them away with lazy gestures of the hand. Franck poured himself a full glass of water and it briefly crossed his mind to empty it over himself, to let the coldness of it jolt him out of his overwhelming lethargy and to see how the others would react, what kind of face the old woman would pull. She had just started eating her eggs, her chin almost in the plate. Jessica suddenly looked at him with a half-smile, her eyes bright, a luminous green like a cat's eyes, almost as if lit from within. Her mother turned to her and was about to talk to her, so she leaned toward Rachel and ordered her in a low voice to eat instead of picking at her food.

He abruptly got to his feet. His chair scraped the floor and the old woman broke off her eating, her fork full, and threw him a hostile look, then shook her head in irritation or contempt and went back to her food. He left the table with all the little noises of their meal ringing in his head, and as he walked out of the kitchen he turned and saw all four bent over and silent, gathered together and held by that half-light like a single strange organism with sporadic gestures, a calm monster capable of digesting its prey before devouring it. A creature that mustn't be looked in the eyes, a monster whose poisonous caresses you mustn't give in to, however much you lusted after them.

5

The man selling the car was a master plumber the old man had done a few favors for a year earlier. He was a tall, taciturn, pensive-looking man, who seemed not to listen to what was said to him and only answered after a few seconds' thought. You didn't know if each time he was weighing up the pros and the cons or if he simply had difficulty understanding. For now, stooping slightly, he opened all the doors of the little Renault, lifted the hood, and took a plastic case containing starter cables from the trunk. He explained in a low voice, as if talking to himself, that the car belonged to his wife, who had just left him for an electrician, a guy he had known for fifteen years. That was why he was selling off her car—so she wouldn't have the nerve to come back for it one day, the bitch. He cursed between his teeth and insulted her and vowed to take a blowtorch to them one of these days, her and that motherfucker. He said this through clenched teeth, hitting the bodywork with the flat of his hand from time to time.

While the old man took a look at the engine, Franck slid in behind the wheel. He moved the seat back and put his feet on the pedals. Everything was clean, as good as new. The odometer indicated 68,000 miles, but the rest seemed straight from the factory. You could have eaten your food off the floor rug. A deodorant shaped like a fir tree hung from the rear-view mirror, giving off a smell of mint. He felt good here. As if he were at home. He passed his fingers over the radio and grasped the knob of the gear shift. A deep, calm joy overcame him, bringing a lump to his throat. He had never really had a car of his own. He hadn't had time, and he hadn't had the money, so he'd taken the ones he'd been lent for a few hours, always feeling as if the guy it belonged to were lying in ambush in the back seat keeping an eye on his driving and ready to yell as soon as he overtaxed the engine a little or made the tires screech.

The jilted plumber didn't even look up when they hooted the horn as they drove off. He was too busy counting, for the third time, the fifteen fifty-euro bills that his act of reprisal had brought in. Franck watched him getting smaller in the rear-view mirror, still focused on his money, then disappearing around a bend. The car ran very smoothly. He didn't care about the make, the model, the engine. It was his and his alone, the papers were in order. Now he felt completely free. He had the impression as he drove that he had left prison a long way behind him, once and for all. The old man turned left to go home, and he kept straight on for Langon, alone on that straight road where a little of the shade of evening was already falling from the tops of the pines. Through the open windows, smells of pine resin and heather and sand reached him, smells he'd loved so much when he was a kid, when they drove through the forest to the dunes, the noise of the ocean sometimes rising toward them well before they saw it. He and Fabien would start running, crying with joy every time, never blasé, as soon as that infinite expanse opened up in front of them.

He drove for nearly an hour in the arid solitude of the pine forest barely softened by the gilt of the sunset. After a while, he stopped at the entrance to a firebreak and got out of the car just to hear what the noise of the engine and the whoosh of speed had prevented him from hearing: the silence of this desert. Its crackle of insects. That scent of dry grass and dust. He took a few steps in the ash-gray sand. The earth seemed scorched. The pines, the ferns, the thickets of gorse all appeared on the point of catching fire. At present everything was silent. Nothing moved. Franck slowly turned around in a circle to get a better sense of it.

I'm alive and everything else is dead. Or else the opposite.

That was when he had the idea of taking out the phone he had bought that morning. He entered the code from the card— *180 minutes including 60 free*—then dialed Fabien's number.

Hi, this is Fabien. Leave a message after the beep or call again later.

Tears came to him when he heard his brother's voice. There was that casual, insolent tone he always affected, that way he had of shrugging off problems, even big ones, even those you can't easily dismiss, like those tough characters you sometimes run into at night, as if, as far as he was concerned, nothing was important or serious, as if life were a kind of game in which you could afford to play for high stakes and lose and keep losing, because a day was bound to come when you could make up for your losses.

"Hi, bro, it's Franck. I've been out for five days but I didn't get a phone until today. I'd really like to say . . . They tell me you're in Spain, what the fuck are you doing down there? You could have waited for me to get out and we'd have gone together! Because here . . . Well, anyway, you can tell me all about it. I'll ring off now. Will you call me back? Love you, bro."

He hated answering machines. Speaking into the void. He never knew what to say to these machines. Once he'd hung up, he realized that he was bathed in sweat and his heart was pounding.

He took from his wallet the piece of paper where he had noted down a few numbers of old friends, the three or four who'd bothered with him when he was in the can, who'd written to him or passed a message to him through his lawyer. The first two were no longer reachable. There was no name against the third. No. Later. I'll call you later.

He dialed the number. He hoped he would get an engaged signal. Or else a recorded message, in which case he would hang up.

"Yes?"

"Hi, this is Franck. How are you?"

A TV was blaring away.

"Wait, let me turn it down, I can't hear you . . . That's better. Where are you?"

"I'm out. I got out five days ago. Some friends of Fabien are putting me up."

"Where?"

"Out in the sticks. Near Saint-Symphorien."

"Right. How's it going? How's your brother?"

"I haven't seen him yet. He's in Spain, he'll be back in three weeks. What about you?"

"What about me?"

Franck heard his father's heavy breathing. He tried to imagine what he might be doing while he was on the phone. If he was by the window or if he had one eye on the silent TV set. He would have liked to know if he'd aged, if he walked with a stoop. He remembered seeing him sitting on the public benches on the last day of the trial. Freshly shaved, his hair cut short, looking impressive in that charcoal-gray suit he'd never seen him wear before. He remembered those eyes. His father's eyes, so pale it was as if the alcohol and the tears had washed them clean. Those eyes had remained on him throughout the hearing.

He tried to get the conversation going again. "I just wanted to know how things were."

"They're fine. I tinker with this and that."

"The garden?"

"Yes, the garden. And other things. There's lots to do around here."

Silence again. The hole became a chasm. Franck had to take a deep breath to continue. He choked back the bitterness rising like a ball in his chest.

"Okay. I'll ring off now. It must be time to pick the tomatoes."

"I pick them in the morning. It's better then."

"Bye then, speak to you later."

"Sure. Speak to you later."

As he was moving the phone away from his ear, he heard:

"I love you both."

He hastened to say I love you, too, but his father had hung up and Franck spat out the sob that was stopping him from breathing and wiped his eyes and sat down on the ground because his legs were shaking. He let the images of childhood jostle and scatter, the voices, the laughter, his parents a little tipsy one Christmas Eve, both beaming. Joy, simple and dumb. He realized after a moment that he was smiling at these memories, sitting on the ground, no bigger than when he was eight.

He got back on his feet and shook his head as if the memories, caught in his hair like wisps of straw, were going to fall at his feet. He had to talk to someone. He had to hear a friendly voice, warm and smiling. You can hear a smile in a voice.

The voice that answered him was surprisingly curt and hostile, but soon frayed into a little cry of joy when he said his name. It was Nora. She couldn't stop telling him how pleased she was to hear from him. "Fuck, it's been a while, you must come over, we'll have a drink to celebrate, Lucas will be so happy!" Lucas was *her man*, as she put it, he had literally carried her off from her home one evening when her father Hocine, crazed with booze, was threatening to kill her and her mother and her sisters with a nail gun he had brought back from the construction site where he was working. Lucas had knocked him out with a chair, then, with Nora's help, had nailed him to a door by his shirtsleeves and his pants legs, with his arms outstretched, and advised the women to leave him there all night to sober up, which they had done, managing to sleep in spite of his moans and curses and threats. A month later, Hocine fell from the third floor of an apartment building and was impaled on the steel reinforcement bars fifteen feet down. No flowers, no wreaths. His wife had quickly had the body sent back to his poor peasant family in Morocco.

Talking to her about prison and Fabien and the people who were putting him up, Franck rediscovered Nora's rough, husky voice and recalled the hatred she still felt toward her father. She talked about him often, her mouth full of insults and curses, regretting that she hadn't stuck a knife in his groin all the times he'd come a bit too close to her or her sisters.

"So, when are you coming? We have heaps of things to tell you, too. There've been some changes here. I won't say anything now. You'll see when you come."

A child started crying behind her, it didn't sound very old, but Franck didn't dare say anything because all at once he felt an impulse to hang up, disappointed, though he wasn't sure by what. He wanted this conversation to stop, this illusion of a reunion to vanish, the way you give up running after a train you've missed. He explained that he had a whole lot of things to do, problems to sort out, it'd take a few days, but he'd come to see them, her and Lucas, he couldn't wait to give them a hug. She gave him a big kiss through the phone and he promised her he would bring champagne and they hung up simultaneously.

Franck felt like flinging the phone in the bracken because the damn thing only reminded him of all that was gone, all the bridges burned between his past and him. He had never thought about these things and now he was overcome with strange feelings he couldn't put a name to. There was a lump in his throat. He was as sad as an abandoned child.

He got back in the car, took off at top speed, and drove fast, happy to assert his mastery of the machine and the confidence of his reflexes. After a while, he let out a yell through the open window, and he didn't know if he was yelling into this gray-brown desert out of pleasure or loneliness.

When he pulled up outside the house, the old man got up from the bench where he had been sitting with a can of beer in his hand and came shuffling toward him.

"So, what do you think? Goes well, doesn't she? They're good engines, these. Not too much electronics, you don't need to have three computers to repair them."

He walked around the car with a satisfied air as Franck got out. He waved his beer at him.

"Go grab yourself a beer, we'll drink to the car!"

The skin of his face was shiny, taut, and pink, and his eyes with their reddened lids were watery. He moved about with a forced joviality brought on by the alcohol, and at the same time he seemed exhausted by the heat, so that Franck didn't know if his hooded eyes expressed deep sadness or fake bonhomie. He expected the old man to either burst into tears at any moment or start threatening and insulting him.

He thought again about his father. He'd been like that on his bad days—in other words, often. He and Fabien would observe him on the quiet when he came home, trying to figure out if he'd been drinking, and above all how much booze he'd downed. It was best if he arrived completely drunk because he was quite cheerful when he was drunk, he would smile stupidly and ask them eagerly what they wanted to eat and stagger into the kitchen and sway in front of the open fridge, before going and sitting down in front of the TV, telling them he needed to rest and falling asleep almost immediately.

The days when he came back not quite drunk and not quite sober, on the other hand, he didn't talk or else just muttered things, a bit stiff on his legs, and he had that sad, nasty air and he went all over the house, opening then slamming the doors. He never said so, but he was looking for her. The two boys had realized that immediately, and they heard him muttering indistinct, furious things and sometimes ending up sobbing. Then without a word they would lay the table and heat a frozen meal in the microwave, hoping he would like it so that they didn't have to see again a plate or dish smash against a wall and crash to the floor. And they would stop moving and keep quiet, not daring to look at anything, eyes down.

He walked into the kitchen and it took him by surprise, so deeply engrossed had he been in his memories, still sitting over his plate under the yellow lampshade, listening to his father's labored breathing, looking at his big hands shaking, reassured by Fabien's presence. The coolness of the open fridge, the hiss

of the beer can as he opened it finally brought him back to the
present. The half-light through the partly-closed shutters, the
smell of stagnant water rising from the sink, the buzzling of a
few flies.

He hadn't seen Jessica or her mother since morning. They
had planned to go shopping in Bordeaux. They had to take
Rachel with them to take her mind off things, Jessica had said,
she'll turn into a real savage if she goes on like this. He went out
into the corridor, to the foot of the stairs. Through the silence
he heard their voices, outside on the other side of the house,
near the swimming pool. He hesitated about what he wanted to
do, then walked toward them.

The low sun was still beating down hard above the forest.
Not a breath of air. Jessica was lying on a deckchair, in a swimsuit, and when she saw Franck she stood up and took out the
earphones of her cell phone.

"So how was the car?"

She was smiling, eyes bright. She let her arms dangle by her
sides, her shoulders back, standing firmly on her slightly parted
legs, and for Franck she couldn't have been more naked, offering herself up to his gaze, knowing he was looking at her. He
took a swig of beer and nodded.

"Brilliant," he said. "I took it for a spin."

"Let me have a sip."

She came closer and reached her hand out for the can. Their
fingers touched. The scent of her sun cream hovering between
them. She looked at him as she drank, a smile in her eyes. A
little beer ran down her chin, and she tried to lick it off with the
tip of her tongue. Next, she rolled the cold can over her belly
then slipped it inside the elastic of her bikini bottom and took
it out again almost immediately. She was still looking at him,
gently biting her lower lip.

"There you are," she said in a low voice, giving him back his
beer. "I'm sure it's warm now."

"Why are you playing games?"

She stopped smiling and raised her head, her chin toward him. "I'm not playing games."

Her voice shook a little. For two or three seconds she didn't move, her vague, fixed look resting on him, although probably incapable of seeing him. Franck thought she was going to start crying. Then, abruptly, she seemed to come back to her senses.

"How would you feel about going clubbing?"

"When? Tonight?"

"Yes, tonight. In Biscarrosse. I'll introduce you to some people. You have to get out and about!"

"That's a two-hour drive, isn't it?"

"No, not as much as that. If we leave early enough, we can get there and have a bite to eat before we go dancing, we can sleep on the beach and get back tomorrow morning after breakfast. What do you say?"

She shimmied in front of him, hands on hips. He gave a start when he heard the old woman's rough voice calling Rachel. She was nicer when she spoke to the dog. Jessica shrugged.

"It's nothing. She's like that. She doesn't know how to be nice. She isn't easy to get along with. But deep down, she likes people. She just doesn't show it. She'd put herself through fire for Rachel."

Franck preferred not to reply. He couldn't think about anything apart from the two hours they were going to spend alone in the car. The stop they would be bound to make after a while, in the middle of nowhere. He had the impression she was having a lot of difficulty stopping herself from leaping on him. He thought he could smell that smell, that desire, over and above the scent of the sun cream. And he wondered if he would have resisted such an assault, even with the old woman and Rachel close by.

"I'll go get ready."

As he turned his back on her, he deliberately touched her thigh with the tip of his index finger and he tore himself away from that intimacy because it almost hurt.

They were driving in the lengthened shadow of the pines along straight, deserted roads, and the still-warm air rumbled around them. The only times they spoke was when Jessica gave Franck directions. She sat slumped in her seat, headphones in her ears, often sliding her finger over her cell phone to choose a piece of music that never seemed to satisfy her. One foot up on the dashboard, a little gold chain around her ankle. When Franck had asked her if it was gold she had replied, without looking at him, "What do you think?" and he hadn't known what to say to that because already she was bobbing her head in time to whatever she was listening to and he had been content, hands tight on the wheel, to look on the sly at her legs in tight-fitting white pants, her upper body in a kind of black bolero, her sullen mouth. He would occasionally glance at the quiet side roads, the isolated fire breaks where they could have stopped and thrown themselves at each other, but she had barely looked at him since they had left, and the electric tension that had run through Jessica's body earlier had receded, extinguishing even the gleam in her eyes. The perfume she had sprinkled herself with covered her skin in an artificial veil and masked the aromas of desire and sex he thought he had smelled when they had stood so close together earlier.

When they got to Biscarrosse, the sun was reddening on the ocean above bands of mauve clouds. They parked on the sea front, facing the dunes. Franck was disappointed not to see the sea, which was hidden by the expanse of sand. People were coming back from the beach through a gap, towels over their shoulders, parasols or iceboxes in their hands. Franck looked at them enviously. He imagined the low tide, the last bathers lifted gently by the calm swell. The breeze cooled him down and erased his tiredness. He'd have liked to run to the water and dive straight in, fully clothed, feel the shock of the cold water and cry out and kick his feet and thrash about like when they were kids, but he knew that Jessica was getting impatient behind him, the soles of her shoes squeaking on the sand scattered across the blacktop. He turned to her and immediately she started walking to the center of town, saying she was hungry.

The heat still hovered between the houses, rising from the roadway, emanating from the walls. The shop windows were lit up, as were the signs and lanterns outside the restaurants. Young people were distributing menus, invitations, vouchers for special offers. In the crowd of vacationers, Franck felt dizzy at the proximity of all these scantily-clad women, some of them stunning, all of them free, and he sensed an arrogance in the casual way they displayed their breasts and shoulders and bellies and thighs and he felt like a starving man staring at a buffet he wasn't allowed to touch. Tanned faces, windswept hair. Half-opened lips, bright smiles. Scornful or brazen looks. The night that was about to start abolished modesty, reduced distances. It seemed to him that all these bodies would soon touch, jostle, mingle, and he stiffened his shoulders to stop his hands from plunging at random into the crowd.

Jessica suddenly clutched his arm.

"Where the fuck are you going?"

Her face was against his, tense and waxy in the blue light of a crowded restaurant terrace.

"We'll eat here. I know the place. It's quieter inside."

A very young girl showed them to a table in a corner, beneath a wall light imitating a ship's lantern. Franck was about to sit down facing the room, to still see all that bustle and maybe calm his dizziness, but Jessica stopped him dead.

"No. I'll sit there. I want to see who comes in."

She hung her tiny handbag on the back of the chair then sat down and immediately started reading the menu. Hanging on the wall behind her was a fishing net with plastic fish and starfish caught up in it. Franck looked around him at the customers at their tables, the coming and goings of the waitresses, the ice buckets from which bottles of white wine stuck out, the trays of seafood, and he tried to remember the last time he had eaten in a real restaurant, not a fast-food joint, and he recalled a trip to the Basque coast with Fabien, they had set off to the south as soon as they had managed to get that old Peugeot started and had stopped in Ciboure, pretty much at random, one stormy evening, and they had devoured stuffed *piquillos* and watched the waves crashing at the foot of the Fort of Socoa. They had also drunk, too much, and had come out dizzy and staggering in the squalls, blaming the wind for knocking them over. Franck remembered the return to Bordeaux, how they had fought sleep, with the radio almost at full volume, switching from one station to another, the silence in which they had listened to a song by Serge Reggiani, his plaintive voice: *"C'est moi c'est l'Italien / Est-ce qu'il y a quelqu'un / Est-ce qu'il y a quelqu'une."*[3] He was their father's favorite singer, the one he listened to sometimes when he was drunk, slumped in an armchair, tears in his eyes, dismissing them with an absent wave of the hand when they came looking for him to sit down for a meal. Fabien had switched off the radio at the end of the song and for a moment there had been nothing else but the night drowned in rain and the rumble of the engine and the monotonous swish of the windshield wipers.

Jessica put her menu down and stood up abruptly. "I have to make a phone call. I'll have a steak tartare with fries and a Coke."

She hurried to the exit with her head down, already fiddling with her cell phone. Franck caught a glimpse of her outside on the sidewalk, with her back to him, the phone glued to her ear. She lit a cigarette, then her shoulders drooped and she moved a few steps away to talk. Franck went back to the menu, unable to decide. He was hungry, and everything looked appealing. Shellfish and seafood. Fish.

A waitress approached and he ordered Jessica's steak tartare and for himself *gambas* à *la plancha* and mussels and a carafe of white wine because the bottles struck him as too expensive.

[3] It's me, it's the Italian/ Is there someone/ Is there some woman?

"What's this wine like?"

The girl shrugged. She was a pretty brunette with gray eyes. She was wearing a black linen apron over red pants. She gave him a kindly smile. "I can't tell you, I don't drink wine. But we've never had any complaints."

"Well, if nobody's died, it should be all right. Oh, yes, and a Coke for my friend."

"A Coke," the pretty brunette said, scribbling on her note-pad. "Got it."

The room was humming around him. He looked again at all these people who seemed happy to be there. At one table, on the other side of the narrow aisle along which the waitresses came and went, a little boy was solemnly pursuing a winkle at the bottom of its shell while around him the four grown-ups present were talking loudly and eating oysters. When he had captured the thing, he looked at it closely, made a face, then put it down on the rim of his plate. He did the same thing twice more until the man sitting on his right asked him if he didn't like it. The boy shook his head, his hands between his thighs, his nose at the level of the table. Look, the man said, and with his fork he speared the piece of brown flesh and swallowed it whole, rolling his eyes. It's really good, you should try it.

The waitress returned with a carafe of white wine streaming with condensation. Franck took it and let his hand rest for a few seconds on the coldness of the glass then poured some for himself. The first sip was so good it brought tears to his eyes. He emptied his glass greedily, as if it were water. He realized that he was hot. The sweat was making his shirt wet at the base of his back. His head felt heavy, as if he were drunk. The noise of the restaurant, the loud voices, the snatches of conversation he could hear weighed on him and he felt crushed by all these presences, by this bustle, this chaotic merry-go-round.

He poured himself some more wine, drank a little, then turned to see what Jessica was doing. There was no sign of her, just people passing along the street, some standing in front of the board where the menu was displayed. The waitress set down in front of him half a dozen *gambas* and a large glass of Coke. He was embarrassed by the empty chair facing him. He felt like such a loser, sitting alone in this noisy, crowded room.

When he stood up, the waitress, who was some distance away, looked at him in surprise. "It's that way," she said, pointing to the door of the toilets.

"No, I'm going to look for her. I'll be right back."

The girl nodded and turned her back on him, her arms laden with plates and dishes, then thrust open the swing door leading to the kitchens.

Outside, night had fallen, and all that was left of daylight was a bluish pallor at the end of the street, toward the ocean. He saw Jessica immediately, some twenty yards away, sitting on the edge of the sidewalk in front of a clothes store. Legs folded under her, head resting on her folded arms. In her right hand she held her cell phone. When he asked her if everything was all right, she didn't react. He crouched by her and stroked her head, but with a soft movement she shied away. People passed them, indifferent. Franck could see their legs, and hear their shuffling steps, the slap of their bare heels on the ground. It struck him that the two of them were like dogs, having fallen so low, because he didn't know what to do, lost in this moving forest. He kept his hand over Jessica's hair without daring to touch it. He wished he could just run away. Leave her there with her mood swings. Then she looked up at him and her pale eyes were full of tears and he put his arm around her shoulders without trying to pull her to him, making an effort not to put his full weight on her.

"What's going on?"

She wiped her cheeks with the back of her hand. Her chest rising again with a few sobs. "Nothing. It's my business."

"Is it that serious?"

"No. It's nothing."

She looked around her at the people strolling and the lights

of the street with an alarmed expression as if she had just woken up on this sidewalk. She got to her feet, almost swaying.
She glanced at her cell phone then followed Franck back to the
restaurant. She seemed to hesitate in the doorway, then walked
over to their table. The waitress watched them pass and smiled
at Franck.

"Why is that bitch eyeing us like that?"

"Ignore her. She was wondering what we were up to, she
didn't know if she should serve us or not. She's nice."

As soon as she was seated, Jessica emptied half her glass of
Coke. She put her phone down next to her and looked at it
again.

"Is there a problem with Rachel?"

"Rachel? What are you talking about?"

"I just thought—"

"You thought what? Leave Rachel be. This has nothing to
do with her. I told you, it's my business. So drop it."

The waitress arrived with the steak tartare and the fries.
Jessica gave her a hostile look and the girl turned on her heels,
wiping her hands on her apron.

"Enjoy your meal," Franck said.

Jessica didn't reply. She cast a circular glance around her then
busied herself with her steak tartare. As he shelled his shrimp,
Franck watched her. She seemed engrossed in her food, nibbling at a fry from time to time. All he could see were her long
lowered lashes, her tight lips. The rapid, precise gestures.

Not once throughout the meal did she look at him, nor did
she say a word. She observed the tables around her, staring at
half the diners until she had to lower her eyes or turn away as
soon as someone noticed her insistence. She even smiled at the
occasional burst of laughter from a table a short distance away.
She checked her phone countless times, peered closely at a few
fries she was getting ready to eat.

She might as well have been alone, or facing a wall.

Franck wondered if he still existed. Or if the white wine had made him invisible. He thought about getting up and leaving, just to see if she would notice. He wanted to slam her face in her plate. He looked at her and tried to find the slightest trace of charm in her. He knew everything about her body, its perfection, its intimate recesses. He remembered what they had done, the frenzy of it, he recalled their wild orgasms, so close to perdition. But he wondered now why he had been so eager to do it again, because there opposite him sat an impossible, almost unreal, perhaps unimaginable creature. An artificial being. One of those robot women he had seen in movies, who tried to kill the Terminator and his protégé. Maybe that afternoon of lovemaking only existed in his imagination. A terrifyingly real hallucination.

He busied himself with his confused thoughts and said and did nothing, just to see how far she was capable of going, assuming that she was playing this game deliberately. After a while, she called the waitress over because she wanted a dessert. She ordered profiteroles and Franck asked for another carafe of wine.

Jessica threw herself on the dessert, without a word. She smudged the outside of her mouth with chocolate, and didn't bother to wipe it away, just like a little girl. Once she had finished, she again checked her phone and sent a few texts. When he was no longer capable of swallowing a drop of wine, Franck stood up and went over to the counter to pay. At the second step he made, he felt the whole weight of his body fall to the bottom part of his legs, transforming his sneakers into lead boots. A blonde with tanned skin, big golden rings hanging from her ears, held court behind the cash register. She asked Franck if he'd enjoyed the meal and he said yes, it was very good. He felt an acid liquid stewing in his stomach and a migraine rising inside his skull. It seemed to him that it was suddenly darker, despite the ceiling lights casting a harsh glare on the bar.

"Are you paying?"

Jessica had placed her chin on his shoulder and pressed her belly against his buttocks.

The blonde wished them a pleasant evening as she closed the cash drawer and Franck walked to the exit without bothering about Jessica. It was almost eleven and there were fewer people on the street. Franck headed straight for the beach. He didn't know if he should go and throw himself in the water and collapse into the waves to wash himself of this dampness, this unhealthy sweat he had been secreting all evening long, or else take the car and drive with all the windows down in the night along deserted roads in the middle of nowhere, leaving behind him this girl who scared him, unpredictable, unfathomable, poisonous. He heard her walking behind him and he reflected on all these ideas that came to him, he thought about certain carnivorous plants and the strategies they used to trap their prey, he had seen that on TV one evening in the can, and he remembered that guy, Hamid, who had looked at a flower as long and deep as a champagne flute and said that it was "best not to put your dick in that," and they had laughed, the three of them there in the cell, laughed as they had never laughed before.

"Where are you going?"

"I'm going for a swim."

"Now?"

He headed for the gap leading to the beach. His stomach heavy, he was breathing through his mouth, the migraine beating behind his eyes. Jessica caught up with him and took his arm and let herself be dragged along for a while, lazily, saying she was cold. He did nothing to hold her against him but she clung to him, stumbling sometimes in the sand. They left the lights of the parking lot and plunged into the darkness. Couples, groups of teenagers were coming and going and their words and their laughter were muffled by the dunes, but suddenly the murmur of the ocean covered all the voices, mixing them together into a trivial noise, and Franck walked faster toward the water, then broke into a run. In the moonlight he could see the swell rise slowly in a bright roller then subside into a calm glow. For a brief moment, it seemed to him that his nausea was wearing off, but then his stomach contracted as if he'd been punched and he bent double and threw up. He fell to his knees and continued vomiting. Like a dog. His belly plowed with cramps, his back hunched with the effort.

"Are you all right?"

Shut up. Let me finish my sandcastle and I'll get up again. He preferred not to say anything. She was above him.

"Here."

She was holding out a paper handkerchief. He pushed her hand away. He was crying. Because of that death-like taste stuck to the back of his throat. Because of the acidity burning his esophagus. He saw the line of foam six feet from him and he got to his feet, he walked and took off his shoes and rinsed his mouth with sea water. He spat, he gargled, sickened by the salt he brought out some loud belches with the few last spasms and he coughed in a kind of groan of anger and disgust.

At last, he was able to rise to his full height and look at the shiny black expanse in front of him, that vast, calm sweep that blew the night wind into his face. Jessica put a hand on his shoulder. He ignored it and went back up the beach toward the dunes. His legs were heavy and his steps, in the soft sand, hesitant. He heard Jessica struggling to keep up with him.

"Are you angry with me?"

When they reached the light of the street lamps, Franck stopped and watched her approach. The glistening skin of her shoulders. The low neckline of the top, the roundness of her naked breasts beneath it. She huddled against him, her hands around his waist.

"I wasn't feeling well. I heard some bad news."

She pressed her pelvis against his and buried her face in his neck. Franck pulled away.

"Is that why you've been treating me like shit all this time? Like I didn't exist?"

"I'm sorry. Sometimes, I'm too sad and I don't know where I am."

She was now rubbing herself against him and he was getting hard and he pressed on her ass with the palms of his hands. He tried to pull her toward the beach but she resisted.

"No. Not now. We'll have plenty of time later. And anyway, we'll get sand everywhere."

She touched him through the cloth of his pants as she said this, and gave him a look that was meant to be provocative. He would have liked to fuck her there and then, but he didn't feel strong enough to try to drag her away, let alone to start arguing. Come to think of it, he didn't feel strong enough to do very much of anything. Actually, he didn't know quite which word was best suited, strength or will.

"Let's go dancing. I'll introduce you to my friends."

She took him by the hand. She walked in front of him, stepping lightly. He had dined in front of another woman. He had thrown up that meal and now a different creature appeared. He didn't know what to make of such a rapid change, not that he really wanted to think about it. What he wanted was to sleep. When they came close to the car, he almost told Jessica to go to the club by herself and have fun there with her friends. He would wait for her in the car for as long as it took. He could already picture himself settled on the back seat, lying huddled up, the windows half open to let the cool air in, his shirt wedged under his head. Fast asleep.

Jessica must have replied that they wouldn't stay long, that she had promised. He wasn't sure anymore. Once again, the drunkenness was confusing his thoughts and beating in his skull. He caught up with her and took her gently by the shoulder, just to touch her skin in that taut round spot that glistened in the light of the street lamps. He let his hand slide down to one of her breasts, but merely brushed it with a finger or his palm. She let him do that for a while then broke away when they came within sight of the club.

Some thirty people were waiting patiently in front of the entrance. The bouncers were in a dominant position at the top of a flight of three or four steps. One of them, a massive black guy, was talking into his headset, looking toward the end of the street and ignoring the people waiting below him. Franck assumed he was a boxer because of his broken nose. A heavyweight to judge by his build, his long, muscular arms, the way he moved his broad, supple shoulders.

"It's all right, Cyrille's here," Jessica said.

She pointed to the other bouncer, who was shorter and thinner than the boxer and was looking at the little crowd with a suspicious or hostile expression. Black hair pulled back in a ponytail. Severely cut mustache and goatee. For the moment, he stood motionless, his hands joined in front of his groin, almost cramped in his light-gray jacket, like a cop assigned to protective detail, minus the dark glasses. Jessica got up on tiptoe and waved to him, calling "Cyrille!" The guy looked her up and down, indifferently, then turned away, meeting Franck's gaze as he did so. Franck lowered his eyes.

"Do you know him?"

"Of course. I know lots of people here. Why do you ask that?"

The people in front of them started to move forward. The two bouncers quickly inspected the bags, eyeing the people, male and female alike, without saying anything. They remained inscrutable, expressing themselves in gestures or in monosyllables. When Jessica reached the one she said she knew, she asked him if someone called Pascal was already there. The man replied without looking at her, pushing her toward the entrance and already signaling to those behind to move forward.

"Which Pascal? I know lots of Pascals."

"Schwarzie."

"Yes, he's here."

Franck paid the admission charge for both of them, then Jessica pushed him forward with impatient little cries.

Immediately, the sound hit him in the pit of his stomach as if someone had taken advantage of the darkness to land him a punch in the solar plexus. There weren't many people. He could make out a few groups sitting on imitation-leather banquettes around low tables, a dozen figures on the dancefloor, shattered into pieces by the strobe lighting and the glitter balls. Jessica walked over to the bar with the self-confidence of a regular and started peering into the intermittent shadows to see if she could find those she was looking for. Behind the counter, two pretty girls in tight red T-shirts with the logo of the club were dancing sluggishly as they wiped glasses, while a tall fair-haired young man rolled a cocktail shaker over the well-developed muscles of his arms.

Franck had occasionally been to night clubs, but most of the time he'd been too drunk by the time he left to remember much about the atmosphere or the sensations. He and Fabien went there to look for girls, spending part of the night ogling them, rubbing up against them, sweet-talking the least shy among them, though having to yell over the sound system, and sometimes they managed to entice some lost souls as drunk as they were out to the parking lot or into a car and indulge in some fumbled lovemaking, rushing to finish, to achieve a fleeting, animalistic orgasm, stupefied with booze.

At the bar, he ordered an alcohol-free cocktail because there was still acid swishing around in his stomach, occasionally burning his esophagus. The girl who served him gave him a broad smile. Her breasts moved loosely beneath her T-shirt. She had nice teeth and big, gentle blue eyes. Looking at her did him good. Spotting a free seat, he sat down and started drinking, raising a discreet toast in the direction of the girl, who replied with a wink and a mute burst of laughter drowned by the noise. He sipped his cocktail. It was cold and sugary. He felt his drunkenness wear off. He would have liked silence, or else just the sound of the sea, a little wind. A peaceful darkness.

"Are you staying there?"

Jessica had come to the bar and was leaning with her elbows on it next to him. He hadn't seen her because he had been watching the two waitresses, who chatted as they prepared drinks and arranged bottles in ice buckets.

"They're over there, at the back."

She pointed to a corner to the right of a little stage with chrome-plated poles on it. There were two men and a woman. Despite the dim light, Franck could see that one of them was a bodybuilder type in a tight-fitting black T-shirt from which his long thick arms emerged, bulging with muscles. Jessica seemed to hesitate for a moment, then strode across the dance floor swinging her little handbag with determination. Franck took his glass and followed her. Leaving the counter, he gave a little wave to the barmaid, but she ignored him. The bodybuilder stood up when he saw Jessica and reached out his arms to her and embraced her effusively, kissing her on the neck and hair and eyes and mouth, and she returned his kisses as she huddled against him.

Then she made the introductions: Pascal, known as Schwarzie—Franck, Fabien's brother.

Pascal shook Franck's hand eagerly and asked him how he was doing. The other man remained seated, watching the scene with an amused or mocking air. He had very short hair, blond or gray, and it was hard to guess his age. Forty-something, maybe, or maybe a lot younger. A young girl with dark brown skin and thick scarlet lips was leaning against him, one hand on his thigh. He was drinking a mojito through a straw and greeted Franck with a simple nod of the head. Jessica leaned over to kiss him, and when she stood back up again he rested his light-colored eyes on Franck.

"And this is Franck, as I was saying earlier. Fabien's brother. I told you about him."

The man stood up and shook his hand across the table. "When did you get out?"

"About ten days ago."

"We should drink to that. I'm Ivan."

He signaled to the girls behind the bar. The one who had served Franck came over. Still smiling. Franck wondered how you could smile like that, with such a fresh, open smile.

"Bring us some champagne, we have something to celebrate. And make sure it's nice and cold, okay?"

They sat down. Franck looked around the room, which was starting to fill. The DJ was encouraging people to come and dance, to clap their hands and raise their fists, and the crowd was obeying him, while rows of spotlights revolved, seeming to cast their bodies onto the ceiling or against the walls when it was only their shadows that were being projected. Two girls climbed onto the platform where the turntables were and started swaying to the music. Franck didn't know if they were customers or members of staff employed to warm things up. They were dressed in mini shorts and off-the-shoulder tops that left their navels bare and they swayed their hips, spurred on by the DJ and the yelling crowd.

"They dance well, don't they?"

Franck turned to the brown-skinned girl. It was the first thing she had said. Her face was very close to his and her fleshy lips glistened in the lights with a strange bluish tinge. She smelled of honeysuckle. She had a shrill voice with slightly inane intonations. Franck wondered how old she was. Maybe fifteen or sixteen, although her make-up and her curves made her look older.

"What's your name?"

"Farida."

"Do you come here often?"

"No. The Serb brought me. He's a great guy."

"The Serb?"

"Yes, Ivan. That's what they call him. The Serb."

The waitress came with the champagne. Ivan handed her two fifty-euro bills and told her it was fine, he would open the bottle himself.

They toasted Franck's release, his return to the land of the living, and wished him every happiness and success. For a while they exchanged platitudes about prison and freedom and some of the pleasant things in life, like champagne, a well-filled joint, a line of coke, a nice orgy.

"It's better than jerking off," Pascal said, underlining his words with the appropriate gesture.

They all laughed in approval. Everyone's eyes started shining a little brighter in the intermittent light that was as violent as bursts of machine-gun fire. Franck kept his eyes on Jessica, who occasionally collapsed onto Pascal when she laughed. For a second or two, he doubted the reality of all this. It occurred to him that he was going to wake up in his cell, surrounded by the snoring of the other two, the lights on the walkway showing blue through the skylight. He tried to remember each of the days that had passed since he had come out, but all that remained was the heat and the light and a feeling of suffocation, of being unable to breathe. An almost painful glare.

Nobody was talking now. They were each sipping their champagne and watching the people move about on the dance floor. Franck looked at these strangers and wondered what was stopping him from ditching them right now and going for a walk on the beach, but he felt weak and heavy, stuck on this excessively-soft banquette. From time to time he caught the Serb looking at him curiously, perhaps suspiciously. Then Jessica leaped to her feet and urged the others to come and dance. She held out her hand to them and pulled them to their feet, one by one. Franck was the last to stand and his migraine exploded inside his skull and forced him to sit down again, dazed and groggy. Farida expressed concern about him, and he signaled to her that he was fine. He drank a mouthful of already-warm champagne and watched as the others moved away into that bedlam that was alternately blinding and dark. Two girls came and sat down next to him, out of breath, glasses in their hands. One of them turned her round, breathless, dazed face toward him, beads of sweat glistening on her upper lip. He collapsed back on the banquette and closed his eyes. He heard the two girls laughing noisily. He wondered if they were laughing at him, then decided he didn't give a fuck.

When he opened his eyes again, the girls had gone. In their place, a man was sleeping on the banquette, leaning right back with his mouth open, a half-full glass in front of him. Franck looked at his watch. It was after one in the morning. He moved the joints of his shoulders and neck to get rid of the stiffness in them. He had the feeling he was wearing forty-pound headphones through which the highs and lows of the music reached him in a muffled fog. He got to his feet. The guy who'd been sleeping sat up abruptly, his eyes wide open, then collapsed onto the place where Franck had been sitting.

He took a few steps toward the dancing crowd. From where he stood, he saw a herd of heads moving in all directions, bombarded with flashes of white and colored light as if the violence of the sound was striking them and making them bounce against each other. Faces appeared, some smiling manically, others solemn and inscrutable, their eyes closed. Arms raised. Fists waved in time to the music. He looked for Jessica, thought he glimpsed her in a flash of light, then lost her, seeing only an unknown face. Nor could he see the two guys, Pascal and Ivan, although he wondered if he would recognize them anyway. He walked around the room, passed the bar, to which a cluster of people clung, yelling their orders at the waitresses. Two barmen were busy making cocktails and pouring them into big glasses half filled with ice cubes.

At the end of the counter, he spotted Farida, being sweet-talked by a young guy with a soccer-player hair style—shaven temples and a lock of bleached hair falling over his ear.

When he approached, Farida pretended not to see him at first, then smiled at him with an embarrassed air.

"Have you seen Jessica?"

The girl twisted her mouth then shook her head.

"Are you sure?"

The young guy, who was behind him, grabbed him by the arm. "Hey, she said no, so why don't you just beat it?"

He didn't see it coming. Franck grabbed him by the throat and squeezed his Adam's apple with his thumb and index finger. The guy tried to press down on his arm, but he was already choking, his face swollen, his eyes popping out. His blood was throbbing beneath Frank's fingers, and Frank could feel his muscles and tendons quiver and harden.

"Stop moving. In thirty seconds you're going to faint. And if you insist, I'll crush your throat. Did you get that, or shall I show you right now?"

He was talking in his face. Around them, people were still yelling and laughing and bustling and taking selfies, and not one of them saw the young man shaking his lock of bleached hair as he tried to get free of Franck's grip.

"All right," he croaked. "Stop."

Franck let go of him and he took a step back, knocking into a girl behind him, and started coughing, holding his throat, bent double, wheezing to get his breath back.

Farida hadn't moved from her place, a glass of gin and tonic in her hand, sucking on her straw as she watched the guy struggle against suffocation.

"The three of them left ten minutes ago. They told me to wait for them here."

Franck lit out of there as if escaping from a bramble bush. He found himself back out on the street, feeling numb, as if enclosed inside a hot, humming bell. A few smokers lingered here and there, chatting in low voices, their laughter muffled. A little farther down the street, two sloppily dressed men were staggering along, trying to drag with them a third man who was stumbling and bellowing that he was going to murder that scumbag and then fuck his bitch of a mother and all his family. They moved off into the distance and turned a corner, but the night echoed for a long time with the drunk's cries of rage and the voices of the other two yelling at him to calm down.

Franck walked back toward the two bouncers, who were busy inspecting the handbags of two girls.

"Did you see Jessica come out?"

The shorter of the two, the one with the ponytail and the goatee, replied without looking up at him, "Jessica who? Who are you talking about?"

"Pascal's friend. She spoke to you earlier."

"Oh, yes. She went that way. She didn't look very well."

He pointed to the far end of the street. Just as Franck was turning to walk away, he added:

"Forget it. She's out of your league."

"Forget what? What do you mean?"

"Nothing. Now beat it, we have work to do."

Franck started back toward him, and the big black guy stepped in.

"That's enough now, monsieur. Let us do our work. Come on."

A calm voice. A hand held up, as wide as a no-parking sign. No contact. This man knew what to do in every situation. Franck looked up at his strangely benevolent face, as reassuring as a final warning.

Walking back down the flight of three steps, he started to imagine what was happening. He dreamed of going back to his car and getting a wheel crank so that he could smash the skull of one of those two guys. Kill him maybe. Probably. But what then?

He launched himself in the direction indicated by the bouncer with the ponytail, shivering all over in the cool air. He stopped at the first intersection, listened out in the silence that crept along the sidewalk. A car door slammed a little farther on, on his right. A man's voice. A brief laugh. He ran and the migraine came back and hit him in the forehead, and he hurled himself on because even banging his head on a block of concrete wouldn't have caused him more pain.

It was a BMW crossover, the driver's door open, a man leaning inside. Franck saw the figure rise to its full height just as he came level with the trunk. It was Pascal. The almost insignificant gun at the end of his big, muscular arm. The blow caught Franck on the ear and he cried out and went down flat on his stomach. The barrel lodged itself between his shoulder blades and he didn't dare breathe again, in spite of his breathlessness.

"Keep quiet. If I shoot, you'll die, or you'll be paralyzed from the neck down. I'd rather not do that. None of this shit is your business, so stay out of it. Got that?"

Franck nodded and tried to say yes. The word came out as a groan.

"Spread your arms. Now keep still."

He felt the cold fall on him and pin him to the ground, and he started peeing without being able to hold back the shameful warmth running between his legs.

"Okay," the other man said with a snigger.

He barely heard the voices echoing above him. They were talking calmly, almost in low voices. Have you finished? What about him? We'll see about him later. A slamming of doors. The car drove away in a muffled purr. Then silence. So deep, he might have been at the bottom of a pit, an abandoned mineshaft. Dead underground. Pain was twisting the auricle of his ear. He lifted his hand to it, but it hurt so much he immediately pulled it away, surprised not to see any blood on his fingers. He got up on all fours. It seemed to him that he could breathe again, so he got to his feet and took a few steps in the middle of the street, and he heard movements and then a moan in a narrow alley between two houses.

He didn't immediately grasp what he was seeing. He went closer and made out Jessica lying flat on her stomach, naked from the waist down, her pants rolled up in a ball next to her.

"It's me. Franck."

He was about to ask her what had happened, very nearly asked her how she was.

"Can you turn around? Sit up."

She moved onto her side, leaning on an elbow. Her right cheek swollen, lower lip split. A little blood on her chin.

"Does it hurt?"

She shook her head. She was breathing hard, sniffing, wiping her nose with the back of her hand. He took her pants and held them out to her. She looked around her in the darkness, then leaned on her arm to sit up. She inserted her feet into the legs of her pants, with effort, breathing hard. He helped her to her feet. She tottered, her pants still down around her ankles. Franck kept his open arms around her as a safeguard, not daring to touch her, then squatted and started pulling the pants up over her knees, then her thighs. That was when he saw the blood. With his face just a few centimeters from her belly, it seemed to him that he could smell the odor of blood and cum they had left on her. He clenched his teeth and stood up to finish adjusting her pants, but she abruptly grabbed the pants by the waist and finished pulling them up and buttoning them herself. Then she stood there motionless, her eyes lowered, and he asked her if she was all right.

"My bag. Where is it?"

Franck switched on his cell phone and the screen lit up and he searched the alley where they were. The little white handbag had been thrown at the foot of a brick wall at the end of the alley. Jessica's panties had fallen beside it.

"Here." He held out the bag. "Do you want these, too?"

He pointed to the panties, without daring to touch them. She shook her head and walked to the end of the alley. She looked right and left along the street, then turned to Franck.

"This way. No point going back past the club."

They walked slowly, without saying anything. Every now and again, one or the other sighed noisily. Now Franck felt the cold dampness on his thighs and it seemed to him that his pants had gotten tighter, stretched over his skin like a sign of his shame. Jessica took him by the arm. She was crying, and with each sob her fingers tensed on the material of his shirt.

On the sea front, they got back to the car and stood for a moment in the cool air blown in from the ocean. They had their backs to the town, looking in front of them at the cold brightness of the moon. Jessica had stopped crying and held herself stiffly, her back arched. Franck took his pack of cigarettes from his pocket, but it was damp, so he crumpled it and threw it away in disgust.

"I stink. I pissed my pants when that other motherfucker pointed a gun at me. Does it hurt?"

"Sure. Don't forget, I'm the one who got fucked."

He shuddered. He felt stupid and heavy, as he so often did. Pitiful, wretched. He searched for something to say, but Jessica went straight to the car.

"Right. Shall we go?"

Her exhaustion was clear in her voice, soft as it was. As he reversed the car, she put her hand on his arm.

"Not a word to my parents. This is my business, you keep your mouth shut."

They drove in silence, the night around them, the pines like a race of giants in the headlights. Franck opened his window after a while to try to stay awake, and an acrid smell of dry grass rushed into the car along with the warm air rising from the earth after a whole day of burning. Jessica was asleep, slumped against the door, her hands together between her legs. They could have gotten lost, but some obscure instinct guided them home. No doubt because they were already lost.

Jessica didn't want to sleep in her room. She didn't have the strength to climb the stairs, and besides, she was afraid of waking her parents and Rachel. I'll sleep with you. Franck almost carried her to the trailer and let her collapse on the bed. He cleaned himself with a washcloth and changed. Then he slipped in next to her and fell, like her, into a deep sleep.

6

I fell when I was dancing. I was a little bit plastered."
Jessica twisted her mouth as she drank her coffee in order to avoid the cut that had made her lip swell up during the night. On the other side of the table, Franck could smell the perfume she had sprinkled on herself after her shower. The old woman shook her head and gave Frank a sidelong glance. Franck said nothing, busying himself with buttering a slice of bread then covering it with jam.

"What about you? Were you there?"

"I was around but I didn't dance."

The old woman looked at them in turn, forcing herself to smile. "One of you is lying."

"Why do you say that?"

"Why do you think? I know my daughter. I know what she's capable of making up to get herself off the hook. But I don't know you, and I don't know what you're capable of."

Franck was about to reply, but he met Jessica's eyes looking at him, forbidding him to speak.

"I fell, I told you. Stop pissing me off about it."

The old woman plunged her nose into her bowl of coffee and drank, grimacing because it was hot. She lit a cigarette and started coughing and wheezing to get her breath back, tears in her eyes, beating her chest with her fist, angry and choking. Franck watched her coughing her guts out and it occurred to him that these attacks of hers were probably the only times he would ever see the old bitch cry. One day, maybe, she would fall off her chair, thrown to the floor by one of her coughing fits. Once again, he thought that when that happened, he wouldn't lift his little finger to help her. He stared at her as she caught her breath and their eyes met. Hers were wide open from the strain and they stared back at him as if in reproach.

Rachel came in, muttering a good morning to which only Franck replied. She was wearing a little red dress and dragging her feet in espadrilles that were too big for her. Jessica held out her arms to her and Rachel came to her and let herself be covered in loud kisses.

"Good morning, sweetheart, did you sleep well?"

She nodded, then broke away gently from the embrace and looked at her mother. "Did you hurt yourself?"

Jessica lifted her hand to her split lip. "No. It's nothing. I fell."

"And what about me? Aren't you going to say good morning to me?"

The old woman put her cigarette in the ashtray and took her granddaughter in her arms. Outpouring of affection, smacking of lips. Rachel planted two silent kisses on the old woman's hollow cheeks, then came and sat down next to Franck.

"Would you like me to make you a slice of bread and jam?"

She said yes, looking straight at him. Franck was always trying to read the expression in those dark, almond-shaped, almost Chinese eyes. It was hard to distinguish the sadness in them from the panic. There was a permanent shadow there that he couldn't name. He spread butter on a slice of sandwich bread and added jam. The old woman got laboriously to her feet and walked out. Rachel watched her go, surprised or curious, and continued for a while to stare at the door, which moved occasionally and creaked when there was a draft.

Jessica served her her milk then announced that she was going to do a little washing. She stroked her daughter's hair and left the room, but Rachel didn't look up from her bowl and continued stirring her hot chocolate, making the spoon chink slightly on the enamel. Franck looked at her, so sweet and nice in her red dress. He would have liked to talk to her, but he didn't know what to say or how to say it. It had been like that for a long time—words didn't come and what he meant to say slipped away from him like water or sand.

After a while, she got to her feet and picked up her bowl, gripping it tightly in both hands. She liked to finish her chocolate in the sun, sitting in the doorway.

"Can I ask you something?"

She turned, looked at him, and waited.

"Was Fabien good to you?"

"No," she said in a clear voice. She turned on her heels and slipped through the half-open door with her bowl.

He thought to catch up with her, get her to tell him more, but he knew it was pointless. He went out on the other side and joined the old man in the vegetable garden, where he was picking tomatoes. He had torn out some weeds.

"Here," he said. "Look at this."

Between two rows of French beans lay a huge dead grass snake with a black back and yellow sides. Maybe four feet long. Its head had been crushed and almost separated from its body. Franck couldn't help a shudder running down his spine.

"It's the second one this year. Must be a nest of them somewhere."

Franck couldn't take his eyes off the snake. It seemed to him that at any moment, that long black cylinder might resume its sly, dangerous slithering.

"You're not scared, are you?"

"No, but I don't like them very much."

"Nobody does. That's why I smashed its head in."

The old man finished filling his crate with tomatoes. He blew hard each time he had to bend down and clenched his teeth as he lifted his load.

"What happened last night?"

"Nothing. Jessica slipped while she was dancing like a crazy woman and landed badly."

"She landed badly, did she?" The old man put the crate

down on an old wooden bench. "Don't bullshit me. She got herself in trouble again, as usual."

He picked up the snake, holding it in his fist like a length of rope, then walked up to Franck.

"She's been like that since she was fifteen. She attracts trouble the way shit attracts flies."

"When she was fifteen? What about before?"

"Before, she was just annoying. But nice. She didn't do a damned thing at school, she was always getting punished because she talked in class and answered back. But she was smart. All the teachers said so. A memory like an elephant, and always asking questions that weren't the kind a girl her age would ask. They said she was too mature. At twelve, she was pretty much the way she is now, well developed and everything. Gorgeous and horny. Her mother tried to beat it out of her. Forget it! And she didn't get any better as the years went by. We took her to see doctors, shrinks, all those sons of bitches with their miracle pills . . . Anyway, why am I telling you all this? It's all in the past . . . Well, not quite the past." He broke off and glanced suspiciously at Franck. "Anyway . . . I have to throw this in the woods. Will you take the tomatoes?"

Franck lifted the crate. The old man walked in front of him, swinging the dead snake against his leg. The dog appeared and came over and sniffed at the corpse and started nibbling at it.

"Do you want it?"

The old man threw the snake into the distance and the dog ran and took it in its mouth then shook it as if trying to break its back, after which it lay down and started eating it, beginning with the head, with a great snapping of its jaws. Franck stopped to watch the animal tear off long strips of pale meat and chew them, with what remained of the reptile wedged between its paws. Dog and snake. He wouldn't have wanted his hand anywhere near either of them.

"He'd eat anything, that dog," the old man said.

"Or anyone."

The old man squinted to see the dog where it lay at the foot of a wall. "He's all right with me, I know him and he obeys me. But I never overdo it. Try scratching between his ears. All dogs like that, but him, after five seconds, he starts growling and showing his teeth. I didn't want him here. It was Maryse who brought him one day. He was still young, and hanging about at the side of the road. Someone must have thrown him out of a car. We took care of him but it wasn't easy. My wife and Jessica insisted on us keeping him. They do what they like with him, he lets them. Maybe he's like me, he prefers women. But anyway, I'm not going to shoot him for that."

He spoke about the dog in the same flat, resigned tone he used to speak about Jessica, as if both were a habitual risk, a calamity you had to get used to. Franck started walking back to the house, but the old man's voice stopped him.

"I believe you. Last night, Jessica landed badly. On a man's dick, I'd say." His eyes shone in the sun between his almost closed eyelids.

"Why do you say that?"

The old man laughed silently. "You're well suited, you two. You like to take people for idiots. From her, we're used to it. But you, I thought you were like your brother. That you were someone we could trust."

Franck didn't have any answer to that. If Jessica had decided to lie to her parents, that was their business, the three of them, caught up in their tangled family relationships.

The old man opened a door and admitted Franck to a kind of shed with shelves full of empty glass jars thick with dust. All kinds of junk were piled up here: Formica chairs with rusty legs, kitchen cupboards, old gardening tools, their blades and tines sheathed in spiders' webs. The place smelled of dust and mildew. Franck put the crate down on a shelf.

"There was a time when Maryse made jams and preserves. When we first moved in here. She always said she'd grown up in the country and knew all about it. Yeah, right! Two years, it lasted. Now, it rots on shelves or in crates . . ."

Franck heard the front door slam and its glass vibrate and Jessica's car drive away at top speed. The old man straightened up and listened, then shook his head and sighed bitterly. Franck left the shed, sneezing. He rubbed his head to get rid of the dust and the spiders' webs which he thought he could feel down his neck. He wanted to take a shower again. Since the previous night, he had felt dirty and pitiful. He saw himself lying flat on his stomach on the blacktop, and could still feel the pressure of the gun on his vertebrae. And then the warm urine between his legs and down his thighs, the smell in the car, the windows lowered to let in the cool night air, Jessica slumped against the door, perhaps asleep. He left the old man surrounded by his junk and headed for the trailer.

He crossed the perimeter of fire separating the barns from the house, and it was then that he saw Rachel run across the path, closely followed by the dog. He had time to glimpse her bare shoulder, the strap of her dress hanging loose. He ran to join her, but when he turned the corner of the house he found himself facing the dog, which had been lying on the path but now leaped to its feet. Rachel was farther on, sitting in the doorway of the house, in a shady corner, as she often did.

"Rachel?"

The dog turned to look at the girl. When Franck took a step forward, it growled and its chops quivered.

"Rachel, what's the matter?"

The dog looked at Rachel and stretched its muzzle toward her and then, after a glance at Franck, walked away. Franck went closer to Rachel. She was keeping her head down, her black hair tumbling over her knees.

"Are you sad?"

He lifted the brown mass to see her face. Tears everywhere. A bump on her forehead was turning blue. Her cheek was red. The strap of her red dress torn off.

"Who did this to you?"

The dog had lain down some distance away and was watching them, its head resting on its paws.

Rachel was sniffling and Franck searched in his pockets for a handkerchief he didn't have. With the back of his hand, he wiped Rachel's nose, from which came an endless stream of transparent mucus. His hands hovered over her bowed head without knowing what to do.

"We should put some ice on it. Come on."

He stood up but she remained seated, her forehead on her knees, lifted occasionally by a big sob. He said to her, "Come on, Rachel, come on, we have to see to that." A strangled voice. His hand held out to her. Rachel raised her eyes to him. He leaned down and put his hands on her shoulders, his face very close to hers. He felt like kissing her hair gently, stroking her shoulder uncovered by the torn strap, but he didn't dare. He found it too intimate, or out of place. He wasn't familiar with such soft, gentle gestures. She stood up. Standing, she was as tall as he was crouching.

He took her to the kitchen and got some ice cubes from the refrigerator and wrapped them in a table napkin left on the back of a chair.

"Now keep that on your cheek for a quarter of an hour, and it'll go down. All right? Does it hurt?"

Rachel shook her head. "Thank you," she said.

Since he had bent to talk to her, she placed a kiss on his cheek before walking out. Franck quivered. Watching her move away then leave the room, he realized that it had been a long time since he had felt such a strong desire to take someone in his arms and hug them.

Just then, the old woman arrived, shuffling her feet, her red hair in a mess.

"What happened?"

She saw Rachel with her ice pack on her cheek and squatted by her to take a better look.

"Was it your mother?"

Rachel answered with a flutter of the eyelids.

"She just left," Franck said. "I heard her car."

"It's starting again. I know where she's gone."

The old woman planted a quick kiss on Rachel's forehead then straightened up. Rachel got up and went to the living room. They heard the TV—shouts, the screaming of police sirens, snatches of news, sound effects from cartoons.

The old man came in, scratching his groin through his faded shorts. A stained old T-shirt clung to his bony shoulders. "Where did Jessica go?"

"Guess."

The old man splashed water on his face at the faucet in the sink. All Franck could see of him were his stooped back, his thin frame. His face was in shadow, gray, his unshaven cheeks bristling with white hairs.

"You have to go get her."

Franck looked at the old woman. She had walked away toward the table and was lighting a cigarette.

The old man turned to him. He was wiping his hands on a cloth, leaving dirty marks on it. "You have to go. She'll go with you without making too much fuss."

The old woman's voice turned hoarse and she started coughing. "Forget it! Why should she go with him? He slept with her, so what? He wasn't the first, and he certainly won't be the last! It's true she went with all the men who fucked her, you know how she is, she'll never change! But what's so special about him, apart from being the other one's brother?"

She was leaning on the table and smoking. Franck walked over to her, took the pack of cigarettes she'd put down next to her and lit one, facing her. She looked at him without moving.

"Where does this guy live?"

He spoke without turning around, sustaining the gaze of the old woman, who was almost panting with anger, her eyes popping out, crazy, her face stretched toward him as if she was going to head-butt him.

"Come with me, I'll show you."

They went back to the workshop. The old man wrote the address on a piece of paper then unfolded a 1/25,000-scale map. It was in Lacanau, in the Médoc. Franck remembered the interminable ride, the traffic jams on the way home in the evening, before, in his other life.

"I've been there twice. You go through the town center and turn left here. The street is here. It's on the forest side. You'll see. A big house surrounded by trees. His name is Patrice Soler. He works in telecommunications, something like that. Some kind of engineer, I'm not exactly sure. He makes money, anyhow. But be careful. He's not aggressive, but when he's done drugs he can be nasty. The last time, I went there with Serge, and he kept quiet. If you like, I'll go with you. We can leave early tomorrow morning, when it's still cool. Tonight, there's no point."

Franck shook his head. He wanted to be alone. To get out of here, at least for a few hours.

"No. I'll go on my own."

"It's up to you."

The old man opened an iron closet with a key he'd dug up from the bottom of his pocket and took out a shotgun and a box of cartridges.

"Take this in case. It's small bore, but it should shut him up if he gets excited."

He broke open the shotgun and loaded it.

"Here."

He gave Franck two extra cartridges. Franck took the weapon, which was cumbersome and heavy, and put the cartridges in his pocket. He wasn't too sure how to hold the shotgun, so he put it down on the workbench.

"Why does she go to see this guy?"

"She's known him for years. I'm not sure where she knows him from. He supplies her with drugs for free. She pays him in kind, I don't need to draw you a picture. I don't know exactly what happened to the two of you last night, but it's sent her off the deep end, so she's gone for fresh supplies. When that happens, and nobody goes to fetch her, she comes back a week later completely high, crazy as a jaybird. At other times, she's clean. The occasional joint, that's all. You just have to put up with her mood swings. They're like the weather. In the morning, you never know if it's going to be raining buckets or if it'll be fine, even if it'll last all day. And when buckets are empty, sometimes they hit you on the head."

Franck was tempted to tell him about last night, but he changed his mind because he didn't want to hear the old man whine about that disaster. Without a word, he left the workshop and took the shotgun and the road map to his trailer.

The next day, the old man again offered to come with him, saying that with two of them there it would be easier. Franck told him not to worry and closed the car door and felt good, confined and alone in the already overheated interior of the car. Driving away, he saw Rachel watching him go. As he turned onto the road, it seemed to him that she was waving him goodbye.

He got there toward noon and he was hungry. He found a spot in the vast parking lot facing the ocean before going for a bite to eat on the terrace of an open-air café for vacationers. The crowds he passed were the same as the other night, only with added children, screaming or running around. Dark glasses and parasols. Iceboxes. Straw hats and baseball caps. Tanned skin, shoulders so red they looked almost raw. All languages spoken. He glanced at the beach, covered with people as far as the eye could see. The sea was like oil. Bathers gathered right on the edge, water up to their knees.

A pleasant young guy served him a beer and a tuna and vegetable sandwich overflowing with mayonnaise, which was hard to eat because the garnish escaped every time he bit into it. In the burning shade of the awning, he sipped his beer, watching the stream of summer visitors treading on their own shadows

beneath the vertical sun. He tried to remember how it used to
be in the old days, when he was a child, and despite himself his
eyes closed from the torpor and he found himself expecting to
see all four of them pass by, his parents, Fabien and him, in the
middle of this calm crush, loaded down with their beach gear
like everyone else. He felt himself slipping into a state of half-
sleep where reality merged with visions, in which he imagined
Fabien coming and sitting down next to him and not hearing
him when he spoke, just looking at him and smiling. He unfolded his map and tried to get his bearings. He stood up and
walked in the direction of the beach, like everyone else, surrounded by the noise of conversation, laughter, people calling
to each other. Dressed as he was, in jeans and T-shirt, he felt as
if he'd come from a distant world and landed here amid this
almost naked tribe.

He found the street, then the house, lost amid arbutus and
mimosas, barely visible under the oaks. Two huge pines leaned
their dark tops above it. He climbed over the gate, somewhat
hampered by the shotgun, and landed on a ramp that led down
to an underground garage. He walked over Japanese steps
across a dried-up lawn lined with red dahlias. In front of the
main door, he listened out but couldn't hear any noise from
inside. He was afraid they might have gone out, maybe to the
beach, and he was starting to think about where to place himself
to wait for them when he pressed on the latch and found that it
yielded. It was dark and cool inside. The little entrance hall led
directly to the main room. Leather couches, deep armchairs,
home cinema, paintings and prints on the walls. Franck had the
impression he was looking at an illustration from a catalog or
one of those interior decoration magazines. It was an invitation
to sit and have a cocktail with your friends, exclusively pretty
women or cool, elegant men.

He was surprised that Jessica hadn't brought the chaos
that went with her everywhere to this TV-show set. Maybe she
hadn't had time. The silence was deep and calm. There was no

threat, no tension, in this three-dimensional photograph, and he felt ridiculous, with his shotgun in his hand and his pockets full of cartridges. Through the picture window, he could see a terrace and the turquoise surface of a swimming pool. Franck was going closer when a brief laugh, a man's laugh, startled him. He took up position slightly back from the window and craned his neck to look and was startled to see Jessica run out and jump into the water. She was naked. Now she was floating on her back, eyes closed, beating with her hands and feet, and the water splashed up around her in a glittering din.

Franck slid the window open. The pool was about twenty feet away. Jessica hadn't seen him, and on his right, the man lying on his stomach on an air mattress couldn't see him either. Franck walked toward him, and at that moment Jessica cried out:

"What the fuck are you doing here?"

"I'm here to fetch you. Come on out of there."

She swam to the other end of the pool, as if to take shelter.

"Get lost, you fag!"

The guy on the mattress turned and sat up. He was in his fifties, with short salt-and-pepper hair. Athletic, tanned. He had a massive hard-on. Next to him were two almost-empty bottles. Gin, whisky. And cans of soda. And a salad bowl with ice cubes melting in it.

"What does he want?"

Franck raised his shotgun. "Are you Soler? I came here to fetch her. Get her out of the water."

Through the bead, the man appeared to hesitate, perhaps embarrassed. Then he stood up, his hard-on now at half-mast.

"Who the fuck are you?"

"Get her out of the water. Hurry up about it. I'm taking her with me."

Soler walked unsteadily over to the pool. Jessica was floating on her back, motionless, her eyes closed.

"Come on," the man said, one hand held out toward her.

Jessica opened her eyes. "No. No way. Not with that bastard. I'm fine where I am."

Her voice was thick, her face frozen in a fixed smile. She closed her eyes again. She didn't seem able to keep them open.

"Come on out. He has a shotgun."

"Let him stick his shotgun up his ass."

Franck walked over to the man, his shotgun trained on him. He had him almost at point-blank range now.

"Get her out of there. Dive in and get her out."

Soler swept the space behind him with his arm, trying to grab the barrel of the shotgun, but Franck dodged away and struck him on the ear with the flat of the butt. The man fell into a sitting position, moaning with pain, one hand on the side of his skull, examining his fingers to see if he was bleeding. He grimaced and groaned. Franck lowered his shotgun because the tanned, slim body he had seen on his arrival had become that of a timid, trembling animal, turned in on itself, pitiful in its nakedness.

Jessica started beating the water with her hands, rather as if she was attempting a butterfly stroke, but she made no progress, her head sometimes under the water, wheezing and coughing to catch her breath. The man had crouched at the side of the pool and was watching her with a distraught air, his hand still on his ear. Franck ordered him to jump in the pool and go get her because she wasn't feeling well, but he didn't react, even when he pressed the barrel of the shotgun to the back of his neck, shit, she's going to drown, you scumbag, get her out of there, but the man didn't move, so Franck jumped in without even taking off his espadrilles, his shotgun in his hand, although he let go of it immediately, and he reached Jessica and took her under the arms just as she was going under for a fourth time, struggling less and less, without even the strength to gasp for air. He pulled her toward the chrome-plated ladder and grabbed onto it, but was pulled back by the weight of her limp body. Her hands were no longer able to keep hold of anything. He tried to tighten his grip on her, but she slipped away and started to sink straight down, and he had to dive to catch her before she hit the bottom. When he came back up to the surface, he saw the man standing with his back to them, motionless, apparently either thinking things over or emerging from his stupor, then he walked to the house and disappeared through a glass door, which he closed again slowly behind him.

Franck laid Jessica down on the tiles, on her side. He didn't know what to do and was watching her breathe weakly when she suddenly started coughing and spitting and spewing out water. He sat her up and grabbed her under the armpits and shook her violently to help her get rid of everything that was still clogging up her insides. He had the feeling he'd seen this done somewhere before, but he couldn't remember where. In the end, she started breathing normally and regained enough energy and lucidity to push his hands away, letting out a groan as she did so. It was at this point that the man came back toward them with a baseball bat in his hand. He had put on shorts and a T-shirt and was walking heavily, dragged down by the alcohol and the products they must have both taken.

Without knowing why, Franck dove down to the bottom of the pool to retrieve the shotgun he had let go of while rescuing Jessica. When he came back to the surface, Soler was waiting for him at the side of the pool, swaying a little, brandishing his bat. Franck aimed the barrel at him and pulled the trigger. There was a crackling sound, and then the barrel started smoking. The other man froze as if waiting for the shot to finally happen. Franck took advantage of this to scythe at his ankles with a sweep of the shotgun butt, and the man fell on his ass, screaming with pain, his bat rolling beside him.

Franck hoisted himself out of the water and grabbed the bat. The desire to smash this guy's head in and hear his skull crack as he hit him was so strong that he started shaking as he stood over him, out of breath. Soler looked up at him with a helpless, imploring expression, as if understanding the threat. Franck threw the bat in the pool and kicked Soler in the temple. The man slumped onto his side and his head hit the tiles with a dull thud.

Jessica was trying to get back onto her feet, but she tottered then fell back on all fours, moaning. Franck helped her up and supported her as far as the picture window and laid her down on a white leather couch.

"Where are your things?"

She was nodding gently, breathing in a labored fashion, massaging her breasts. She watched him through her half-closed eyelids, pouting like a sick or frustrated little girl. He ordered her to keep still, knowing full well that she wouldn't be able to take two steps without collapsing, and set off through the villa, opening door after door until he discovered a huge bathroom, covered in blue ceramic tiles, where two bathrobes were hanging. He grabbed one, which still smelled of conditioner, and took it to Jessica and put it on her. Her flaccid arms and inert, heavy body made it all the more difficult. She moaned and groaned and insulted him unintelligibly. He wanted to slap her, to wake her up but also to hurt her and give vent to his anger and disgust. "Stupid bitch," he kept saying under his breath, her thin body slumped against his while he struggled with the tails of the bathrobe.

When she was dressed again, he let her stretch out then went outside to see how Soler was doing. The man was still lying flat on his stomach at the edge of the pool, but moving slightly as if trying to swim to it. Franck pinched his cheek, hard, and he moaned with pain. He had a big bruise on his forehead, one black eye, swollen and bleeding.

"What did you give her?"

Soler moved onto his side, in a fetal position, his head resting on his arm. He laughed nervously. "What do you think? She had the same thing as me. I told her not to swim."

"What did the two of you take?"

Soler sighed. "I don't know. The usual things . . ."

He raised himself onto his elbow then fell back heavily, and suddenly he was convulsed with silent laughter, his eyes closed.

Franck grabbed one of his ears and twisted it, his fingers slipping on the damp skin. Soler tried to get free of his grip, but there was no strength in his arm and it fell back weakly.

"I'm going to throw you in the water. You'll sink like a stone, you scumbag."

Soler stopped laughing and looked at him. "That's not a good idea." He laughed again, and his laugh was a kind of squeal. "The dumb bitch had never tried opium. Can you believe that? With all she's put inside her over the years I've known her, she'd never touched the stuff."

Soler laughed again, then seemed to fall asleep suddenly. Franck kicked him in the shoulder, but he didn't react, and he glanced around at the setting in which he found himself and which he had only ever seen in movies or on TV shows: a villa of 2,000 square feet, a vast garden, a swimming pool . . . He went over to the deckchairs with the bottles next to them and took a handful of almost-melted ice cubes from the salad bowl and filled his mouth with them and crunched them and emptied the remaining water over his head. He had the feeling that his skin and bones had hardened at this icy contact, and this shook him from the fatigue that was starting to replace his anger. A red linen bag was lying on the ground. He took a look inside and found a whole hodgepodge of female stuff in it, cigarettes, a billfold containing Jessica's papers.

When he came back to the living room, Jessica was asleep on the couch, the loose bathrobe spread around her in a large pale green corolla. Her hands folded over her belly, her calm, open nakedness making her look like the model for a painting—goddess, virgin or whore—although Franck didn't know where he could have seen something like that.

He slung his shotgun across his shoulder and lifted Jessica, who was completely limp, her arms dangling, her head thrown back. He was afraid her neck would snap so he pulled her to him and her face, masked by hair stuck down by sweat, came to rest on his chest. She weighed almost nothing, like a child he had come to save and whom he had to get out of here as quickly as possible. He contorted himself to open the door and almost ran to the car. He laid Jessica down on the back seat. A convertible passed, with three girls inside who all turned to look at him, their sunglasses flashing. Before, he would have waved at them and hailed them and arranged a vague meeting on the beach, to the right or left of the lifeguards' station, opposite the flag, attracting scornful looks, maybe a burst of laughter. Before, he would have tried to hitch a lift when he saw them coming, dreaming of being seated next to their almost naked bodies.

He waited for them to turn the corner of the street, then looked around him to make sure nobody was watching him, but all he could see were the roofs of the villas, surrounded by trees, and there was no way of knowing if anyone was spying on him behind the hedges or the mimosa groves. He got in behind the wheel and set off, keeping an eye on the rear-view mirror. He was expecting to see a car emerge through a gate and start to chase him, or a guy in shorts, his belly sticking out in front of him and his hand shielding his eyes, carefully recording his license number.

Jessica remained unconscious for more than an hour, until she said in a strangled voice, "I'm going to throw up." Franck asked her to hold on and sped to the rest area about a mile from there. He was able to park between two tourist cars and as soon as he opened the door, Jessica clambered out, got down on all fours on the asphalt, and vomited on the wheel of a Mercedes. Franck helped her up and supported her as far as the toilet block. With each step, her knees gave way beneath her, which made her look like a sluggish automaton or a drunk on the verge of a coma, and the people they passed got out of their way, repelled by the vomit soiling her bathrobe, or turned to look at the nakedness glimpsed through the opening in the robe.

She let out a bellow when Franck splashed her with water to clean her face and rinse the bathrobe. He insisted, but she struggled and started to strip. In that din of cicadas and water flushing and doors creaking, surrounded by the comings and goings of vacationers, he felt like leaving her there by the wash-stands, the way you leave a dog you don't want anymore. She was swaying in front of him, one shoulder and one breast bare, her hand tense on the fabric, incapable of continuing her strip. Franck pulled the bathrobe up over her shoulders and took her by the arm. She was walking a little better now, but weighed on him more, and coughed and spat to get rid of whatever was still clogging her throat. She collapsed onto the back seat and he had to fold her outstretched legs to be able to close the door.

He drove with all the windows down in an attempt to dispel the smell of vomit that clung to her. She sat slumped in the back seat, naked, the bathrobe thrown off her. He hoped there wouldn't be any cops at the tollbooth, standing guard after the gates, peering at the insides of the cars and the faces of the drivers. As they approached the toll area and its lines, he asked Jessica to cover herself but she didn't react. Even though she was sitting up now and her eyes were open, she looked like someone under hypnosis or like one of those people in a deep coma who don't see or feel anything.

When he got out of the car, the old woman immediately emerged from the house and opened the car door to help her daughter get out. Jessica looked around her and seemed to re-gain consciousness. She pushed her mother away with a mut-tered curse and staggered to the door. The old woman followed her, her hands held out, ready to catch her if she should fall. Two minutes later, she appeared at the bedroom window. She threw a contemptuous glance at Franck then closed the shutters. Behind her, he could hear Jessica crying with animal moans.

7

The old woman came out of the kitchen to take a bowl of coffee and a slice of brioche up to Jessica. When they were alone with their bowls of coffee, the old man poured some more for Franck and asked him how things had gone the day before in Lacanau. Franck told him in a few words. The old man was worried about the shotgun, which would have to be taken apart, cleaned and greased.

"I could have killed the scumbag. I came this close."

"That's all we needed."

The old woman returned. Her husband gave her a questioning look.

"She's better now. She slept well and took her medication. Now she's wide awake and hungry."

She glanced up at the ceiling and lit a cigarette. Nothing more was said for a while. Franck looked at the two of them, subdued, lost in thought, worried. He wasn't too sure what worried them the most.

"She didn't have time to take too much of the drugs, she should recover."

The old woman blew her smoke out hard and shrugged. "Oh, that's what you think, is it? Because you know all about that crap."

"I don't know a damned thing about any of it. But what I do know is that your daughter keeps some pretty bad company."

"Starting with your brother and you, right?"

"Raped one night, stoned out of her mind the next day. That wasn't down to my brother and me. Because those two bastards we saw the other day were people she knew before she ever met us."

The old woman was about to say something in reply, but Rachel came running in and filled a glass with water from the faucet in the sink, standing on tiptoe. She was behaving exactly as if she were alone, drinking facing the window where the treetops were moving. Between two gulps, she asked if she could use the pool. The old woman checked the time on the big clock and said yes. Rachel put her glass down on the drain rack then hopped out. The old man stood up after her. Franck had had time to see the bruises on the girl's cheek and shoulder. He found himself alone with the old woman, who stood up and started rummaging in a drawer, with her back to him, in a metallic clatter of flatware being shifted about. He told himself she was quite capable of taking out a knife and threatening him with it if he didn't leave the room. He would have liked to see her try, just for the pleasure of smashing a chair over her head. Since nothing happened, and the one thing she wanted was for him to go, he stood up and left her to rage to her heart's content. He stopped at the foot of the stairs and listened out for sounds from Jessica's room. He heard a scraping on the floor, the creak of a door. He climbed the stairs and was surprised not to find the dog lying in front of the door. He asked if he could come in.

"What do you want?"

"I want to talk to you."

He heard her moving, coming and going, as if she was putting things away.

"Talk about what? I don't feel like talking."

"Even about Rachel?"

The door opened abruptly, and he was hit with the acrid smell of stale tobacco. Jessica stood there, barring the way, one hand on the latch. Loose T-shirt, track pants. Eyes creased with anger and tiredness. In the draft, the smoke from her cigarette, which lay on an ashtray, slowly drifted out through the open window.

"What about her? Are you going to give me advice on how to bring her up?"

"She still has marks on her face and body. Did you even see?"

"Her skin marks really easily. And anyway, so what? I must have hit her a bit too hard, that's all! She'll make sure she doesn't mess around next time. She was playing with her crummy dolls in the middle of the corridor and I almost broke my neck! And when I told her, the little brat just sighed! Hell, who does she think she is?"

"She's a kid! You can't just hit her like that!"

Jessica shrugged and opened her mouth to say something, then changed her mind. She turned her back on him and walked over to the window. In the stream of light shimmering around her, she was only a frail, dark silhouette. Shaking. Facing him, the cracked mirror of the wardrobe split her reflection in two.

"Even when she was really small, she was complicated. She didn't sleep, I had to give her syrup. The doctor didn't agree, he said it was bad for her, but he wasn't the one who woke up in the middle of the night because she was having nightmares or because she'd stand at the foot of my bed and watch me like she was some kind of zombie until I woke up with a start! And I still give her syrup sometimes, when she's too weird or excited. She's going to need it tonight!"

Running out of breath, she fell silent and leaned on the windowsill with her elbows.

"Who were those guys the other night?"

"You don't need to know."

"Oh, really? They stuck a gun to the back of my neck, and I don't have a right to know?"

"As long as they didn't stick it up your ass, you don't have that much to complain about. I'm the one those bastards raped, and I'm not crying about it."

"Well, I'm going to the cops to make a complaint. I have their license number."

Jessica turned and stared at him. "You're not serious?"

"Of course I am. You're beaten up and raped, I'm threatened

with a gun, I think that's enough reason to make a complaint, don't you? The girl who was with them, Farida, she should be easy enough to find. Pascal and Ivan, that was it, wasn't it? Ivan the Serb and Pascal known as Schwarzie. They seem to be well known in the club. And probably also in the cops' records. I'm going to tell them everything, it'll be a change for them from chasing drunks or investigating thefts from cars."

"And are you also going to tell them that you pissed your pants? Like a fag? They're bound to like that, too."

She turned toward the wardrobe to put away some clean linen. When she opened the door, the broken mirror cast a white flash on the walls. He should have rushed at her and knocked her against the wardrobe door, but he wanted her to talk, so he waited until the anger that was taking his breath away subsided.

"You won't go."

She wasn't looking at him. She stood there motionless, her hands resting on a pile of sheets.

"Why's that?"

"Because if the cops stick their noses in it, the Serb and his friends will slaughter us. You don't know them. So just keep calm and let me sort things out in my own way."

"Have you known them for a long time?"

He went to her and grabbed her by the shoulders.

"Answer me. Have you known them for a long time?"

She planted those pale eyes of hers in his, without blinking. "Let go of me. I said, let go of me. And get out of here."

"I'm not going anywhere. You can scream all you like, you can bang your head on the walls. Tell me everything or I'm going to the cops. That's all there is to it. I'm listening."

"You're another son of a bitch. Just like your brother. It's not surprising."

She smiled, mouth twisted, pleased with herself. She was challenging him with her eyes, nodding sardonically. She didn't see the back of his hand coming. It struck her on the cheek and threw her to the floor. She sat up and slid backwards to the foot of the wall, under the window. Franck walked toward her and grabbed her by the hair and moved his face close to hers until their noses were touching. She clenched her jaws, her lips pinched, and looked him straight in the eyes, tears overflowing from her eyelids. He banged her head against the wall, without force, dully.

"I'm the one who's going to slaughter you. Did you know that? Son of a bitch, you said? I'm going to make you eat those words along with your own shit."

He was speaking in her face, giving her little head-butts, and each time her head hit the wall. He had wedged his knee between her legs and now raised her a little and felt her hard pubis through the cloth but also the softness lower down. She grimaced in pain and the tears started running.

"Your pussy still hurts, doesn't it? They should have fucked you harder, those two scumbags, they should have torn you up so you could never use it again."

She collapsed onto her side and huddled at the foot of the wall, her hands between her thighs, weeping with long sobs.

Franck got to his feet and watched her moaning and choking. It was unbearable. There were three knocks at the door and the old woman's voice rang out:

"Are you all right in there? What's going on?"

Jessica sat up abruptly, leaning on one hand, and replied that everything was all right, she just needed to be left alone.

"Are you sure you don't need anything?"

"I'm all right, I tell you!"

They heard the old woman's steps as she descended the stairs. Franck bent over Jessica and put his hand on her neck and caressed the back of it, under her hair. She wouldn't stop crying, with sharp little strangled sobs, the kind that children have. She took Franck's hand and pressed it to her cheek.

"I'm sorry," she said. "I didn't mean it."

He sat down next to her. He pulled her to him, and she let herself go, her wet face in his neck.

"Did I hurt you?"

"No."

She took hold of his hand and moved it down between her legs and pressed it and squeezed her thighs together.

"Not anymore," she murmured. "There. Yes."

They remained like that for a moment, their breaths mingling, in the light falling on them from the open window. Then, with a spasm, Jessica moaned and gently pushed him, and he moved away from her. He didn't understand why her eyes were full of tears, the sadness overwhelming her, he didn't understand anything anymore.

"They'll be back. They told me they'll be back."

"When?"

She shrugged. "It doesn't matter when. This afternoon, tonight, in two months. I thought I could come to an arrangement with them last night, but they didn't want to know anything about it. They're also looking for Fabien. They know he's in Spain, and they'd like him to come back."

Franck rubbed his arms, which were shaking. He would also have liked to massage his heart, to calm its wild beating. He made an effort to breathe deeply. He stood up and his eyes were dazzled and the room went red around him. Jessica remained seated, her back against the wall under the window.

"Pass me a cigarette."

He looked around for the pack.

"There, on the night table."

They started smoking in silence. Heat filled the room, thick and stifling.

"Now explain."

"I owe them money. Well . . . my parents and I."

"How much? Since when?"

"Thirty thousand. It's been six months."

She flicked her cigarette ash into the ashtray on the floor between her legs. Her fingers were shaking.

"What money was this? What was it for?"

"Actually, it wasn't money. It was drugs. A little bit of coke, shit, pills. I had a plan to sell it in Bordeaux."

"What was the plan?"

"The guy you hit yesterday. Soler. He knows people. People with money in lots of different circles. Here, and on the Basque coast—in Paris, too. So they gave me the drugs in return for a deposit, 20%, something like that. It was Fabien who paid. He'd hardly touched the money from your hold-up. He thought it might work. But that bastard Soler chickened out and sold almost nothing, so then the Serb got impatient and started putting pressure on me. The other night, I arranged to meet with him, I had three thousand euros to quiet him down, but he wasn't interested. That's also why I went to see Soler. For him to give me something in compensation, if you like. And also because I needed to get really high, and he has everything you could ask for. I told myself he might have a solution."

She got back on her feet and went and took another cigarette, then leaned on the windowsill. The dark contours of her body seemed about to dissolve in the stream of light.

Franck had the impression he had put his hands into a sack filled with snakes. "What about Fabien? Is he in Spain to sell the rest of the stuff? Is that it?"

Jessica nodded, blowing the smoke out hard in front of her. "He had some genuine contacts near Valencia. It was Serge, the Gypsy, who told him about them. He thought it was worth a try, so he left. He knows we're at their mercy here, and he's going to do what he has to."

"Why hasn't he been in touch? That's odd, isn't it?"

She shrugged. "Because he's careful. He doesn't want to get caught. And another thing is, he likes to be left alone. He must be seeing lots of girls, he said he'd take the opportunity to enjoy himself. This isn't the kind of business that can be settled in three days, just like that. When he's ready, don't worry, he'll call."

She stubbed out her cigarette in the ashtray as if it were

some filthy or poisonous insect, then turned her back on him and started to make her bed.

Franck felt like shaking her some more so that she would tell him everything. "What are you planning to do? Wait for them to come back here and attack your parents or Rachel?"

"Let them come, the bastards. We can defend ourselves. What do you suggest?"

"I suggest going to see them and showing them what we're capable of. Not letting them do what they like . . ."

Jessica turned and gave him an ironic look. "We? Who's we? Who are you? You're here to sleep and eat and wait for your brother to get back. The rest is our business, so don't butt in."

"I'm the brother of a guy who's involved up to his neck in your business. I'm a poor idiot who wonders what's become of him, and even if he's still alive, so you see, your business is my business, too, got that? The money he put into this little deal of yours is as much mine as his, because we both took it and I did five years in the slammer for it because I kept my mouth shut. Don't you get that? So I'm going to stick my nose into this mess, and I'll kick up as much fuss as I like until Fabien gets back. And if I have to go to the cops, I will. If you don't tell me the whole truth, I'll tell them the little I know, I don't care."

Jessica shrugged. She had put her hands in the pockets of her track pants and was shaking her head, looking at him with disdain. "Is that it? Have you finished?"

"Tomorrow morning I'm going to the cops. If you haven't told me anything else, I'll let them have the whole story. I'm also going to take a trip to Bordeaux to see a friend. Someone I trust, it'll make a nice change. Think it over carefully in the meantime. Have you got that, you stupid bitch? Tomorrow."

He went out without giving her time to reply. On the landing, the dog, which had been lying full length, now got up so abruptly that, standing there, it seemed to Franck even bigger and more massive than ever. The animal followed him with its eyes, its nose on the level of the floor, its back rippling with muscles. When he got to the foot of the stairs, Franck saw its huge head stretched toward him, sniffing the air as if to detect the traces of his fear.

Once outside, he walked through the house looking for Rachel, but the sun was starting to chase people and shadows away with its light. He looked up at Jessica's window. It was a dark rectangle crossed suddenly by a vague gleam of light, like a will o' the wisp, as she closed the door of the wardrobe with the broken mirror. The silence was total. Between the wrecks of cars and agricultural machinery, the dry grass crackled as if threatening fire. He went into the trailer to lie down and try to digest everything he had just learned and to distinguish what was true from what was false, and it all started going around and around in his mind like a crazy carousel, the horses kicking and rearing and biting those they knocked into until they bled, thrown one against the other as the carousel rolled about wildly, but after a while he woke with a start. That dream of horses had slipped into his half-sleep, so he got up and went and splashed his face at the little washstand. The water was lukewarm at first, then he shivered as it got colder and for a moment or two he kept his head under the faucet, wetting the back of his neck and his arms.

Standing in the middle of the trailer, he thought about his hand between Jessica's thighs earlier and he now regretted not having had her right there, on the floor, to flush out that mixture of pain and pleasure that made her weep and contort her face. He didn't know if she felt pain when she came or if it was the pain she felt that made her come. She struck him as a collection of pieces gathered together in the same body, a body that was merely an envelope and meant nothing to her. When he spoke to her, he sometimes had the impression that he didn't know who he was addressing. In the bedroom, in that light that blinded them, he might have thought that another woman sometimes came to replace her as she slid into his arms or insulted him to his face.

He had to talk about her to Fabien. He had to know how she was with him, what he thought of this complicated girl. Could it be that she reserved her mood swings for him, Franck, because she sensed that he was weaker and more vulnerable than his brother? Maybe she was all honey with Fabien because he knew how to handle her and how to be respected.

He dialed Fabien's number. It rang eight or ten times before he heard the recorded message. He hung up and almost threw the phone in the sink, then changed his mind. He thought again about Lucas and Nora.

Nora's voice. She recognized his immediately and started purring. Talking about the heat, the sweat, the darkness she had been curled up in since morning, when Lucas had left.

"Where are you staying now?"

"Where Fabien lives, near Bazas. He told me to come here. Except he's not here, he's gone to Spain, so I'm waiting here until it gets back."

"That's just like him, never where you think he'll be. Yes, he told us about those people. He's been at their place for a year now. He met them through Serge, the Gypsy."

"Are you sure? I didn't like the guy. Was he in business with Fabien?"

"Yes, I think so. You just have to ask Lucas, he knows all about it. The less I know . . . I don't give a damn about their crap anyway."

She suddenly fell silent. Franck heard her sighing and breathing hard.

"Fuck it, I'm hardly dressed and I'm hot all the same, can you imagine? I take an almost ice-cold shower every hour and it hardly cools me down! But then it's always worse in town than in the country. What about you? How's it going? When are you coming to see us?"

"This afternoon, if that's okay with you. When will Lucas be back?"

"Around five, he told me. It doesn't matter, you can stay and

136 · HERVÉ LE CORRE

eat with us, it's been such a long time! We can have a few beers while we're waiting for him. Do you know where we live? It's the same place as before."

"I'll be right there."

He didn't dare ask her if she would receive him with almost nothing on, or if she would invite him to take a shower with her in the heat of Bordeaux. He recalled that evening with her when, during a party, while Lucas, Fabien and a few others were slumped half-comatose, he and she had found themselves together in a room and had done it on the floor, quickly and not well, almost without pleasure, because they were scared that someone might catch them and Lucas would murder them because he was quite capable of that, because ever since he had taken Nora away from her crazy family, he considered her his exclusive property, rather like a dog or a cat you save and treat for the blows it has received, or that you've found limping, weak and trembling at the side of a four-lane highway. Woe betide her and any man who let her rub up against his legs or begged for her attention. Lucas said it frequently to anyone who would listen, with the fixed smile of a madman on the verge of doing what he threatens. Everyone got the message loud and clear, like a warning free of charge, the first one and the last. At such times, Nora would lower her eyes and draw her legs closer together, a Mona Lisa smile on her lips.

Franck heard the tires of a car crunching the gravel on the path and saw the old woman's lousy face as she passed in her Japanese car, clinging stiffly to the wheel. She was leaving for the retirement home, to "play the maid," as she put it, in other words, to help with the dishes and the cleaning, substituting for staff on their summer vacations. She went there three times a week to work four hours in a row, morning or evening, and came back disgusted and contemptuous because of all those dirty and confused and sometimes lecherous old people, she'd talk about it some nights, the porn magazines found in the room of an almost mute old guy, a depressive former teacher who'd already tried to kill himself twice, who'd been saved without any difficulty because he'd gone about it so badly—"Frankly, what's the point of stopping him if he wants to kill himself? It'll make room for those on the waiting list, who are pissing their children off, won't it?"—or else the love letters she'd found once in a drawer of a practically blind old granny who wrote them to an unknown person and then didn't send them—"The kind of letters you write when you're twenty, well, not me, I wasn't the kind of girl who wrote crap like that, and anyway, who would I have written them to, for that you have to love someone and when I was twenty all I wanted was a guy between my legs who could at least do the business just so I could know what it was like to take the plunge, what it was that could make you want to climb the curtains barking like a bitch, but what did I get? Zilch. Anyway, I don't need to go on." While doing the rooms, she and a colleague sometimes rummaged in the residents' things to find their little secrets, their private diaries, their correspondence, the yellowed photographs sometimes kept between two books, and they would laugh a lot at their expense—"Look at this, granny in a swimsuit at the age of forty, fuck, how she's changed"—despising the time passed and other people's youth without any pity.

One evening, over dinner, she had let out all her bile, expressing in her harsh voice all her dreadful disgust at those she called zombies—"There are some who can't even find their dicks to pee, frankly after a certain time they should decide that it's over and put them to sleep for good, and it'll be a good thing for everyone, I mean, what's the point of it, really? I swear to you, if one day Roland forgets where his dick is I'll put rat poison in his coffee, and it'll all be over! I've already started wondering if he still has one . . ." The old man had sniggered and poured himself a glass of white wine. "When I see your face, I actually wonder what I'd do with it!" They both started laughing and clinked their glasses and drained them in one go, and then a grim silence fell around the table, broken only by the buzzing of moths and mosquitoes.

Franck heard the car move away, jolting over the path, then accelerate along the road, and he waited without moving until it faded into the silence. When he walked outside, he smelled fire in the air and he looked to see if he there was any smoke billowing above the trees, but the sky was as white and blinding as molten steel. The fire could just as well have fallen from the sky, he thought, like in those stories about the end of the world.

*

He got a little lost in the sad maze of a deserted suburb, yellowed by dryness, before coming to the familiar six cubes of concrete that made up the project where Nora and Lucas lived. In the almost empty parking lot, a white van without wheels was resting on hubs, its windows covered in cardboard. In the silence, he could hear the distant murmur of the beltway and very close, on a balcony, the solitary song of a bird in its cage.

Nora opened the door to him almost immediately. She was wearing a mauve djellaba, her hair gathered on the top of her head in an untidy bun from which wisps of black hair escaped. In the gloom of the corridor, her smile lit up the whole of her brown face with its big bright eyes. She put her arms around him and hugged him and kissed him on the neck and mouth, squealing with joy. She was heavier and rounder than before. Franck's hands couldn't find the curves and slopes he had loved to feel beneath his palms, loved to stroke at the slightest opportunity.

"Come on, let's have a drink. Lucas will be here soon. He's helping out a friend on a construction site, strictly off the books. Plastering, painting, electrics. Lucas can do anything, you remember. If that idiot wanted, instead of getting into shady stuff all the time . . ."

She walked ahead of him to the kitchen. As she swayed in her loose dress, he sensed that her hips were broader, her thighs thicker. All the shutters were closed, but white light filtered through the smallest crack, the narrowest gap, as if about to knock down any obstacle that stood in its way and come rushing into the rooms and burn everything to a cinder. There was a heavy, damp heat here, and the fans merely moved it around, as if churning tar. A heady smell of incense made the atmosphere almost nauseous and Frank asked Nora if he could smoke, just to smell something other than that sweet, pungent odor.

"Yes, of course you can smoke. You can even offer me one."

She took two beers from the fridge and then they went into the living room, which was furnished only with a couch and three armchairs arranged in a semi-circle in front of a huge TV set. She put the beers down on a low table consisting of a large, hammered brass tray supported by four bricks. They clinked their aluminum cans together in a toast, then swigged their beers without saying anything, looking at each other, exchanging smiles. Nora lit a cigarette then wedged herself into the bottom of an armchair, moving the hem of her djellaba up her legs.

"I'm so pleased to see you. It's been a while."

"More than five years. You haven't changed."

"Of course I have. And so have you."

All at once, he didn't know what to say anymore. Or how to say it. He had thought so much about what he'd say when he got out of prison to all those he knew that the words now struck him as inadequate, too weak to express what he felt, this anger, this sadness, and at the same time this joy at seeing the world around him stretch as far as his eyes could take him, without walls, without warders, without the faces of the other convicts, their steady eyes pressing on him, their bodies like so many obstacles to avoid if he wanted to go on his way. Nora was getting ready to speak and he knew what she was going to say and he preferred her to keep it to herself.

"But anyway, that's all over now."

He spoke quickly, hurriedly. She understood. She put a finger to her mouth and nodded. They finished their beers in silence and stubbed their cigarettes out in the ashtray.

Nora hadn't taken her eyes off him. She was staring at him, her lips half open, and at that moment it seemed to Franck that her long, brown face was perfect, her big dark eyes with the thick lashes, and he didn't know what to do. Before, at a moment like this, he would have stood up and they would have come together immediately, without a word, with that gentleness that had always been part of their embraces. Now he merely looked at her, taking direct advantage of the beauty of her face, and he couldn't understand why he remained so still beneath her calm, deep gaze. He couldn't understand what was stopping him from approaching her. Maybe all the time that had passed without anyone waiting for him, with only inaccessible memories remaining.

"And how is it with those people? Everything okay?"

"Do you know them?"

"I don't, but Lucas does. He must have gone there once or twice when he had business with your brother. The old man used to do business with the Gypsy, you know? Serge. I'm not too sure what they did. I'm not interested in their shit. Why do you ask me if I know them? Is there a problem?"

"It's the girl."

"What about the girl? Don't tell me you fucked her as well?"

"What do you mean, as well?"

Nora shook her head and gave a disappointed smile. "You're all the same."

They suddenly heard a baby crying. Franck didn't know if it came from the back of the apartment or from the neighbors', but Nora was already on her feet.

"She's woken up. She doesn't sleep well in this heat. I'll be back."

As she passed him, she lightly touched his cheek with her fingertips. He should have taken her arm, held her back, lifted her dress, and plunged his face into her lower belly, then made her sit on him. Instead, by the time he raised his hand to touch hers, she was almost out of the room. The next moment he heard her talking to the baby in a little girl voice and the crying abated and all that could be heard was the voice of a mother talking in the silence, saying nonsense words mixed with unintelligible singing and sucking noises and little laughs, all meant to express happiness and love.

Franck tried to think. He told himself that without those five years in prison he might have been the father of the creature that had been whining there, at the end of that corridor, and he thought again about the time he and Nora had fucked, bodies glued together, arms and legs intertwined, mouths joined, almost without moving, holding their breaths so that the others in the next room, floored by gin and pills, slumped in a spasmodic coma, shouldn't come back like zombies from their momentary death and tear them apart and punish them.

Nora came back into the room and placed a little living thing in his arms, a thing almost naked apart from a pale-blue diaper, a thing that gesticulated and babbled and flailed with its feet and its hands, which were sometimes rolled into fists, sometimes with fingers parted.

"Let me introduce Clara, nine months old. The love of my life. I'll leave her with you while I get her bottle ready—the breast is never enough for her."

The baby's eyes were black, like her mother's. They lingered on Franck's face, and for a few seconds she stopped moving and looked stunned, then a big toothless smile came to her, after which she suddenly grimaced and started twisting in all directions to free herself from the arms and hands that were barely holding her, not daring to tighten around her.

Nora was in the kitchen, where loud voices came from a TV.

"What's wrong?" Franck whispered in the baby's ear.

But she continued struggling and arching her body and moaning, and beneath the warm, tender skin Franck felt the hardness of her tense muscles. He stood up and held her close and the baby pushed with her head as if trying to propel herself away from him. He would have liked to hug her even tighter to prevent all movement and neutralize her, the way you immobilize a guy when you get him on the ground. With one hand he flattened her against him and with the other took her arms and legs and held them still. "That's enough now, all right?" He put her head against his neck, and for a few seconds the little body stopped moving. Franck felt only her halting breath beneath his palm and then was suddenly aware of the panicked beating of her heart through the tip of his thumb. "What should I do, dammit, what should I do?" So he relaxed his pressure on the baby and immediately a cry went up, hoarse and torn, a cough, a spit, wind and fear at last expelled after being held in, then sobs shook the child's sweaty body and Franck, who was trying to kiss the little reddened face, saw tears run from those eyes that were no longer looking at him.

He went into the kitchen and Nora, who was standing in front of the TV screen, turned to look at her screaming daughter. "What's the matter with her? She was in a good mood just five minutes ago. God knows what goes on in those little heads of theirs."

"I don't think she likes me."

"Lucas says the same. That's why he passes her to me all the time and I have to manage by myself. Give her to me. She's hungry."

She threw her cigarette in the sink and took the baby in her arms and whispered sweet things to her in a mysterious language, kissing the fine black hair stuck down by sweat. The sobs subsided and the baby placed her head on her mother's chest, sucking her thumb and staring into space, still tearful.

"I'd better go," Franck said. "I'll leave you to it."

Nora unbuttoned the top of her djellaba and took out one of her breasts. Franck instinctively turned his eyes away. This was no longer the kind of nakedness he had desired to see and caress.

Nora smiled. "It's all right, you'll get over it."

Franck shrugged, affecting indifference, and made an

effort to concentrate on Nora's face as she looked down at her daughter.

"Stay a while, Lucas won't be much longer, he said he'd try to get back earlier if you were here. In any case, I have to leave for work. I do the four to ten shift at the Auchan supermarket. Hell, someone has to bring in enough to buy diapers and food for her. Do babies scare you?"

"No, I scare them. I have to go."

Franck went to Nora to kiss her. She still had her daughter on one arm, and with the other hand was holding her breast to the baby's mouth. She held out her cheek to him, and suddenly there was no longer anything between them, if there ever had been anything. He placed his lips on the skin of a mother whose body now seemed to exist only in connection with this other tiny, fragile body, carrying it, feeding it, protecting it, given over entirely to this life that captured all her capacity for love and diverted her sensuality to its own needs. Leaning toward Nora, Franck smelled the baby's smell, that sickly-sweet mixture of moisturizing cream and disinfectant and milk, and he knew he had to go. He gently squeezed the baby's tiny hand and left the room without hearing what Nora was saying and found himself on the landing, his throat gripped by invisible hands, and he hurried down the three floors, as if escaping after a job that had gone wrong. He almost ran to his car and shut himself in the overheated interior, almost panting, and suddenly had a desire to see how long it would take him to faint from dehydration and die.

He thought again about the baby he had held in his arms. He could have squeezed her so hard to stop her resisting him that he might have choked her to death. What could have happened in him to be tempted to do that? he wanted to know. He felt disgusted with himself, and he remembered the pedophiles in prison, men who hugged the walls in the workshops or gathered together in a corner under the protection of two warders, he remembered his scorn and hatred for those people, who were so discreet and always talked in low voices, never a word louder than any other, risking only furtive, sidelong glances around them, presumably to evaluate the threat weighing on them even when the other convicts were silent. He loathed their polite airs, their honeyed tones, their good manners, the books they came to get from the library and which they pretended to leaf through as they waited by the doors while the warders pulled back the bolts and made the iron hinges squeak. What they had done to children, everyone knew. It spread through the corridors and the cells like the smell of shit whenever a newcomer arrived, and the reasons for his incarceration were known even before the guy had finished putting his toothbrush on the washstand. It would be whispered outside as he walked around the exercise yard, and everyone had their own exclusive information about him, which they'd gotten from a warder—the victim was his daughter, his son, his nephew, a nine-month-old baby, a schoolkid, an altar boy, and so on. And occasionally, when you passed one of them in a gangway, closely guarded by a warder, you spat at his feet or muttered an insult or threatened a punishment, and of course none of them reacted to the affront, just continued on their way, dragging their feet, their hands in the pockets of their track pants.

He was no better than those perverts. Something had risen inside him, something barbarous and dark and bestial. The anger of a frustrated young boy. He had been able to control it in time, that was all. He hadn't broken that living doll struggling against him. He had often dreamed that he was killing someone. With a gun or with his bare hands. But in those dreams he never went all the way. The bullets moved slowly, in a curve, as if he'd thrown paper balls, and just as his hands were squeezing the life out of someone he would wake, always with a start, and his hands would relax, although his heart would continue to pound with anger, or with relief that he wasn't a criminal. But with that baby in his arms, he hadn't been asleep. He had tried to overpower her as if he'd been fighting with a guy his size and weight. It would only have taken a little more pressure on that little body and he could have killed her.

He gave a start when someone tapped at the window. A big signet ring was hitting the glass.

He didn't immediately recognize Lucas, with his shaved head and hollow cheeks. He was dressed in threadbare jeans, white with plaster and spattered with paint stains, and a color-less T-shirt torn in places. The door opened and the air from outside rushed into the car, almost cool, and Franck started gulping it down as fast as he could.

"What are you doing in there? You're going to croak! A little bit longer and I wouldn't be talking to you now!"

Franck felt Lucas's big hand grab him by the shoulder and pull him out of that furnace. The light forced him to close his eyes and he had to lean on the car in order not to fall.

"Were you leaving, or did you just get here?"

Franck gradually caught his breath but his dry, swollen throat stopped him from speaking.

Lucas took him by the arm and pulled him toward the building. In the lobby, the shade was red and he felt the sweat running down him like rain. He lifted his fingers to his forehead because it seemed to him suddenly as if his skin was oozing blood. When they reached the landing, Lucas was breathing hard, his face streaming with sweat.

"I smoke too much," he breathed.

"I was just leaving," Franck said at last. "I stayed with Nora for a while, we had a drink, she introduced me to the baby."

"Oh, really? And you were leaving without waiting for me?"

Lucas opened the door with an abrupt gesture, as if some-one was resisting on the other side. Nora was waiting for them in the corridor. When she saw Franck, she came to him and raised a hand to his cheek.

"What happened to you?"

"I felt faint in the car. It must be the heat."

"Go stick your head under the faucet," Lucas said.

He opened a door and pushed him into the bathroom. When he was alone, Franck sprinkled his face and drank out of the palms of his hands. He splashed water over the back of his neck then put his head under the faucet, panting. Shivers were running down his back. For a moment he stood and looked at the pale face in the mirror, that wild-eyed creature streaming with water and sweat.

He went back into the living room where the TV was muttering away, throwing pale gleams into the semi-darkness. Lucas was slumped on the couch, dressed in shorts and a short-sleeved shirt open on a hairless chest and firm abdominals, a joint in his mouth and a beer in his hand. The baby was lying next to him, wedged between two cushions, her little feet beating on her father's thighs.

"Are you feeling better now? Fuck, you scared me, shut up inside your car like that. Wasn't five years in the slammer enough for you? Grab yourself a beer. It's nice and cold."

Franck grabbed a can from the low table then looked at the baby, who was moving with slow gestures, her four limbs flailing the air around her. She made him think of someone drowning in dark water.

Lucas took the tiny foot resting on his thigh between his thumb and index finger. "It's weird, isn't it? However much you tell yourself you didn't want one, you get attached to it all the same. Isn't that so, my little pisser? Your daddy's little sweetheart, except when you scream at night!"

The baby caught the finger he was waving in front of her and squeezed it in her fist then lifted it to her mouth. He took the pacifier that had fallen next to her and stuck it between her lips.

"It was Nora who wanted a kid. I have to take care of her a little bit."

"Where is Nora?"

"She's gone to work. She says she wants an honest job. She works like a slave, check-out girls like her work ridiculous hours, but still, it's what she calls an honest job. She says she's doing it for the baby . . . Anyway, tell me, what's happening with you?"

Franck shrugged. "A poor bastard just out of the can. Nothing very original. You know how it is, anyway."

"Hell, try not to look so happy. Anyone would think you're going back there tomorrow."

"Have you heard from Fabien?"

"No, not since April, or May, I can't recall. He'd found a job down there, over toward Langon. He was in charge of warehouses, trucks, I can't remember what he told me. He was working at night, with a dog. You see the kind of thing. And then he left for Spain at the beginning of the month, to do what I don't know."

"Is he the one who told you?"

"Yes. He told me he'd be away for three or four weeks, max. Since then, I haven't heard from him. He hasn't called. He hasn't even been in touch with the Gypsy even though they were always doing business together."

"How long have you known the Gypsy?"

"Two years. It was your brother who introduced us. They included me in their business when I came out of the slammer. The cars. It's Serge and a cousin of his and the old man you're staying with who disguise them. Afterwards, they go to Romania or Poland. It doesn't bring in a lot of money, so we have to get by in other ways. We handle metals, copper. Catalytic converters. That pays well. There are guys who recycle platinum. But it's hot because there are teams of Bulgarians, entire families with a father who gives all the orders and a whole bunch of brothers and cousins, they want it all for themselves, they don't like anyone stepping on their toes so we have to be careful. Even the Gypsies steer clear of them, they're a nasty bunch."

He turned to the baby, who was asleep, one hand raised above her then falling again gently at her side.

"If she sleeps too much now, she'll be bugging us tonight. I don't care, it's her mother who'll get up."

He put his joint down in the ashtray and stood up and placed the baby in her Moses basket. He stood there for a few seconds looking down at her, shaking his head and sighing.

"What are we going to do with you?"

"Why do you say that?"

"No reason. It's just that she doesn't have much of future. What with me and her mother, she's drawn two bad cards. A thief and a junkie."

"I thought Nora was clean"

"Except when she slips back. But it's true, most of the time she holds out."

Lucas took a long drag and kept the smoke in his lungs for a long time. He grabbed the remote control and cut off the murmur of the TV.

"I'm really pleased to see you and Nora again."

Lucas stubbed out his joint in the ashtray then lit a cigarette. "You don't look like it. Why did you come? To be honest, you seem strange to me."

Franck made an effort to smile. He glanced at the sleeping baby, so quiet now, and thought again about the strength with which this tiny little thing had rejected him earlier.

"I still have to get my bearings. It's not easy."

"And how are things over there, with the old couple and Jessica?"

"You know her?"

"I used to see her around with Fabien, at parties, that kind of thing."

"And?"

Lucas gave a silent laugh. "And she's crazy."

"What do you mean, crazy?"

"Don't tell me you haven't noticed!"

"She's a little bit strange, but . . ."

Lucas shook his head, looking at the silent TV screen, where young men and women in bathing suits were coming and going between the vast spacious living room of a villa and the side of a swimming pool.

"Look at those whores . . ."

Franck also looked. The people seemed to be arguing, moving with abrupt gestures. He told himself that he would have liked this villa just for himself, in Miami or somewhere else.

"So as far as you're concerned, Jessica's just strange . . . Even your brother told me there were days when he didn't recognize her, when she made him feel nine inches tall, and the next day she would have given him blowjobs all day long and wanted them to get married and have kids. He told me he sometimes had the impression there are two of her. Not to mention all she's capable of taking when she's not feeling good. Booze, dope, meds. Fuck, in comparison, Nora was a homeopathic addict."

The baby moaned in her sleep and Lucas bent over the Moses basket and put his hand on her round little belly.

"Shit, she's hot. I'll take her back in the bedroom, it's cooler there. Grab yourself a beer, there are some in the fridge. Get one for me, too."

Franck watched him walk away, the big basket with the sleeping baby at the end of his big muscular arm. He wondered if Lucas still lifted weights, still boxed at the gym. He stood up and went to the kitchen, trying to let a little air circulate over his damp skin to dry it. The fridge blew its coldness in his face and he stood in front of that artificial godsend for a few seconds and the memory of the air conditioning turned up to full strength in the factory for vacationers on the highway came back to him. He took the beers and closed the door again in a clatter of bottles. Lucas was watching him from the doorway of the kitchen.

"Okay," he said. "What's the problem?"

He told him. The debt of thirty thousand euros, the unsold drugs, Fabien going to sell some of them in Spain, near Valencia. The guy Jessica knew and who claimed to have a ready market then chickened out. And the Serb who was losing patience, and what had happened the other night in Biscarrosse.

Lucas listened to him, wedged into his couch, arms spread across the back, shirt gaping open on his broad torso, looking like some kind of slovenly godfather sure of his hold over his visitor.

"That's it," Frank concluded. "That's the mess I'm in. Tomorrow, I'm going to the cops and telling them everything."

Silently, Lucas brought his hands up behind his head and stared at Franck through half-closed lids. "For a start, you can forget about the cops. If you want to go straight back inside, sure, go see them. But don't ever come and say that to me here, in my home. Got that?"

"No, I just meant—"

"Do you know where to find those sons of bitches?"

Franck felt something start that he could no longer stop. Like a mechanism, slow at first but whose parts gradually, inexorably swing into action. He didn't know yet if he himself would be crushed in the process, if he was witnessing the awakening of a mechanical monster that once up and running would devastate everything around him before tearing him to pieces.

"Why do you ask that?"

"Because I think we should have a little talk with them, quiet them down, don't you think? After what they did the other night? You're dropping the whole thing without reacting, like some kind of fag? Plus, as far as the money is concerned, apart from a bank loan, I don't see any way to pay them back. So if you can't pay them back, you scare them so that they drop it until Fabien gets back, and you also save your honor and your girlfriend's."

"Jessica must know, but she won't want to say."

"Your Jessica attracts trouble the way a piece of meat attracts wasps, but that's no reason to do what they did to her."

Franck stood up. He couldn't find anything to say in answer to that.

Lucas looked at him, hands on thighs. "Get her to talk, and we'll go there. If need be, I'll ask the Gypsy to help us out. He can be pretty tough when he puts his mind to it."

"I'd rather keep him out of this. I don't think he likes me very much. I saw him the other day with the old man and it didn't go well."

"You must have said or done something to upset him. You should have kept your mouth shut."

Lucas now also stood up. Franck had the impression he was taller, stronger, more imposing. His skin glistened, his muscles rippled on his torso. He brandished his fist close to Franck's face, his jaws clenched.

"You'll see, we'll give them such a hammering, they won't be back!"

Franck walked to the door and Lucas followed him. He could hear him breathing through his nose with anger or hate and smell the scent of his cologne mingled with the odors of beer and tobacco. On the landing, he turned and shook his hand, which was as hard and dry as cardboard, and huge, imprisoning his fingers in a burning-hot vise. Lucas wasn't smiling, he had his eyes fixed on his as if wanting to extract a promise from him.

"All right, I'll let you know," Franck felt obliged to say. "As soon as I have the address, we'll go."

Lucas didn't say anything. He turned away, merely nodding. It was as if he didn't believe a word of it. He quickly shut the door, although without slamming it, and immediately turned the key in the lock.

8

J essica had fallen asleep on top of him, her legs around his thigh, and was snoring softly, her head on his shoulder, and Franck stroked the hollow of her sweat-soaked lower back. The house was silent, and behind the closed shutters the heat was alive with the buzzing of insects. Every now and then, a cicada would start to sing in a pine somewhere then stop, as if overcome, and everything would fall back into the stifling torpor of the afternoon. The old folks had left early in the morning for a drive to the border to buy cigarettes and booze from a *venta*, and they'd taken Rachel with them, promising her they would go to the aquarium in Biarritz.

She came for him as soon as her father's Mercedes had driven away along the road. She came into the trailer dressed in her mini shorts and a kind of cropped T-shirt that hung loosely around her breasts. Without saying a word. Barely looking at him. He was lying on his bunk, fiddling with his cell phone, and she started collecting the glasses and cups that had been left lying about and put them in the little sink, as if she was about to do the dishes, then took the pot from the electric coffee maker and poured herself a drop of cold coffee and stood at the window, sipping her coffee and watching the birds moving about in the dust outside the barn.

He immediately knew what she wanted. He could sense it, he could sense *her*. With her lips resting on the rim of her cup and her pensive air and the brightness of her eyes capturing all the light from outside, she was more beautiful than he had ever seen her. He sensed that deep in her body she was quivering with longing for what they were going to do, a longing as explosive as a fit of temper that can't be contained for long but has to be allowed out, and he was expecting to see the crotch of her shorts get wet, he imagined it filling with fluid on the verge of oozing out. He changed position, because his jeans were becoming almost painfully tight. She couldn't be unaware of his move, but she continued looking outside then put her cup down on the drain rack.

"Well?"

"Well what?"

"You went to see your friend. How was it?"

Franck sat down and looked at her. She finally turned to him, with her hands in the patched pockets of her shorts. She had that waxy, inscrutable look he had seen before, and her bright agate and turquoise eyes were fixed on him.

"He agrees. We're going to see those guys to quiet them down. If you know where to find them, you have to tell us. You know him. Lucas."

"The boxer?"

"Yeah, the boxer. I trust him. He and Fabien were like brothers."

"They were?"

"Fuck, yes, and he hasn't heard from him since the beginning of the month and can't understand why."

She crossed her legs, leaning forward slightly, and bit her lower lip. "It's too hot in here. Come upstairs, it'll be more comfortable."

He followed her. She walked slowly, head down. He wanted to touch her. To pin her against the wall, right here, in the sun, and take her and make her scream. On the stairs, he had her ass within reach of his mouth. He could have eaten her there as she clung to the banister. He could think of nothing else. He followed her, he sensed her, he sensed her flesh, her pussy, that wet softness that would soon slide over his fingers. Nothing could have torn him from the attraction of that body. From the desire to which his whole being abandoned itself. When they reached the landing, Franck noticed a figure at the foot of the stairs. He thought of a child, the apparition of a child, suddenly appearing as if back from the dead, and he shuddered at the idea of a ghost. It was only the dog, sitting there with its muzzle raised toward him.

He joined Jessica in the bedroom. She was lying flat on her stomach on the pale-blue sheet.

She woke up and turned abruptly onto her back, her eyes wide open and fixed on the ceiling. Franck turned to her, but she ignored him, and he wondered if she even remembered that he was there, next to her. She slipped a hand between her legs then took it away and examined her fingers, which were moist and glistening, then got up and left the room, slamming the door behind her as if she was in a temper. The stairs creaked as she walked down them. Then he heard the water pipes rumbling.

She came back five minutes later, glancing in his direction, although he couldn't have said if she'd seen him because she didn't say anything and turned her back on him and got dressed. He still wanted her, so he pulled the sheet over him because it embarrassed him to have a hard-on when faced with such indifference. Did she even remember that she had screamed, that she'd begged for more, begged him to hurt her? Once again, he had the impression that the girl who was getting dressed with her back to him and was still just as naked, just as available, wasn't the same one he'd thought he was losing himself in half an hour earlier. A twin might have replaced her while he had dozed off, or come back upstairs from the bathroom to play that role. He must have seen that kind of story in a movie, where a woman and her double screw with the hero's head until he's almost crazy.

Or else she was the one who was crazy. Two in one. Alternately possessed and dispossessed. He wasn't sure. He didn't know anything about human beings or the baggage they carry around on their backs, the pits in which they take refuge or go astray.

He had learned in prison—and before, too—that you shouldn't trust them. One minute they were pitiful, the next dangerous.

She looked for her pack of cigarettes, found it, and lit one. "So, your boxer? When does he want to go there?"

"As soon as you tell me where to find those guys."

"Call him."

*

From the start, Jessica insisted that she wanted to come along, to get her own back for what the other guys had put her through. That was her condition for coming out with an address. Lucas didn't try to dissuade her. They arranged to meet outside Pascal's, the one nicknamed Schwarzie. He lived on the right bank, in the Bastide district, a two-storied house with a dilapidated façade, iron shutters streaked with rust. Lucas parked a little farther along the street and joined them immediately, a baseball bat in his hand. Seeing him walking in the middle of the road, swinging his strong, supple shoulders, Franck thought he looked so invincible, so formidable, that nothing bad could happen to them. The street was full of parked cars, some mounted on the sidewalks. Through the open windows, TVs let out a muted clamor. Above them, swallows flew across the washed-out blue of the sky, emitting cries, their bodies occasionally gleaming gold in the setting sun.

Behind the door, a child could be heard chattering and a woman in another room answering him, raising her voice. When Franck rang the bell, both voices ceased, and almost immediately a little boy of about ten came and opened the door, and on seeing him Franck recoiled and told himself it was best to drop the whole thing. The boy looked at them in turn, with the door ajar, but Jessica pushed him back and asked if his father was there.

"Mom!"

Jessica shoved him aside and he stumbled back and leaned

against the wall and Lucas came in after her and rushed upstairs, telling Franck to follow him. Franck met the boy's terrified eyes but couldn't think of anything to say to him because cries and curses and the noise of broken dishes could already be heard from the kitchen.

They opened the doors to three bedrooms, searched closets, looked under the beds, but didn't find anyone. Everything was clean and tidy and smelled of fresh linen and lavender. Franck found it hard to imagine that brute in a place like this, in this calm interior. They came back down on the double because it seemed as if the screams and cries of the two women below might alert the whole neighborhood.

The boy had taken refuge beside his mother, who was standing by the sink, a knife in her hand, trembling and moaning. She held her son against her as she brandished her knife in their direction, but she was shaking so much with sobs and shudders that it was obvious she might let go of it at any moment. Jessica was barely three feet from her, her monkey wrench raised, and she was asking where that bastard Pascal was. "Tell us, for fuck's sake, or I'll beat you up in front of your kid!" Meanwhile, Lucas opened the fridge and started emptying the contents onto the floor and kicking the cans and packs, which rolled in all directions and burst. He found two cans of beer and threw one to Franck, who almost missed it, then opened the other and started drinking in long gulps, his bat resting on his shoulder. He finished the beer belched, crushed the aluminum can in his hand, and threw it at the woman, hitting her on the forehead.

The screaming stopped abruptly, and Jessica swept her monkey wrench through the dishes drying on the sink. The woman shuddered and closed her eyes and dropped her knife at her feet. Franck went closer to get a better look at her. Beneath her smudged make-up and her tangled hair, which had fallen in front of her face, she was younger than he had first thought. She smelled of perfume and sweat. The damp skin of her neck and upper chest glistened.

"Calm down. We don't have any beef with you. We just want your scumbag of a husband."

"He isn't my husband," she sniffed.

"Who cares? We need to talk to him about what he did to our friend here the other night. It's best if that doesn't happen here."

The woman was still gasping in panic, hugging her son to her. "What do you think, he always tells me where he goes?"

"Then call him and get him to tell you where he is."

Franck took the boy by the arm and pulled him to him. The woman screamed, but he grabbed her by the throat.

"Shut up and nothing will happen to him. Do you have a phone?"

"In the next room."

Franck let go of the boy. They followed the woman to the living room, which was on the other side of the corridor that divided the house in two. She took a telephone from the low table and looked at them in turn. They didn't move, just stood there, keeping her at a distance, and all that could be heard was the faster breathing and sniffing of the boy, who had come into the room and again clung to his mother.

Then Jessica went behind the woman and stuck the blade of a pocket knife under her throat. "Say one word too many and I'll cut you. Understand?"

Yes, she understood. She nodded. She looked in the faces of Franck and Lucas for expressions of disapproval or embarrassment, but they were masks of fear, frozen in the moment, their eyes fixed on the knife blade.

She dialed the number and in the silence they heard the beeps of the dialing followed by the regular rings. Franck went closer and listened.

"Yeah, what's up?"

"Where are you?"

"At Samir's, why? Why the fuck are you calling me? We're in the middle of a game!"

"It's Jordan, he isn't well. I think he caught sunstroke. I wanted to know if you'd be back late."

The boy looked up at his mother in surprise, but she reassured him by running her fingers through his hair. There was a silence on the line, then the distant voice resumed:

"I'll be back when I want to be back! You're not my mother, right? I don't know, put some ice on him! Don't bug me with things like that, for fuck's sake! All right, okay, see you later!"

Lucas left the room and they heard him searching in a cupboard in the kitchen. He came back with a roll of adhesive tape, some cotton thread, and a cloth. Jessica didn't let go of the woman. She pressed her mouth against her cheek to talk to her.

"Where does this Samir live?"

"In Talence. Les Lilas project. Block C. I don't know the number."

"Don't worry, we'll find it. What's his surname?"

"Kheloufi."

Lucas and Franck unrolled some of the tape and tied her hands behind her back and then her feet, then gagged her with the cloth. Lying on the tiled floor, she started moaning and writhing and kicking, so Jessica came back and pricked her throat with her knife and she calmed down long enough for Franck to immobilize her by tying her wrists and ankles. The boy let them do the same to him. They didn't say anything to him, they were gentle with him, they didn't tie him too tightly, leaving him a little bit of wriggle room. They put tape over his mouth and sat him down on the couch. His tear-filled eyes rolled crazily then came to rest on his mother, who had her eyes closed.

Lucas looked around him as if checking that everything was in order, then turned to Jessica. "Like we said, you stay with them. The guy has to wonder what we're going to do to them. We'll call you anyway."

Jessica sighed. She was standing in the middle of the room, arms dangling, her knife still in her hand, and she was staring at the woman and the boy, as if not quite there.

"Take it easy," Franck said in her ear. "We have no beef with them."

"Don't worry, I'm not going to cut their throats right away."

Franck and Lucas left and once outside they both paused for a moment in surprise, perhaps because night had fallen, then started running to the car as if suddenly time was short. An engine revved up at the corner of the street and headlights pinned them to the spot and the screech of tires made them jump apart, each to one side, and walk bent down past the parked vehicles. Franck flattened himself against the side of a van just as two doors slammed and yells echoed. He took out his club, but felt so helpless that his impulse was to throw it away and go talk to the guys, to calm things down. Then he heard them yelling at Lucas to get down flat on his stomach and stop moving and already he could hear the dull thud of the blows falling along with the curses then Lucas screaming and moaning and his begging them, stop, stop, and Franck thought of Jessica, who must have heard and could probably see it all through the window, of Jessica with her knife in her hand and the woman and the kid at her mercy. He ran to the house and knocked at the door, and it opened immediately while his fist was still on the door and he leapt back on finding himself face to face with the woman, white with fear, the knife held under her jaw and the blood already emerging from the cut, Jessica behind her holding her by the hair and addressing the street, the night full of cries.

"I'm going to bleed her, you motherfuckers! Get out of here or I swear I'll cut her throat!"

Franck didn't know what to do anymore, he turned and saw Schwarzie in the middle of the roadway, in the light of the headlamps, aiming a gun at them, and at that moment he thought they were all going to die here, on both sides, one way or another.

"The kid's name isn't Jordan, it's Dylan," Jessica said behind him. "That's how she warned him, by using the wrong name, the bitch."

Franck also grabbed the woman and brought her out onto the sidewalk, Jessica still clinging to her, and he managed to yell at the guy to let go of his weapon and retreat and the guy took two steps back but at the same time he tightened his grip on the gun. A short distance away, Lucas had gotten to his feet and was swaying and punching the space that separated him from the other man, who was also stunned and propping himself against a car, and in the yellow light of the street lamps they looked like two drunks horsing around.

"Drop that gun," Franck said.

"Let go of her first, because I'm going to blow that bitch's brains out and yours afterwards."

His voice was firm, almost calm, but his arm was shaking and it was clear he was making a superhuman effort to keep his gun properly aimed. Franck saw Lucas collapse onto his guy and they rolled, locked together, against a car then onto the hood of another before collapsing between the two vehicles. There was the terrible sound of a skull hitting the asphalt, then Lucas stood up again and charged at Schwarzie and smashed into him the way you see in rugby and they fell to the ground, tangled together, one pulling the other down in his fall, heavily, almost slowly, without a cry. Franck rushed forward and tore the gun from Schwarzie's hand. Schwarzie didn't even resist, and Franck smashed his face with a blow from the club and screamed, come on, let's get out of here.

Jessica flung the woman against a wall and ran to him. He helped Lucas to his feet and they limped toward the cars. The siren of a police car could be heard in the distance and they hurried as best they could.

"I can drive," Lucas breathed. "Go on."

With the back of his hand, he wiped the blood streaming from his nose and the cuts above his eyes and threw himself on his seat.

Franck took the wheel of the other car and got out of the parking spot, knocking the cars in front and behind, setting off an alarm. In the rear-view mirror, he saw Lucas reverse toward the avenue and disappear. He swerved to avoid Schwarzie, who still lay motionless on the roadway. There was a squeal of sheet metal, and an external rear-view mirror smashed into pieces. Just as he turned the corner of the street, he saw the blue flash of a revolving light, then nothing more because he launched the car down a narrow street without knowing where he was going. Jessica had put her knife on the dashboard and sat huddled on the passenger seat.

At every intersection, he expected to see police cars suddenly appear and set off in pursuit of them, but nothing happened, they sped away and got lost in housing projects and deserted streets, and despite the mildness of the summer night nobody was hanging about outside the apartment blocks or the houses and soon they were able to get their bearings and get back on the beltway to return home. On the highway, the darkness seemed to close behind them, wiping out all trace of them. Jessica hadn't moved since they had set off. She might have been asleep. Turning onto the country road, speeding between the dark masses of trees, he felt alone again, and imagined that he was drifting amid empty shadows without dimension. He tried to reconstruct that evening's events and could only recall a few fleeting images, like those of a dream that escapes us, torn by cries.

The house loomed up in the headlights, and the surprise drew him out of the dreamlike state he'd been in during the ride, and it was as if a space-time bubble had conjured him away and propelled him here. Instinctively, he checked that Jessica was definitely there next to him, and when he saw her unfold her legs and stretch her arms, then get out of the car without a word, he knew he was back to reality with a vengeance, and in getting up in his turn, he felt the jagged steel edge of the gun against the small of his back. He didn't even remember taking it and he removed it from his belt and looked at it in the strange clarity of this moonless night, beneath the swarming stars. The steel gave off no gleam. The weapon seemed to absorb all light into its unfathomable blackness.

He looked up, suddenly dizzy. Some distance away, Jessica was watching him, a pale figure. She shrugged, then walked nonchalantly toward the door. The dog appeared at the corner of the house, over toward the barn, growling. "Shut up," she said to it in a husky voice before pulling back the bolt and disappearing into the entrance hall. The dog lay down, its head on its paws, its ears up. Franck waved the gun at it. And he had the impression that the animal sank a little into itself, as if fearful.

All was silent, apart from the whispering of the breeze. An owl sang, very close by, on the edge of the forest. When he and Fabien were kids, they had tried to call to those they heard, raising their hands to their mouths like conches and blowing into them, and they waited a long time for them to respond. Another bird replied, farther away. Franck took a deep breath of the gentle air of this perfect moment, then walked to the trailer, crushed with fatigue. He passed close to the dog, which didn't move.

9

Franck smelled the tobacco before he saw the two women. They fell silent when he approached. They were sitting on garden chairs in the shade of the big oak behind the house, drinking coffee and smoking. Jessica threw him an indifferent glance, then stretched her legs in front of her. Her mother was plucking her eyebrows. Franck caught her aggressive look in the little mirror she was holding up close to her face. Passing behind Jessica, he lightly touched the back of her neck with the tip of his index finger, but she brushed it away with the back of her hand as if it were a troublesome insect.

"At least it didn't stop you sleeping."

"Actually, it did. That's why I tried to catch up this morning. I thought you were going to bring me coffee and croissants."

"There's some coffee left in the kitchen. It's probably not very hot."

"I hear you measured up last night," the old woman said.

She had turned to him and was looking at him frankly, with a sudden benevolence he had never seen in her before.

"Let's just say we didn't come out of it too badly, given the shit we were in. We were royally fucked. The guy was nearby, he got there almost immediately, we barely had time to get out on the street. Plus, he had a gun."

They all three jumped at the cries coming from the forest. Rachel. She burst from the shade of the trees at a run, screaming. Jessica rushed to her. The old lady had sat up on her chair, craning her neck to see better, then leaned down to take a cigarette from the pack she'd put down at her feet. Franck stepped onto the path that led across the meadow and caught up with Jessica, who was crouching with Rachel in her arms.

"A snake!" the girl was crying. "A big one, over there. It came after me."

"No, no. It's all over. It didn't bite you, did it?"

Rachel shook her head. Her mother examined her ankles, her arms.

"Why did you go into the woods on your own?" Franck asked. "Aren't you scared, all on your own in there?"

Rachel turned to look at the forest and for a few seconds seemed to peer into the dark tangle as if some monster might emerge from it. "No," she said. "I'm not scared, but . . ."

Jessica straightened up and took her by the hand. "Come with me. You're burning hot. I'm going to cool you down and give you something to drink. Come on, sweetheart."

Franck watched them walk away, Rachel frail and unsteady, twisting her feet because of her badly-fitting espadrilles, then he turned back to the forest and caught himself also peering at the dark rim into which the path plunged, trying to see what it was that Rachel had been afraid of seeing.

"What now?"

The old woman was staring at him, her face twisted, one eye closed because of the smoke from her cigarette.

"What do you mean, what now?"

"War has been declared, hasn't it? What do you suggest we do now?"

"You talked to Jessica, didn't you? I thought you people were the ones who make the decisions. Since when have you cared about my opinion? I still can't understand why you haven't kicked me out."

She nodded her head as he spoke, without taking her eyes off him, as if weighing every word he uttered. "Because you're Fabien's brother and he's a good man, and we owe him that. We made him a promise before he left. Do you like that for an answer?"

The woman had poured herself more coffee. It must be cold. She drank it in one go.

"And I don't see anyone else around here who could find the guys who raped my daughter and make them pay."

For a moment, they had been hearing dull metallic blows coming from the old man's workshop.

"What about him, can't he do anything? He knows people, he could sort it out in a few days, don't you think?"

The old woman lit a cigarette and stood up and came toward him, chin thrust forward, heavy breasts bouncing beneath her sleeveless blouse. "You're scared, is that it?"

She blew smoke in the air through her twisted mouth, lifting a lock of red hair. A smell that was a mixture of tobacco and lily of the valley wafted over to Franck. He stared at that glum expression, that mask of bitterness, the slit of the mouth, the uneven teeth that overlapped like the posts of a fence after a storm. Her creased eyes scrutinized him, perhaps looking for one more reason to despise him.

"Yes, that's right. I'm scared. You really nailed it."

He left her there and went back inside the house. He heard her muttering and clearing her throat, expelling and spitting the resentment and stupidity that seemed to control every beat of her heart and keep her on her feet.

Jessica came out of the bathroom where she had been cooling Rachel down and consoling her. Rachel was now eating chocolate ice cream from a little tub. Her eyes were still shiny with tears as she looked in Franck's direction, but she gave a slight smile when she saw it was him, and it struck him that it was the first time he had seen her smile.

"We're going shopping," Jessica said. "Want to come with us?"

The car drove occasionally through patches of shade where the forest still breathed a little coolness in through the open windows. Rachel was sitting quietly in the back seat, on her lap a little red bag from which hung a tiny blue rabbit she was holding between her fingers. She, too, had put on big sunglasses with red frames, and her tanned face, her black hair gathered on her head in a hasty bun from which wisps of hair straggled, made her look like a miniature film star. At an intersection, a police car was parked on the shoulder and two cops in dark glasses, standing on the median strip, watched them as they passed and continued to watch them for a while as they sped away down that interminable straight line. Franck's heart had started pounding and he'd felt the hairs on the top of his head stand on end.

Jessica put a hand on his thigh. "It's all right. They're often there doing nothing. From time to time, they watch the cars through their binoculars."

In the distance, light shimmered on the asphalt. When they got out of the car in the parking lot, the heat was there, heavy and compact, laid over all things as if the night hadn't dispelled it. Rachel wanted to sit on the shopping cart but her mother told her she was too big for that, which angered her a little, and she dragged a few feet behind them as if she was strolling alone through the store. The air conditioning must have been turned up to maximum and the customers pushed their heaped carts in front of them with a calm slowness, perhaps to take advantage of this temporary interruption in the heat for a while longer. Jessica walked along the aisles and threw boxes and cans into her cart almost without looking at them or slowing down. Every now and again, she would compare two prices, shrug, and resume her progress along the endless aisles where kids moaned or cried or stamped their feet in front of the product of their choice while their mothers turned their backs or pretended not to hear and made to walk away in the hope they would follow.

Rachel would occasionally bring back a pack of cereal or a bag of candies and submit them to Jessica's reluctant approval then carefully place them in the cart. In front of the freezer cabinets, Franck felt a great shiver run down his back and saw the same gooseflesh on Jessica's bare arms. As so often, she was wearing almost nothing: the same old shorts cut from a pair of jeans, a light white cotton blouse through which her black bra was visible, a pair of thongs, fuchsia-colored toenail polish. She filled an insulated bag with frozen ready-meals then turned to him.

"I swear to you I would have cut that bitch's throat last night. It's a good thing you were there."

An old woman, who was hesitating by the pizzas on the other side of the thick glass door she had just opened, turned and stared at them. Franck met her gaze and smiled at her and she limped away on her swollen legs. Rachel got down a box of ice cream bars then left again. Franck told her not to get lost but she pretended she hadn't heard and disappeared behind a pyramid of packs of coffee in front of which an employee was attracting the customers, promising a trip to Peru to those who won the prize draw.

"Of course you wouldn't have cut her throat. You don't just kill people like that."

"Well, if you say so . . . In the meantime, we need meat."

There was almost nobody at the fresh meat counter, only a tall blonde who had kept her sunglasses on. Tanned skin, lips visibly botoxed, giving her mouth a permanent pout, fingers covered in rings. She was having some entrecôte steak sliced, checking the thickness of the slices to a fraction of an inch, and the butcher, a pudgy man in his fifties, was scrupulously following her instructions. When Jessica approached, he started to ogle her, his eyes glued to the top of her thighs and the triangle tightly held in by the fabric of her shorts. Franck saw the moment when he was about to leave the tip of his finger in the middle of the blonde's entrecôte, but the woman leaned a little farther in toward him, her elbows on the glass partition, and pointed an imperious finger at him, and he went back to cutting the meat with the delicacy of a surgeon.

The blonde picked up her package and walked haughtily away without a word, on high heels as sharp as ice picks.

"And for madame?"

The butcher had turned to Jessica, letting his gaze travel all over her body as if she were naked in front of him. She bent forward to touch her knee, perhaps to scratch it, and gave him her order in that position, and the man's eyes started rolling over the curve of her breasts visible in the neckline of her blouse. He grabbed the quarter of meat from which he was going to cut slices of sirloin and stroked the yellow fat with the flat of his hand, digging his thumb into the soft, dead flesh. His nails were incrusted with blood and his knuckles turned white with the effort he was making as he pressed on the blade of the knife. He wiped his hands on his apron and took a sheet of paper to wrap the slices he had cut.

"Brilliant, fantastic," Jessica kept saying in a throaty voice during the weighing.

"Anything else?"

She was now glued to the display window, rising on tiptoe. Franck half expected her to go behind the counter and roll around on the floor with the guy in the middle of the cold meats. He thought he detected a sickly-sweet smell of blood in the air, and he moved away a little, vaguely nauseated. He looked at the almost empty aisles and in the distance saw a little boy holding his mother by the hand and he started searching for Rachel along the rows of aisles but couldn't see her anywhere, so he went back to Jessica and waited for her to finish her act in front of the butcher, then when she turned to him, beaming, he found it hard to tell her straight out that he couldn't find her daughter.

"That bozo took ten euros off the price. His tongue was hanging out so much, he could have licked his own dick."

She took the cart from him, pushed it a short distance, then stopped dead.

"Where's Rachel?"

"No idea. She must be hanging around the candies or toys."

"Fuck."

She threw her bag down in the cart and set off at a run, calling Rachel's name. Franck followed her with the cart, telling her, wait, don't yell like that, she isn't far, but he was starting to have a nasty sense of apprehension. He remembered the boy they had terrorized the day before, threatened, tied up. He ran toward the exit, past the rows of checkouts, bumping into two women emptying their shopping items onto the conveyor belt, and he ignored their protests and emerged onto the parking lot, convinced that he would see a couple of guys bundling Rachel into the trunk of a car, but the glare of the sun on the roofs of the cars was blinding and he could see nothing but dark figures shimmering in the light, so he went back inside the store where the only thing that could be heard were the cries of Jessica calling her daughter. People stopped as this crazy woman passed, shoving the carts she encountered and sending them crashing into the rows of shelves, leaving in her wake a trail of packages collapsing onto the floor. Franck caught up with her and grabbed her by the shoulders to make her calm down and listen to him, but she pushed him away and swept a whole row of cans on her right, which crashed to the ground with a dull rattle. She started running again and at that moment Franck cried out to her, over here, come over here instead of yelling, look! Rachel was sitting in a corner of the bookstore aisle, absorbed in a book. She lifted her nose from the pages, saw them rushing over to her, then resumed her reading as if nothing had happened, engrossed, heedless of everything.

Jessica grabbed her arm and pulled her to her feet and threw the book away, then slapped her so hard that Rachel fell to the floor. She grabbed hold of the top of her dress and pulled her back up and hit her again, on the back, on the face, letting out a kind of angry groan with every blow she landed. Rachel let herself be beaten without reacting, as inert as a rag doll.

Franck said to Jessica, stop, shit, you're completely crazy, but she didn't listen to him, so he seized her around the waist and threw her to the floor and interposed himself between her and Rachel, fists clenched, I swear to you that if you dare do anything else to her I'll beat you to a pulp. Jessica had stopped moving and lay curled up in a ball, shaken with sobs. Franck helped Rachel to her feet and took her in his arms. She wasn't crying, wasn't complaining. Her eyes were wide with terror and her face was pale and shiny with sweat.

"Come on, Rachel."

He took her by the hand and they left the store while people stared at them and whispered comments that buzzed in his ears as they passed. Outside, a short distance away, there was a man selling ice cream and Franck asked Rachel if she wanted one. She said yes, head bowed, clutching her little bag to her and sniffing and wiping her nose with the back of her hand. Franck looked in his pockets to see if he had a handkerchief but couldn't find one. Rachel pointed to what she wanted in the brightly colored tubs—strawberry and pineapple—while Franck chose chocolate. They sat down on a concrete bench that was still in the shade. The sun fell on their feet and Rachel moved her toes in her sandals and her pink toenail polish shone slightly.

They sat there for a while without saying anything, the sun gnawing at their legs as it rose toward its zenith. A little dog dragging a leather leash attached to its collar came and sniffed at Rachel's ankles, and when she held out her hand to stroke it, it leaped back in fright, then started barking. Franck stood up and shooed it away with an abrupt gesture of his arm.

"Come here!" a shrill voice cried.

It was a woman with red hair, rather like the old woman's, pushing a cart filled to the brim.

"It's all right, he doesn't bite."

"But I do," Franck replied with a big smile on his face.

The woman recovered her dog then walked away along a path of the parking lot, bending down to talk to the animal, perhaps telling it to be more careful, and the dog raised its head toward her and trotted on its short legs that seemed to sink and disappear completely into the burning asphalt.

Jessica passed them with her cart. A guy in his shirtsleeves, but with a tie, presumably the manager of the store, was closely behind her, perhaps seeing her out.

"Shall we go?"

She had only slightly slowed down and they stood up to follow her. She hesitated for a moment, long enough to spot her car, then walked more quickly, the big steel cart rattling across the blacktop. She opened the overheated trunk and threw in the contents of the cart in no particular order.

Franck put Rachel in the back seat, leaving the doors wide open, then went to help Jessica but she had almost finished. She didn't look at him once, pretending to be engrossed in her task. Feeling his eyes on her, she straightened up, panting.

"Don't say a word. Keep your mouth shut. Now's not the time."

The ride back took place in silence. Rachel fell asleep as soon as they set off, curled up on the seat. On the path leading to the house, they passed the old man just leaving in his Mercedes. He waved to them then disappeared along the road.

The old woman was waiting for them in front of the house, baskets and bags around her, and as soon as they stopped she rushed to empty the trunk of the car, moaning because her daughter, as usual, had put things in just any old how. Jessica took Rachel out of the car and carried her to the house, distributing kisses in her hair, and Rachel clung to her, still stretching in her sleep. Franck went up to the old woman, who was muttering away, bent over the trunk.

"And where's your husband going like that, in this heat? Couldn't it have waited?"

The old woman poked about in the bags a few seconds before answering him. "He has to see Serge, if you really want to know. And Serge doesn't like to be kept waiting."

He let them go back inside the house. The crazy whore and

her martyred child and the withered old bitch. He suddenly realized that he had nothing more to do here. He would leave tonight. He'd made up his mind. He would stay in a cheap little hotel not far from Bordeaux and get by. He would explain to Fabien that the situation here was no longer tenable, that this house of crazy people was turning dangerous. A nest of rattle-snakes. When he got back, they would figure out what to do about this drug business. This toxic family wasn't theirs. Let the Serb and his team do whatever they wanted, cut them to pieces, burn their house down, he didn't care. It really wasn't his concern anymore. He was sorry about Rachel, but with a little luck they wouldn't do anything to her. She would just be a witness to the horror. It was quite possible she'd seen things as bad, to be so sad and quiet, as if she couldn't find the words to tell her story, and was scared to do so anyway. With her whore of a mother and her alcoholic grandfather who'd probably let his oil-stained hands wander occasionally, it was likely she'd al-ready experienced too much for her age. In the meager shade the front of the house provided against the noon sun, he started imagining sordid scenarios, terrible explanations for Rachel's silence. He imagined her gritting her teeth, eyes filled with tears, beneath her mother's blows or the old man's hateful ca-resses. After a while, he told himself that was enough of twisted ideas and disgusting thoughts, the old man couldn't be such a bastard as to dare do that to the girl. He'd seen pedophiles in prison. Their perversion was as plain as the noses on their faces. Whenever he and other convicts passed one, there was always somebody who said, look at that guy, look at his face, you can see it. Whereas the old man . . .

He remembered those faces and nothing was clear to him anymore. The masks everyone wore in prison, thanks to its rumors and its nursed hatreds and the wretched comfort that came from having found someone lower or more disgusting on the scale of social disgrace than you were—those masks were falling. The more he thought about it, the more Franck had the impression that he was living through the day after a carnival. Those guys didn't have all their miseries and their misdeeds written on their foreheads. In prison, you never look like what you really are. Revealing yourself is like stripping naked, it's getting yourself screwed, one way or another.

Appearances can be deceptive.

The sun finally pinned him to the wall, so he moved and dismissed all these thoughts with the back of his hand. They were too big for him to deal with. Since he wasn't really hungry, he gave up the idea of joining the others in the kitchen. He went to his trailer, found a pack of cookies, ate three or four, and drank some water. He grabbed his bag from a chest and opened it, determined to fill it soon with his meager possessions. Without this heat, he would have done it right away and left without even going to warn them. He told himself that at the point he'd reached, two or three more hours wouldn't make much difference to the situation.

He lay down on his bed, and thought suddenly about Lucas and Nora. He remembered Lucas's bloodstained face, the punches and blows he had received when the other two had jumped him.

Nora answered immediately.

"*How's it going?* You ask how it's going, you son of a bitch? Badly, that's how it's going. Right now, Lucas is in the hospital, and I'm outside there with my baby having a smoke while he has a scan. Because the fractured jaw is nothing. They're talking about cranial trauma, you get the picture? So whatever lousy plans you and that bitch have in mind, keep them to yourselves. When he got back last night, I thought he was going to die! He practically didn't sleep, and this morning I didn't recognize him, can you imagine? He looks as if he was beaten up for hours. And yet he knows how to take the blows, I've seen him after fights he lost. But this was a bloodbath."

"I didn't think it would turn out like that. We were just supposed to intimidate this guy, and then—"

"That's enough, Franck. I don't want to hear anymore. I'm going to hang up. Just forget about us, okay? Or else I'm going to the cops. When you were inside at least we had some peace, without you or your brother coming around and getting Lucas involved in something every few days."

She hung up and Franck looked at the screen of his phone as if he could see Nora's angry face on it. He threw the device away and lay down, shivering. His whole body was aching, as if he had the flu. He remembered what had happened the night before, Lucas's screams, the guy bending over him, raining blows on him, Jessica's uncontrollable rage, the blade of the knife on the woman's throat, already drawing blood, and the other guy waving his gun in the middle of the street and those few fractions of an inch by which everything had hung in the balance, between the finger on the trigger and the bullet leaving the gun, between the wound to the skin and the perforation of an artery.

His heart was beating faster, thinking of what might have happened, had nearly happened. Those few seconds of hesitation, those few fractions of an inch where there was a margin of error. He shivered again. Outside, everything was still and silent. He listened and couldn't make out so much as a quiver in the air, the trembling of a leaf. He thought about what had happened afterwards. He could already see himself turning onto the road without looking back and accelerating, as relieved as when you free yourself from a bramble bush, in spite of the scratches and the splinters that will have to be removed later.

Then he wondered where he would sleep tonight. He thought about the few people whose doors he could have knocked on, but nearly five years later, not having heard from any of them, what was the point? Would they even recognize him? Nora and Lucas would have been the only ones . . . The road lay in front of him, free but winding, and he didn't know where it would lead him. Get out of here, a voice throbbing inside him kept repeating, almost making him tremble.

Above him, the ceiling was haloed in damp, drawing a pale archipelago in an ocean of mud. He tried to see familiar shapes in it but could make out nothing and closed his eyes. He let childhood memories come back to him. Moments he'd never thought about again, things he hadn't expected to find. All those faces. Lucie, Amel, Mohamed, Quentin . . . His best friends at school. Solid, intimate, fraternal. Amel's smile. The most beautiful girl he'd ever known, without any doubt. Infatuated with another boy, older, stronger, funnier. The painful desire to know what had become of her brought a lump to his throat. He would have loved to hug her like they did all the time in the old days, miming lovers' embraces then breaking away from each other abruptly, almost embarrassed at the desire rising inside them, as if they were siblings and were recoiling from the taboo of incest. If he saw Amel now, he'd definitely sweep away those rules, he'd be able to tell her . . . But it was too late now, of course. Their lives had gone in different directions.

For a while, he mulled over these thoughts, their false promises, and their guaranteed disappointments. He was ten, fifteen years older, he couldn't turn back the clock, his attempts to go back in time and relive it all, knowing what he knew now, as he'd seen people do in movies, merely brought him back to the present. He caught himself whispering the names of all those he missed. When he named his mother, her figure took shape on the overcrowded screen of his memory, but her face remained blurred and all he could make out was the sad smile she had so often, toward the end.

He stood up, his heart heavy, as alone as he'd ever been, and he resented this little boy's sorrow, this lost child's helplessness, and he hated the narrow space of the trailer, wondering how he could have felt free in it during his first days here, how his very solitude could have seemed to him an ideal expanse, without walls or borders.

Then he heard voices echoing on the other side of the house, toward the forest, and water moving in the swimming pool, and he realized it was after five, so he went out, forcing himself to take deep breaths in order to get rid of the lump in his throat.

The sun was still high and all he saw of them at first was their heads sticking out of the pool, Jessica signaling to him to come and join them, and Rachel, turned toward the forest, diving in, so that all you saw of her then were her feet.

"Come and have a swim," Jessica said. "It'll do you a lot of good!"

The dog was sitting between him and them, panting, its tongue drooping with thirst. Its lusterless black eyes never left Franck, following him as he moved over to a deckchair. The old woman's cigarettes lay on the ground. He took one and lit it then collapsed into the deckchair and looked up at the deep blue sky, a sky so pure that he wouldn't have been surprised to see a few stars come out.

"You're making a big mistake."

He felt drops of water falling on his legs and opened his eyes. Jessica was standing over him, barely covered by a scanty bikini, legs apart, shaking her wet hair with one hand. Then she came closer and sat down astride him, then lay down, rubbing herself against him, and he opened his arms without daring to touch her, his cigarette at the end of his fingers, seized at first by that coolness then overwhelmed with embarrassment because he could see Rachel swimming in circles in the pool, taking a deep breath with each stroke, her eyes closed.

"Stop it, the kid's there."

She kept right on, moving her pelvis back and forth two or three times, then leaped to her feet.

"It doesn't affect you anyway, so what are you scared of? And she doesn't care, look at her!"

For another moment or two, she stayed close to him, slowly swaying her hips, then sighed and went back inside the house. Franck stubbed out his wet cigarette and took another from the pack he'd put down next to him. He smoked it looking up at the sky, where clouds with white caps were now advancing like a huge flock of sheep. He heard the voices of the two women in the house through the open windows, one husky and harsh, the other deep, nervous, halting. He tried to hear what they might be talking about but all that reached him was the grating of the one, the prattle of the other. Tonight he wouldn't have to hear them any-more. He'd be far away. Miles away. He wouldn't have to lower his eyes beneath the old woman's hostile gaze anymore, or to guess if Jessica was in a mood to let him fuck her or stick a fork in his belly. He let himself slip into the sweetness of that deci-sion, the first real decision he had made since he'd left prison.

The sky was becoming overcast but the heat didn't let up. In the distance, in the forest, a bird called, a single bird, and there was no response. Even Rachel, in the pool, seemed to respect the silence of nature. Franck wondered what she was doing, resting perhaps in her red rubber ring, as she often did, content to float with her eyes closed, so he sat up but couldn't see anything, not even the top of her head and her black hair, and when he stood up all he could make out was the blinding glare on the still surface of the water and the empty ring. He ran to the wooden rim and bent over it and moved the water, crying out as if he could wake the girl asleep at the bottom, then jumped in and seized the inert body. It weighed nothing but started to struggle and pant as soon as they were both out in the air. For a few seconds he kept Rachel out of the water at arm's length, as she writhed and arched her back and tried to catch her breath, then he clasped her to him and hoisted himself onto the ladder then down onto the concrete paving and laid her on an air mattress. She sat up, coughing and spitting, and he grabbed the towel and wrapped it around her shoulders. He tried to take her hand but she pulled it away. He told her reas-suring things in a low voice, but she seemed not to hear, her big wide-open eyes staring into space.

The dog had come closer and was watching all this with its nose to the ground as if trying to analyze the scene.

"What's the matter?"

Jessica came running. She kneeled next to her daughter and took her face in her hands and turned it toward her and kissed her on the eyes and the mouth, what's the matter, sweetheart?

"I found her motionless at the bottom, her eyes closed. Shit, I was scared."

"She's always doing that. It scares me, too, sometimes. Do you hear that, Rachel? You mustn't do that again, do you understand? You could drown, you could die, do you understand? So stop scaring us like that, do you hear me?"

Rachel nodded, eyes lowered, chest lifted occasionally by a deep intake of breath or perhaps a sob.

Jessica stood up. She looked at Rachel and shook her head irritably, her cheeks swollen in a sigh of weariness. "There are times when I really don't know what's going on in that little head. She's really weird."

"She's not the only one."

"Why do you say that? Do you mean me?"

Franck shrugged. "No, just saying . . ."

In front of the house, a car door slammed. The old man exchanged a few words with his wife, then came toward them, a beer in his hand. "What's wrong with her?" he asked, indicating Rachel with his chin.

"She almost drowned," Franck replied. "She wasn't moving at the bottom of the pool."

"Is that true?"

Rachel hadn't moved, still sitting with her arms around her knees, looking fixedly in front of her. She responded to her grandfather with a slight shrug of the shoulders.

"But you can swim, can't you?" The old man turned to Franck. "Playing the fool under the water like she does all the time, it's not surprising she sometimes scares herself. Eh, Rachel, what is it we're always telling you?"

"It's like talking to a stone," Jessica said. "Look at her. She hasn't said a word since she came out of the water."

Franck was sitting next to Rachel. He pushed her hair

behind her back to see her face. She was very pale but had stopped crying and was moving a little black pebble about between her feet.

"Are you feeling better?"

She nodded, then whispered, "I was asleep."

"What do you mean, you were asleep?"

Above them, the old man and his daughter were talking about the heat, the long ride from Bordeaux, the car's air conditioning, which wasn't working properly and needed repairing.

"In the water. It's like I was asleep. And then I got scared."

She wasn't looking at him, now busy rolling the pebble in the palms of her hands.

"Scared of what?"

Rachel shook her head then pulled it down between her shoulders, as if seized with a great shiver. Franck stroked her cheek with his fingertip and she closed her eyes.

"Wouldn't you like to play a game?"

She threw off the towel that had been placed on her back, then stood up and ran to the house.

"Where's she going like that?" Jessica asked.

"She's going to look for a game. It'll take her mind off things."

"I said she was weird. Her stupid father was the same. Moody. You never knew what he was thinking."

They played for nearly an hour on a console on which you had to drive a little car very fast and get it to negotiate hairpin bends or leap across collapsed bridges. Rachel handled it like an expert, then handed the controls over to Franck and watched him crash into the obstacles. She sometimes made a move as if about to come to his aid, but then merely sighed in frustration. Two or three times, she giggled at his clumsiness and he assured her that he had been better than that before, that he used to play all the time with his buddies, and Rachel pretended to agree, clearing her throat and taking the console from his hands.

Franck admitted his defeat, and Rachel didn't insist on

inflicting him with yet another loss. From her little bag, she took a fuchsia pink phone and switched it on. The screen showed the photograph of a kitten with ruffled fur and a surprised look on its face. Rachel started scrolling through her messages, eyes glued to the device.

"Do you use that often? Do you get messages?"

"Mom gave it to me but she doesn't like me to use it too much."

"Has anyone written to you?"

"My friends from school. Sometimes I get sent things."

She laughed as she read a couple of lines that Franck couldn't make out.

"Do you want my number?"

She looked at him in surprise. "To do what?"

"To call me if you need to. And then just to have it."

She handled the phone with the same dexterity as when she'd been playing. "Go on."

He dictated the ten figures to her, and she typed them in without making any mistakes, then put in FRENCK, very fast.

"With an *a*."

She sighed and corrected it.

"That way, you can call me whenever you like, if you're scared of a snake or whatever, and I'll be there."

She nodded, frowning, as if thinking this over.

"And what's your number?"

She recited it with her eyes closed, hesitantly, and he had to get her to repeat it. As she got up and went back inside, he repeated the number to himself, inventing a mnemonic to avoid forgetting it. And this tenuous link suddenly reassured him. It seemed to him that in this way he wasn't abandoning her to the pack.

*

In all this time, Jessica and her parents didn't put in an appearance, Franck assumed they were talking about the meeting with the Gypsy, and he felt pleased to be leaving them behind, leaving them to their life of dirty tricks and crummy deals. Fabien would be back soon. Presumably informed that things were starting to go wrong here, including for his own brother, he'd be back to restore a little bit of order by bringing them back their money. That would quiet them all down. The Serb and his dogs, Jessica and her parents.

He had confidence. He would leave tomorrow morning. He had to tell Rachel that he would soon be back to get her. While watching her press the buttons on her console, he searched for the words he would have to use to tell her these complicated, improbable things. Making a promise he might not be able to keep, but he had to do it before leaving her alone with them.

During the meal, among the butterflies and mosquitoes attracted by the light, they more or less ignored him, exchanging news about people he didn't know, and he made no attempt to involve himself in the conversation. The old man didn't talk much, he seemed anxious, and was drinking a lot, keeping the bottle of white wine in front of him without offering it to anyone, before going to fetch three beers which he arranged around his plate. The old woman was excited, pushing her shrill voice to the point of extinction, bent double by coughing fits, and occasionally lighting a cigarette before she'd even emptied her plate. Every now and again, Franck met Jessica's gaze, but she would turn away immediately and pretend to take an interest in what Rachel was eating. Just before ten, as the sky in the south was lit up with summer lightning, he went to bed and they barely replied to his goodnight.

From the trailer, he heard them talking in low voices for a long time and he wondered what crummy scheme they were dreaming up this time. He put his things away in his bag, the few books, already read, whose covers and titles no longer meant anything to him.

Later, he heard a car door slam and Jessica's car drive off.

It might be a storm approaching. A distant, muted rumble. The image of Rachel alone in the middle of the dried-up meadow faded along with his dream as he opened his eyes on the blinding light bulb above him.

His cell phone was vibrating under his pillow. FABIEN.

"Did I wake you?"

"Fabien?"

Behind the rough, muted voice, there was music. Maybe from a radio. How was it possible, even after five years, that he didn't recognize his brother's voice? There was breathing at the other end, halting, as if impatient.

"Fabien? Is that you?"

A sharp little laugh. The pain wasn't immediate, like with those very thin needles that gradually penetrate until the pain strikes.

"No, it isn't Fabien. He can't talk to you."

"Who is this? Pass me Fabien."

"Are you stupid or what? I told you he can't talk to you. And you know why? Because we killed the son of a bitch."

Franck looked around him. The cramped space of the trailer. The wall cupboards above the bench seats, the little stainless-steel sink. His closed bag ready for departure. Through the window, the darkness of night. He made sure that all of this still existed and wondered at what moment this narrow universe was going to be wiped out. He had to say something, he needed to hear the sound of his own voice to ward off the emptiness. He shook his head and rubbed his hair as if to rid himself of a spider's web.

"Oh, yes? How do I know you're telling the truth?"

On the other side of the world, the man sighed. "Wait, let me have a look."

Suddenly, the music stopped. All Franck could hear now was the man's breathing and a kind of electronic hum on the line.

"Okay. Are you still there?"

He spoke with a maddening calm. As if he were checking an address book or an order form.

"Right, what I've got here is a guy who's six feet tall, according to his identity card, which was issued by the Prefecture of the Gironde on March 12, 2002. His address is 28 Rue des Bouvreuils in Talence. He has brown hair, almost shaved, and a tattoo on his . . . left shoulder, that's right, a tattoo of a tiger showing its teeth, wow, it's really scary! What else can I tell you? Let's see . . . Ah yes, there's this ring. It's silver, with something or other engraved on it, and inside there's the words *NEVER DEFEATED*. Going to have to change that, I guess. It won't be cheap, but it's worth it, it's a good ring. I'm not going to ask you to come and identify the body, we aren't in a movie, but anyway, that should be enough. Time of death five or six hours ago, no more than that. Multiple cuts on the chest, caused by a sharp weapon, most likely a kitchen knife. Quite a lot of blood all around. The face bears marks of blows, likely cranial trauma. The victim was probably beaten before being killed. Is that enough for you? You see, TV is useful! Those American shows with their experts and all that shit. That way, we can use the right words when we break the bad news to the nearest and dearest. Don't you think?"

Franck wiped the tears from his cheeks with the back of his hand. He listened with his eyes closed to that voice stabbing him with every word and he tried to imagine his brother's dead body as the man described the details, but he could only see Fabien alive the day he'd come back from the tattoo parlor, the tiger's head coming alive with each movement, its mouth seeming to open a little more with the contractions of the muscles, and he saw again the little house at 28 Rue des Bouvreuils where they had grown up, and he remembered that he had envied Fabien that ring he'd bought when he was fifteen from a gypsy woman they said was a bit of a sorceress or witch, Carmen, the grandmother of his best buddy Esteban, a ring adorned with strange arabesques, maybe runes, that were supposed to protect him from the *mala suerte*. They had thought of the *Lord of the Rings* and had joked about that, so to make sure of total protection Fabien had had those words engraved inside it before putting it on his finger and never again taking it off because one day it had become impossible—you would have had to cut off the ring or the finger.

"You're dead," Franck breathed.

"No, no, you don't understand, it's your scumbag of a brother who's dead. Right here, on the ground. Listen, I'm slapping him a few times to wake him but the bastard has stopped moving."

Franck heard the blows given with the flat of the hand, ringing out loud and clear.

"Stop!"

His cry was muffled by the plastic partition walls. There was nobody to hear him apart from this guy. He walked up and down the warped linoleum. Two steps, then two more. Caged animals behave like that, without even dreaming of throwing themselves against the bars. Born in a trap. Captured before birth.

"Why did you do it?"

"You ask why? Don't you have the tiniest idea? Don't you remember what happened last night? You gave my friends a rough time. A very rough time. You know what I'm talking about, don't you? Your whore tried to cut the woman's throat, and your pal beat up a guy who's like a brother to me, and now they're in custody because thanks to you the cops came and stuck their noses into their business. We think that's already quite a big deal, but on top of that your brother still hadn't come back, we didn't know what to think anymore, he was screwing us every which way. So there you are. Tell your host family we'll be coming over there to get compensation for the money they owe us, and that we'll take it in kind, to even things up. There are three women there, aren't there?"

"No, there are two."

"Oh? Didn't that bitch have a daughter? You know the

bitch I mean, the one you're fucking, what's her name? Jessica? So make sure you tell those degenerates that—"

Franck threw the phone down on the bench seat and sat down and cried. There was a hollow inside him that collapsed and opened up a chasm echoing with screams. He wept, he bawled, he let the tears and the mucus run, he sat back on the seat with his hands on his thighs and gave himself up to the grief that was drowning him. Next to him, the man's imperturbable voice hissed through the phone.

He picked it up. He was shaking so much, it was hard to hold it against his ear. That low voice was still there, droning, painful. He heard the click of a cigarette lighter, and thought he caught the crackle of the tobacco catching fire, the breath of smoke being exhaled.

"Is that you whining like that? Did you whine like that in prison, in the shower?"

Franck stood up and took a few steps. He coughed and ran some water onto his hands and wet his face. He was starting again to feel something other than that empty sensation inside him. "I don't understand . . ."

The man laughed. "No, that's for sure, you don't understand. You should never have gotten yourself mixed up in this shit. There's too much money at stake, and nobody's going to just sit on it. One way or another, the bill has to be paid. Anyway, I think we've said everything there is to say. I'm not going to have the body sent home, that'll just be more expense."

The man hung up and all that remained was the silence. Franck dialed Fabien's number but the ringing echoed in emptiness before a message said something in Spanish that he didn't understand. Franck watched his phone go off then sat down on the bench seat and leaned on the collapsible table, wondering if he would ever have the strength to get up again. The tears kept flowing, and he didn't do anything to wipe them away. He had the impression he was sitting at the edge of a cliff with his feet in the void, waiting to jump and let the waves carry his body far out to sea.

He thought about his father. He shuddered at the thought that he would have to tell him about Fabien's death. He pictured himself facing him, searching for the words to tell him.

After a while, the silence and darkness around the trailer became too heavy, too thick, threatening to trap him like one of those insects you see in blocks of amber. He laboriously got to his feet and wiped away whatever was running over his cheeks, mouth, and chin with his T-shirt. When he was sure his legs would carry him, he looked in the little cabinet in the bathroom for the gun he had recovered the previous night. It was warm and heavy and reassuring. He took out the magazine and saw the dull sheen of the cartridges jammed into the steel case like a necklace in a strange casket. He reinserted it in the grip and checked that the security was on properly. The barrel bore the inscription CZ 75, Czech Republic. That reminded him of video games and the references to the arsenal placed at the disposal of the players, those brands, those macho acronyms, those calibers of ammunition and their magical numbering. He slipped the gun into the belt of his jeans and left the trailer.

As soon as he was outside, he was surprised to feel cooler air flutter over his arms and neck, even though it was still warm. The full moon cast its gray and blue light into the darkness. He walked past the dark mass of the house, past the former hayloft where the old man had set up his workshop, its iron door closed at this hour, with a huge lock on it. The meadow was bathed in a whitish light that just about allowed you to put one foot in front of the other but wouldn't let you see where you were going. He took the path leading toward the forest, whose black outlines he could see against the star-filled sky.

Not a sound. Even the trees were silent and still. Franck could still feel those flutterings on his skin, and yet there was no breath of air, either around him or in the nonchalance of the leaves, and as he got close to the woods the thought that it might be the souls of his dear departed crossed his mind, so lightly that it didn't even scare him.

Lowering his head, he went in under the cover of the trees. He didn't think of anything except advancing along the path without twisting his feet in a dip or stumbling over a root. The occasional pale patch of light fell in this darkness, and above his head a bluish vapor hovered in the foliage. In places, though, it was so dark that he had the feeling he might be drawn into a pit of absolute blackness. The path, sometimes of beaten earth, sometimes of heaped sand, was distinct and easy enough to follow. He knew that it led to the pigeon trap and its strange circle, where witches might come to dance on nights like this, when the moon illuminates as much as it conceals.

The construction in the clearing appeared between the trees, looking in the pale light like the bony body of a sleeping monster. But no figure danced there, shaking her hair about, half naked, available and crazy. Franck went closer and found himself in the middle of a network of galleries that were nothing more than the ramshackle fortifications of a drunkard's war against birds. He couldn't see the moon from here, only the luminous vapor and the silver edges of the passing clouds. To his surprise, he found it beautiful, even though it was a night like hundreds of others he had known, which had scared him when he was a kid, when he had loved to stay out late with his pals, protected by that huge mantle under which everything seemed permitted and of which Fabien had taught him a few rituals and secret places. Now, he wasn't sure if he found this moment unreal or perfect. He was the only thing moving, and the silence was total. He had expected to hear noises, rustling, the cry of a night bird, but nothing seemed to be living around him, as if he had unwittingly stepped across a border and found himself alone in a land he didn't dare name. He did an about-turn, checking to see if luminescent eyes weren't spying on him through the window slits of the galleries. Nothing. Just emptiness. Accustomed to the darkness now, he could make out details he hadn't noticed the first time he had come here. He looked for his shadow at his feet but realized that it wasn't there.

"Let's go."

His own voice, with no echo. He wondered if he had really spoken.

This seemed like the right place, here in the middle of this clearly cursed circle. He took out the gun and inserted a cartridge in the chamber. He raised his arm and held the gun close to his face, but didn't know what to do. He knew that because of the recoil it was easy to miss. The barrel jumping, the bullet skidding, taking away half your face and leaving you alive. In movies, he had seen guys put the barrel in their mouths and spatter the wall behind them with their brains. Instantaneously. He placed the block of steel between his teeth and the smell and taste of the metal filled his mouth and the back of his nasal passages, and his teeth chattered against the steel and the bead hurt his palate. He felt his eyes fill with tears. He was holding the grip with his right hand, his index finger on the trigger guard.

That was when he saw it come into the clearing. He saw its coat glistening with flashes of blue, its shoulder muscles rippling. Without a sound, moving fast, its body close to the ground, the dog disappeared into the darkness and vanished like smoke. For a long time, Franck stared at the place where he had seen the animal swallowed up by the night and tried to hear the dull hammer blows of its strides, but there was nothing, not a quiver, not a sound. He thought the animal might retrace its steps, panting, and come toward him with its nose to the ground and that sly air it had, its quivering skin running with a fierce electric charge, ready to leap on him, so he waited for a long moment, hardly daring to breathe, but nothing happened. He realized he was still clutching the gun in his hand. He felt like throwing it into the bracken, but then he ejected the cartridge and slipped it into his pocket and wedged the gun into his belt, against his lower back.

He had to go back to the house. He would have to keep going. How and why, he didn't know. But he knew that Fabien would have slapped him if he'd seen him with the barrel of that gun in his mouth. He would have thrown him to the ground and beaten him black and blue and screamed at him that he had to live, had to keep going, that it was the one obligation to which he had to submit absolutely. When his mother was dying and she had seen the two of them in tears at her bedside, she had made them promise to live in her place, and to take good advantage of it because she would so much have liked to continue in this world. "I won't be able to," Fabien had said. "I won't have the strength." She had grabbed hold of his shirtsleeve with her bony hand and found the strength to pull him to her and given him a fearsome look, filled with anger and sadness, and said, "I forbid you, do you understand? I forbid you to say that. You're going to live and you'll be happy, for me. You'll take all the happiness possible and send it to me in your thoughts, all right? So stop saying that. I want you to promise. And you too, Fransou. You're both my life. My life will continue with you."

She had fallen back, exhausted and out of breath, and they really had thought she was going to pass away then and there, before their eyes, after telling them that. But since her closed eyelids were still quivering, and her chest still rising and falling under the sheet, they had moved close to her and put their heads on the pillow and promised her and kissed her hollow, burning temples, feeling the distant throbbing of her blood in them.

Franck ran his hands through his hair, shook his head as if to release himself from a fit of dizziness, then set off back along the path. When he came out into the meadow, the sky was starting to lighten in the east. He couldn't see the time on his watch—he didn't think he'd stayed all that long in the woods. Gradually, with every step he took, it seemed to him he was returning to the usual space-time continuum, to a world of hard blows and sorrows.

10

The old man was working on an engine at the workbench, struggling to take off the cylinder head gasket. He grunted, his body bent over his work. When Franck came into the workshop, he broke off for a second, listened, but didn't turn. Then he resumed his efforts, more noisily, more ostentatiously. There was a smell of oil and iron and sweat. The old man was wearing a grimy undershirt and a pair of gray shorts on which the streaks and stains of grease took the place of printed patterns. There were black marks on his arms, his shoulders, and even his neck.

Franck felt a strong desire to smash the old man's skull against the block of steel, then turn his bloodied face around and continue to wipe out his features with a hammer. He felt an almost painful quivering on his skin. Fatigue knotted all his muscles, weighed on his shoulders and the back of his neck, as if he were carrying someone.

"What's the matter?" the old man asked, still without turning.

Franck went and stood beside him at the workbench. He picked up a long screwdriver and started tapping with the wooden handle. "What's that engine for?" he asked.

"The Citroën ID19 behind you. It's for a guy who collects them. He pays well, so I'm refurbishing it for him. They're good, these old engines."

Franck turned. The car, resting on jack stands, was concealed beneath a tarp, its hood wide open.

The old man glanced at the screwdriver that Franck was holding. "Here, will you help me turn it over? I have to drop the oil pan."

The old man turned the bracket of the hoist and they slid the belts under the engine. The chain creaked when they pulled on it. The engine slowly tipped over and the pan, oozing with oil, became accessible.

Franck looked around for a cloth and saw one on the floor, in front of the car. He took a deep breath and managed to blurt it out:

"They killed Fabien."

The old man turned to him. His hands were black. He held them away from him. Franck threw him the cloth, which he caught in midair but did nothing with. He seemed to be thinking about what he had just heard, as if he didn't understand or was weighing up the repercussions. "Shit," he said at last. "How did you find out?"

"They called me last night on his cell phone. They described his body to me. The tattoos, everything. His ring. They told me he owed them money and that they didn't like that raid of ours the other night."

Franck caught his breath. He was trying to hold back the tears and sobs choking him. The old man wiped his hands, looking at him as if overwhelmed.

"They also said they were going to come here and make you pay, one way or another."

The old man shook his head. He threw his cloth down on the workbench then went to a little fridge and opened it and took out two bottles of beer. He held one out to Franck, who refused.

"We have to talk seriously."

He pulled a grease-stained garden chair toward him and collapsed onto it, breathing hard. He opened his bottle and took a long gulp.

"I'm really sad about what they did to your brother. I'm sickened . . . disgusted . . . He was a good guy. Straight. When Jessica brought him here, we wondered what kind of guy he was, because she'd gotten us used to seeing her bring home just about anybody, guys like her, misfits, junkies, alcoholics, that kind of thing . . . Sometimes we even had to go and bring her back half unconscious from hovels where you wouldn't have let a dog sleep . . . But Fabien was quiet. And that quieted her down, although she occasionally had her relapses. You've seen how she is, always changing, one day up there, the next day as far down as you can go. She really gave us a hard time, I can tell you . . .'"

The old man wasn't looking at him anymore. He was peering into his beer bottle as if a fly had fallen into it, moving his feet about uneasily, shifting his ass on the shapeless plastic chair. Franck knew by now that Jessica was crazy, and her past escapades and excesses no longer interested him. He had a strong feeling that the old man was beating about the bush, hesitating to come out with what he had to tell him.

"What did you want to say to me that was so serious?"

The old man raised his eyes toward him and stared at him, twisting his mouth, as if to say: *Well, if you really want to know.* "I went to see Serge yesterday. He knows where to find the Serb."

Franck's heart skipped a beat. He gulped for air like a fish thrown into the sand, mouth torn by a hook.

"I didn't want to tell you, but—"

"Where is he?"

"I asked the Gypsy to find out. He's been hiding himself since your little excursion the other night. The friend of his whose face you smashed in is in custody and they know that faggot is going to spill the beans. But anyway, that bastard the Serb is known as the white wolf. If the cops could get their hands on him . . . It's possible he'll spill the beans, too, and they'll leave him in peace. In fact, he—"

Franck banged on the workbench with a wrench that was lying there. "Where is he?"

The old man shook his head and sighed. "In Cenon," he said as if reluctantly. "He's staying with this guy who minds the drugs for him. A cousin of Serge's knows his son. It's in a little street under the high-rises. We'll take care of it."

"*We*? Who's *we*?"

"I mean Serge. And with Serge, it's like I'm talking about myself. Let him get on with it."

"And how exactly is he going to take care of it?"

"Just let him get on with it, I tell you. Stay out of it."

"They killed Fabien. They had him killed down there in Spain. I won't even get to see his body. I'll never see him again, for fuck's sake. I'm in this shit up to my neck. And I'm going to make them eat that shit, I'm going to drown them in it, do you understand?"

The old man nodded his bony head. He relit his little cigar. "And I say drop it. Serge will make him pay for what he did to your brother, what he did to Jessica. He gave me his word. I know you don't like him. But when he finds out they killed Fabien, he's going to go crazy, because he really liked your brother. When there's a debt of honor, gypsies always pay them, or make sure they're paid. And this isn't about business anymore, it's about honor, it's about friendship."

"Give me the address. I don't give a fuck about this honor crap. I don't need your fucking Gypsy to settle this. As soon as you have a problem, you call him—what's that all about? What's his stake in all this?"

"He doesn't have a stake. It isn't a game, and you don't understand shit. But what the hell? It's up to you."

The old man searched in his pocket. With the tips of his dirty fingers, he took out a piece of paper. Franck tore it from him.

"You're making a mistake."

"I'm out of here anyway. I've seen enough of you and your whore of a daughter and her bitch of a mother."

The old man leaped to his feet, sending his plastic chair flying. He took a hammer from the workbench and waved it over Franck. "I'm going to beat you to a pulp! Is that how you treat us, you son of a bitch? We fed you, we put a roof over your head!"

He was foaming with rage, his twisted mouth giving off a foul stench of beer and tobacco.

Franck grabbed the raised arm and kneed him in the gut, and the old man fell to his knees and let go of the hammer. Franck slapped him and he collapsed noiselessly onto his side, mouth open, gasping for breath.

Franck walked around the outside of the house. He heard the old woman bustling in the kitchen, the TV at full volume, plates and flatware being moved about. He walked past the swimming pool and glanced at the still water, which was barely disturbed by a wasp struggling at its surface.

Farther on, the dry meadow in the white light. Rachel in her red dress, her back to him, wearing a large straw hat he had never seen on her before. She was beating the scorched grass with a stick, making big, broad gestures. She was more or less the way she had been in his dream: alone and small in that blinding, desolate expanse. He wanted to call her, then changed his mind because he wouldn't have known what to say to her. Just as he was about to retrace his steps, she turned, arm in the air, and looked at him solemnly, her brow furrowed in the shade of her hat. Franck waved at her, which could just as well have meant hello as goodbye, but she didn't reply, merely looking at him and blinking as if to see him better. Then she turned her back on him and again began beating the grass, indifferently, in the burning air.

He ran and collected his things from the trailer and threw his bags in the car and got in.

He drove, dazed for a long time by the overpowering light of the meadow, the figure of Rachel sometimes trembling there when he tried to recall her in her red dress. A strong desire to cry out took him by the throat. But the farther he got from the house, the weaker the image grew, and a deeper and larger sadness took hold of him, his heart raced, and the thought that he was going to surprise that guy in his hideout and kill him sometimes made him shudder and his teeth chatter.

He crossed the Garonne without seeing it and drove at more than sixty past a wall of loud, stinking trucks. The river below him flowed slowly, compact and brown, like a gigantic mud-slide, absorbing the rays of the sun without any reflection. He had to break free of the stupor into which his anger and grief had thrown him in order to leave the highway and regain a sense of direction. He had been here before, a long time ago, two or three times. Definitely drunk, at night, pounded by loud music in the back seat of a car where there was wild yelling and laugh-ing. He could no longer remember what he was here for. He had to stop to look at a map, and a few minutes later he found the street where the drug dealer lived. Cautiously, he passed the house twice, an ordinary little house, behind a hedge of bay trees. Everything seemed normal. Shutters half-closed, gate open. He went and parked in the street at right angles to this one, so that he wouldn't have to maneuver to get away again. He took the gun from his bag and put it in his belt and immedi-ately the weapon bothered him, hitting a muscle or a nerve with each step he took. After a while, the image of Fabien's body came into his mind and he had to stop as if he had banged his head on the lintel of a door that was too low. Curled up, blood beneath him. Shapeless face frozen in a grimace.

Franck moaned and clenched his teeth and stooped in the heat of the deserted street and hastened toward the house. The door opened noiselessly. He pushed it and listened out on the threshold of that silent half-darkness. He lifted the security and inserted a cartridge in the chamber. It seemed to him that the metallic click could have been heard from the other side of the street and he pulled his head down beneath his shoulders.

To his right, a kitchen, cupboards gaping open, doors torn off, drawers thrown to the floor. Cans of food, packs of cereal, all kinds of provisions strewn over the floor. Broken plates and glasses. Only the table and the chairs standing neatly around

196 · HERVÉ LE CORRE

it had withstood the destruction. He walked along a corridor, keeping the gun down against his leg, his finger on the trigger guard. All the doors were open and led to bedrooms that had been laid waste. Wardrobes emptied, bedding turned over. And yet it all still smelled of sleep and stale tobacco. He stopped and listened, as if the silence was going to whisper an explanation for all this in his ear. He looked at his gun, which he clutched in his sweaty hand. Then something moved. Then a moan, be- hind that door, the last one, almost certainly the bathroom. He kicked it open, gun pointed. In the bathtub there was a man. Feet and hands tied. Above him, streaks of blood on the pale green tiles. He was bare-chested, dressed only in his under- pants, and there were dozens of deep gashes on his skin.

Franck didn't immediately grasp what he was seeing. The face was nothing more than a shapeless mass turned toward him, mouth open and ravaged. A hole shiny with blood and phlegm. A gelatinous mass ran between the half-closed eyelids of the right eye and lay frozen on his cheek. On the other side of the face, a reddish globe, wide open. Franck recoiled and knocked against the door, which was still open behind him. He bent double with nausea but was unable to spit out anything but an acid liquid that burned his throat and sinuses and he coughed and spat some more and rushed to the washstand, which was soiled with brown marks, and drank greedily from the faucet and rinsed his mouth some more. He managed to recover his breath and rise to his full height and keep standing. He took a deep breath and went back to the eyeless man, and it was then that he saw the tattoo on the right shoulder and arm down to the elbow. Crossed daggers held together by a red snake with its mouth open, threatening black fangs.

Franck bent over the Serb. He couldn't look away from that ruined face, those hollow eyes. He wiped the tears that were running down his cheeks. He thought about Fabien and what they had done to him. And he wept over the shattered body of this accomplice of his brother's executioners. He would have liked to curse him, mock his suffering, piss on his raw wounds. He gathered enough air to be able to speak.

"Why did you kill Fabien?"

The Serb let out a shrill moan, like a child's. And he shook his head and moved his legs and his whole body seemed to say no.

"You didn't kill him but your friends did, is that it? In Spain . . ."

The man arched his back and puffed out his chest in an effort to speak, and a groan that was almost a cry came from him.

"Of course it was your people! Who else? You're half dead and you're still lying! Lying to the end, you motherfucker!" Franck aimed his gun at him. "I'm going to give you a present, you son of a bitch! I'm going to finish you off! You can't go on living like that! You see, I'm taking pity on you!"

The Serb slumped to the bottom of the bathtub and turned his head to the wall. His body seemed to relax and wait.

Franck sensed a movement behind his back. Turning, he saw a man with a baseball bat and immediately a blow on his shoulder jolted him and flung him against a little cabinet, causing the contents to clatter and rattle and roll about. The man raised his weapon again, so Franck, off balance against the tottering cabinet, fired at his stomach and the man left the room backwards, without a cry. Straightening up, Franck glanced at the Serb, who was still in the same position but had stopped moving and perhaps even breathing.

In the corridor, the other man was lying in a fetal position, his hands tight on his wound, teeth clenched, grimacing. Without a moan. He was looking at his reddened fingers and breathing hard. Blood was spreading beneath him. Then someone cried out from the street: "What's happening, for fuck's sake?" Franck ran to the end of the corridor and opened a door leading to a garden in the quiet shade of a silk tree and passed under a pink and blue portico from which hung two swings. He clambered over a wooden fence that shook and bent beneath his weight and almost fell into an inflatable swimming pool, in which a little boat and some plastic figurines—warriors bristling with spears and swords—were floating. He went into the house through a sliding picture window and came across two little boys sitting in front of a huge screen, playing on a console. Volleys of gunfire rang out. A man was on the floor, in a pool of blood. Franck hesitated, looking in turn at the children and the screen, the children staring at him in astonishment, immediately peering at the gun he was holding in his hand.

"It's all right," he said putting his index finger to his lips.

He crossed the living room behind the couch where the kids were sitting looking at him, their weapons and the corpses on the frozen screen forgotten. He passed in front of an open door to a garage, where he heard someone bustling about beneath a dim fluorescent light, a woman's voice saying: Everything all right, sweethearts? Then he went out into the garden and at that moment the alarm from a police car rang out in a neighboring street. He tried to figure out which direction to go in to get back to his Clio. Left, then left again, it seemed to him. The cops were getting closer, a car sped past at the end of the street, its noise making him jump. In five minutes they would be everywhere, he had to venture out onto the sidewalk. He thought about going back into the house where the two boys were, pointing the gun at their mother and getting her to hand over the keys to her car, which must be that old Peugeot 205 parked out front, but the woman just had to resist for two minutes and the trap would close in on him, so he stuck his gun in his belt, behind his back, and walked looking straight ahead like an onlooker approaching an accident. From the corner of the street he saw a police car that had stopped across the roadway, roof light flashing, doors open. He stopped for five seconds and listened to the calls and yells coming from over there, then got back to his car and rid himself of the gun that had been bothering him by sliding it under his seat. He twisted his body to recover the key from the pocket of his jeans and he noticed that he was shaking and having difficulty inserting it in the ignition. He was trembling like a leaf in the furnace inside the car and when the engine started his foot slipped on the clutch pedal to the point where he was sure he would stall when he tried to drive off. Some distance away, a cop appeared armed with a shotgun. He opened the trunk of his car and took out a bullet-proof vest and held it out to a plain-clothes colleague with a pistol in his holster, carried high, almost under the armpit, who started to put it on.

Franck released the clutch pedal, rolled down the windows, and breathed in. The air wasn't quite so hot outside, and there was even a slight breeze. Then he drove off without any difficulty, leaving the two police officers waving their arms about to get their vests on. Two hundred yards farther on, he passed an unmarked car speeding noisily along with two men inside, a sun visor marked POLICE making it even more obvious to the few people passing by on the sidewalks. He was suffocating. He wasn't sure he had thought to breathe since he'd left, so he took two or three deep breaths to rid himself of the sensation. He drove for a while at random beneath signs announcing highways that didn't lead anywhere he wanted to be—it would be the same everywhere anyway. Though actually, he would have liked to head straight for Spain, for Valencia, hoping to get there early in the morning and track down his brother's body and take it in his arms and bring it back here to bury it beside their mother, but he shook his head as if to wake himself up, because even in thought this meager consolation was inaccessible to him, to them, and it seemed to him that many things had been forbidden them or stolen from them during all those years when their childhood had collapsed like a sandcastle besieged by the rising tide.

He had the waning sun in his eyes and all he could think about was shielding himself from it, until the road became a straight ribbon shaded by pines. He stopped at a little supermarket to buy water and something to eat, then resumed

driving until he got to the maze of lanes and parking lots serving a seaside resort and parked as far as possible from the main
access routes by which vacationers came away from the shores
of the ocean. He got out of the car. The still air hummed with
the song of cicadas and smelled of resin. He took a few steps
toward the dunes, the dry pine needles crackling beneath his
feet. He continued through a thicket of dead trees stifled and
gradually overrun by the sand. Franck advanced awkwardly
amid the undulations of the soft, warm ground, which occasionally gave way beneath him. Then he saw the blue of the
horizon with a blinding patch in the middle that forced him to
screw up his eyes. A cool, gentle breeze was blowing, and he
felt overwhelmed by the well-being that it lavished on him.

Low tide. The sea was like oil. It rolled gently some hundred yards from him, lying there like a crumpled tablecloth. He
stripped and ran to the water and took a few steps into the cold
thickness that held back his legs and sapped his strength. He
let himself fall into it and turned over onto his back, panting,
looking up at the sky, licking his salty lips, and thought about
nothing, not because he was incapable of thinking, but because
here and now there was no point to it—he was no longer in any
danger, he was out of reach, lying in the blue and cradled by the
sweetness of the world.

He got out of the water when he started to feel numb and
threw himself, shivering, under what remained of the heat of
a slanting sun. He had the impression that he had slept and
looked around him with the curiosity of a man who wakes up
and isn't very sure where he is. The beach was deserted. He
could just about make out some dark figures in the distance.
Silent seabirds came and pecked at the wet sand.

He went back to his car and ate and drank what he had
bought on the road. He tried to think about the weeks he had
lived through since leaving prison and his present situation,
and it seemed to him he was like an animal caught in a ditch after the booby-trapped soil has collapsed beneath it, waiting for

someone to come and get it out of there only to truly confine it. It seemed to him that captivity would be less painful than this hole in which he was going around in circles, tiring himself out in trying to climb the steep, crumbly walls.

He lay down on the ground and watched darkness fall. He smoked two or three cigarettes, letting the thoughts and memories come and go, and he felt both sad and serene. It was always his childhood that came back into his mind. He could see them, the two of them, that woman and that man, smiling and handsome in photographs he had looked at a lot, later, when things weren't going so well anymore, photographs that must now be lost. He tried to go back in time, as if he could weave the fabric all over again, mend it where it was torn, and pick it all up from the point where they had left off, recover the life they should have had, the life that had been stolen from them.

He talked to them under his breath in old words, words from before, words he no longer uttered except in secret, when he was alone. A little wind kindled the stars, which lit up in glittering streaks. He dozed off and woke again beneath a black sky sprinkled with light. Since sleep seemed determined to take him, he settled in the back seat of the car, with all the windows down to capture the smells and noises of the forest.

He saw again the Serb's tortured face, his gouged-out eyes oozing blood, his gashed body slumped in that bathtub. He shuddered. He knew that people suffered horrible tortures, and always had, everywhere in the world. He had seen movies, videos, with friends, appalled, and there was always one who pressed stop or went to close the window, and another one to complain in frustration, and they then commented on what they had seen, stunned, with the few meager words of indignation or disgust that they possessed. He had seen blood flow, he had fought hard and dirty. But just a little while earlier he had leaned over the guy he would have liked to subject to the most horrific tortures and he had wept and shaken at the sight of that butchery. He had heard the man's labored breathing, the wheezing of his bronchial tubes, and that slimy groan, that strangled moan that had risen to him to deny Fabien's murder, even though he was almost dead already. He had wanted to finish him off, but would he have pulled the trigger if the other guy hadn't arrived with his bat? The question didn't bother him. He preferred to ask it of himself than to have answered it.

He dreamed that a huge wave rose from the ocean and overflowed the dunes and came crashing down on him. He woke with a scream in the first light of day, his heart in his throat. He seemed to hear the great calm beating of the sea, and the terror of his nightmare faded as he fell asleep again.

Children's voices dragged him from the torpor that resembled sleep. It was broad daylight. Car doors were slamming, people calling to each other. When he sat up, he watched them load themselves with parasols and beach bags and iceboxes. It was nearly nine and the air was mild and when he got out of the car he had to move his joints, which were aching from the awkward positions he had been in during the night, then after the vacationers disappeared into the dunes he found himself alone again in the breeze that ran along the tops of the pines, and it took him a few seconds for the full reality of his situation to come back to him and send a shiver down his spine. The tortured Serb, the guy in the corridor with a bullet in his belly bent double over his wound, the cops, the ride here, to what now appeared to him like a dead end. On one side the dunes, on the other the circular lane serving the parking lots.

He got back in the car and drove along an almost deserted road until he came across a café where he ordered breakfast, convinced that the kind of permanent vertigo that held him captive was caused by hunger. He found a seat on the terrace, not far from a group on a cycling vacation—German, perhaps or Dutch—big rucksacks next to them, their bicycles overloaded with saddlebags a bit farther on, devouring slices of bread and butter dipped in tea, passing around a road map.

A newspaper had been left on the next table. Franck opened

it and glanced at the headlines about war and terrorism, cynical and horrible politicians, along with lists for the benefit of vacationers staying in the region, lists of music festivals and of traditional summer fairs where people could drink to their hearts' content. He remembered the alcohol-fueled excursions that he and Fabien and a few others had made, and especially one time a guy had stood on the guardrail of the Saint-Esprit Bridge in Bayonne and proclaimed to the assembled company that he was quite capable of jumping off and that you needed balls to do that. He had finally fallen on the right side, on the sidewalk, and thrown up, then fallen asleep in his own vomit, surrounded by passers-by who stepped aside and walked hurriedly away.

Franck folded the newspaper and watched the cyclists get on their machines, as heavily laden as donkeys, and ride away, almost reeling with the effort. He calculated that he had about three thousand euros left and that he could still get by. He just had to find a quiet place to take the time to think. A quiet place where there wouldn't be anybody around. He started thinking about the Massif Central as a wild country full of abandoned villages and impenetrable forests, and he told himself that he could go to ground there, deep inside a wood, and even get a job as a lumberjack. He left a ten-euro bill on the table then stood up, almost relieved. It was nearly eleven. He hadn't been aware of the time passing.

In the car, he was pleased to see his things around him. He set off, vowing to throw away the gun at the first opportunity, once he was in the middle of nowhere.

Then his cell phone rang. For some seconds, he groped in his bag for it. It was Rachel. She was speaking in a low voice, trying hard not to shout.

"You have to come! Help! Come quickly!"

WOLVES

11

As soon as he turns onto the path, the house appears, windows gaping, front door wide open. Franck starts shaking and rushes inside with a moan. In the hall he stumbles over the body of the dog, huge, stretched out full length. The top of its skull has been blown away, and all that's left of the head are the half-open jaws, the eyes are gone, the teeth bared in a final blind rage. Only those teeth, that square muzzle, that biting apparatus. Blood and brain matter are spattered all over the tiled floor and the foot of the wall. There is also a smooth pool of blood that's spread as far as the foot of the stairs. Earth and fragments of a broken flower pot and shards of glass—the entrance door has been smashed in—are scattered across the floor.

To get into the kitchen, he has to step over the oversized carcass and he can't help dreading that the animal will wake up and attack him suddenly while he's balanced on one foot. He opens the door, and it is there that he finds the old woman. She is lying flat on her stomach in a round pool of blood as distinct and shiny as spilled paint. She has fallen in front of the sink, which is full of dirty dishes, and on her left foot, hanging from her big toe, she still has one of those slippers of hers, the slippers he heard her dragging throughout the house all day long, carrying with her the acrid smell of tobacco, shaking the ash from her cigarette everywhere. He looks around for the other slipper but can't see it. The dead woman is wearing white track pants she soiled when her bladder let go. Between her shoulder blades, the shot has hollowed a jagged crater as wide as a saucer full of raw meat. Her red hair is spread in a corolla around her pale face, which rests on one cheek. The eye that can be seen beneath her hair is half closed. She often looked like that when she kept her cigarette in her mouth and got smoke in her eyes and gave people sidelong glances, her half-closed eyes expressing suspicion or contempt.

He bends over the body and has to lean on the worktop in order not to be thrown to the floor by the vertigo that has taken hold of him. The woman's scarlet lips have remained half open on her last breath, drawn back in a bad-tempered snarl that makes her look a little like the dog. He pushes her with the tip of his shoe then gives her a little kick in the side. "You finally croaked, you bitch." He has only whispered it but his voice echoes pathetically in the silence. He thinks it's stupid to talk like this to a corpse, but right here and now it does him good. Sweat is running down his back. He wipes his forehead with the back of his hand. There's a sour smell under his armpits. He glances through the window, where the light is already harsh enough to force him to screw up his eyes. The ancient tractor, the carcasses of cars, the van, all the scrap iron heaped up there over thirty years, everything has that sallow, lusterless hue, the color of things that have begun to disappear, slowly destroyed by the erosion of time.

In the next room, the living room, furnished only with shapeless couches and armchairs in cracked imitation leather, the huge TV set is softly diffusing its multi-colored light. Sitting in front of it, the old man is huddled over his hands holding his stomach, bent double as if watching his body empty drop by drop between his feet through the foam rubber seat of the armchair and spread on the floor beneath him. He has pretty much the same wound in the middle of his back as his wife— an uneven hole the size of a saucer—leaving a huge bright-red dahlia in the back of the chair.

Franck leans forward a little and sees the eyes, the open mouth, the lower lip drooping in a startled, idiotic way. There hovers around the body an odor of shit mixed with powder. A sudden fit of nausea forces Franck to spit a little bile, then he leaves the room, where the old clock is still ticking, their lousy clock that dates from 1850, they always said, left there as security by a shady antique dealer along with a whole consignment of old furniture and paintings now rotting in the barn.

He walks out of there and steps over overturned chairs, drawers flung on the floor, clothes scattered in the corridor, thrown from the gaping cupboards, and climbs upstairs to the bedrooms. All the doors are open. A chaos of searched and emptied wardrobes, broken mirrors, lifted mattresses lying across the springs.

Except Rachel's. On the sky-blue door there's still that cut-out of a big orange cat looking at you with a hostile air, arms crossed over its pot belly. Franck shoves it with his shoulder in case it might be locked or something might be blocking it, and he finds himself in the middle of the room, gasping for breath, his heart beating like crazy. Nothing has been touched. The bed is made, the soft toys lined up on the golden-yellow counterpane with their backs to the wall, blonde dolls installed in their pink and sequined setting amid their accessories: an RV, a picnic table, a little palm tree. Images on the walls, posters of cartoon characters, a shelf with a few books and monstrous figurines with pig noses. Green and blue. Wallpaper with plant-like patterns. The goldfish in its aquarium, turning in circles in the middle of a plastic decor.

He remembers the day he caught Rachel tidying her room, humming, a cloth in her hand. That meticulous, almost persnickety order she restores every morning. "When she's grown up, I'll get her to tidy the house, it'll make a nice change from all this mess," Jessica often jokes, hugging Rachel, while the girl stands there, solemn and silent, head bowed, arms dangling like those of a rag doll.

Franck feels reassured by this intact spot where there still hovers the light mint and lavender scent of shower gel that Rachel always carries with her, in her hair and on her skin, when she comes and huddles in your arms, without saying anything, then suddenly frees herself from your embrace, almost abruptly, and runs away without looking at you, like a moody cat. It seems as if nothing bad can ever happen to her, because this order she maintains around her, in her little world, may actually protect her from the surrounding chaos. That and the silence in which she encloses herself and which now hums in Franck's ears.

He feeds the goldfish. It swims up to the surface and swallows the dried insects. "Of course, you don't know where she is."

He carefully closes the door again and stands by it for a moment, listening out for the slightest sound. He hears only the murmur of the TV, and remembers with a shudder the corpse of the old man slumped in front of it. His back torn out, his stupid air, bent over his own death.

"Rachel?"

His head is spinning, buzzing as if he's landed in a hornets' nest. He thinks he's going to wake up and escape from one of those terrifying but vivid dreams in which something irrevocable has often happened, something that pursues you in the dark even after your eyes are open so that for a few seconds you wonder if it all really happened. But he isn't asleep, and reality is asserting itself in all its blinding clarity. He touches the wall with the flat of his hand, takes his car key from his pocket, and looks at it closely as if it's an object he's forgotten how to use, making an effort to think about what has happened and to find in this carnage and chaos signs of the vague structure he has been making his way through, the loose, rotting floor across which he has been limping and stumbling for the past few weeks. Through the door of Jessica's room, he glimpses clothes heaped up in front of the wardrobe, drawers tipped out onto the floor in the livid light thrown by the window. He takes a few steps in the direction of this disarray then turns back to the other door, where the huge ginger cat peers at him defiantly.

They haven't turned over Rachel's room. They should have done. It's what he would have done in their place. He even thinks to search under the mattress, or among the clothes in the wardrobe to try to find what's there, then dismisses the idea, he couldn't do it, he thinks with disgust, it would be as if he were sticking his fingers inside Rachel's panties. I haven't become like them.

What they were looking for could very well have been under that mattress, and may still be there. Money, drugs. Rachel might have been sleeping for days or weeks on wads of bills or smack or grass hidden under her bed or in a skillfully restitched soft toy. And they didn't touch a thing. Maybe they weren't looking for anything. Maybe they came only to demand a final payment of the debt one last time, a settling of accounts, revenge for the Serb.

The telephone starts ringing, making him jump. He takes a step toward it, thinking to pick up, then changes his mind. It rings seven or eight times and he stands there in front of it, motionless, during the outgoing message, then panting when he hears the breathing of someone who decides not to leave a message and hangs up. He doesn't dare move, he barely breathes, as if they can hear him or sense his presence. When the phone falls silent, he convinces himself that they know he's here. They may have seen him turning onto the path. He goes and stands in the doorway and looks out at the empty road, the trees and bushes glistening in the sun, the dark, ugly pines, the whole of that still landscape, paralyzed by this summer morning. From where he is, he can't see the trailer but he supposes they looked there, too. He walks around the Mercedes, takes a few steps toward the deserted meadow, gazes at the forest, and thinks again about his nightmare, picturing a tidal wave of vegetation about to come crashing down on the house. He retraces his steps. Anxiety between his shoulder blades, pressing like a fist.

The door of the trailer has been closed again, and the idea crosses his mind that it might be a trap, a man waiting in ambush inside with a shotgun in his hand, so he hesitates before turning the latch. He thinks it's ridiculous. A guy sweating in a trailer just to put a bullet in his head. Attacking him in the house would be so much more practical. And this guy and his accomplices must have let Jessica go and attacked him. Why not? But the old man and the old woman bore the brunt of it. And her? Where was she in all this time? With Rachel? He doesn't understand. He tries to think, his hand on the latch of that fucking door, behind which . . . But he doesn't come to any conclusion so he pulls the door toward him as if about to tear it off.

The closets and chests have been opened and emptied. The cushions on the bench seats lifted and ripped open. His books scattered on the floor. He picks up three on which he has stepped and puts them on the worktop in the kitchenette. He strokes the soft covers with his fingertips, and flashes of memory cross his mind and he stands there motionless for a moment, assailed by the shadows and the figures he once imagined looming out of the words. Then as the air thickens around him and numbs him, he moves his shoulders and runs a little warm water over his hands, his arms.

When he goes out, the sun falls on him and forces him to stoop. In a daze, he makes out the house through his almost-closed eyelids, a dark, impenetrable mass. He could set fire to it so that nothing remains of this cursed castle straight out of a horror story, and the cops will find the charred corpses of the two old people in the ruins, still smoking in the middle of the wrecks of cars and all that mess rotting on palettes and under tarps. For a moment, he considers going to the shed and looking for a jerry can of gasoline. He really would like to see the first flames burst out through the smashed windows and hear the pitiless growling of the fire, ready to devour it in one go, a crazed monster with a hundred hungry mouths. He would like it to finish like this, in a huge blaze that would cleanse everything. As if fire could purify anything. A medieval belief. Charred bodies, lost souls.

He stands there in the white light, surrounded by a terrifying silence. An emptiness, a void that hums in his ears. It is death speaking to him with its immense mouth open. He is afraid suddenly, and he runs to his car and sets off at high speed, tearing up pebbles and dust beneath the wheels. As he drives away, just before turning onto the road, he looks to see if anyone has come out of the house to follow him.

12

He drives for a while in the hope of seeing Jessica's car around a bend or in the distance on the highway. He speeds toward Bordeaux, pushing the old engine of his old Renault to the limit. Three times he dials the number, three times he gets the outgoing message, and he always leaves the same message in return: "Call me back, I don't know where you are."

When the phone rings, he very nearly swerves and cuts in front of a truck. Jessica almost screams through the din of the engine, the whoosh coming in through the lowered windows.

"Have you been there?"

"Yes. I saw. What happened?"

"How did you find out?"

"Rachel."

"Fuck, I don't believe it! What did she tell you?"

"To come. So I came."

"Obviously."

"Are the two of you all right? What—?"

"We're both fine. I'll tell you. Meet me in the parking lot of the drive-in Carrefour in Mérignac. I'm not far from there. I'll wait for you."

She hangs up. On the beltway, trucks and RVs, cars laden with trunks, bicycles. Franck remembers that the country is on vacation. They're all leaving, even if it's just to swap one routine for another. He envies these people he glimpses in their cars. He envies the little habits toward which they are driving, the ritual of the beach, watching TV under the canopy of the trailer, the 7 P.M. drink taken in turns with your neighbors on the campsite, going out to dinner every now and again. Since yesterday, he's been drifting from one bloodbath to another and all he would like right now is to be in one of those cars taking the highway to Bayonne, to Spain, a little boy dozing off or glued to the window, or even a brooding, frustrated teenager slumped against the door with headphones on. Safe. Letting himself be transported without a care toward another world, even if it's a fake one.

Jessica is where she said she would be. He parks behind her and she doesn't move and he has to get out of his car and go to hers and lean down at the door for her to turn her head to him. Her features are drawn, her eyes shiny, and her hands on the wheel make it look as if she's about to drive away at any moment. Her cheek is swollen and bruised. He doesn't see Rachel in the back seat. Only a big traveling bag.

"Isn't Rachel with you? Where is she?"

"Did you see what they did?"

"Where's Rachel?"

"She's safe with friends. Don't worry."

She opens the door abruptly and he has to dodge back to avoid getting it in the legs. She grabs her little red linen bag and takes out a pack of cigarettes and lights one, leaning back against the car, then looks over at the people washing their cars with high-pressure hoses.

"What happened?"

She shakes her head. She swallows air then sighs. "They arrived around eight. I was upstairs and I heard my mother scream and right after that a shot and then another. I locked Rachel in her room and I stayed there on the landing not knowing what to do, I had to stop myself from screaming. Fuck, they were killing my parents and I was there and I couldn't do anything!"

She breaks off and wipes her tears with the back of her trembling hand and takes two drags of her cigarette.

"They were yelling that they'd come to do to us what we'd

done to the Serb, I didn't understand, and just then two of them came up the stairs and saw me, so to distract them, because I didn't want them to find Rachel, I went to them and started hitting them. Forget it! They threw me down the stairs and stuck the barrels of their shotguns on my face. I couldn't see their faces, they had me pinned to the ground and I couldn't move. One of them said, She's hot, let's fuck her! And the other one replied, You go ahead, I'm not going to dirty my cock in her rotten pussy. I told myself, if they fuck me, they won't kill me, I was thinking about Rachel in her room and I'd rather fifty of them had me even if they tore my insides out, anything rather than that, and then all at once I heard one of them say, What the fuck's that? I realized when I heard the dog growling, I yelled, Attack! But they fired and I felt this wet, heavy thing fall on my legs and I realized right away that it was the dog, I felt like throwing up, I really couldn't figure out what was happening, do you understand? My parents dead, me with a gun stuck to my head, and my kid up there, I couldn't put it all together and think, not that it would have helped anyway . . . Meanwhile, I could hear them turning everything upside down, they must have been looking for money and they ransacked everything and I was scared they would attack Rachel, and there was this big bastard on top of me pointing his gun at me and asking them if they'd found anything and them yelling no . . . After a while he pulled down my panties and stuck his finger in, it hurt but I told him yes, it's good, go on, I wanted to distract him and take his shotgun, I swear to you I would have made mincemeat of those sons of bitches, I wanted to do everything to distract their attention and get them to leave Rachel alone, you taste good, he said, that bastard licked his fingers, don't worry, you'll catch hell when the others get here."

Even though they are full in the sun, Franck is shivering, he leans against the front fender of the car because he has the feeling his legs are going to give way. Listening to Jessica, he sees it all again, the bodies, the chaos, and he wonders what lucky chance stopped those guys from breaking down Rachel's door. When he asks Jessica the question, she looks at him at first as if she doesn't understand, then sniffs and lights another cigarette and blows the smoke out effortfully as if the words won't come.

"After a while, they went back down, this guy was talking dirty and I was saying to him, Go ahead, dammit, if you have the balls, and he was growling like a dog, I'm sure he was jerking off all the while he was pinning my head to the floor with the barrel of his shotgun. There was someone who said, What about her? I knew they were all eyeing up my ass and hesitating, they must have been looking at each other to try to make up their minds. And then they decided to leave. I got a kick in the ribs and it winded me, and just as I was turning to see what they looked like, they grabbed the dog and threw him at me saying, Here, if you're so horny, why don't you fuck this one? It was so disgusting, you can't imagine, that dead dog on top of me, dribbling on me, and the smell of shit . . . I didn't dare move until I heard them drive away, then I got up, all covered in blood and dog shit, and then I heard Rachel crying in her room and that gave me courage, I went up and told her I would open the door but that she had to wait, I couldn't let her see me in the state I was in so I threw my clothes outside and I went and took a shower, I must have stayed twenty minutes in the boiling water, I rubbed and rubbed and if I could have taken my skin off I would . . . Afterwards, I went to see my parents, I couldn't believe they were dead, I just hope they didn't suffer . . ."

Jessica slides to the ground and sits there, her forehead against her knees, shaken with silent sobs. Franck looks at her, withdrawn and so small she could be any little girl overcome with sorrow. The people coming to collect their shopping glance out from behind their rolled-up windows in their air-conditioned bubbles, then park and open their trunks and wait for their orders to be brought to them, forgetting everything else.

"What about Rachel? She must have heard something! The

shooting, the yelling! Didn't she see anything when you came downstairs with her?"

"I'd given her some of her syrup to sleep. When I went up-stairs, she'd fallen asleep again. She didn't wake up until we were in the car. I don't dare imagine what I would have done to stop her seeing all that."

Franck squats beside her. He takes her by the neck and places his mouth on her hair, but she resists and pushes him away gently.

"Come on," he says, "we can't stay here. Let's go get Rachel and then figure out what to do. At least they don't know where we are."

"I think I saw a car behind me earlier. A 4×4 like the Serb's. They may be following me. But you're out of the picture anyway."

"Out of the picture? I'm in it up to my neck. Because I went to see the Serb yesterday. They killed Fabien, in Spain. Did you know that? So your father told me where I could find that bas-tard. And when I got there, he was lying in the bathtub, hacked to pieces and with his eyes gouged out. Do you understand any of this mess? That's why they came this morning. To avenge him, because they think I was the one who did it. There was another guy there, and I had to shoot him. You get the picture now? See how fucked-up it is? One thing's for sure, if they find out where we are, they won't let us go."

Jessica shrugs. She sniffs once again and raises her head, without looking at him. "What do you suggest?"

"We go get Rachel and then hide out somewhere and think."

She smiles ironically and shakes her head. "Think, huh? Think about what?"

"About what we're going to do. The cops are going to be involved and things will get even more complicated. I left my prints everywhere in that house, including the bathroom. And then there were two little boys who saw me. They got a good look at me. Tomorrow, my face will be in every police station in the country, the cops will have it on the dashboards of their cars."

"Why should that bother me? It's you they're looking for."

Franck shudders and gets to his feet. He shakes himself as if trying to rid himself of the electric charge that's running through his body. Once again, that desire to hit her, to destroy whatever devil is inside her. But there are those shoulders, those breasts he glimpses over the top of her T-shirt, those thighs, all that caramel-colored skin the sun has given her. And those eyes that gather all the light filtered by her thick, long lashes.

"Okay. In that case, I'll hand myself in and tell the police everything."

"That's right. Go on, tell them everything, you've been wanting to do it for a long time."

Franck gets in his car and drives off. In the rear-view mirror, he sees her move away then disappear, and for a long time he keeps an eye on the traffic behind him, hoping to see the red hood of her Renault reappear. He is on the beltway when his phone rings.

"Where are you?"

"I'll be at the police station in two minutes."

"Idiot. Where are you?"

"There's a hotel along the beltway. Exit 13. I'll wait for you in the parking lot."

Six or seven cars are parked there. All with license plates from outside the region. No shade. He rolls down all the windows, opens the doors, and waits at the wheel. Every now and again, a little air stirs the furnace. Jessica arrives fifteen minutes later. She gets out of her car, her big bag in her hand.

"Is this where we're going to say? Are there rooms?"

There are five left, on the third floor. Franck pays for two nights in advance, in cash.

No sooner are they in the room than they're on top of each other, weighed down by their bags, squeezing past the bed. They pile their things in a closet then without a word Jessica lies down in a fetal position, like a sulking child. Franck enters the small bathroom. He first rinses off the sea salt that's puckering his skin then soaps himself with the sample provided by the hotel. When he comes back into the bedroom, she's probably asleep; she doesn't react when he talks about going to get a bite to eat because after that, they'll be able to think more clearly. He dresses and walks around to the other side of the bed, noticing that her eyes are wide open and she's staring straight ahead.

"What are you thinking about?"

"Nothing."

"Rachel?"

"Nothing, I said. All right, shall we go eat?"

They drive to a nearby shopping mall, where they walk past empty stores where assistants stand looking bored, then they go into a cafeteria and order the set meal of the day and find a table far from the employees on a break, and start to eat without saying anything to each other. Every now and again, Jessica glances over at the entrance as she picks at her food, and each time Franck turns his head and sees only shoppers pushing carts or teenage girls idling in front of the windows.

"I keep thinking they're going to come for us."

"Are you sure they followed you?"

She nods. "Yeah . . . They caught up with me on the highway."

"Why did they leave you in the house if they were going to follow you later? Are they stupid or what?"

"How should I know? You're pissing me off with your questions! You sound like a cop! They murdered my parents, my father and my mother, can't you get that into your thick skull? And my kid was there, shut up in her room, all alone upstairs, while they looked for their money or God knows what! And obviously all because they were looking for you, because you stuck your nose in their business. So I don't give a fuck about the whys or wherefores! I saved my skin, and my daughter's skin, I don't even want to know how."

She pushes away her plate and looks around them at the people having lunch and talking in low voices. Breathless, her eyes shining.

"If it's me they're looking for, why did you call me?"

She hesitates, shaking her head, her eyes lowered. "Because with you, I'm not so scared. You're all I have left, now that they're dead."

"And Rachel."

"I don't feel safe with Rachel. Right now, she's more trouble than anything else."

She looks him straight in the eyes, waiting for his reaction. Her pupils seem to gather all the brightness from the fluorescent lighting and glow like a cat's eyes. He forces himself not to let it show, but he feels like slapping her or slamming his plate in her face.

"So by taking her to these people, you've put her somewhere safe and gotten rid of her at the same time?"

"Does that shock you?"

He shrugs. "She's your daughter."

Franck prefers to keep silent. He has the sudden impression that they're sitting on the edge of a ravine, a forest in flames behind them. And that the crazed arsonist is sitting right next to him.

As they drive back to the hotel, he dismisses these thoughts from his mind. They're on the run, their legs trapped in brambles, and he estimates their chances of getting out somewhere between very unlikely and almost nil. The most sensible thing would be to go to the cops and try to tell them everything. The whole story. The drugs, the debt, the Serb's men, Fabien's death in Spain, right up to today's bloodbath. The two of them caught up in all this, trying to defend themselves. And the Gypsy, who seems to know more than anyone else. Maybe being honest, telling it the way it is, might speak in their favor. He dismisses this idea immediately, picturing the cops sniggering behind their desks or leaning on a table with their arms crossed as if they don't believe a word of it, occasionally showing him the fingerprints they've found, mainly his own. And then at the end, there's the slammer. The images and memories coming back into his mind make him tremble. He stands by the window, watching the traffic on the beltway, while Jessica, who's lying on the bed, has switched the TV on and is channel hopping and asking him what he's thinking about, and he replies, Nothing, I'm just looking, that's all.

Then he thinks about Rachel. The survivor from a bloodbath, dropped two hours later in someone's house like a bothersome package. And soon, when they're arrested by the cops, or the others catch up with them . . . He remembers again the image of Rachel in her red dress in the middle of the dried-up meadow. Alone.

Jessica switches off the TV and gets up. He hears the springs of the bed creak, the door of the closet open. When he turns, she is naked, taking her toiletries from her bag.

"I'll be back."

His body understands why she said that before he does. He listens to the water running, he hears each of her gestures, follows the movements of her hands. He lies down and waits for her. He wishes he could reject her, he wishes he could despise that supple, languorous body, break free of its spell. In the impasse he finds himself in, he wishes that all desire could be extinguished, that all his energy could be devoted to escape or to looking for a way out, instead of being subject to his animal instincts, like a dog. But he also knows that in the worst circumstances, in the most extreme situations, people still find the strength to come together and make love, even in the depths of despair. There's nothing animal about that. Only life stubbornly persisting. He really doesn't know anymore. He decides to just let go.

Jessica comes out of the bathroom, her still damp skin glistening in places. She stares at Franck, as if she's thinking of something else, and he wonders if she even sees him right now.

She stays like that for a few seconds then smiles sadly at him before lying down on top of him.

They wrestle in silence. He wants to hurt her, she opens up, gives herself, without ever looking at him, a stranger to him. They come violently, teeth clenched, as if they are in a rage. Barely out of breath, she immediately gets up and goes to take a shower.

They spend the afternoon in the room, dozing, watching TV. They don't talk. Franck tries to think over the situation, but the only conclusions he comes up with are discouraging. He sees the walls around them as their only prospect, the hundred square feet of the room as their only space for maneuver. He is awakened by the voice of Jessica speaking on the telephone, having fallen asleep without realizing it.

"Yes . . . What's the matter with her now? Did she say anything? I'm not surprised . . . She never eats much . . . Is she being nice to you at least? Not a word? Right. Can I come over there this evening? I'll tell her . . . Oh, yes, of course . . . About 7:30? Okay. See you later."

Jessica turns to Franck.

"We're invited over for a drink."

"Who was that?"

"Delphine. The friend I left Rachel with."

"How is Rachel?"

"We have to go there. She won't speak, she's refusing to eat, she's locked herself in the toilet."

"Does your friend know about your parents and everything?"

"No. Delphine doesn't ask questions. Neither does Damien. I just told them that it would help me out if they could keep her for me for two or three days because I had some problems, and they agreed right away. I've known Delphine for ten years. She's like a sister. And besides, I didn't tell Rachel anything either. What could I have told her anyway? She didn't ask anything, I think she was still woozy because of the syrup, I don't think she heard anything from her room. I told her we were going on a trip and that her grandpa and grandma would join us later, because right now they had a lot of things to do. You know how she is. She doesn't say anything, she just does as she's told. She got her little things together, and of course she took that old cell phone I gave her last year and called you with it, and we went out the back way, she didn't see a thing. So she's not going to tell them anything. And anyway, I wonder sometimes if she quite understands what people say to her. She's really weird. She scares me sometimes, you know, like those kids in horror movies, who walk down the corridor at night and stand at the foot of the bed with a knife in their hand. She did that sometimes when she was smaller. Come in in the middle of the night without saying anything and watch me sleep."

"Your father says, or rather, said, the same thing. Have you ever wondered why she's like that?"

"The teacher at school last year found that strange. She said she was intelligent and everything, but really couldn't figure her out. We even had a visit from a social worker . . . I got some of the same treatment when I was a kid. They like to stir the shit and try to get you into trouble, those people. But anyway . . . Why are we talking about this?"

"We started talking about Rachel."

"Oh, yes . . ."

Jessica remains pensive, her eyes staring at the TV screen, which is off, then snaps out of her daydreaming. She puts on white pants and a black off-the-shoulder top and ruffles her hair with her fingers. She is suddenly radiant, and she turns to Franck with a smile that defuses his anger and mistrust.

13

I t's a high rise on the southern outskirts of the city. They live on the eleventh floor. The elevator smells of urine, its steel walls covered in obscene drawings, logos, insults. Jessica and Franck stand apart, staring at this banal wall art. The corridor they emerge into smells of fried onions and spices. Rap music plays behind a door, someone bursts out laughing. Delphine opens the door to them, in a basketball top and shorts, barefoot. She is blonde, her frizzy hair gathered on the back of her head in a huge yellow clump. Dull skin, fleshy lips. She puts her arms around Jessica, and they kiss and rub against each other like lovers. When they've finished, Delphine first shakes Franck's hand, then decides to kiss him.

Rachel is at the end of the corridor, motionless. Franck sees her and calls to her and she comes toward them with small steps. Jessica goes to her.

"Well? I hear you haven't been nice to Delphine and Damien?"

Rachel comes and squeezes her mother's legs in her arms and presses her head to her belly.

"Come on, that's enough now."

She gently pushes Rachel away, rubbing her head with the flat of her hand.

A tall guy as thin as a rod, in Bermuda shorts and a Portugal soccer shirt, advances toward them, holding a cell phone in his hand. He takes Jessica in his arms and lifts her off the floor. Groans of effort, little cries of pleasure. He greets Franck warmly, squeezes his hand in his own big, strong hand, then ushers them into the living room for a drink. Two children are at a table. A little girl, in a baby chair, in front of a red plate filled with vegetable purée. A little boy turning his nose up at a tomato salad. He has his head down, his napkin around his neck.

"He's being punished," Delphine explains. "His Lordship doesn't want to eat anything, so he can't leave the table. He'll stay there when we sit down to eat later. Since he doesn't want to eat, he's not allowed to be at the table with us, but he isn't allowed to get up. His name is Enzo. The girl is Amalia."

The little boy raises his eyes to the newcomers and Damien's voice cuts through the room like a knife. "What did I tell you?"

The boy immediately lowers his head and starts crying in silence, his shoulders heaving with each sob.

"I'll have to try that method with Rachel," Jessica says. "She never wants to eat either."

Little Amalia bursts out laughing, waving her plastic spoon then starts to pick at her purée with her fingers and proudly show her dirty hands to the adults. Her mother goes to her and makes her eat two mouthfuls, explaining that this is how it's done. She wipes her fingers, puts the spoon back in her hand, and gives her a kiss on her forehead.

Rachel has sat down at the end of the table and is looking at all of them, children and grown-ups, with what might be a surprised expression, before moving her eyes closer to her little games console.

Damien brings drinks and nibbles and they sit down on plastic armchairs around a garden table. Damien explains that they'll be getting a leather suite in the fall. Then they drink and nibble and talk about this and that. Jessica and Delphine mention some of their mutual acquaintances. They laugh, sometimes expressing surprise, sometimes anxiety. Every now and again, they explain things to the listening men. Damien is in charge of the drinks. Beer or gin and tonic? Franck drinks two Belgian beers and eats peanuts. He feels heavy, slumped on his chair. Damien asks him how long he's known Jessica. So Franck tells the story. Prison, Fabien, Jessica and her parents, the dog.

Nothing else. No mention of the drugs, the debt, the gunfire, the bloodbath. Oh, a dog? Damien loves dogs. It's one of his great passions in life. He would have liked to be a dog handler for the police or the army. He used to have a Rottweiler, before he got together with Delphine. But that stupid dog couldn't stand children, and they didn't want him to attack Enzo, who was a baby at the time. Oh, no, Enzo isn't his son. They had to get rid of it. The dog, of course. He gave it to Bilail, a friend with a kebab joint that had been robbed twice in six months.

This boy was a gift from her life before. Well, a kind of gift. Not that he's bad, no. But he's stubborn, he zones out and doesn't say a word for days. Yes, a little bit like Rachel. And I get tired of it. That's why I told Delphine one was enough, that's why she called Jessica earlier.

The two women have fallen silent and are listening to him. Delphine glances at her son, who is playing with his fingers and sniffing.

"I get you," Jessica says. "She's not easy. She's my daughter, sure, but frankly there are times when I find her hard to take."

"I knew right away that it wouldn't work out. As soon as you left, she sat down on the floor in a corner with her bag and refused to move. She made like she didn't hear us, like we didn't exist! And don't get me started on lunch. She didn't touch a thing, didn't take any notice of us! There are kids who are a little bit like those dogs that stop eating when their masters aren't there anymore."

Jessica nods her head in approval. She seems to be reflecting intensely on what has just been said.

Franck looks at Rachel. Her head is resting on her folded arms, as if she's asleep. He'd like to leave. He could get up, say to her, Come on, Rachel, let's go, get your things, and he would get out of here, he would drive all night with Rachel sleeping in the back seat and in the morning she would wake up in a new place, in front of a vast landscape, a deep valley, mountains in the distance . . . Just a slight breeze in memory of the night . . .

He gets up abruptly and the others are surprised to see him on his feet.

"I'm going out on the balcony for a smoke."

He opens the sliding glass door and closes it again behind him and feels relieved not to be hearing them anymore. It's mild. There's just a slight breeze blowing, like the one he was just dreaming about. He listens to the voices, the snatches of music, of TV shows. The town stretches at his feet, lights up with the coming night. Bordeaux in the distance, the bridges over the river.

"Aren't you smoking?"

He hasn't heard Jessica arrive. He lights their cigarettes.

"Are you all right?"

"Why do you ask?"

"I don't know. You don't look good. You seem strange."

"Like Rachel, you mean?"

"We're taking Rachel. That should please you."

"When are we going?"

"They've ordered pizzas, we'll eat and then go."

They wash down the pizzas with beer and Coke. Rachel eats a piece with gusto, even saying thank you when Delphine serves her.

"She's talking and eating!" Damien says.

Jessica looks at her daughter and laughs. "What were we saying earlier?"

All Franck can see of the boy being punished is his back, which lifts occasionally in a big sigh.

"Doesn't he want a piece?" Franck asks.

"If he wants to eat, he has a plate waiting for him in his usual place. Then he'll be able to sit at the table properly."

Saying this, Damien doesn't even look at the boy, but then he turns to him.

"Shit, just go. Go to bed. And make sure you don't wake your sister."

The boy leaves the room without a word, looking down

at his feet. Franck tries to meet Jessica's gaze but she lowers her eyes to her empty plate and makes a show of picking up a few crumbs with her fingertips, lifting them to her mouth and crunching them. He'd like to know what she's thinking right now, as they hear the little boy dragging his feet along the corridor, he would like to read in her eyes some sympathy for the kid, some sadness at this cruelty, but she seems to be increasingly withdrawn into herself, locked into her armor of flesh and skin. Her parents were killed this morning, practically in front of her. They are going to rot there, not even hidden under the earth as befits the dead, and the vision of their carcasses rotting away in that house he knows, where he thought he might be able to regain his freedom, makes him break out in a sweat—he thinks he can smell the pungent odor. He doesn't know how she does it. There they are, on the run, stuck with a little girl, trapped. And she's chatting and laughing, as if all this is merely the logical extension of a story begun a long time ago, as if she doesn't care how it's going to end up. She's running across a void, like those cartoon characters who realize too late that there's no more road left, no way out.

He realizes that everyone has fallen silent around the table, listening perhaps to the boy's steps moving away. When the bedroom door closes almost noiselessly, Franck has the feeling he can start breathing again, and Delphine comes back to life, like a humanoid creature that's been recharged, and suggests coffee.

So they have coffee. A joint circulates, and Jessica drags on it with forced enjoyment. Franck hasn't smoked dope since the slammer, and along with the smell and the taste of the dope other sensations come back to him. The stench of sweat, the reek from the toilets, stinking breath blown into your face. When the joint comes around for the second time, he refuses, thick-tongued, and washes away his nausea with a long swig of beer.

When they leave the building, Franck has the feeling he's escaped from a deadly mechanism of walls gradually closing in on them until they are all crushed. With Rachel asleep in his arms, he hurries to the car, anxious to get away from this place as quickly as possible. Jessica lags behind, slightly drunk, laughing to herself. She collapses onto the passenger seat while Franck settles Rachel in the back.

"Did you know that boy, Enzo? Had you seen him before?"

Jessica rolls down the window on her side and lights a cigarette. "No, I'd never seen him before. In the old days, when we were having a good time, it wasn't really the place for a kid. Mind you, I must have seen him once or twice when he was a baby. But she was hitting the sauce too much to bother with a child, so she used to give him to his grandmother to look after."

In the hotel, the receptionist peers at Rachel, who's still asleep in Franck's arms, but says nothing. They put her to bed without undressing her to stop her from waking up. Franck lies down on the carpet, a blanket under his head, and hears Jessica fall asleep immediately. In her sleep, she moans faintly like a little girl.

The last time he checks on his cell phone, it's after three in the morning. Above him, in the darkness of the room, the light on the TV set is a red star in an empty sky.

14

Rachel devours her slice of bread with chocolate spread, the chocolate forming a mustache under her nose. After a while, she asks her mother if they're going to the beach and Jessica looks at her, holding her cup of coffee in the air, and says, "Yes, of course we are, but not today. Franck and I have things to sort out." Rachel nods, she seems content, then resumes eating, her eyes turned to the window, the lawn yellowed by drought, the three anemic trees succumbing to the lack of water.

"We can't stay here like this. We have to make our minds up. The three of us in this room. And it's expensive, we can't keep spending money on crummy hotels. We'll start attracting attention."

Franck listens to her. She speaks slowly, looking him full in the face, her eyelashes fluttering with anxiety. She looks fresh, the skin under her eyes smooth, not the slightest wrinkle of exhaustion. Regenerated.

"What do you suggest?"

"You're not going to like it."

"Tell me anyway."

"We go to see the Gypsy, Serge. He's the only one who can help us. My father trusted him, and it was mutual. And he's always liked me . . ."

Franck can well imagine in what way the Gypsy likes Jessica. Despite himself, a shadow of doubt passes across his eyes, betraying his thoughts, and she leans across the table and plows the back of his hand with her nails.

"It's not what you think. You know, there are guys I haven't slept with."

She says this in a low voice, with tears in her eyes, then turns her head away and stares at the far end of the room. Rachel looks at them in turn, eyes wide open with curiosity or surprise, then almost imperceptibly shakes her head, apparently upset. Franck leans toward her.

"Are you all right, Rachel?"

She nods, staring out through the window.

Franck doesn't recognize the route he and the old man took. Even when they leave the beltway, he has the feeling that Jessica, who's driving in front, doesn't know where she's going anymore and that they're losing their way. Nor does he remember this area of forest and abandoned fields cut across by expressways and strewn with industrial parks where the western outskirts of the city break up. A plane passes some 300 yards away, descending over the trees, slow and heavy. Rachel, her face wedged between the two front seats, asks him what it's like to fly in a plane and he replies that he doesn't know, he's never done it.

When they enter the camp, three women who have been chatting under a tree watch them get out of their cars and don't move and don't take their eyes off them until Jessica approaches them and asks them if Serge is there. None of them answer. The youngest, with bleached yellow hair, a basket of washing under her arm, walks away toward the nearest house but stops when the Gypsy appears on the terrace, in the shade of the eaves. He doesn't move, hands in the pockets of his khaki pants.

Jessica walks in front, swinging her handbag at the end of her arm. Franck has taken Rachel by the hand and Rachel lets herself be dragged along, as if she doesn't want to follow. People, children especially, have come out into the doorways of the other two houses and the trailers to watch. Two men, who have been unloading lumber from a small flatbed truck, stop their work and light cigarettes, ready to watch. Serge nods to them and they lean back against the cabin of the truck and smoke unconcernedly.

He takes Jessica in his arms and embraces her for a long time, without a word, then turns to Franck and shakes his hand. "I didn't think you'd ever show your face here again."

"Neither did I, but—"

"That was before," Jessica cuts in. "Everything's changed."

"And who's she?"

"Rachel. My daughter. You know I—"

"Come in."

Jessica hesitates, glances at Franck, then turns back to the Gypsy. "He's with me, you know."

Serge's gold-flecked eyes come to rest on Franck and look him up and down. He spits on the ground then holds out his hand toward Jessica. "I said come in."

She turns to Franck. "It may be best if Rachel stays outside, given what I have to say to Serge."

She follows the Gypsy into the house. Rachel and Franck stand there on the terrace for a moment, then Rachel spots a rocking chair and sits down in it and rocks, watching two little girls playing under the canopy of one of the trailers. Franck sits down on a bench next to her.

"Are we going to the beach?"

"Yes, but not today. You heard your mother."

The two little girls stop playing and look at Rachel, then they say something to each other and burst out laughing. Rachel turns her eyes away and concentrates on a lizard that has climbed on the tiles and is now still, head raised.

"What was the matter with Grandpa and Grandma?"

She has asked her question without taking her eyes off the lizard. Franck feels his stomach sink as if from a punch.

"Why do you ask that?"

She doesn't reply. She stops rocking, stands up, and slowly approaches the lizard, which looks up at her.

"Is that its heart?"

"Whose heart?"

"The lizard's. You can see it beating on the sides. Look."

She points at the animal, but the lizard scurries away and stops a little farther on.

"I didn't see. Come and sit down."

She obeys, sitting down with a sigh. She plays with her fingers. Eyelids lowered, her long lashes shading her eyes, she makes Franck think of an embroiderer bent over her work.

"When are they coming back?"

"Who?"

"Grandpa and Grandma, of course."

"I don't know. Soon, probably."

She looks around the vast esplanade surrounded by five trailers and three houses. A woman in a yellow scarf passes, pushing a shopping cart full of empty plastic bottles that creaks and rattles over the stones.

Franck wishes Rachel could be quiet now. She's never talked so much in such a short space of time, and he has the impression his throat is getting tighter with each word she utters. He glances at the door through which Jessica and the Gypsy disappeared, wondering what they're telling each other, what they could possibly be doing in there. It seems to him they've been there for at least half an hour. He looks at the time on his cell phone—it's just after twelve. They got here twenty minutes ago. Turning his back on Rachel, he stands up, leans on a post, and lights a cigarette.

A car arrives and brakes abruptly, raising dust. A BMW, quite an old model, but looking as good as new. Two young men, barely twenty, get out and run to Serge's house and stop on the threshold.

"Hey, Serge! You have to come!"

From inside, the Gypsy asks what's going on.

"You have to come, the heat's on, for fuck's sake!"

"I'll be out later!"

"No! Now! We're in deep shit !"

"Stop breaking my balls! I said I'll be out later, so go home and have a drink!"

One of the young guys drags the other to their car, cursing through clenched teeth. They get in and drive slowly for about thirty yards and park in front of an immense mobile home.

"Maybe they're dead."

Rachel has said these words under her breath, as if to herself.

Franck shudders. He makes an effort not to turn around, he doesn't know if he should react, because he won't be able to pretend, because the little girl will guess if he's hiding anything or lying.

Jessica and Serge come out, talking in low voices, and unable to bear it any longer, Franck takes the opportunity to move away from Rachel and walk toward them.

"My cousin and I will go there this afternoon. I can't leave Roland and your mother like that. The dead don't forgive us for treating them badly. I'll put them where you told me, that way you'll be able to find them again. Okay, girl. Take care. I'll deal with the others afterwards. I need time to think."

He takes her in his arms and kisses her on the forehead. Then he turns to Franck and holds out his hand.

"Take good care of them. We're on the same side now."

His hand feels dry and hard in Franck's. A firm handshake. In his gold-flecked eyes, the glint of a smile, or of irony. Franck doesn't know what to say. He merely nods, his throat dry.

Rachel has come closer, and the Gypsy strokes her hair. "Never be scared, all right?"

"You're not scared, are you?" Jessica says.

Rachel looks down at her feet. "No," she says firmly. "I'm not scared of anything."

For an hour they drive through former marshland along the estuary of the Gironde, a few miles from the nuclear power plant, on straight, deserted roads lined with drainage ditches and hedges, occasionally passing a dirt road leading to a ruined shack or farmhouse. Franck follows Jessica in her abrupt stops and about-turns, and he can see perfectly well that they're in the middle of nowhere, that they've plunged into a featureless landscape where all directions merge and cancel each other out. They'll never get out of here, he's sure of it, never leave this quiet hell, this swampy desert. Every now and again, Rachel gestures to him through the rear windshield and he responds by pulling faces or waving his hand and making an attempt to smile. He ought to take her far from here, take her somewhere safe, but in the heat blowing through the lowered windows all the impossible solutions that he envisages scatter like the smoke from his cigarette.

Then Jessica turns abruptly onto a path beneath a small white sign with the words SAINT SARAH in clumsy lettering. She stops the car in front of an immense mobile home beneath three big acacias and hurries out of the car and opens the back door and asks Rachel to come out and see the new house. She turns to Franck, jumping up and down.

"Not bad, is it?"

He gets out of the car and joins her. He turns around, examining the surroundings. Buzzing of insects. Stench of stagnant water. The path continues in a wide curve, lined with thickets and bramble bushes. The mobile home is on a concrete slab, mounted on cinder blocks. In front of it, a vast terrace strewn with dry leaves. An electricity line descends from a wooden pole to a meter box.

"All mod cons. It's like being on vacation."

"Yeah, sure," Jessica says.

She takes some keys from her bag and goes to open. The door resists a little, then creaks on its hinges. Rachel doesn't move. She looks around her, frowning in the sun. Franck holds out his hand to her.

"Want to come and see?"

"Are there snakes?

"No. I don't think so. And if there are, I'll kill them all and we'll be fine."

Rachel walks toward the mobile home, careful where she

places her feet. Inside, Jessica has been opening the windows.
She comes to the door.

"It's really big! Come see your room, sweetheart."

Rachel goes and stands in the doorway of a small room taken
up almost entirely by a bed. The mattress is bare, pale blue, a
square of light resting on it.

"Well?"

"I'm thirsty."

Franck has remained in the doorway of the mobile home,
brought up short by the smell of mold and the oven-like heat.

The only water available is from a well some twenty yards
from the mobile home. Not for drinking and sometimes runs
red, the Gypsy warned them. Make sure you keep your mouth
closed when you take a shower. They have to prime the pump
and hope the filter isn't silted up. The liquid that comes out is
brown at first, then gradually turns clear. It looks almost drink-
able. But for cooking and drinking, it's better to fill up with water from the fire hydrant at the entrance to the village, near the
stadium. In a solidly-built shed, Franck finds three five-gallon
jerrycans and a wrench, then sets off on his errand. On his way
back, he buys three packs of bottled mineral water. While he
busies himself with these organizational tasks, he doesn't think
about anything else. He's streaming with sweat, dazed with migraine. In addition to the water, he buys a pack of cold beers
and drinks one on the way and for a few minutes, refreshed
by what he has drunk, he dares to believe that they still have a
chance.

Jessica has found some garden furniture, two deckchairs,
and a big parasol, which she has set up in the shade. She has
swept the leaves away. Franck hears her bustling about inside,
opening and closing closets, humming. Rachel is lying in one of
the deckchairs and he goes up to her and asks her if she wants
a drink. She opens her eyes, her forehead glistening, her cheeks
red. Her face contorts as if she's about to cry. Franck opens a
bottle of water and helps her to hold it and she drinks greedily

and it runs over her chin and down her neck, then when she's finished she takes a deep breath.

Once night has fallen, after they've eaten—the food warm and soft because the fridge hasn't had time to get it cold enough—they have to retreat into the mobile home to escape the clouds of mosquitoes plaguing them. All evening, Jessica plays housewife, making Franck think of a little girl using a life-sized toy for the first time. By the end of the meal, Rachel is dropping from exhaustion and falls asleep, moaning softly, on the mattress where Jessica has laid a kind of sheet found in a chest. Then they drink the beers, which have stayed cold, slapping their thighs and arms and necks to kill the mosquitoes that have come inside. Franck finally finds an insect spray at the back of a closet, and as the pungent, toxic smell spreads, Jessica tells him about her conversation with the Gypsy, who promised her on the graves of his dear departed that he would give her parents a burial and that he would then deal with the Serb's gang, making them pay for everything they've done. She says it's going to be all right, that soon everything will be the way it was before. Before what? Franck asks. She doesn't reply. Then after a long moment of silence, she adds that she couldn't have done it alone. Take their bodies and bury them, she means. She passes the cold can over her neck and the top of her chest then sits back in her chair and puts her feet up on the table, legs apart, and says she's hot, fuck, she wants to strip off completely. The fatigue and the migraine and the anxiety throbbing inside him like a background noise stop Franck from going and sticking his mouth to the triangle of light cotton he glimpses between her thighs.

They lie down, exhausted by the heat, naked on the rough cloth of the mattress. In the darkness, as sleep descends on him, Franck feels as if he's lying at the bottom of a well, bound hand and foot, crushed beneath his own weight.

15

During the night, Rachel woke them with a scream. She'd had a bad dream and they stayed with her for a while, waiting for her to get back to sleep. She was shivering, burning up. Franck cooled her down by placing a washcloth filled with ice cubes on her forehead. Jessica stroked her hand, her eyes closed, almost falling asleep.

"It's all right, it was just a nightmare. Come on, leave the light on for her, it'll be okay."

"Go back to bed. I'll stay for a while."

Rachel turned onto her side, with her back to her mother and her hands in front of her. She fell asleep almost immediately. Through the windows, Franck could see the gray dawn. Lying down, he half opened a window and the cool air came in and he let it rush over him.

Now, Rachel is drinking her bowl of hot chocolate on the edge of the terrace, facing the hedge that makes the edge of the area. She's watching the insects, following their crazy flight, occasionally looking up into the branches of the trees above her head.

Franck hears Jessica moving things about inside, slamming cupboard doors, noisily shifting flatware, muttering to herself angrily. She comes out onto the terrace and sits down, then pours herself a big cup of coffee and slams the coffee pot back down on the table. She says nothing at first, staring over the bushes, then asks Rachel if she's eaten and when the girl doesn't reply she screams:

"Fuck it, Rachel, I asked you a question, so answer me! Would it burn your fucking tongue to answer when you're spoken to?"

Rachel turns and stares at Jessica with that mixture of fear and compassion she displays increasingly often when she looks at her mother. They stare at each other for a few seconds then Rachel lowers her eyes and turns her back, muttering, "Yes, mom, I ate some melba toast with jam." Jessica sighs, lights a cigarette, and glares at her daughter's back.

"Yes, she ate," Franck says. "I was with her."

"Did I ask you? Can't I have a quiet conversation with my daughter without you butting in?"

Franck doesn't know what to say to that, so he says nothing, just looks at her and wonders what's stopping him from hitting her. Maybe the fact that Rachel is there. Or the fact that he's tired. Just as he suppresses the desire to throw himself at her, he sees again his mother's terrified face after she's been flung to the floor by a slap, her lip slit. Fear and surprise and an immense sadness all together on her contorted features, tears smudging her black eye make-up, blood running down her chin. Her husband, the love of her life, yelling, his hand raised. Franck remembers the sudden silence, Fabien rushing to his mother to help her up, his father straightening then slumping on a chair, his face in his hands, weeping.

He never again raised his hand to her. There were tears, apologies, hugs, loving words. But an invisible crack had started to work its way between them, against them. And the sadness never again left his mother's face, like a pale foundation that no smile could erase. Until months later, illness cleansed her skin, smoothed the rough edges of her forehead and cheekbones, turned her eyelids red. Her cheeks alternately freezing or burning. A desperate terror gradually coming to rest on her.

Later still, all barriers now down, he had reserved his fists for his sons. And for the walls, his head befuddled with booze.

"Why are you looking at me like that?"

Jessica's voice is almost gentle, surprised, as if she's seen the ghosts he's summoned.

He gets to his feet, a bitter taste in his throat. "No reason. I'm sorry."

Rachel looks up at him and smiles. As a result, the tears don't well up and he comes and sits down next to her. He gives her a little nudge with his shoulder, and she tightens her grip on her empty bowl and sighs, You're silly. Occasional gusts of wind bring vague smells of stagnant waters and decay, and Rachel holds her nose and waves her hand in front of her face like a little fan. They sit there like that for a moment, without saying anything. Jessica has gone to take a shower. In the far distance, a dog can be heard barking.

"Are there people here?"

"Yes, but a long way away. This place is deserted."

Rachel nods thoughtfully. Franck leans toward her and whispers in her ear: "What was your dream about last night?"

"What dream?"

"The dream that woke you up. When you were scared."

She doesn't reply. She examines the bottom of her bowl, turns it around in her hands.

"Don't you want to tell me?"

She shakes her head. "It was too scary. Like it was true."

She stands up and goes to clear the table, then does the dishes. Franck sees her through the window: diligent, methodical. Just then, Jessica comes out of the bathroom and runs a hasty hand through her daughter's hair. She is naked. Franck goes back inside the mobile home because he wants to look at her. She dresses in front of him, without taking her eyes off him.

"All right? Getting a good eyeful?"

Rachel turns toward them. A cup rolls and clatters at the bottom of the sink.

"Be careful, or else let me do it," Jessica says.

She grabs her cell phone and goes out and walks away in the sun. Franck watches her move her arms, shrug her shoulders, shake her head as she speaks, then hang up testily. She immediately calls another number, and seems to calm down. She turns toward the mobile home, looks at the time on the screen of her phone, then nods at what she's being told. After hanging up, she seems more relaxed, as if reassured, and the features of her face have regained a little softness. Rachel comes out of the mobile home with her games console, and Jessica takes her in her arms and hugs her and kisses her noisily on the cheeks and forehead and hair, as if seeing her again after a long absence.

He has to stock up on provisions. They agree on a list of essentials so as not to have to venture out every other day. They write it down on a piece of paper, with Jessica drumming constantly on the table, irritated by the time wasted in writing all that. Sighing and breathing hard because Franck isn't writing quickly enough.

"Shit, are you going to draw little flowers as well?"

When he stands up, he brushes against her arm in reaching for the pen and she gives a start as if he's touched her with an electric prod. Before he goes, he apologizes, leaving her listless, head down, an extinguished cigarette between her fingers.

He drives for half an hour before finding a supermarket far enough away, eyes glued to the rear-view mirror, the gun under a big plastic bag. He knows perfectly well that the others will never find them here. They haven't followed them, they can't possibly know the Gypsy's directions. All the same, he expects to see the 4×4 he passed one day at the old people's place appear behind him and not let him go.

You don't always believe in what you know. What he's certain of is that they're trapped. They've reached the end of the road, they're standing on the edge of a precipice. What he knows is that he'll have to jump off. In ten days, in three months, he'll fall. Even the big shots get caught, for all their hideouts, their networks, the money they distribute. And he doesn't have any of that, he left prison and landed in a nest of vipers fighting with rattlesnakes.

He goes over all this in his head as he crosses the overheated asphalt of the parking lot, his cart in front of him, and he tells himself he could easily attack a check-out girl and get himself caught red-handed. Instead, he lets himself be enveloped in the air conditioning and strolls past empty stores where assistants stand behind cash registers, looking bored, or busy themselves placing hangers on clothes rails. He wanders for a moment as if in a strange land, passing dark figures briefly silhouetted against the harsh lights of the shop windows and then immediately erased despite their slow pace, while the plastic mannequins look on icily. He has the impression he's come from another world, a parallel or underground world, and has to get back there as soon as possible, to take shelter or to lose himself.

He fills his cart with packs and cans, adds some ice cream for Rachel, and hands his cash over to a pretty, smiling blonde, feeling her cool fingertips in his palm as she gives him his change. To get out, he walks along the check-outs and passes a security officer, a huge guy with an earpiece, and feels his eyes follow him, and when he arrives outside, blinded by the sun, he fully expects two guys to grab him but sees only three employees near a service door, smoking.

On the way back, he loses his way amid the vines, glimpses the dull, brown estuary, the muddy arms of the ocean, as he turns a bend, and finally gets back onto the isolated road that leads to their refuge. When he gets out of the car, he's struck by the silence and he knows immediately that they aren't there. The windows of Jessica's car are down, the door of the mobile home is wide open. He calls out just in case, listens, then resolves to carry the provisions inside and puts them away any old how in a closet and in the fridge. On the table, three cigarette butts in an ashtray, beside a pack of cigarettes and Jessica's little green lighter. Everything is tidy. The dishes Rachel has washed are drying on the drain board by the sink.

He goes out, listens again to the silence. No birds singing. Not even a breath of air in the foliage above him. Just the buzzing of insects in the hot air. Then on his right, in the distance, Rachel's screams, followed by weeping. He runs and gets his pistol from the car and hurries along the path between the hedges. He steps over ruts with mud at the bottom. The tracks disappear from time to time beneath grassy clods and patches of bramble. The weeping has stopped. He stops and hears a dull moaning. He starts running again and comes out to a pond lined with dry reeds and little acacias. He sees Rachel and her mother on the other side, very close to the water. He doesn't understand what they're doing. Jessica has her back to him, a thin stick in her hand, and Rachel is standing stiffly by the pond, arms glued to her body. He asks them if everything is okay and Jessica turns abruptly and throws her stick in the water. He stuffs the barrel of his gun in his jeans pocket so as not to scare Rachel and walks toward them along an indistinct path that seems to run all the way around the pond.

"What happened? I heard Rachel yelling and crying."

Rachel turns and looks at her mother resentfully, her cheeks still wet with tears.

"Nothing happened. Little Miss here started screaming for no reason, she thought she saw a snake, she scared me half to death! I lost my temper, and there you are! Then she's surprised and starts crying."

"You slapped her?"

"Yes, why? Do you want me to slap you, too?"

"I'd like to see you try."

He advances toward her. She would have to make a move to slap him for him to have a good reason to hurt her. In his arms, he feels that desire to hit her. Rachel still doesn't move, then turns to the pond, which is nothing now but a mirror filled with blue sky.

At that moment, he sees red streaks on Rachel's calves and he goes to her and crouches.

"Did you hit her with the stick you were holding? Are you crazy or what?"

Jessica walks away along the path then turns. "Hey, you don't know. You piss me off with your fucking cop questions.

She scratched herself on the brambles. I don't know if you've noticed, but there are lots of them here."

She sets off resolutely and soon, on the other side of the pond, her dark reflection moving across the water is like that of a witch or a drowned woman.

Franck asks Rachel if she's all right but she doesn't reply, and when he takes her hand she refuses to let him keep it in his and strides ahead of him.

They feed on a can of ravioli and a few tomatoes. Jessica barely touches her food, she's silent and withdrawn. She watches Rachel, who's eating slowly, with a kind of application, and two or three times Franck meets her gaze and she turns away immediately. After a while, she stands, takes her chair with her, and settles at the end of the terrace to smoke.

The heat of the afternoon seeks them out and they take refuge against the wall of the mobile home, where the sun pierces the shade and casts medallions of shifting light on them. They doze. Jessica moans in her sleep, curled up on a mattress thrown on the floor. Rachel is slumped in her deckchair, eyes open, staring at the foliage above her. Franck doesn't know if she's asleep or sunk into a kind of panicked inertia. When he asks her in a low voice if she's thirsty, she doesn't react, just flutters her eyelashes weakly.

Time stops passing, as still as the burning air, as the stagnant water filling the ditches and ponds around them. Life has run out of gas. Their bodies nailed down by tiredness.

A sharp, regular noise wakes them. Jessica reaches out her hand to her phone and picks up. She listens and mutters at first, then sits up.

"What did you say?"

She glances over at Franck, shielding her forehead with her hand.

"How did you manage?"

She listens some more, silent, slowly nodding, then thanks the Gypsy profusely. The dead will be quiet there under the trees. She'll be able to visit them when all this is over. How can she ever thank him enough? She'll pay him back, for sure. She also thanks the cousins who played undertaker and did the digging. She moves the phone away from her mouth and can't stop saying thank you and see you soon because she won't forget what he's done, then hangs up and puts the phone down beside her with a sigh of relief. She stands up and shakes her T-shirt around her to dry the sweat, then wipes her armpits and breasts through the cloth. She goes into the mobile home to get her cigarettes and sits down in the doorway and smokes, without saying anything at first, then starts talking under her breath, as if to herself.

"Good, it's done. They put them under a big oak tree my father loved, on the edge of the woods. Every fall he used to pick mushrooms there. Shit . . . When I think about it . . ."

"What about the dog?"

"What about him?"

"What did they do with the dog?"

"I'm talking to you about my parents and you think about the dog? What the fuck do I care? They threw him in the woods, as far as I know."

"Fucking dog."

Franck thinks about the old woman, how she will rot beside her husband, and he wonders if her skull will be any uglier than her face when she was alive.

Jessica gets up and throws her cigarette butt away. In front of her, in her deckchair, Rachel has closed her eyes. She stands looking at her daughter with a pout, but doesn't go to her. She shrugs. "Right. I have to go."

"Go where?" Franck asks.

She doesn't reply and goes back inside and starts rummaging in a closet and slamming doors and turning faucets on and off, humming the theme song from *Titanic* in a thin, high-pitched voice as she does so. When she comes back out, she's dressed the way she was on the first day, when she came to pick him up from prison. Shorts cut from jeans, a man's sky-blue shirt. She carries her usual bag on her shoulder, that black linen saddle-bag adorned with big mauve and red flowers. No make-up. Just her tanned skin, the pale immensity of her eyes. She hesitates for a moment by Rachel, her car keys in her hand, then walks away.

Franck watches her. The sun is still blazing, even though it's already low.

"Where are you going?"

She opens the car door, throws her bag on the passenger seat, and sighs. "If anyone asks you—"

"Don't you think it's risky? You might run into them."

She stares at him in surprise, as if she doesn't understand. "No, I won't. And besides, I can't stay here anymore, in this rat hole. I can't stand it! I have to take something or I'll go crazy. I have to see a friend who has just what I need."

"Don't get back too late. Rachel will be worried."

Jessica glances at her daughter then smiles ironically. "Worried, her? You don't know her. And don't start giving me advice, you're not my husband. I'll get back when I want to. Just don't wait for me to have dinner."

She gets into the car and slams the door and drives off immediately. She reverses toward the road and turns onto it without taking any care. The engine races and the tires skid, raising a little dust. Silence falls again abruptly, as if the car has been sucked into another dimension. When Franck turns, he almost knocks into Rachel who has been standing behind him.

"All right, sweetheart?"

She stares in the direction her mother has vanished and doesn't reply.

"Shall we play a game?"

She shakes her head then goes inside. He hears her open the fridge. She comes back out holding two ice-cream bars.

"Here," she says.

They eat their ices, standing facing the hedge that limits their field of vision, the foliage quivering in the slight breeze. Toward the west, the sky is growing heavier, milkier. Cooler breaths mix with the hot air.

"There's going to be a storm. Are you scared of storms?"

"No. Lightning is pretty. Thunder's a bit scary but it's nothing."

"So we'll make sure we're nice and safe when we look at it."

She looks up at him, blinking. She doesn't smile, but turns her soft, calm face toward him.

"What's the matter?"

She doesn't reply and goes back to her deckchair and picks up her rag doll. "I have to tell Lola. It's a secret."

She walks away, dragging a plastic chair behind her, clutching the doll to her chest. She sits down at the foot of a tree, settles Lola on her lap, facing her, and starts whispering then breaking off and assuming an attentive air, as if listening to the doll's answer. Franck finds himself taking advantage of this peaceful moment. The air is getting cooler, the sun dissolves into the gray mass rising above them. Life could be like this, a succession of silent moments in which the only thing to be heard is the whispering of a child.

A bird call drags him from his daydream and he falls back into the bitter anxiety of the impasse he's in, and he again starts listening out to the murmur of the wind, the distant sound of an engine, maybe of a tractor, the barking of a dog, and he realizes that the bubble that was around them has just been burst by these tiny vibrations, dispelled like an illusion. He takes a few steps across the grass, goes to the car, and opens a door to let out the whiff of confined air, the smell of stale tobacco and plastic. He should leave and drive far from here and stop in a place where an old couple will welcome them and offer them a safe haven without asking any questions. He read a story like that in a book when he was in prison, a woman pursued by men whose brother she's killed, sheltered for a few days by an old woman who doesn't ask her anything but has guessed everything and lets her regain her strength then leave again. He also recalls her encounter with a trapper in the wild harmony of the mountains. He tells himself that if you can imagine it in stories, it's because it can happen in real life and he tries to think about that, about how true novels are even though they're made up, but he gives up because everything gets mixed up in his mind and already the sky toward the south is rumbling and thickening and now seems to come down on them like a tarp.

After eating, they watch darkness fall and the lightning in the distance flash behind the clouds and rumble in the dark. Franck sees the time go by on his watch. It's already more than three hours since Jessica left. During the meal, Rachel asks suddenly if her mother will be back soon and since Franck doesn't know what to say to her, she pushes her plate away.

"Grandma often scolds her and sometimes they even fight."

"What do you mean, they fight?"

"They slap each other and sometimes I hear them shout at each other and make noise in the kitchen."

"Does that happen often?"

"When she comes back late and doesn't sleep in the house."

She jumps a little at a close thunderclap, then puts her hand on Franck's arm.

"Where are Grandpa and Grandma?"

There are two simultaneous flashes of lightning, and the wall of the mobile home shakes behind them. Rachel squeezes Franck's wrist.

"Let's go back inside, it's getting nasty."

Franck takes a torch from a chest and checks that it's working.

"I'm turning out the light. Don't be scared. We have the torch."

They sit down on the bench seats on either side of a square table, the torch between them. Franck pulls back the curtains so that Rachel can see the storm.

For almost an hour the sky wages war on them. Franck

250 - HERVÉ LE CORRE

occasionally has the impression that a flash of lightning will split their fragile refuge in two in one blinding chopper stroke. At times, Rachel switches on the torch to check the ceiling and the corners, then turns it off again with a sigh.

"Are you looking for something?"

He almost has to scream to cover the hammering of the rain on the roof. Rachel shakes her head. Then, as the storm seems to finally be moving away, while the wind and the rain are still battling outside, she leans toward Franck.

"Where are Grandpa and Grandma?"

Franck smiles and takes the torch and lights it and aims it at her, and she struggles against the beam of light.

"Was it them you were looking for with the torch?"

She sighs, her lips quivering, and looks at him in disappointment. "Don't be silly!"

"They've gone away for a few days. Didn't they tell you before they left?"

Rachel lights the torch again and sticks it under her chin. Lit like this, her eyes wide open, she looks like a little ghost.

"You're scary like that."

She laughs and makes a face. Then there's a muffled sound mixed with that of the rain and the wind. A car passing on the road. The hiss of tires on the wet surface. It may be Jessica coming back, drunk or high, but he doesn't believe that, he's stopped believing it, he knows that right now she's lying on a couch or a bed somewhere, stupefied, with some guy between her legs, presumably taking his payment in kind.

"Switch it off!"

She obeys. She listens out, too, barely breathing. With the lightning gone, it's darker now and he senses more than he can see. He senses her eyes resting on him, clinging to him. The lapping of the rain. The storm rumbling in the distance.

"Don't move."

Franck grabs the gun from the high closet he put it away in after getting back from the pond, then opens the door. Outside, the coolness, the cold rain make him shiver. He takes a few steps and realizes that in this total darkness he can't even see his feet. A long way away, the lights of the village cast a pointless orange haze into the sky. Dead light. He goes back inside and in the dark, he doesn't see Rachel at first and he calls to her in a strangled voice. She replies by lighting the torch against her hand. She's sitting under the table, her doll next to her, her little bag over her shoulder.

Franck doesn't know what to do to keep her safe. He crouches next to her and asks her if she's all right. She nods and gives him the torch. He looks for something to protect her better from what is going to happen, he ought to take off a cupboard door, he gets back on his feet, opens the pantry next to the fridge, pulls on the door and manages to loosen one hinge but not the other, and just then he glimpses the flash of a torch at the entrance to the area, just enough to guide the steps of whoever is holding it. He opens a window in the back of the mobile home and slips outside, falls awkwardly over a cinder block and twists his ankle and hobbles the first two steps toward the corner of the mobile home and there he hears slow footsteps on the entrance path, then on the grass, maybe about thirty feet away. He can't see anything, and he keeps his gun flat against his thigh, stiffening his arm to control the shaking.

For a few seconds nothing happens. He can no longer hear the man walking, he assumes that he, too, is on the alert, and abruptly the cloud cover is lit up by a flash of lightning and Franck makes out the figure standing with a shotgun in his hand and he fires by guesswork into the darkness and the man lets out a cry and falls. When Franck lights his torch, he sees him lying on his back, arms outstretched, one hand still holding the shotgun, and he rushes to him and grabs the shotgun and throws it onto the terrace. The man is wounded in the chest, on the right-hand side. He doesn't move, his eyes wide open, panting, in a state of shock. Blood soaks his T-shirt under his sleeveless vest, which is full of pockets. In one that's buttoned up, there are five cartridges. In another, a switchblade knife. Franck throws it all away. The man has a square face, with close-cropped jet-black hair and light-colored eyes. He's young. Franck doesn't know where he's seen him before, but he's sure he has. As he slowly moves one arm, searching perhaps for something to grip, Franck smashes his nose with the grip of the pistol, using it like a hammer. The guy moans and shudders and looks around him in panic as if wondering where he is. Franck now remembers the two young guys who came looking for the Gypsy yesterday.

"Was it Serge who sent you? He's the only one who knows where we are. Why?"

The man turns his head left and right, eyes rolled halfway up, lips bared over bloodstained teeth. He moans, trying perhaps to talk, blinking in the rain that's falling on him.

When the headlights emerge from between the gate posts, they strike Franck as if the car has knocked into him and he falls to a sitting position, letting go of the gun. In the time it takes him to get back on his feet, he hears the car going into reverse and sees the sidelights move away and the engine revving up, the gearbox creaking with each change of gear. He runs along the road and sees the lights disappear and he stands there for a moment, expecting to see the car come back, but there's nothing now but the rain, the cloud cover turned white at times by drowned flashes of lightning on this night of water.

He walks back toward the mobile home. By the light of the torch, he sees the man still lying there, slowly moving his legs, one knee bent. He turns his head toward Franck and watches him with terror as he approaches. When he moves, his face contorts with pain.

"Why did you come? It was Serge, wasn't it? He's cleaning up after that crazy woman, is that it?"

The man closes his eyes and sighs, then coughs, blood on his lips. He opens his eyes again and manages to lift his head. "I don't know and I don't give a fuck! You're dead, whatever happens."

He talks as if his mouth is full, as if he's about to throw up.

Franck points his gun at him, he sees the half-closed eyes behind the bead, in the weakening light of the torch, and he doesn't know if they express contempt or exhaustion. It would be so easy to wipe out all expression from that face and no longer wonder about what this guy and his associates are thinking and planning. Pull the trigger and wipe out everything with one gunshot. But his hand is shaking too much. He aims a kick at the man's leg, which is also shaking, then slips the gun into his pocket and walks away. He picks up the shotgun, which is long and heavy, and finds the cartridges that he threw away earlier. Going back inside, he switches on the light and looks around for Rachel and finds her still huddled under the table.

"We have to go, darling. Do you know where your things are?"

She stands up and goes into the bedroom and he hears her opening a closet. He recovers his bag, the two or three items of clothing he's taken out of it, his dirty linen, thinking to leave as few traces as possible. He knows it's no use, but he tells himself it will complicate the work of the cops for at least half an hour. Rachel is ready before him. She's waiting for him at the door, a sports bag at her feet.

"Did you get everything? Wait for me. Don't go out."

He hoists his gear over his shoulder and pulls Rachel toward the car and throws bags, shotgun, and cartridges in the trunk. Rachel peers into the darkness, where the wounded man is still moaning. When Franck makes her get in the back, she resists a little then settles. He maneuvers the car to get out. In passing, the headlights illuminate the body then return it to the darkness.

"Is he hurt?"

"Of course he's hurt. He wanted to hurt us. So I stopped him."

In the rear-view mirror, he sees Rachel kneeling on the seat, turned toward the rear windshield, trying to see something.

It takes him almost twenty minutes to get back onto the A63 highway and once on it, at least for a few miles, he has the feeling he's left his troubles behind him.

Rachel is standing between the seats. She puts her hand on his shoulder, and when she does that, tears rise to his eyes. He doesn't know what to do next, it's as if a bird has taken refuge with him. He turns a little and sees her eyes, wide with curiosity, staring beyond the windshield.

"Where do we go now?"

"I don't know yet. I'll tell you. We have to sleep."

She doesn't move. Then after a few minutes' silence, she asks him if he wants her to sing him a sad song.

16

Rachel has finally lain down and fallen asleep. He drives in the darkness of the highway, the world around him reduced to the trajectories of light that he passes or overtakes, and he feels powerful and desperate, like the last man on earth. He grabs his cell phone and has to make two attempts to dial the number. Listening to the ringing, he takes a deep breath and tries to calm the pounding of his heart. At this hour, he tells himself, his father won't hear or won't answer, then when the voice echoes against his ear, so close, so clear, he gets a lump in his throat.

"Franck, are you all right?"

He has rushed to the phone. He knew it was his son. Anxiety quivers between the words.

"Yes, I'm all right. Can I come?"

"Of course you can come. When?"

"I'm on my way. I'll soon be on the highway to Pau."

"Do you know where it is?"

"I have a vague idea. In the Ossau Valley, that's all I know. After Laruns, before Artouste."

His father explains. Repeats the names of places, the changes of direction. Franck hears again that calm, slightly husky voice. The precise diction. He remembers doing homework, his father trying to explain to them things he himself was making an effort to understand. Sitting at the table, side by side. Their mother would come in from time to time and tell them to come and eat, their minds would be clearer afterwards. We're getting there, we've nearly finished. Franck can hear it all: the voices, the sighs of impatience, the TV chattering away in the next room.

His old life, a ghost he's taken on board, sitting and whispering in the seat next to him.

"If you get lost, call again. Obviously, at night . . ."

"Don't worry."

His father gives a nervous little laugh. "You know perfectly well I never worry about the two of you."

A pang of emotion. *The two of you.* Franck had to take a deep breath in order to continue speaking. "I'll tell you everything."

"Be careful using your phone on the road. Hang up now."

Franck's eyes are filled with tears. He wipes them away with the back of his hand and sniffs. In the back seat, Rachel shifts and moans in her sleep. He is soon alone on the highway, and time starts slowing down and the body of the car shudders whenever he tries to go faster. He tries to imagine his arrival, the first looks, the gestures he and his father will make, and all he can summon up is a scene so distressing that at times he wonders if he shouldn't turn back.

Soon, in the coolness of the air, along walls that tower over him and shadowy masses of trees looming up in the headlights at the entrances to bends, he knows that the mountains are there all around in their vast tranquility, and he starts to think that everything might still work out. Rachel wakes up and asks where they are and leans on the back of his seat. He tells her they're in the mountains, they'll be there soon. She presses her face to the window.

"I can't see anything."

"It's still night. Tomorrow, you'll see how beautiful it is."

"Have you been here before?"

"No."

Silence. She looks at him with her serious air, frowning. He can't see her but he knows she's making a major effort to believe him.

Suddenly, it's there. He's sure of it. A house with all its windows lit up, a small lantern above a door. A man appearing in the doorway, coming forward, standing firmly on his legs, hands in pockets, very upright.

"Who's that?"

"My father."

After that, Franck's breath fails him. He gets out of the car and lets Rachel out, composing himself before he turns. He walks the thirty feet separating him from his father. He's like a drunk, each stone he treads on is like a loose cobble that might make him stumble.

At last he raises his eyes toward that impassive face, those lips half open in a kind of surprise or the hint of a smile. He hasn't aged. The weariness has gone, the bitter lines. They embrace, somewhat stiffly. Franck feels the strong fingers, the thick hand, press on his shoulder.

"And who's this?"

"This is Rachel."

Franck signals to Rachel to come closer and she takes small steps toward them, blinking in the light from the lantern under the canopy. She comes to a halt in front of them, head bowed.

"We can do the introductions later," his father says. "Come inside, it's cold here at night."

Franck looks up at the sky. Despite the lantern and its yellow light, he can make out armfuls of stars above him, ready to fall if you put your hand on them. His throat is still knotted, caught in a net of conflicting emotions.

The smell of a wood fire. The lamp hanging above the table in the kitchen dispenses a golden cone of light. His father hands Rachel a chair on which she climbs in order to lean on the oilcloth.

"My name's Armand. Are you hungry?"

She shakes her head.

"I have milk, if you'd like some."

She accepts. He takes a large glass jug from the fridge, grabs a bowl, and fills it.

"It's good, you'll see. Tomorrow, I'll introduce you to the cow."

Rachel looks up at him, without understanding, still frowning, apparently angry, then she dips her lips and drinks the milk with long gulps.

Armand asks Franck if he'd like anything. A coffee. Something to eat. A piece of cheese.

"I could use a beer."

His father smiles. He takes a glass and goes to fill it from the faucet.

"I quit four years ago, when I decided to buy this place. I looked around the house, and then I sat down on the stone bench outside and looked at the mountains and started bawling. I knew I'd end up here, but walking straight. Not staggering. Not like a drunk. I lost all my fights, all the people I loved, but this is one thing I hold on to. And every morning when I go outside I have that same desire to bawl my eyes out. Not just because it's gorgeous around here. Anyway, you'll see for yourself tomorrow. It's worth a look."

Franck drinks the water in one go, his teeth icy. He would like to say something, but as so often, the words don't come so he watches Rachel finish her milk, her little face almost entirely in the bowl. His father also watches the child and they share that mutual contemplation, aware that it's doing both of them a great deal of good.

When Rachel puts down her bowl, Franck asks her if it was good, and she says yes in a low voice and puts her head on her arm and closes her eyes.

"She needs to sleep," Frank's father says. "Come with me, I'll show you the way."

They climb a wooden staircase that creaks a little and come to a corridor lit by a naked red light bulb, with beams on the ceiling. Armand opens a door and switches on the light of a small room that smells of mothballs and furniture polish. A huge wardrobe, a single bed, a night table with a bedside lamp on it.

"Sometimes in summer, I rent this room and the one next door to some Spaniards. This is where their little boy sleeps."

He opens the door to another room, a larger one.

"And this is yours. There's a little bathroom at the end, there, the blue door. If you want a shower, it's downstairs."

Franck carries Rachel to the room and puts her down on the bed. He explains to her that he's just next door and that he'll leave the door open. She says yes in her sleep then turns her back on him.

Downstairs, his father is standing in the doorway, looking out at the night, smoking a cigarette.

"If you want one, the pack's on the sideboard."

Franck joins him. They smoke for a while without saying anything, the Milky Way clearly visible above them.

"So, are you going to tell me?"

"Now?"

"Tomorrow will be too late. You won't be able to tell me anymore, and I won't be able to listen to you." With a broad gesture of his arm, his father indicates the extraordinary clarity of the night. "There's nobody watching, nobody to see us cry."

"Why do you say that?"

"Because that's also what we're here for. We have just the light we need."

He raises his finger toward the sky and Franck suddenly sees the multitude of stars strewn across the darkness like a protective veil. He doesn't know where to begin. He lights another cigarette, just to gain a few seconds.

"Do you really not have anything to drink?"

His father sighs, stands up, goes back to the kitchen, and opens a cupboard. The clink of glass. He puts a bottle and a glass down in front of Franck.

"Spanish cognac. My lodgers left it for me two years ago. Don't ask me if it's any good. I mean, Spanish cognac sounds quite suspicious, and I don't drink that kind of thing anymore anyway."

He goes and sits down on a granite bench below the window and Franck follows him with his bottle and his glass. The first swig of alcohol burns his esophagus and warms his face like a wood fire. His father is standing against the wall, waiting, staring into the darkness, perhaps at the slope that can be made out behind the barn.

So Franck talks. He starts with the death of Fabien and as he speaks he can still hear the voice of the guy on the telephone, that voice of steel, and his own words fade and get lost in the confusion of that memory and he hears himself through that glass wall and he sees his father lift his hand to his mouth and press on it as if to stop anything at all from coming out, as if not to wail with grief or give vent to his rage, then raise his dry eyes to the sky and blink as if looking for tears that won't come. He stays like that, gazing at the great vault of stars. Franck falls silent and looks at him and shivers because a sprightly little wind takes advantage of the darkness to gallop across the meadows. In that profound silence, nothing can be heard but his father's labored breathing, which gradually calms down.

Armand swallows his sobs and hits his cheeks with the flat of his hand. He rises to his full height and lights a cigarette. "So that's what you came to tell me?"

"You didn't want me to wait before I told you. I can shut up now and leave again tomorrow."

His father places his hand on his arm. "No, not that, especially not that. I lost two sons, I've got one back, and I'm keeping him."

He falls silent again, sighs and coughs. A moan escapes his strangled throat.

"Will we ever be able to recover his body and give him a proper funeral?"

"I don't know. I don't think so."

"What did they do with it, do you think? Did they throw it somewhere, on a garbage dump, or put him in concrete? Or did they—?"

"Stop it. You're just twisting the knife. It doesn't do any good."

His father looks again at the sky. Franck sees his wet cheeks, the weak gleam of the tears in his eyes.

"To think there are some people who believe in God . . . The fools."

Franck also looks up and can read nothing in the deep chaos that glitters up there. He's never asked himself that kind of question. In prison, there were all those idiots who called on their gods, the way you curse when you burn yourself or catch your finger in a door, but they were just bastards who were looking for a good reason to be even bigger bastards after absolving each other with a few magic formulas.

"And where does this girl come from? From the family you talked about?"

Franck tells him about the old man and the old woman, people who had bought that old farm ten years earlier with money that must have seemed like manna from heaven. The old man disguising cars and refurbishing old engines for gypsies or lovers of old jalopies, the hostile old woman, as coarse as emery cloth. And then there was Jessica. He wanted her as soon as he set eyes on her. It wasn't just because of prison, the almost five years without anything apart from jerking off and porn fantasies, the obsessive desire for holes and orifices to be filled savagely. No. Franck doesn't know how to explain it. A trap you rush toward knowing in advance that it's a trap. Or a delicious poison that works its effects slowly and hooks you like a drug. A toxic flower. A sweet beast capable of tearing you to pieces at any moment. And in the middle, that almost mute little girl who played alone and almost never cried even when she was really sad. Even since the bloodbath. She says nothing, she's content to be sad and to watch you on the sly or look at you in that dreamy way, and you feel weighed and judged by those big black eyes that are always disappointed by the stupidity and wickedness of grown-ups. You have the impression that even though she's only eight she knows a lot more than you do about a lot of things.

"Anyway, her mother left for Bordeaux yesterday to look for drugs and I had a pretty good idea she wouldn't be back that night, and this Gypsy sent his guys after us last night, and here we are. From the start, I was conned. They played me. I left traces everywhere they wanted me to leave them, and I'm going to be made to take the blame for everything."

They fall silent. His father is breathing through his nose, loudly, perhaps angrily.

"What are you planning to do?"

"What do you mean?"

Armand turns toward him abruptly, head pulled down between his shoulders. "Here and now, in the next few hours, if you want me to be precise. The little girl you've been lumbered with, her mother who's going to show up eventually, maybe with gangsters on her trail, and the mess you've gotten yourself in. What are you going to do?"

"No idea. I keep thinking about it. Maybe go to the cops and tell them everything."

"And do another ten or fifteen years inside, is that it?"

"Can you see any other solution? Maybe that's where I belong. Maybe it's all I'm good for, maybe I can't do any better. You used to tell us that sometimes. And you'd tell me to stop always following in my brother's footsteps. And you were right. Look where it's gotten me."

"I said and did a whole lot of stupid things. I said that to your brother and you whenever—"

"Stop," Frank says.

His father stands up, rubbing the small of his back. "Whenever I was plastered, whenever I couldn't stand on my feet, whenever I didn't know what to say to people anymore. Whenever I beat you boys and your mother, without knowing why, until I got tired or . . ."

He breaks off, out of breath.

"All the harm I did you . . . And I couldn't help it. I had to drink to divert my anger and avoid going and killing someone, that fucking Dutch CEO who kicked us out from one day to the next even though the business was doing well, do you remember? You were little and your mother would bring you to the factory when we were occupying it, you would play soccer with the other kids. We found out his whereabouts and I swear to you that there were three or four of us who thought seriously about it for six months. We knew how to get hold of guns, we were ready, really, we didn't care. And then Ahmed blew his brains out when his wife left him and that knocked us for six and we went our separate ways and I went downhill but so did my friends, in another way. I had to drink myself senseless or I would have done it all by myself, or else I would have murdered some random rich person outside a luxury hotel, I don't know . . . You can't imagine. There were days when I wanted to destroy the world."

Silence. He stands facing east, his hands in his pockets, and sees the pallor against which the peaks stand out.

"Look," he says. "I may not have late nights, but I do have early mornings. All to myself."

Franck also gets to his feet and comes close to his father and they stand there side by side gazing at the power revealed beyond a horizon as black and jagged as a smashed jaw.

"I wish she was here," Armand whispers.

Franck wants to say yes, but the word sticks in his throat. He takes his father by the arm and holds him close.

"All the things we've lost," Armand says. "My God, all the things we've lost . . . And every morning there's that—that light that comes and chases away the nightmares and the ghosts. I read a book about that kind of thing a while back. Dawn as a kind of second chance granted to us every day. I don't really believe it, I mean in second fucking changes, but I try to take advantage of the moment. Your mother used to love that. The stars, the sky, the sunrise. I used to make fun of her when we were young and she'd say 'You'll get there! I'll teach you, you'll see.'"

He falls silent again, his eyes lowered. Franck feels him shivering and asks him if he's all right. His father replies with a movement of the chin and raises his head to face the coming day, and breathes out two or three times to expel the sadness stifling him.

Franck takes a few steps to calm the memories streaming in, the mixture of images and voices and faces, the whole theater of shadows. His father puts a hand on his shoulder, making him jump.

"I'll make coffee."

"Do you want me to help you?"

His father laughs. "To make coffee? No. Stay here and make the most of it."

Franck wonders how long he would hold out, on the run, under the cover of trees, in the depths of ravines, under promontories or in caves, forced to improvise his own rules of survival, hearing helicopters pass over his head, dogs barking. Images from an action movie come back to him, in which a highly trained ex-soldier, equipped only with a knife, holds off hundreds of pursuers, and he estimates the duration of his run at a day or two, just long enough to wander a little farther into the impasse he's already in and catch pneumonia when the night gets too cold.

His father comes back with the Italian coffee maker and two cups, and they drink their coffee facing the paling sky, the sun still a long way from coming up over the ridges.

"What do you advise me to do?"

"To think it over until this evening. To look at the beauty of things a little bit, because I don't think you've taken much time to do that in all these years. Maybe you'll realize what there is to be gained and lost in what you decide to do. There's just one obligation: to stay alive. You're 26 years old. You still have a lot of time in front of you. I beg you, son—stay alive."

He looks up, turned toward the forest, which is just emerging from shadow.

"It'll be nice to get a little sleep."

Franck looks up at the transparent sky, in which there's nothing more to be seen but a few casual patches of mist. They go back inside, surrendering temporary victory to the daylight. Upstairs, Rachel is sleeping on her back with her arms outspread. The sheet and blanket have fallen to the floor. Franck covers her carefully and she turns her head and half opens her eyes. He's afraid he's woken her but she smiles and her lips form a pout and then she sighs and turns over onto her side.

17

He is woken by Rachel chattering outside, and he sees the sun filtering in through the edges of the shutter and checks what time it is. He has only slept about two hours but he feels rested and calm, perhaps because in coming here he did what he was supposed to do.

Downstairs, the kitchen is full of light, and through the wide-open door he glimpses the dazzling sight of the pale-blue sky resting on the spine of the mountains. He sits down on the bench, and puts his elbows on the oilcloth. The morning echoes in the room, more peaceful than silence. Rachel is playing and chatting in a low voice. He pours himself coffee and butters a slice of bread and puts jam on it and bites into it with gusto, without any restraint or second thought. He can hear his father in the bathroom, the water running, the pipes groaning at times. A fly enters noisily, knocks against the walls, goes out again. Franck leans back against the wall with a sigh of content- ment. He captures these moments and holds them the way we squeeze a little sand in our fists. He knows that when he opens his hands they will be empty.

He goes outside and walks over to Rachel. She's playing with a young cat that jumps and rolls to catch a cork tied to a piece of string. She looks up at Franck and blinks and whis- pers a good morning lit by a smile. The cat flattens itself on the ground, ready to leap, and she lets out a little cry when it takes the cork and plays with it, lying on its back. Franck sits down on the bench where they were last night and closes his eyes on this fragile instant.

His father appears and tells them that he's adopted the cat, which has been roaming the vicinity for two weeks, depositing mangled field mice in front of the door. They ask each other if they slept well. Well, although not very long, but it'll do.

"Does she get washed and dressed on her own?"

"Yes. She does lots of things on her own. She's a big girl. Aren't you, Rachel?"

Rachel nods. The cat is sitting, having lost interest in the game, and she calls it, but now it walks away, sits down again, looks around, lifts its nose in the direction of a passing bird, then starts cleaning itself.

"You should take a shower. I'll show you where it is."

Rachel gets up and follows Franck. "I have to fetch my clean things," she says before climbing the stairs.

He and his father find themselves back in front of the house. They light cigarettes and a sly little breeze wafts around them and shakes the smoke and scatters it far from them.

"So you think her mother's going to show up?" Armand says.

"Of course she will. This is her daughter. She'll want her back."

"And do what with her? From what you told me . . . After that bloodbath, with all the trouble she and you are in . . ."

"I don't know."

They hear a car approaching and Franck's heart skips a beat, then he tells himself it can't be Jessica. It's the postman, who parks and gets out of his car and waves to them. He sticks the mail under the windshield of Franck's car.

"I have to hurry! I'm covering for a colleague at the office, see you tomorrow!"

"See you tomorrow!"

Armand watches him reverse, a big smile on his face. "He's a good man. And we both had more or less the same troubles. He became a postman after being fired from his workplace. He bounced back, as they say. He's a union delegate so they're always after him, but he gives as good as he gets, so for now everything's working out."

"Everything seems so simple here," Franck says.

"Here and now, yes. As for what came before, well you know that, I don't need to draw you a picture. As for tomorrow, who knows?"

Franck can't think of any answer to that. He just wishes that time would stand still. Or at least slow down.

They hear Rachel close the bathroom door and Franck shudders when he sees her appear: she is wearing her red dress, the one she was wearing in the dried-up meadow in the sun, so alone in the middle of the furnace. And in that strange, terrifying dream.

"Right," Armand says, "shall we go see the cows?"

She nods.

"It'll take an hour. It's a bit farther down the valley, toward Gabas. If you like, you can go for a hike. There's a trail that starts down there, behind the caved-in barn. It's under the trees, it climbs gently. With a little luck, you might see a fox."

As soon as they've gone, he starts to feel afraid. He knows the spell is about to be broken. He looks around him at the landscape, so bright in the clear light, as if he's feeling this harmony for the last time before a disaster occurs. The moment before. The last moments of innocence. He decides to do the hike recommended by his father, knowing it will be easier for him to climb than to come back down.

He goes back into the kitchen and pours himself a drop of lukewarm coffee which he drinks slowly, standing in front of this banal untidiness he finds so reassuring. Next to his butter knife, glinting less brightly than the chrome steel, there is that object, in the middle of the breadcrumbs. He sits down as soon as he understands what it is. The inscription on the inside of the ring is the same:

NEVER DEFEATED.

It takes him a good minute to realize what's happening. Rachel put Fabien's ring on the table before leaving. Rachel has had that ring for days or weeks. That ring never left her

grandparents' house. The guy on the phone was only pretending to be a murderer. He doesn't know yet why they wanted
him to believe that Fabien had been killed by the Serb's people. What he knows is that Fabien, like his ring, never left the
house. And is still there. Rachel knew and couldn't say anything. Franck remembers the dog that sometimes stood in front
of her, an instinctive guardian of the pack. He sees again those
black oily eyes absorbing all the light, the mortal density of that
fixed look. He shudders. He puts his hand flat on the table, the
ring in front of him, and his arms and shoulders shake and pain
attacks his stiff neck. He gets up to try and rid himself of that
electricity burning him from the inside like a microwave oven
and his legs shake so much that he has to lean on the table for
support. He slips the ring onto his finger and he has to clench
his fist because it's too wide, then he manages to get it on his
thumb and the magic of that ring starts to work, and he's able
to take a few steps to the door and fill himself one last time with
everything that he will miss from now on. He knows that now,
it is all he knows: the light, the wind, the blue of the sky, the
immensity rising and curving around him.

He is in the shower when his cell phone rings. He may have
been expecting it, but he still jumps and almost lets it slip from
his soapy hands when he goes to grab it.

Jessica is screaming. He turns off the faucet and listens, concentrating on the square of blue sky through the open window.
She is interrupted by a coughing fit and he tells her that she
can come, that Rachel is with him and she's safe. He squeezes
Fabien's ring in his fingers as he tells her how to get here, to his
father's house, in the Ossau Valley.

She sniggers in a husky voice. "Your father the drunk? Hell,
is that the best place you could find to keep my daughter safe?"

"I'll expect you. You'll see how things are."

He hangs up and a desire to throw up forces him to lean
over the washstand, but nothing comes and the nausea recedes.
He finishes washing, letting icy water run over him. He pants

and moans and punches the cold tiles with his fist. He gets dressed, shivering, then is relieved to see the sun again and for a moment he stands there motionless, trying to reflect on what has happened, on what is bound to happen next. He looks toward the end of the path leading to the house, expecting to see Jessica's car come charging up at any moment, even though he knows that she has almost four hours of driving in front of her. He feels as if he's standing in the middle of a field of ruins, a giant puzzle whose pieces he doesn't yet have the strength to put together. He thinks about the hike his father mentioned, takes a few steps toward the caved-in barn, then gives up the idea. Walking for an hour under the trees? Watching out for a fox? He doesn't understand how that prospect could have seemed so attractive barely twenty minutes ago. He feels as if he's waking up from a happy dream, the kind that children have, holding the longed-for toy that vanishes as soon as they wake up. He's fallen back onto the sticky pallet on which he slept badly all these weeks, in sweat and sometimes in tears.

He sits down on the granite bench to wait for his father and Rachel, because it seems to him that their presence will give him back the points of reference he lacks in the heart of this landscape that's become too big for him. And because he's impatient to see Rachel's reaction when she notices the ring on his finger and what she'll say, if she chooses to say anything. For a fraction of a second, he has the feeling his father will arrive and give him the solution, by showing him a way out he didn't know was there, like a lost or helpless child who feels reassured when he sees his parents arrive.

When the car stops, Rachel gets out almost immediately but waits by the open door for his father to also get out and go to the trunk to take out the container of milk. He also brings a piece of cheese wrapped in a sheet of paper and Rachel falls into step with him, eyes fixed on the ground as if taking care not to put her feet just anywhere.

"Well? Getting some fresh air? This girl isn't afraid of

anything! They showed her how they milked the cow, and she already wanted to go under the cow to try! Even the dog followed her, and he can be a bit touchy. He even wanted to be stroked. Isn't that so, Rachel? You're a good fairy, that's what you are! You arrive and everything goes well!"

Rachel nods with a contented smile, but she hasn't taken her eyes off Franck. Armand goes inside, saying something that Franck doesn't catch, doesn't even listen to, and as Rachel approaches, her hands in the pockets of her dress, he shows her the ring on his finger.

"Have you had this ring a long time?"

She shakes her head, looking down at the ground and tracing little arcs in the dust with the point of her shoe. Her hair falls in front of her face and she stays hidden in its shadow.

"How did you get it?"

She bites her lip and takes her hand out of her pocket and wipes her nose with the back of it. "I took it from Mom."

"But . . ."

"She put it on the sideboard once, after she hurt herself with you during the night."

"Why did you take it?"

She suddenly looks Franck straight in the eyes. "Because she scolded me and then hurt me."

"Do you know whose ring it is?"

Rachel lowers her eyes again. She nods, she does know. She has taken both hands out of her pockets and she joins them in front of her and wrings her fingers.

Franck takes a deep breath, trying to find the air he lacks. He would like to run his hand through Rachel's hair to reassure her but he doesn't dare. He would have the impression he was capturing her, and she might struggle. He doesn't know how to ask his last question. Searching for the words, he's afraid she'll run away and withdraw into her silence again.

"Do you know where Fabien is?"

She looks at him again. He doesn't know what to read

into that look: sadness and fear. But a real fear, like a nagging pain that's reawakened when you touch the source of it. She's breathing fast, her chest rising and falling crazily in little gasps and Franck holds out his arms to her, but she takes a step back and sits down, there in the dust, her red dress forming a co-rolla around her. From inside, he hears his father's voice, asking what's going on. Franck stands up to go inside.

"Are you staying there? You'll catch sunstroke."

Rachel doesn't reply but stands up and follows him inside.

"If you like, I'll put the TV on for you," Armand says.

"No, I have my game."

She climbs the stairs and they hear her close the door of her room behind her.

"Fabien didn't die in Spain. It wasn't the Serb's men who killed him. It was them, the family. Jessica and her parents. They buried him in the woods, behind their house. I know what I still have to do."

His father breathes hard through his mouth and turns to the door, which is wide open. "It's not possible," he says in a low voice. "What kind of people are they?" He wipes his tear-filled eyes with the back of his hand. "I'll go with you. And that witch is coming here, isn't she?"

He breaks off, choking.

Franck lets him absorb the blow. Slumped on his chair, his father lets his eyes be dazzled by the light shuffling across the doorway of the house.

"She'll be here in two hours. I'll grab her and take her back there. You can stay with Rachel. I don't know what she saw, but whatever it was, she saw too much. We want to avoid her seeing anything else, don't we?"

His father nods. "It's up to you. But one way or another I'll come and see the place where my son died. It's best if you take care of the woman. Left to myself, I'd just shoot her."

They're silent for a while. In the silence, they hear a helicop-ter flying over the valley.

"Let's eat," Armand says, standing.

"Are you hungry?"

"No. But we have to eat. To get our strength up. We're going to need it. And the girl has to eat, too. I'll open a jar of axoa.[4]"

During the meal, he jokes about the cows who knew that Rachel was their friend, and she listens to him, a smile in her bright eyes. Then he talks about the chamois and the bears, he goes through all the mountain animals, the vultures who can fly without flapping their wings, the foxes with their golden eyes. He tells stories about shepherds, he says that young Fourcade—it was his family's farm they visited to fetch the milk from—is a shepherd and that sometimes he has strange adventures, with noises at night around his hut and his dogs who start to bark, crazed with anger or fear, like this morning when he opened his door in the first light of dawn and found almost his whole flock outside, and the dogs lying there, strangely quiet.

Rachel listens to all these stories with her fork in the air, eyes wide open, her long lashes fluttering sometimes with incredulity. At times, the silence falls again, and all three of them listen out as if trying to hear Jessica's car coming, and Rachel looks at the faces of the two men as if trying to figure out what they're so afraid of. Then Armand tells another story about the old days, a legend about a bear cub, the terror of a village surrounded by wolves one Christmas night, the curse that fell on a hamlet haunted by the ghost of a smuggler killed ten years earlier by a policeman who was born there, and how the ghost appeared at the end of January, the anniversary of his death, making terrible threats, followed a week later by the death of one of the inhabitants.

For a while, it's as if they are somewhere out of time, and Franck would be happy to hear more of these stories where people are snowbound or terrified of the dark, where it isn't good to go out, where the pastures are haunted or threatened

---

[4] A Basque veal and vegetable stew.

274 · HERVÉ LE CORRE

by bears that can't be caught. He doesn't remember his father being such a talented storyteller when they were kids. It was his mother who would make up stories for them, her nose in a book as soon as she had a moment to herself. He wishes he could remember her firm, almost solemn, slightly husky voice. All he can recall are her hands dancing in front of her, painting the characters and the settings.

Rachel has gone to take a nap, his father is tinkering in his shed, mending a chair. Franck is in front of the TV, channel hopping without finding anything to interest him. Time passes with agonizing slowness. When he hears Jessica's car drive up, a TV presenter is asking a woman if the many relationships she has with men, one after the other, are the cause or the consequence of her lack of satisfaction. He switches off the TV at the exact moment the car door slams.

She is no longer wearing the outfit in which she left yesterday. Now she's in a T-shirt and khaki Bermuda shorts. She strides toward him and he makes out her pale face, her shiny skin, her glazed eyes. As soon as she gets closer, he is aware of the smell of her sweat, which she's tried to hide with scent, and another odor, maybe alcohol, he isn't sure. There were nights when his father was in this state when he came home but there was nothing in his vague expression but intense exhaustion, not this bottomless, inexorable madness, which for a few seconds prevents Jessica from speaking. Her lips are tight and her jaws quiver as if she's about to tear his throat out.

"Where is she?"

She steps to the side as if to walk around him but he reaches out his arm to stop her and she stands there leaning on him heavily, as if on a barrier.

"She's asleep. She's having a nap. Calm down."

"Calm down? You take my daughter and you want me to calm down?"

She moves back and faces him, arms down by her sides,

ready for a fight. She's breathing hard through her nose, her nostrils dilated.

Franck feels his heart kicking in his chest. He thinks about knocking her out with his fist, throwing her to the ground, pressing her into the stones. He suppresses the force that quivers in his arms.

"Now's not the time to fight," he says. "And besides, you'd be out of your league."

"Oh, yes? I could murder you! Let me through so I can get my daughter!"

"You won't get her because you're going to end up in jail. You don't even realize it's all over for you."

He raises his hand and shows her Fabien's ring. She recoils. Her eyes leave him, try to fix themselves somewhere, come back to him.

"Where did you get that?"

"I thought it was on the finger of the guy who killed Fabien. He described it to me in detail on the phone the other day. And now Rachel gives it to me! Strange, don't you think?"

"So what? What does it prove?"

"That it wasn't the Serb's men who killed my brother, it was your parents and you. Fabien never went to Spain. You took his money and went into business with the Serb, and you found yourselves in debt toward him. And since he's the kind of person who takes something like that seriously, he was starting to lose patience and wanted to get back at you."

Jessica is looking at him curiously. All anger has left her face. She even smiles, with a kind of innocence. "You're right, we have to talk about it," she says in a soft voice. "I'll go get my things."

She does an about-turn and walks back toward her car.

"Rachel!"

Armand comes running out. He stumbles and catches on to Franck's arm.

"She ran away! I just saw her go up into the woods!"

He points to the tree-covered slope in the distance and Franck tries to make out the start of the path, but can't see anything. The noise of the gunshot makes them throw themselves on the ground and his father holds his shoulder, grimacing, his legs flailing as if he wants to flee the pain nailing him to the ground. He presses his hand to the wound, blood reddening his fingers. Franck crawls toward him in the raised dust. He doesn't hear Jessica pass close to them and run toward the forest. He moves his father's clenched hand out of the way and opens his shirt, uncovering five or six holes in the muscle, a gash above the biceps. With a tail of the shirt he wipes the blood, which immediately starts gushing again. His father clings to his neck and now both of them are rising then falling again with moans of effort, staggering like drunks. When they are on their feet, his father looks at his shoulder and blows on it. He brings his crumpled shirt back over his bruised and lacerated flesh and presses the cloth to it, panting.

"It's nothing, I can manage. I have something to clean it. Go after that crazy bitch!" He sways, sits down on the bench. "It's nothing, I tell you. Think about Rachel. There's a shotgun in the shed, and cartridges in the drawer of an old sideboard."

Franck helps him to his feet, but then he pushes his hands away and tells him he'll be fine. Franck runs to his car and takes out the shotgun and cartridges he recovered last night. He hopes the ammunition hasn't taken in too much water and he loads the weapon and hurries toward the forest.

Silence. Only his footsteps and his gasping in the half-darkness of the firs. The path is broad, quite distinct, furrowed down the middle by the rains. He has to stop after two hundred yards to catch his breath and rest his shaky legs. He sets off again at a more regular rhythm, trying to keep pace with his breathing. The shotgun bothers him, without a strap to put it over his shoulder, and the cartridges in the pocket of his jeans press on the tops of his thighs with each step he takes. The path rises gently without any ledge and slowly wears down his muscles.

He has to stop twice more to recover a little energy, and he urges himself on in a low voice, imagining Rachel fleeing in that dark solitude. He assumes that Jessica is also struggling as she climbs. Or maybe the mad rage that has her in its grip has abolished her fatigue. Through a gap, he glimpses the valley, cars moving noiselessly along the road. He tears away once again, propping himself on big stones as if on a ruined staircase. The sweat streams down his back and his blood beats in his temples. He stops in front of a stream that descends with a murmur and falls from a rock in clear strands. He wets his face in it, drinks a few mouthfuls from the palms of his hands.

Above him, he glimpses the pale green of a thicket of hardwood trees moving in a gentle wind. Flashes of sky. He sets off again, treading on tatters of light, his legs hardened and burning. He turns around two more bends, then reaches the cover of some beech trees and comes out onto a vast grassy slope strewn with huge rocks and trunks of dead trees. The trail is nothing more now than a straight line gently descending. And perhaps two hundred yards away, he sees the tiny figure of Jessica.

He doesn't know where he finds the strength to start running. It seems to him that his run is nothing but a fall and that it's only by chance that he bounces back each time he puts his foot down. A hot, noisy wind descends from the cliff above the meadow, kneading the tall grass, humming in his ears. Jessica doesn't hear him coming and when he's about thirty feet from her she turns and aims her weapon at him and he does the same and the barrels of their shotguns move in time to their panting as if those dark, empty mouths were searching for each other.

"What were you planning to do?"

"Get my daughter back."

They have to talk loudly because the wind scatters their words.

"With a shotgun?"

Jessica doesn't reply. She strengthens her grip on the weapon and wedges the butt on her shoulder, head bent to line her eyes up with the bead.

"How many people are you going to kill? Your parents—that was you, wasn't it?"

She shakes her head. Her finger slides over the trigger guard, comes to rest on the trigger. "It was my mother who started it. She was afraid you'd go to the cops or that you'd get caught at the Serb's, so she started yelling that it was my fault everything was fucked, and that I'd been screwing up her life since I was born, that I always screwed everything up."

Rachel's cry is distant, muffled by the wind and the trees. Jessica turns toward the edge of the wood and Franck throws himself on her shotgun and tears it from her hands and when she tries to grab it back, he lands her a kick that sends her rolling a few yards down the slope. She stops moving, and lies there on her side, curled up, panting, weeping silently or choking with anger. Franck breaks open the shotgun and throws the cartridges away, then flings the weapon into the grass. He undoes his belt. Jessica sits up when she sees him, but he pushes her back down, flat on her stomach, and ties her hands behind her back. She says nothing, just moans and groans. She might be an animal. A wounded, dangerous dog.

He climbs back up along the path and picks up his shotgun. He regains a little strength in his legs and runs toward the forest, which encircles a rocky peak. He goes in under the cover of the trees, and at first sees nothing in the gloom, then makes out the army of dark trunks that stand there as if ready to attack. He calls Rachel and in the renewed silence he hears her cry out again, less loudly, and weep.

He finds her motionless in the middle of a scree, in a patch of sunlight.

"What's wrong?"

She hardly dares turn toward him, her arms down tight against her body. She's sobbing, her hair stuck to her face. "A snake! Over there!"

On a flat stone, a small viper lies coiled, its head resting on its body, its tongue exploring the air around it. Franck takes Rachel in his arms.

"Look."

He throws a stone at the snake, and it slithers away under a rock.

"You see? It was just warming itself. It wouldn't have done anything to you."

Rachel almost chokes him with her arms and he feels her tears run down his neck. He retraces his steps, and during the descent his legs shake and he feels muscles he didn't even know existed grow even tighter than they were. He puts Rachel down and gives her his hand.

"I'll walk in front. But there are no snakes here, I would have seen them."

She says all right. She says she's scared all the same and she squeezes two of Franck's fingers in her sweaty hand.

They get back to Jessica, who's sitting on a rock by the side of the path. She looks up at them, her face smeared with tears and dust. Franck feels Rachel's hand tighten on his. She leans her shoulder against his thigh.

"Hello, darling," Jessica says. "Aren't you going to give me a kiss?"

Without letting go of Franck, Rachel takes a step forward, then hesitates.

"What are you afraid of?"

"There was a snake."

Rachel walks toward her and puts her arms around her and clings to her, then abruptly breaks free. Jessica leans toward her, her hands still tied behind her back.

"Well, are you happy now?"

"Let's go. We'll talk later. Come on, move."

She stands and walks ahead, resolute, erect, a little stiff. At first, Rachel follows Franck then walks beside him as soon as the path allows her to do so. Nobody speaks. The sun has moved over to the other slope, and it's quite cool now beneath the trees. Franck dreams of a chair and a glass of water. He asks Rachel if she's thirsty and she says she wants a glass of milk.

They come within sight of the house and Franck sees a grimy 4×4. He takes down the shotgun he's been carrying broken over his shoulder and grabs Jessica by the arm. They approach slowly. The 4×4 has a local license plate. Judging by the layer of mud incrusting the lower part of the bodywork, the car belongs to someone from the area.

In the kitchen, a man in his shirtsleeves is sitting opposite Franck's father, who's clenching his teeth and sweating. Lying on the table, a kidney dish, a syringe, bottles of antiseptic.

Armand relaxes when he sees Franck. "Let me introduce Dr. Pierre Etchart, state registered vet."

The man doesn't look up from what he's doing. All they can see is his massive back, his thick forearm, his hands in their blue latex gloves.

"Stop moving, for fuck's sake! It's bad enough that I can't see anything."

He straightens up, holding some kind of tweezers in his hand, and drops a small piece of lead into the kidney dish. Only now does Franck notice that there are already five there, all bloodstained.

"There. It's done. Now all it needs is a bandage."

He turns to Franck and Jessica and looks at them. Then his eyes move to the shotgun.

"I don't know what game you're playing, and I don't want to know. But if you could go and have your fun somewhere else, that'd be best for everyone."

"It's all right, Pierre."

"No, it's not all right. Another seven or eight inches to the left and you'd have lost your shoulder. You caught some of the splatter."

He cleans the oozing wounds some more then puts on the bandage and knocks together a sling.

"I'll come and change it tomorrow, as soon as I've seen Lescarret's sheep. Sorry about that, but the animals come first."

He stands up and puts away his equipment in a rucksack. He shakes Armand's hand and walks to the door. As he passes Franck, he jabs his chest with his index finger.

"Don't spoil your reunion. Take care of him."

To go out, he pushes Jessica aside without looking at her. He hurries to his 4×4. The engine races, the tires skid and raise dust and stones.

"Don't mind him," Armand says. "The man's solid gold. He came as soon as I called him. And because he's a friend, I told him what had happened."

He gets to his feet, breathing hard, leaning on the table.

"It's all right," he says. "And besides, it's the left arm."

He sees Rachel, who has her back to him, and calls her over.

"Aren't you thirsty, sweetheart?"

Jessica remains standing near the door, her hands still tied behind her back. She looks at them in turn and there's no expression on her face, it's as if she doesn't recognize anybody, as if she's looking at them from a distance or from a place known only to her and inaccessible to anyone else.

Franck gets out glasses and pours milk and water. His father glances at Jessica out of the corner of his eye. Twice, he gets ready to say something but changes his mind because of Rachel, and he turns toward her and asks if it's good, if she wants anything else. She shakes her head, looks up at her mother, and tries to catch her eyes, but can't because Jessica seems not to be seeing anything anymore, resting a clear, blind gaze on Rachel. Armand suggests to Rachel that she go and watch TV and Rachel gets up and follows him into the next room, her head down. Noises, words and music echo immediately. When Armand returns, he asks what they're going to do now, he tells Jessica to sit and she sits down on a chair he pushes toward her.

"I'm going to find Fabien," Franck says. "She's going to

show me where they buried him and then I'm going to call the cops. This has to end."

For a moment, nobody says anything. The only sound is the TV in the next room. All three of them seem exhausted, stuck on their chairs, around this table, like lifeless puppets.

Franck has the feeling he's just climbing out of a sack in which he's been lugged around roughly for weeks until he's dizzy and worn down, and there are moments when he'd like to go back inside and curl up and ask someone to close it tightly and throw it into a ravine. He leans toward Jessica, who is staring down at the patterns on the oilcloth.

"Was it you who killed him?"

She looks at him at last. Her eyes are filled with tears, her eyelids flutter and overflow, and water runs down her dirty cheeks. "No, it wasn't me." She moves her arms about behind her back, longing to wipe her face. "I don't know," she goes on.

"What do you mean, you don't know?"

"My father. It was my father. The Serb's drugs . . . We needed money, we didn't want to ask the Gypsy, we wanted to handle it by ourselves but Fabien didn't agree."

"What about the rest of the money?"

She shrugs. "We used it. You always need money, dammit."

"And when the Serb started getting impatient, the Gypsy came back into the game. With me as the ball, is that it? And he sent his guys to me to kick me about, is that it?"

"We gave the drugs to the Gypsy to sell but he needed time and the Serb wouldn't wait. So Serge decided to muscle in. And since you were there in the middle, we took advantage."

She continues speaking in a monotonous voice, looking down at her fingers, which she keeps twisting.

Franck listens to her and watches her as if he's in front of a screen, viewing a recording. The Gypsy taking the opportunity to eliminate the Serb. Himself charging headfirst into all the traps laid for him. The machine that kept on grinding with every move he made. He feels no emotion, nothing that could make his heart beat faster or his hands shake. The anger and the grief cancel each other out and merge into a painful lucidity. He barely recognizes the woman who's speaking in that muted voice and looking him straight in the eyes, tears running ceaselessly over her soil-stained cheeks. He sees only the rickety machine from which he's extricated himself before he could be torn to pieces.

He prefers to look away. He stands up because he feels that this lucidity of his is an unstable mixture.

"We have to go back. We'll leave tomorrow."

18

They leave at dawn, without having really slept.

Franck and his father have been in the kitchen since around five, too anxious to sleep, eating and exchanging nothing but the most utilitarian of words. Coffee, sugar, bread. A few sentences about what the weather is going to be like.

They tie Jessica up and lay her down in the back seat. She doesn't say a word, just lets herself be bound and lifted and seated, seemingly absent, completely indifferent to whatever might now happen to her. She refuses the coffee they offer her, but accepts a cigarette. Yesterday, she didn't say anything more after the few confessions she had made, falling back into her silence, withdrawn far into herself. They allowed her to go to the bathroom, then gave her something to drink and cleaned her face, and she submitted to everything without protesting, complaining, or thanking them.

Franck places the gun next to him and puts the shotgun away in the trunk. He's taken a few caliber 12 cartridges with him.

His father watches the car drive away in the same position as when they arrived the other night. Standing firm, his hands in his pockets. Franck waves his hand through the lowered window then accelerates as soon as he's on the road and goes even faster when they reach the valley. He wants to get away from the pull of the mountains, that powerful spell through which he felt his mistrust, his anger, his fears fade and leave him without the unhealthy energy that has kept him going all these weeks. And yet, when it comes down to it, there's a kind of contentment in him. He couldn't say what it is. Perhaps it's that, in coming here to see his father, he did a thing he'd thought he was incapable of doing. The thing he had dreaded the most, even after all he had endured and committed. He'd been afraid he would find an embittered, tearful old man, and instead he found a man who'd been born again in a new country, even though every line on his face is a scar, a man who keeps going in spite of his fatigue, a man who lives with his beloved ghosts and respects death itself, stopping it from coming too quickly. He knows these things in a vague way. That some souls that have passed through hell are granted a second chance.

As soon as they are some way down in the plain, as soon as the noise of the speeding car on the highway isolates them a little more from the outside world, Jessica emerges from her torpor and Franck hears her move for the first time and make the imitation leather seat squeak. When he turns toward her, he sees her eyes fixed on him. The way they tied her, she can't sit up.

"What are you planning to do now?" she asks. Her voice is curt and harsh.

"Whatever I have to."

"Whatever you have to? What kind of answer is that? Do you think you're in a movie?"

"That's it, you're right. This is a movie, but it'll be over soon. Especially for you."

"Oh, yes? What are you going to do, kill me and bury me in the woods? Why didn't you do that yesterday?"

"Not in front of Rachel."

For a while, she doesn't say anything more. Franck doesn't want to turn around, doesn't want to see that transparent, increasingly empty gaze again.

"You are going to kill me, aren't you?"

"Of course not. I'm not crazy like you."

She curses him under her breath then falls silent. As they get closer, Franck's heart races with increasing frequency and he sometimes has to take deeper breaths to get all the air he needs.

They turn onto the highway leading toward Bordeaux. They still have forty-five minutes ahead of them. It's just after ten o'clock. It's Franck who decides to speak. He'd like her to start feeling bad.

"You're going to see your family again. Aren't you happy to be returning to the scene of your crimes?"

"They weren't crimes."

He can't help turning to see the expression on her face as she dares to say that. She's still lying on her side, looking at him with clear, unblinking eyes, convinced of the obviousness of what she's just said.

"Three people dead. What do you call that?"

She doesn't reply right away. She's probably thinking it over. Franck slows down as they get to the tollbooth and he finds it hard to concentrate on what he has to do. Before long, they're on a deserted road that plows through the pine forest and Franck's heart tightens despite the sweet smells of resin and earth that reach him.

"It had to be done, that's all. There was no other solution. I couldn't stand my parents anymore. There had to be a way out."

He doesn't see her, but her steady voice, the calm tone in which she speaks, and that quiet sense of conviction that underlies everything she says give Franck a strong desire to stop the car and leave her tied to a tree to die slowly, thinking about what she's done and what she's just said. He feels like swinging his arm back and hitting out at random as parents sometimes do when they're exasperated by their kids after hours of driving.

They drive the last miles without saying anything more. The house looms up in a harsh light and for Franck its gray facade with the shutters closed has the air of a mausoleum. The gypsies closed the door behind them and it looks as if nobody has lived there for years.

He takes his gun, gets the shotgun out of the trunk, loads it and puts a few extra cartridges in his pockets. He's not too sure why he's weighing himself down with such an arsenal. He doesn't see what threat could possibly disturb what he's about to do but he prefers not to leave any of the weapons behind. He unties Jessica, making sure to leave the rope on her feet, and helps her sit up and then get out of the car. She stands there motionless and looks around her then gazes for a long time at the house, eyes raised toward the windows as if expecting one of them to open. Franck pushes her with the barrel of his gun and they walk around the outside of the building and past the trailer and come to the shed where the old man kept his gardening tools. Jessica walks with her head held high, her hands tied behind her back, just like a condemned man going to his execution.

"Stop. Don't move."

He goes into the shed backwards, the shotgun aimed at her. She continues to look straight in front of her, without blinking. Her lips are tightly shut, her nostrils dilate with each breath. She is fully in the sun, and the heat that falls on her doesn't seem to bother her. A little sweat glistens on her forehead and above her lip. It's as if she's angry and is stopping herself from screaming.

Franck finds a shovel and hoists it onto his shoulder. *Hi-ho, hi-ho*, he can't help singing mentally, remembering the dwarves of his childhood.

"Let's go. You know where."

He has the strange impression that he is at once familiar with this place and totally detached from what he lived through when he was here, remembering only vague, meaningless fragments of that time. They walk across the dried-up meadow, past the clothes line, treading the narrow path he took so often and all he can remember is Rachel running here, screaming with fear. The forest comes toward them as much as they approach it, and soon they are in its shade, which is thicker than he remembers it, and the silence is expectant and Franck grips his shotgun even harder and listens and peers into the underbrush and between the tree trunks.

Jessica stops abruptly and turns toward him. She's out of

breath and her face is shiny with sweat. She looks at the barrel pointed at her, the shovel resting on Franck's shoulder. "What are we doing here?"

"What do you think?"

She shrugs, twisting her mouth to signify that she doesn't know.

"Where's Fabien?" he asks.

"Fabien's dead, isn't he?"

"Don't play that game. Now's not the time."

"He's dead, I tell you. What does it matter where he is now?"

"I want to know where he's buried. I want to recover his body and give him a proper funeral. Can't you get that into your crazy head?"

She smiles. Without any malice. A happy smile. Her face lights up and her eyes grow bigger and Franck sees again that girl, as bright as the sun, who dazzled then blinded him, and for ten seconds he's no longer sure what he's doing here and half expects to wake up from this macabre nightmare.

"You're completely crazy," she says, shaking her head. "It's that way."

She starts walking again, not caring if he follows her or not, and she progresses as fast as she's allowed to by the ropes around her ankles. They come to the pigeon trap and she stops at the edge of the circle of galleries, which looks like the emaciated spine of a dead monster.

"It's here."

With the tip of her shoe, she lifts the carpet of pine needles. The earth looks brighter here, almost white. Franck props the shotgun against a tree stump and takes out the gun.

"Don't pull any tricks. I'm going to untie you, and I swear I'll shoot you if you try anything stupid."

With some difficulty, he undoes the knots at her feet and wrists. He ought to be using both hands. Or a knife. The mountaineer's rope finally falls to the ground. He takes three steps back and throws her the shovel.

"Go on."

Jessica looks at the shovel and doesn't move. It's as if she's never seen one before and is wondering how to use it. Then she gently pushes the handle of the tool with the tip of her foot.

"No."

On the ground next to Franck, there's a fallen branch with a clump of needles and a pine cone still attached to it. He takes it and hits Jessica in the face and hits her again on the back and a cut across her forehead starts to bleed and the threads of her T-shirt snag on dry stumps of bristling twigs and he pulls her toward him and as she spins around, she lets out a scream, loses her balance, and almost falls on her back. She straightens up again. Her face is covered in blood, and amid the scarlet her eyes light up in terror. He hits her again, full in the face, and she staggers back and falls to the ground and bawls like a child reprimanded for no reason.

Franck throws the branch away, his hands sticky with resin, and he raises his gun and aims it at her, straight at that face that's a mask of blood and fear. He's shaking, he can hardly see because the sweat is running into his eyes and because tears are gushing out without his knowing why, so he wipes his eyes with the back of his hand and takes his finger off the trigger because he's within a fraction of an inch of taking her face and cranium off with a bullet fired from such close range.

"You're going to do it! You're going to do it!"

He barely hears himself say that in the din of Jessica's moans and the clamor of hate and throbbing blood echoing inside him.

She gets back on her feet, panting, her jaws chattering. She holds herself stiffly, her arms at her sides like those of a store window dummy, then she lifts her T-shirt and wipes her face and, without even a glance at Franck, starts to dig.

The soil is loose. Jessica throws shovelfuls of gray sand behind her. She clears the surface layer and the shape of the grave appears. A rectangle, about five feet long. She wipes her face again and breathes, the sweat soaking her T-shirt.

Franck stands about six feet from her. Sometimes he forgets to breathe. He knows his heart is still beating only because at the back of his throat, beneath his burning skull, the blood is racing and pounding.

Jessica is in the hole, black with earth, buried up to her knees. She sits down on the edge and puts her head between her knees for a moment.

"Don't stop," Franck says.

She pretends not to have heard him and wipes her face and neck and blistered hands.

He passes behind her and pushes her with a weak kick in the back. He no longer knows who she is, this filthy girl sitting on the edge of a grave. He doesn't even know if she's anyone. His memory of what she was has been erased. As far as he's concerned, right now she's a creature over whom he has complete power. He doesn't enjoy this domination. He doesn't even have any desire to take revenge. Jessica is a living, useful tool. Only one thing is certain: Fabien is here, a few inches beneath the sand, in the earth, already filled with earth.

"Dig."

She gets back on her feet, shaken by sobs that choke her and make her cough. She presses with her foot on the blade of the shovel and clears a more compact clod of earth, then another, and now Franck sees tatters of blue fabric and as she continues to dig, having perhaps not seen what she has revealed, a violent stench makes him recoil. It coils around him then fades, remaining as a pungent odor that hovers over the grave and sticks to his palate. Jessica has stopped digging and climbs back up onto the rim of the grave and spits and throws up.

Franck goes closer and makes out the shape of the body lying in a fetal position. He sees a torn hand, yellow bones covered in a brown crust. He can't take his eyes off these remains even though he can't make them out clearly, mixed as they are with the sand, and he says things in a low voice, you see, bro, I came. He dreads seeing more: the ruins of the face, the skeleton grotesquely dressed in its rags of fabric and skin.

Then he straightens up, emerging from what is perhaps only a nightmare, and looks around him, surprised to see the forest unchanged, that standing indifference splashed with sunshine, and just then on his right something moves in the middle of the pigeon trap, something deeply black that has just frozen and toward which he turns, feeling dizzy. The dog is there, in the middle of the trap, standing on its four legs, staring at him with its bottomless eyes. It looks even larger than he remembers it. Powerful and muscular. Its black coat giving off no light, no reflection, the light dying there. This dog he saw lying dead in the corridor, its face blown away by a shotgun volley. He would like to speak, he would like his words to break the spell at least, but his dry mouth and throat are incapable of emitting the slightest sound. He remembers abruptly that he has a weapon in his hand, so he raises his arm and places his index finger on the trigger. He has stopped shaking. He has to kill this chimera, this vision of all his fears, and he takes aim at the motionless dog, whose sides rise and fall slowly as it takes deep breaths.

The blade of the shovel hits him below the knees, and he feels as if his legs have been scythed off. He falls on his back in the hole and curls in on himself to take his pain and wounds in both hands, feeling the dampness of the blood, and he struggles and writhes, his brother's shattered body beneath him like a bed of branches and stones. He manages to dodge the second blow that Jessica brings down on him, and he pulls on the handle of the shovel and tears it from her. With a cry, she topples over onto him, heavy, slow, and lets her face come to rest on his and he catches himself feeling that softness again, dizzy with fatigue and pain until the moment he feels Jessica's mouth open and her teeth catch his face and plant themselves in his skin. He grabs her by the hair with his free hand but can't manage to push her away and he hears her growling mutedly against him, her teeth locked in his flesh. He slides his hand up to Jessica's neck, feels the throbbing of the artery beneath his fingers, and presses his thumb in as if capable of tearing it with his bare hands.

She falls back, choking, coughing, spitting on him, her mouth full of blood, and he knocks her back with a punch to the temple. He hoists himself out of the grave, crawls a few yards, and gets up onto all fours, his belly shaken with nausea, the stench of death in his mouth like a juice he tries to spit out. When it calms down, he turns toward the baleful shrine and sees nothing now but a patch of sunlight where the dog had been. A short distance away, Jessica is lying on her stomach, her face turned toward him, her eyes wide open, breathing through her mouth, her lips trembling like those of a sulking child.

Franck leans back against a tree trunk and searches in the big pocket of his pants for his cell phone in the middle of the shotgun cartridges. He dials the number, and his father picks up immediately and asks how he is. Franck gets his breath back before replying.

"I'm here. I found him. He's here, very close. I have no strength left. You have to come. How's Rachel?"

"She's playing outside with the cat. I'll be right there."